Praise for Allison Amend's

A Nearly Perfect Copy

"Gracefully wielding a collage of unlikely elements, *A Nearly Perfect Copy* pits authenticity against imitation, deception against personal fulfillment, and replacement against irretrievable loss."
—*The Dallas Morning News*

"Amend creates suspense by charting in wincing detail Elm's and Gabriel's progress through ethically gray areas in the art market to unquestionably illegal acts.... Well-wrought.... The author meticulously delineates [her characters'] yearnings and frustrations.... Cleverly rendered." —*The Washington Post*

"Amend draws sharp characters [and] creates a nicely evolving plot.... What unfolds is acutely appealing: various characters struggling to overcome defeat and failure in their private and public lives.... I got caught up in their problems, their struggles. I loved the lore about the art business. Really, I found this to be a terrifically entertaining novel that never lost its hold on the hearts of its characters or [on] mine." —Alan Cheuse, NPR

"Beautiful.... Amend's brisk, complex second novel focuses on artistic lineage and forgery, loss and replacement, and questions of origin and originality.... Stunningly well-researched, *A Nearly Perfect Copy* is studded with fascinating detail." —*Mid-American Review*

"A flawlessly rendered, totally engrossing, class- and continent-hopping story.... Written with the stunning clarity and great humanity of a true artist at the height of her abilities. My guess is, if you read this book you will soon be shoving it into the hands of someone you love. I certainly will."
—Charles Bock, *New York Times* bestselling author of *Beautiful Children*

Allison Amend

A Nearly Perfect Copy

Allison Amend, a graduate of the Iowa Writers' Workshop, is the author of the Independent Publisher's Award–winning short story collection *Things That Pass for Love* and the novel *Stations West*, which was a finalist for the 2011 Sami Rohr Prize for Jewish Literature and the Oklahoma Book Award. She lives in New York City, where she teaches creative writing at Lehman College.

www.allisonamend.com

Also by Allison Amend

Things That Pass for Love

Stations West

A Nearly Perfect Copy

A Nearly Perfect Copy

A NOVEL

Allison Amend

Anchor Books
A Division of Random House LLC
New York

FIRST ANCHOR BOOKS EDITION, JANUARY 2014

Copyright © 2013 by Allison Amend

The Library of Congress has cataloged the
Nan A. Talese / Doubleday edition as follows:
Amend, Allison.
A nearly perfect copy : a novel / Allison Amend.—1st ed.
p. cm.
1. Art dealers—Fiction. 2. Loss (Psychology)—Fiction.
3. Self-realization—Fiction. I. Title.
PS3601.M464N43 2013
813'.6—dc23 2012020699

Anchor ISBN: 978-0-345-80314-6
eBook ISBN: 978-0-385-53670-7

Book design by Maria Carella

Printed in the United States of America
10 9 8 7 6 5 4 3 2 1

A Nearly Perfect Copy

Part One

Spring 2007

Elm

Sometimes when she closed her eyes, Elm could see the wall of water moving toward her. The hissing of the wave's retraction burned her eardrums, and she shivered as though pinned down again in the wet debris. These were the sensations she returned to, as if by default, the images repeating over and over again.

At three in the afternoon on a May Friday, Elm sat in a meeting with the other department heads of Tinsley's. It was getting dark; the sun had slipped behind the building across the street and the sounds of traffic below were faint through the double-paned windows.

"Elm? Elm?" Ian tapped her shoulder.

"What? Sorry." Elm sat up straighter and rifled the papers on the conference table before her.

"Quarterlies," Ian reminded her softly.

"Right, well, as you know, the first fiscal quarter," Elm began, buying time while she looked for her notes, which she'd put in the folder in front of her, she was sure of it. This is what comes from sticking an art history major in a corporate job, she thought; it's like getting a horse to dance: it might happen, but it won't be pretty.

And then her notes revealed themselves, on top, ready for her presentation. She cleared her throat. "The first fiscal quarter," she repeated, "saw a drop in revenue from last year's recorded earnings from the same period." Colette, an associate specialist from the Paris branch of the auction house, was tapping her fountain pen against her paper, her pug nose wiggling in time.

"How is this possible in the biggest art boom of the century?" Greer asked.

Elm sat for a moment until she realized the question wasn't rhetorical. "Well, it's possible we're seeing the downside of that boom. The energy crisis—"

"Yes, but we're selling art, not pork bellies," Greer said. "At least, that's the theory."

Greer Tinsley never let pass a chance to upbraid Elm in public, capitalizing on his position as CEO of the auction house, and Elm's subordinate post as head of seventeenth- through nineteenth-century drawings and prints. They were both the heirs to the auction house that bore their great-grandfather's name, but the shareholders were in charge now. Though Elm was, in Greer's mind, one of the inferior cousins, she was a Tinsley, no doubt about it, the chestnut hair that would accept no dye, the birdlike nose that no rhinoplaster had ever successfully eradicated.

Elm let her hands fall to her sides. She had found that when being confronted by Greer, the best course of action was to take none.

"I mean, that is the theory, isn't it?" Greer's accent was affected, what some might call "Continental" and what Elm's husband called "international queen." He was the only man she knew who still wore an ascot, though there were plenty of employees of Tinsley's who wore pocket squares to match their ties.

"Yes, it is the theory," Elm said.

"I mean, we're not a museum, are we? Collecting for our own personal edification?"

He seemed to expect an answer so Elm said, "No, no edification."

Greer sighed heavily. "So what plans do we have for improving this trend?"

Ian stood up, coming to Elm's rescue. "Well, Greer, we are ramping up our business-getting, which should permit us to move more volume. There are a couple of commissions that Elm has garnered . . ."

"Good." Greer seemed uninterested when the objective was not Elm's humiliation. "Numbers like this make my—our"—he gestured at Elm without looking at her—"great-grandfather turn over in his grave. Any other business? No?"

Elm breathed a sigh of relief and began to gather her papers. On his way out, Greer approached her. "Elm, I'd like to talk to you. Can you come to my office in a few?"

"Sure," Elm answered, her heart contracting like she was a child in trouble for passing notes at school. She pretended to need to order her papers while she waited until everyone else exited the conference room. Ian was standing just outside.

He always managed to push the dress code envelope. Today he wore a pink and blue V-striped shirt under a definitely purple suit, though Elm thought it might be able to pass for an iridescent black that had been dry-cleaned too many times.

"Thanks, I owe you," she said.

"I'll put it on your tab," he said, and Elm wasn't sure if he was joking or annoyed. "Did you call that woman back?"

"Not yet," Elm said. "Did we determine, is she an Attic?" *Attic* was their term for an old person, almost invariably a woman, who would insist that her grandfather had been Monet's gardener and saved a masterpiece. It was up in the attic somewhere, if they could just send some nice young person to muck around in the cobwebs for a couple of days, effectively cleaning out the woman's attic for her.

"Probably. Upper West Side."

Elm shrugged. Though the really big sales were from major estates and collectors, it was not inconceivable that some rich widow on Central Park West owned a few minor Guardis or Valtats. Enough of those allowed for a comfortable base on which to search for larger commissions.

"You want me to do it for you?" Ian put his hands on his hips. His jacket neglected to bulge, like it was stapled to his shirt.

"Thank you, yet again," Elm said. "You know you're good with the ladies."

"Right. Old ladies and pedigree dogs. Attractive, successful men my own age with a trust fund, not so much."

"Where would I be without you?" Elm asked. "What's more nowhere than nowhere?"

"The East Nineties?"

"Ha." Elm lived on East Ninety-fifth Street.

Ian's cell phone sounded. His ringtone was a trumpet calling for the start of a horse race. "Hello? Oh, hiiii," he drawled, turning down the hall and waving good-bye.

———

Greer's office had a magnificent view of the East River. Even on the grayest day it was suffused with light. Elm had learned to make afternoon appointments, as Greer sat with his back to the view, and the strong morning sun blinded those who sat across from him. His office was decorated in the traditional masculinity of dark wood—wainscoting, panels, built-ins—all of it shiny tobacco-brown oak. His grand desk was a nineteenth-century Chippendale masterpiece, Baroque and ornately carved. On its legs were faces, flowers, vines, and, of course, eagle feet gripping balls blunted on the floor. The top was so polished Elm could see her reflection when she leaned over it, and it was devoid of everything except a telephone and a computer—no pens, blotter, photos, in-box/out-box, nothing.

"Elmira," he said, feigning surprise at her appearance. "There you are. Will you sit?"

"How's Anne?"

"Connecticut," he replied, answering a different question. "Putting up the rosebushes or something. Colin?" he asked. "Moira?"

"Great, both great." Elm smiled. She knew he didn't really want news; he was merely being polite. There was a short silence. Behind him, framed by the bay windows, a tugboat trudged down the East River, stacks of used tires on its bow.

"Elmira," he said. "I'm concerned."

"I know," Elm said. "You mentioned in the meeting."

"No, but I'm *very* concerned." Greer sat back, placing his ankle on his knee. He was reminding her with his body language that he was the real Tinsley, she the interloper. There had been a scandal involving Elm's grandmother's marriage and since then her side of the family got the smallest cottage on the family compound and saw little of the estate's large dividends. Elm's father had made some money in real estate, of all things, which was only slightly better than cleaning toilets in the family's estimation. But then the social order went by the wayside and the company went public and Greer's insistence on family hierarchy was sheer snobbery.

"Elm, please understand you are a valued and respected part of this establishment—"

"And a Tinsley," Elm interrupted.

Greer nodded, pained. "But I don't think Great-grandfather would have wanted it to be run into the ground for the sake of family loyalty."

"I don't think Great-grandfather, as you call him, would have considered me a Tinsley."

"Maybe not," he said. Elm had found out from Greer's brother, the sweet and affable, if prodigal, Will, who was now squandering his fortune on snow bunnies in Aspen, that Greer had objected to Elm's hiring, and was overruled by then-chairman-of-the-board Greer Senior. Elm wasn't sure now if Greer harbored the same set of prejudices that influenced his opposition to her ten years ago, or if he was nursing new ones. Similarly, she wasn't sure what the grounds for objection were. The degree from the lesser undergraduate institution (*lesser* meaning, of course, not Yale or Harvard)? But surely he couldn't argue with the graduate degree from Columbia. Or the fact that she was considered an expert in her field, the go-to person for a *New York Times* quote, the one who took big clients to dinner, a member of the board of trustees of two museums and the art consultant to a trendy, invited-members-only downtown social club. Maybe it was just the fact that she wasn't *close* family—her blood diluted. It wasn't worth thinking about. It was impossible to think rationally about irrational thoughts.

"Maybe, Elm, you want to take some time off." Greer's voice rose at the end of the sentence. He was trying to sound nonchalant, off the cuff.

"To heal?" she asked. She was attempting sarcasm, but she suspected he hadn't heard.

"If you like." Greer looked at his desk, desperate, Elm thought, for something to distract him. Finding nothing, he examined his fingernails. "You've barely taken any time since . . ." He let the sentence trail off.

"And prints and drawings?"

"We'll get someone else to pitch in for a while."

Elm stood. "If you want me to leave, then fire me. But stop this passive-aggressive looking-out-for-my-best-interests crap."

"Keep your voice down," Greer said sternly. "Get ahold of yourself."

"Right," Elm said. "The family creed. Do not show emotion. Do not embarrass the family. Grieve your dead son in silence."

Now Greer was standing too, shocked by the mention of Ronan, her son. "What do you want from me?" he hiss-whispered; he didn't want his secretary to overhear them.

"Nothing," Elm said. Suddenly, the anger was gone, as though she'd been seized by a cramp and released. These bursts came and went, leaving her apologetic and defensive. "Sorry. I'll focus. We'll be back in the saddle by the fall season."

"I hope so," Greer said. "I certainly hope so."

———

At home, Elm's doorman informed her that Moira and Wania had beaten her home. As soon as she opened the door, Moira yelled, "Mommymommy Mommymommymommy," and threw herself into Elm's legs.

"Hi, bunny," she said, shuffling forward.

Wania sat on the couch in front of the television rebraiding a long strand of hair. "Afternoon, Ms. Howells." She was from Jamaica, and Elm understood approximately 30 percent of what she said. Once she told Elm that the "peenters" had come, and Elm asked, "What?" three times until she pretended to understand. It wasn't until that evening, lying in bed, replaying the day, that she realized Wania had meant "painters."

"How was school?"

"Fine," they both answered automatically.

"Andrew was really funny today, *mon*." Moira had picked up Wania's Jamaican slang. It drove Colin crazy, but Elm found it amusing. "He made this noise in art class like this"—Moira blew a raspberry into her forearm—"and everybody really laughed. Even Mrs. Buchner." Elm was half listening, flipping through the mail. Bill, bill, package of coupons, labels from the Children's Aid Society, cable television offer, cable television offer, cable television offer. "And, Mom? It sounded like he farted," Moira explained, in case Elm didn't get the joke.

"Funny," Elm said, placing her hand on Moira's snarled hair, a continual struggle. She had practically come out of the womb with a mess of tangles, and no amount of conditioner would keep them from forming. Elm had given up on attempts to brush or braid it, and let Moira attend her tony private kindergarten wild-headed.

Seeing that her mother wasn't interested, Moira danced around in circles for a moment, and then settled in front of the television.

"You know, Wania," Elm said. "You can go, if you want."

"Are you sure, Ms. H?" Wania perked up.

"Yeah. I'm not going to the gym or anything today. Is there dinner?" Elm lived the ultimate New York stereotype. She couldn't cook, Colin couldn't cook, and their housekeeper/nanny couldn't cook. Instead, Wania bought prepared food at Citarella or Eli's Vinegar Factory every day.

"Chicken fingers," Wania said, pointing to Moira, "and spinach-stuffed chicken breast."

"Perfect," Elm said. "Thank you."

Wania stood and went over to the closet. She put on her coat and took out her woven bag. "Is it rah-nig?" she asked.

Elm couldn't understand her. "Rah-nig," Wania repeated. Elm shook her head.

"Mo," Wania called.

"Raining," Moira said, head glued to the television set, where Dora the Explorer was skipping down the adventure path.

"Oh," Elm said. "No, not yet."

"See you Mahnday." Wania stepped around the couch to plant a kiss on Moira's head. Moira reached around and patted her shoulder without turning. "Bye," Wania said softly, calling Moira an endearment that Elm heard as "beetle nut." "Have a nice weekend, now."

The door closed. It was quiet except for the overexcited television, but the volume was low enough for Elm to tune it out. She went into her room, and sat on the bed to take off her shoes. She put them away, then undressed completely, leaving her suit on her bed. Moira came in while she was in her underwear. "Mom? Will you play restaurant with me?"

"Sure. I'll have the chicken cordon bleu and a Caesar salad." Moira pretended to write this down on an imaginary pad of paper.

"And what do you want to drink?"

"You mean, What would you like to drink?"

"What would you like to drink?"

"Cherry soda, please."

Moira ran into the living room to whip up the imaginary meal. Elm lay back on the bed, crooking her elbow over her eyes. She needed to get up and start reheating dinner and play with her daughter and figure out how to get her sales figures up and how not to be demoted to some honorary position in her family's firm, and how to get over the paralysis that threatened to overtake her at every moment.

But for now it felt so good to close her eyes and let herself be empty. She wasn't anything, not mom, not boss, not wife, not friend. She was driftwood, a cloud, and she gave herself three minutes of unconscious-ness that wasn't sleep but rather absence until the cordon bleu and cherry soda were ready and Elm flooded back into herself.

———

"Where's Wania?" was the first thing Colin said when he walked through the door. Elm fought a frisson of jealousy.

"Sent her home," she said, watching his face, suspicious.

"Oh," he said. The little hair he had left, white blond, clung to his head like seaweed. His face was inscrutable. Elm realized he was just commenting on the scene, performing a "find the differences in the two pictures" exercise.

He popped a carrot stick in his mouth, and then tried to kiss Elm on the cheek clumsily. "Where's Shrimp Salad?" he called.

Moira ran out of her room. "Daddy, I asked you not to be so silly," she chided.

"Ya did, did ye? Be not remembering that, I wasn't," he said, putting on his Irish hillbilly accent. Moira loved it, copied it like a mynah bird. It was almost their secret language. Elm understood it, but was unable to reproduce the sounds or words. She knew she should find it sweet, but she felt left out.

He picked Moira up. "I'm silly? *You're* a silly silleen gob, y'are so." Colin let her slide down his body to the floor. He asked Elm in his "reg-lar" voice (as opposed to "Daddy" voice) when supper would be ready.

"Whenever," she said. "I'm just chopping carrots for salad. I can warm the chicken up anytime."

"I'm hungry now," he said.

"Then we'll eat. Moira, set the table, please."

A silence set in while they ate. Dinners were always like this. Elm didn't understand why the family was reminded particularly of Ronan during dinner. They had rarely eaten together before; this was a new phenomenon. But his absence was acutely felt, his memory respected by a silence they had all tacitly agreed on.

Moira took one bite from each end of the three chicken fingers on her plate. She liked the ends, with the extra breading. She would have to be coaxed to eat the middle. Elm didn't have the energy to fight this battle again. She was so tired that even her toes felt fatigued, as heavy as doorknobs.

As if she knew what Elm was thinking, Moira said, "Mom, do I have to eat the middle part?"

"What do you think I'm going to say?" Elm asked.

Moira didn't answer. She took a large bite and chewed it with snarled lips.

Colin shook his head, snapping out of a daydream. "Guess what," he said to Elm.

"What?" Moira answered automatically, looking at the three chicken fingers intently, willing them inside her stomach.

"It looks like Moore is buying Omnard's prescription brands."

"It's going through, then?" Elm decided there was too much salt in the ricotta stuffing of the chicken breast. She began the delicate process of unstuffing it.

"Inked today. As of tomorrow Maxisom, Norafran, and Extardol are all ours."

"What's that, Daddy?" Moira had gotten down to two chicken finger middles, the point at which her mother usually gave up trying to make her eat them.

"Medicine to make people feel better."

"And what happens to their PR departments?" Elm asked.

"They get folded into ours, I suppose. We'll have to see how it'll shake down."

"Shake out."

"Excuse me?" Colin poured them each another glass of wine.

"Shake down is extortion. Shake out is seeing how something will turn out."

"Right," Colin said. "Are you going to eat those, Ballyreal?"

"No," Moira answered seriously. "I don't think I'll be eating these."

"Should we be worried?" Elm asked.

"About the chicken fingers?"

Elm narrowed her eyes. "About the shakeout."

"What good would worrying do us now?" He balled up his napkin and threw it at Moira, who squealed and jumped off her chair to pick it up.

"No good at all, which doesn't mean I shouldn't do it." Elm stood up to clear the dishes. "Do you want to give M her bath?"

"No bath!" Moira screamed. "I already took a bath."

"No, you didn't," Elm said.

"But I don't want to."

"Yeah, well, we have to do a lot of things we don't want to do in this life, don't we?"

"Come on." Colin picked Moira up. "We can sing the bath time songs."

Immediately, Elm regretted speaking so harshly to her daughter. Sometimes the little girl's spoiled nature irked her, but if it was anyone's fault it was Elm's. Nannies, lessons, only-child-hood—no wonder Moira felt put out by any request that went contrary to her wishes.

That night in bed, with the rain falling heavily again and the tires sloughing off water twelve floors below on the wet streets, Colin snuggled up against Elm, breathing into the hair on the back of her neck. "Y'all gonna give us some somethin' somethin'?" he asked.

"Who's that voice?" Elm asked. "You sound like a deaf frog."

"Thanks."

There was a silence. Colin ran his hand over her stomach slowly, polishing it.

"What are we going to do this year?" Elm asked the ceiling.

"About what?"

"Ronan's birthday."

Colin's hand abruptly stopped. He pulled it back to himself as though she'd bitten it. "I don't know."

Elm said, "Maybe we should go away."

Colin turned, giving her his back. He was angry, hurt, Elm didn't know which. Why could she still not read his silences after ten-plus years of marriage? Was she not allowed to talk about Ronan? "Maybe."

After a silence Elm spoke. "I was going to say that I think I want to have another baby," she said. Until that moment, she didn't realize that she'd been thinking about getting pregnant, wondering if having another child might somehow ameliorate her grief.

"Really?" Colin said. "Is this the right time, do you think?"

"I'm over forty now. I don't know how long it'll take," Elm said. "And I don't want to regret not having started sooner. Or having waited too long."

"I don't know, Elm. Things are just so up in the air right now."

Elm looked at the headboard. The veneer was beginning to chip away, revealing the particleboard underneath. "I just feel like I'm ready." She shrugged. "We're ready."

"Let's see how things shake down at Moore first."

"Meaning . . . ?"

"Meaning you can let that worry you to sleep tonight."

His tone may have been harsh, Elm wasn't sure. Was he angry at her for wanting another child? Because she could explain to him that she wasn't trying to replace Ronan. Rather, she wanted the distraction of a new baby, the joy of creating a life. She would let the idea sink in and they could revisit it another time when Colin wasn't so worried about his job. She stared at the molding where the ceiling met the wall, slippery white painted wood like waves. She willed her mind still and concentrated, concentrated, until her gaze clouded over and she slipped among them.

———

That Thursday night Elm and Colin were supposed to go to a party. Elm didn't know the people and didn't want to go. All afternoon she grew more and more angry at Colin until she erupted while they were getting ready to go out.

"I don't know these people. *You* don't even really know these people. Budokon class at the gym does not count as a place to know people from."

"Come on," he'd returned. "You drag me to work events all the time."

"Yes, but you've *met* those people." Elm stopped straightening her hair and went out to the bedroom where he was picking a tie. "And, I don't have a choice. It's for work."

Colin said nothing. He tried on a jacket, then took it off and threw it on the bed. He surveyed his closet again.

"And are we tallying now?" Elm refused to let it drop. "Because I think Christmases in Galway count for a lot more than weekends at Pine Lake."

"Drop it, Elm. If you don't want to come, don't. I'll go alone."

Now Elm looked out the window of the taxi sulkily, imagining her face illuminated in the taxi's window as it reflected the buildings of Midtown. Why was she being so petulant? Because she was tired, she told herself. And she was too old to meet new people. The point of getting married, she argued with herself, is that you don't have to go to parties anymore if you don't want to. And here she was being dragged downtown to someone's TriBeCa loft. Any normal people would live on the Upper West or Upper East Side, unless they were artists or showoffs or fake bohemians. Elm went downtown only to see art openings and to shop, and, frankly, both were better above Fiftieth Street.

She realized when they exited the cab at Duane and Church that these gym friends of Colin's were going to be fake bohemians. The door was covered with half-scraped stickers of businesses past. Inside, Elm could see a lobby no bigger than a phone booth (she was dating herself, she knew, referencing things that no longer existed), and a small elevator that would inevitably smell of urine. Then they would get off the elevator directly into someone's multimillion-dollar apartment with spectacular views of what used to be the Twin Towers but was now a pair of missing teeth on the horizon and what would someday, maybe, be the Freedom Tower.

Colin was always doing this, making new friends. Part of it was his Irish accent. People thought he was friendly because he spoke with a lilt. It invited "Where are you from?" and then bred a false intimacy when they mentioned the time they'd traveled to Ireland and Colin feigned interest. And there was his smile, which, Elm admitted, was what attracted her to him in the first place. If she had to sum up Colin in one feature, it would be his mouth. A lopsided grin that made everyone else smile back, just the hint of teeth, like he was laughing because you were the funniest person on the planet. The mouth was so attractive that Elm hung out with it for weeks before she turned to him, outside a movie theater where they had seen a particularly sexy thriller, and said, "So are you going to kiss me ever?" and he looked somewhat stunned. Then he bent over to kiss her.

Ronan had inherited the same winning mouth. It made it nearly impossible for Elm to punish him, which he knew and exploited. He would smile goofily at her, and she would laugh, and his time-out would dissolve into giggles. He had a whole arsenal of expressions: the Puppy Dog, which always netted him ice cream; the Affected Pout, when he was exasperated by Elm; the Elvis, in which a curled lip meant he was humoring her attempts to cheer him; and the Toothless Glee, which, even when his teeth grew in, Elm always thought of as bare-gummed.

Elm had been wrong when she imagined that the elevator opened into the living room. Instead, there was a small mud room. They hung their coats on hooks and Colin rang the doorbell.

The door was opened by a man with a barrel chest so protuberant that Elm was reminded of a pin cushion, his arms and legs emanating like needles. His hair was long, though it only sparsely covered the putty-smooth crown of his scalp. He held a glass of champagne in his left hand. "Colin! Come in!" He swung the door wide and took a sip from his glass. Then he handed it to Colin and gestured for him to come in.

"You're the wife," he said.

"Elm," she supplied her name. She held out her hand to shake, but the barrel-man leaned forward and kissed her on both cheeks quickly. Elm felt the color rise to her face.

"I'm Dick," he said. Elm fought a juvenile urge to laugh.

Behind him, a large loft was fenced in by huge factory windows. On the walls hung several excellent pieces of modern art. Though Elm didn't particularly care for any work completed after 1920, she had to admire the collection: Basquiat, Rothko, Dine, and a couple of artists she didn't recognize. Guests posed on the various couches and chaises; they were universally attractive (though not prohibitively so), comfortable, well dressed.

"Ellen," Dick called. "Colin and his wife are here."

"Hello," said a woman walking toward them. She was wearing black cigarette pants and a blouse made out of a sort of shimmery silk. "So glad you could come. We've heard so much about you."

"Oh," was all Elm could think of saying. Ellen's hair was also long; it fell down her back in curls and waves. The temples were going gray. Elm disapproved of long hair on older women. So too the uncovered gray was a lie, the "I'm okay with my age" a mere front for the same insecure pore examination every woman over thirty performed every time she looked in a mirror. Anyone who pretended otherwise was a big phony.

Ellen drew Elm into the room while Dick poured Colin another drink. Elm met a few of the couples, who bore names that sounded like they'd made them up for the party: Kiki and Boris, Monique and Elvis,

Geraine and Enjay. But, she reasoned, her name probably sounded ridiculous to those who didn't know it was short for Elmira, a Tinsley family name that dated back to the seventeenth century. She felt Colin's reassuring presence at her back and accepted the glass of red wine he proffered.

"You should see this man's high kicks," Dick said. "Watch out!" He swung his leg in the air, spilling some of his drink.

Elm forgave Colin immediately. She even inched toward him, as though they found themselves marooned in unexplored New Guinea being stared at by indigenous tribesmen. It reminded her of when they were first married, and right after Ronan died, when, for different reasons, they had clung to each other so tightly that the rest of the world seemed mere window dressing, incidental.

And yet Colin was in his element. He and Dick were laughing about their Budokon instructor, a muscle-bound lothario named Giorgio who would "crush ya as soon as look at ya." Giorgio liked his class to find their "inna kick-ass" as well as their "levitational attitudes." Originally from Queens, Giorgio was an inveterate name dropper; he had been trained by Billy Barken, who was some sort of guru, and Giorgio's private clients included a nightclub impresario, several minor actors, and a reality television celebutante.

Elm sipped at her wine and smiled when it was appropriate. Exuberant people forced her into herself, to retreat back to her core. Colin expanded like a sponge. He did his Giorgio imitation, which Elm had never heard (had she?). All of Colin's impressions were hilarious, if only because the accent was so ludicrous.

Elm looked over the shoulder of a short, curvy woman toward the Basquiat on the wall. It was one of his later works. Almost without realizing it, Elm left the circle, which had moved onto exercise trends of past and present—Fluidity, Jazzercise, aerobics, step aerobics, Tae Bo, Pilates—to examine it up close. It exuded a peculiar artificial lemon smell. Elm supposed it was from the cleaning supplies used in the house. Sometimes a canvas or a varnish will take on characteristics of its environment, the way people begin to look like their dogs. Elm followed a brushstroke while it dipped and whorled, then disappeared.

The curvy woman said, "Isn't their art collection amazing? It would be easy to hate them, except they really love these paintings."

"Well, then, I guess it's money well spent."

The woman extended her hand. Her nails were long and painted a bright shade of pink. "Relay," she said.

Elm's brow must have knit, because the woman added, "Seriously, that's my name."

"Elm." The woman's hand was warm.

"Well," she said, as if to chide Elm for her equally preposterous name. "You want the tour?"

"Sure," Elm said. "Are you? Do you . . . ?"

"Art adviser."

"Oh," Elm said. She debated telling Relay what she did for a living. It inevitably changed the tone of the conversation. Art advisers relied on galleries for most of their purchases, since the clients were usually interested in contemporary art, but Elm's auction house got occasional communications from those interested in the older works in which Tinsley's specialized. If this woman knew that Elm was the specialist in Tinsley's drawings department, she would probably butter her up in the hopes that Elm could tip her off if there was something undervalued hitting an auction, or a real find that was somehow underpublicized. Of course, this kind of insider trading was illegal but widely practiced. Elm made a habit of not consorting with the salesmen of the art world.

Relay took her into a long hallway with doors on one side. On the left was a large Pollock, an early work. She opened the last door and they entered the study. Across from a leather couch hung an enormous flat-screen television, and for a moment Elm wondered if that was the art she was supposed to see. Then Relay turned and pointed at an equally large charcoal drawing by Renoir, a study for *Luncheon of the Boating Party*. The table was more prominent in this sketch; it covered about 60 percent of the paper's surface, and the "lens" was bigger, showing the table legs and feet wound around them, complete with two more Yorkshire terriers tearing at a piece of bread. A young woman who didn't appear in the finished painting sat next to Aline Charigot, looking overwhelmed by the spectacle. In the back stood a boy whose features, blurred though they were by the wide swath of the charcoal, coalesced unmistakably into Ronan's face. The same nose Elm had, Colin's curly hair, the slight build, the insouciant posing. Elm gasped.

"I know," Relay said. "It's beautiful, right?"

Elm nodded her head and forced back the lump in her throat that threatened to explode into tears.

"This is really their best piece. Very few of his sketches are still in existence. I heard he liked to burn them once the painting was complete. He felt they took the mystery out of the final product."

Relay took her into the bedroom and showed her the Joan Mitchell triptych and Chihuli vase that stood proudly in the corner, hovering near a pair of embroidered Louis XIV chairs. Elm made all the admiring sounds she knew were appropriate to the situation, but she was still thinking about the Renoir. She was always picking Ronan out of crowds, and Colin or Ian would tell her she was imagining things. Yes, it was a boy with curly brown hair, but, really, he looked nothing like Ronan. He was obviously part Asian, or his lips were too full. She persisted, though. It gave her comfort to imagine him walking down New York streets, or little parts of him finding their way into other children.

Relay opened another door, which revealed a marble bathroom. Between the his-and-hers mirrors was an oil portrait of a Rhodesian Ridgeback. The dog was sitting stiffly in front of the Chihuli in the bedroom, head tilted quizzically at the viewer. It was a very realistic portrait, and completely devoid of any artistry whatsoever. Representational, not imaginative.

Relay said, "So many of my clients are into pet portraits these days. I have this woman on the Upper East Side who can paint from photographs if she has to. She met Dishoo before he died, though. Isn't he adorable?"

Elm opened her mouth to say something noncommittally positive. She wondered if Colin was looking for her. They'd been gone awhile. Her empty wineglass was warm in her hand.

"They loved this dog. In fact, I was talking to Ellen and they are thinking of having him cloned."

"What?" asked Elm. She was tired. "Cloned, like in bronze?"

"No, actually cloned."

"We're looking into the possibility, Relay. Don't tell tales out of school." Ellen stood in the doorway, silhouetted in black against the frame like a cameo.

Relay didn't look remotely embarrassed. "Devotion like yours to a pet is rare."

"Dishoo was a special dog." Ellen walked between the women to air-kiss the portrait. "So smart. Once, when the neighbor's apartment was on fire, and for some reason the smoke alarm didn't go off, he barked until we woke up and were able to call the fire department. On 9/11 I had to sneak past the barricades to get him out. We loved him so much."

"Was he old?" Elm managed to ask.

"Heart gave out. We had him put to sleep. A kindness we can't give humans, but at least Dish died painlessly in my arms. This portrait was painted a few years ago, when he was in his prime. And now, thanks to the miracles of modern science, we may have him back."

"You can't be serious," Elm said. "Isn't that illegal?"

"Not in Europe!" Ellen said brightly. Then her face hardened, and Elm could tell she was just remembering that someone had told her that Elm's son had died. Elm knew this look on people's faces, when they caught themselves either alluding to their own inconsequential troubles or reminding Elm of her dead son, as if she had forgotten, even for five minutes, as if she would ever forget. Ellen recovered quickly. "Has Relay shown you everything? The Renoir?" Ellen leaned over toward Relay and stage-whispered, "Elm's at Tinsley's, I hear, a specialist."

"Drawings and prints," Elm confirmed reluctantly, "seventeenth-to nineteenth-century."

Relay looked impressed, though not astonished. Perhaps she didn't have a surprise gene, or had she already known?

"We'll have you back when Dishoo's . . ." Ellen searched for the word. "Reincarnated, so to speak. You can compare the portrait to the real thing."

Elm laughed, but the other women didn't join in. She turned the laugh into a smile. "Could I trouble you for a refill?" she asked.

"Certainly!" Ellen replied. "Did you enjoy it? Dick and I love this vineyard and we bought up all the 2001's." Relay turned out the light before Elm could get a last glimpse of the silent dog.

In the living room, Colin was holding court, drinking a cocktail glass full of brown liquid. Scotch, most likely. He was on his way to getting drunk, which didn't upset Elm. He was a hilarious drunk, laughing loudly and telling stories. His personality was amplified with liquor. It was a testament to his fundamental good nature that this temperament was kind and gentle, if a bit boisterous. Elm got quiet and sulky with liquor, so she made sure to limit her intake. Since she'd had the children she'd lost her tolerance, and after a couple of nights celebrating Moira's weaning, lying in bed with the apartment building spinning around her precariously, a balloon of nausea attempting to climb her esophagus, she limited herself to a couple of glasses of wine. Thus, she was the designated driver, which, in New York, meant the designated cab finder.

When he saw her he extended his arm and spun her around so she fit against his shoulder. "Where've you been?" he asked her.

"Touring the art."

"Big artsies, these ones."

"They're cloning their dog."

"What?"

"I said, they're cloning their dog. It died and they had a portrait painted of it, and now they're going to have the dog cloned. In Europe."

"Too much money, not enough sense," Colin whispered. "But the scotch is excellent. Want a taste?" Elm shook her head.

After refilling her glass, Elm went to sit on the sofa. Another woman joined her and Elm discovered that the woman's sister had also gone to Wesleyan, but she was older than Elm and Elm hadn't known her. The woman asked how many children Elm had, and she paused before answering that she had just the one. They discussed private schools, then babysitters. A man joined them, the woman's husband. Elm did her impression of Moira aping some teenage pop star, innocently changing the lyrics from "love me up" to "love me 'nuff" and "wanna crash your party" to "wanna crash your potty," which always made her giggle.

The woman's face was open, with wide-set eyes. The left was slightly bigger than the right, though she had tried to disguise this with makeup, painting a wider swatch of eyeliner on the bigger one. Someone had given her lessons, and from far away it worked. The man's body was half youthful strength and half pot-bellied middle-ager. He had beautiful salt-and-pepper hair. Elm wondered if that's how people saw her and Colin, a nice couple, well groomed, well suited. Or, she wondered, was their tragedy apparent? Had it aged them or matured them in a way that was perceptible, even to a stranger?

She felt Colin's hand on her shoulder. She introduced the couple to him, and said that their daughter was born the same year as Moira, and was attending the school they had almost decided to send her to. It was superior to the one they ended up at, but they thought they wouldn't have the energy to schlep all the way across the park and down fifteen blocks every morning for fourteen years. At least Moira was close to home.

"Almost ready?" Colin asked her. "It's nearing midnight."

"No," Elm gasped in disbelief. Had she been forced to guess the time, she might have said ten p.m. "It was lovely to meet you," she said to the couple. "We have to relieve the babysitter. She has science club in the morning or something."

They said their good-byes, and this time both Dick and Ellen kissed Elm's cheeks. Relay slipped her a card; Elm put it in her jacket pocket without looking at it. "You'll come back and meet Dishoo, right?" Ellen called as the elevator door closed.

"Wouldn't miss it!" Elm said.

"Who's Dishoo?" Colin asked. The elevator gave a lurching start.

"The dog they're cloning. Rhodesian Ridgeback, maybe?"

"Am I pissed or am I missing something? How are they cloning their dog?"

"I think you're pissed *and* missing something," Elm said. "I don't know. I didn't ask. Europe, maybe. I think it's legal there?"

Colin shook his head. "Crazy as fucking loons, the rich are."

Gabriel

The letter was florid and embossed. Nothing French was official without raised lettering, which required paper solid enough to withstand the pressure. This letter had a particularly ornate seal, a ring of flowers and a headless crown. "We regret to inform you, despite the excellence of the submitted materials, and with extreme sadness due to the number of deserving candidates who will not have the opportunity to realize the experience doubtlessly anticipated in the solicitation of this prize, that your entry was among countless worthy applications that have not been awarded the 2007 Prix des Artistes Émergents."

A lot of verbiage to say, "Fuck off."

He wanted to murder the messenger: to crumple up the page or rip it into indistinguishable pieces. But violence to paper was against his nature. Paper was delicate, precious. Even modern paper, readily available and inexpensive. Even paper delivering bad news.

The sun was shining, a rare occasion in rainy Paris, and Gabriel fingered the letter in his pocket as he walked down the Rue St. Joseph on his way to work, threading his way among the garment racks and bolts of cloth. The men in orange jumpsuits were out in droves at this hour, hosing down the sidewalks and urging the water toward the gutters with plastic fronds. Gabriel stepped around one man wielding a lethal-looking brush, scrubbing particularly stubborn dog shit stains.

Why did Gabriel still bother to apply for these prizes? It was embarrassing to be still looking for emerging artist grants when he was more than fifteen years out of school. Every year's rejection resulted in a resolution not to humble himself before the prejudiced committees again, but when each deadline came around his dire financial straits prompted him to send in his work, open himself up to yet another round of disappointment. It was a particularly unfortunate day to receive bad career news; his friend/rival from his days at the École des Beaux-Arts, Didier, was having an opening for his solo show tonight at a well-regarded gallery. Gabriel quickened his step so he wouldn't be late to work.

Though not the most renowned gallery, Rosenzweig Gallery was nonetheless located in the fashionable Marais district, and dealt mostly in older drawings. Édouard Rosenzweig hired only École graduates to be his assistants. In exchange for horrendous hours and little pay, he offered a crash course in the business side of art. Business was a practical matter untaught and unmentioned in the École—anyone uncouth enough to care about paying rent was either a poseur or a capitalist.

Édouard had originally chosen Gabriel because of his surname. Connois was not his real name—it was the name of his illustrious ancestor Marcel Connois, a major Spanish painter from the French school of Hiverains and a contemporary of Degas. Gabriel's actual name was Holgado y Rodríguez, hardly evocative and, well, Spanish. Marcel Connois's work was displayed in all the major museums of the world, and Gabriel's mother used to swear that two major works had hung in her childhood house, both now owned by the Hermitage: *Adam Leads Eve from the Garden* and *Portrait of a Muse.* His ancestors had come from France at some unknown point in time, bringing with them the French surname (not unusual in Cataluña).

Gabriel had obviously inherited his relative's talent; he had won a full scholarship to the École, beating out dozens of better-trained artists who were technically superior, at least initially. Gabriel had enjoyed five student years in Paris, living in the garret apartments provided by the school, eating *menus fixes* and drinking cheap plonk that invariably gave him a terrible headache. Then, somehow, fifteen years had passed and he woke up one morning feeling the weight of his age, the absence of accomplishments as heavy as their presence might have been.

Along the way there had been crumbs of success, tantalizing tastes: group shows, purchase of his work by regional museums, a write-up in an avant-garde Barcelona magazine. But he still ate *merguez* waiting for the month's paycheck to arrive, he still had to beg for supplies, and recently, disconcertingly, his lower back had been paining him, tight across the top of his buttocks, and no amount of stretching or icing would relieve it. And he was still working a full-time job for The Man, eking out an existence as a gallery slave and desperately searching for time and money to work on his art.

Inside the gallery, the light was muted by the window screens. Gabriel left the grate pulled halfway down, a signal to passersby that someone was in but not ready to receive business. Then he made coffee with an Italian percolator, standing and drumming his hands on the counter while he waited for the gurgling to stop. He spilled sugar on the counter and used his hand to sweep it into his coffee. The staccato grinding of the lifting grate was followed by the unmistakably unhurried footsteps of his boss.

Édouard was dressed uncharacteristically in a suit and tie, the former of a pistachio color popular among panelists on television current events roundtable programs, the latter a muted solid saffron. He wore a Kangol cap with the bill in front and carried a black, seemingly empty briefcase.

"Ahh, café," he said by way of greeting.

Gabriel handed him the *tasse* without speaking and unscrewed the percolator, retracing his steps. Édouard flipped through the morning mail, leaving it in an untamed pile on the counter.

"So," he said, acknowledging Gabriel with a flick of his chin. "Today we have an appointment at noon."

Gabriel leaned against the counter; his tight black jeans didn't allow him to sit down fully. He had worked for Édouard longer than any other assistant, longer than he should have. On his ten-year anniversary with Édouard, his boss bought him a cake and gave him a miniature drawing, some scrap of a Piranesi sketch. It was easily the most valuable thing Gabriel owned.

"He was recommended to me through Jean-Marie as a dealer of some importance," Édouard continued.

"You should have told me," Gabriel said. "I would have dressed."

"You're fine the way you are." Édouard smiled approvingly. The wrinkles around his eyes grew deeper. They sat in bags of skin, like a Shar-Pei puppy, while the rest of his face remained unlined, as though his eyes were older than the rest of him. "If you could prepare some of our pieces for inspection . . ."

Gabriel nodded, tossed back his coffee. He knew the stock better than Édouard did, better than the inventory list. He walked into the storeroom and put on the white cotton gloves. He should pull out a representative sample of their good work, not their best. Something should be held back. A little reticence could be sensed. It would not do to seem overeager.

The visitor's appointment would explain Édouard's outfit. This was someone to impress. But Édouard had dressed flamboyantly; obviously Jean-Marie had told him that the dealer's taste admitted novelty. From the locked cabinet, Gabriel removed a couple of eighteenth-century drawings from the Italian School, a sketch after Rubens, and two well-preserved seventeenth-century etchings of a Brueghel drawing. He complemented the selection with a lesser-known Corot and a not entirely successful landscape by a young Cézanne.

Nearly every time he performed this task for Édouard he remembered the Rembrandt preparatory sketch for a self-portrait the artist completed the year he died. It was early in Gabriel's extended apprenticeship, and he had fingered the yellowed paper carefully, holding the watermark up to the light. The paper itself was beautiful, thick and uneven, rough like a winter beach. Worms had eaten through the page in a couple of places, and when Gabriel turned it over, despite the thickness of the paper a faint ink line showed through. Also on the back was Rembrandt's signature, the pregnant *R* and the perfectly aligned letters, followed by the date: 1667.

And, ah, the drawing itself. The sure, strong lines centered the bulbous face. The background was cross-hatched into a darkness the artist would later imitate in oil, his gray hair curled from underneath his cap. In the sketch, the artist wore a wry smile, which he replaced with a tired grimace in the final portrait. Gabriel had eased off one of his cotton gloves and lightly traced the rounded chin, imagining, for a minute, the complete confidence of the master's hand. He was not supposed to touch the drawings—the oil from his fingers could compromise the graphite or the paper, but just being that close to such a master draftsman sent a frisson of pleasure that was not unlike a sexual thrill down his back.

In comparison, these sketches were anemic, and Gabriel found the task menial, rote. As he arranged the chosen stock on the light table, he was confident that his choices would please Édouard. He hoped the collector would be interested in the pieces; someone, at least, should have a good day.

————

Despite his best efforts to ignore the hype, it was clear to Gabriel that Didier's show at Galerie de Treu was eagerly anticipated by art critics and collectors. There were actual advertisements in *L'Officiel des Spectacles,* which Didier showed him proudly at the studio, and a short article in *Paris Match.* Gabriel had debated whether to go to the *vernissage* at all, but Didier had come to his studio, his smile making him look like the kid he had been when they had met more than twenty years ago, telling Gabriel how much this show meant to him and how it was a triumph for everyone who didn't sell out or quit. At de Treu's gallery, Didier's career seemed suddenly assured. Gabriel assumed that Didier could look forward to enough income from sales of his work to permanently quit the asinine job he'd been holding.

That night, Gabriel met Hans outside the *métro.* Wordlessly the two artists began to walk toward the gallery, shuffling, Gabriel thought, like condemned men on the way to the gallows. He should be happy for his classmate. He knew that Didier's success should suggest to him that his own was still possible.

Hans tripped over a lose stone. "Christ, I'm drunk."

"Already?" Gabriel asked.

"I told Brigitte that it started at five. I don't get to go out at night that often."

The gallery was as crowded as Gabriel had feared it would be. The title of the show was painted on the window: "Aching Thighs." The small over-the-door air conditioner chugged futilely, blowing like wisps of breath on the sweaty faces of Paris's art community.

Didier was dressed in what Gabriel considered to be a simulacrum of artist-wear, a tuxedo jacket paired with a James Dean white T-shirt, jeans, and gaudy orange sneakers. He was surrounded by a gaggle of admirers, de Treu himself (the Salvador Dalí mustache was unmistakable) guarding against the crush of intelligentsia. No one could have seen the art even if they wanted to, but all eyes were trained on the crowd, not the walls.

Rather than fight to greet Didier, Hans and Gabriel made their way to the bar. Unusual for an opening, this bar was fully stocked. Hans ordered a whiskey. Gabriel held up a finger, indicating he wanted one too. Hans made a big show of removing a twenty-euro bill from his wallet and dropping it into the tip jar. The bartender, in recognition, poured them doubles and winked. It would never have occurred to Gabriel to tip so grandly at an open bar. But of course that was what got you the biggest drinks the quickest.

Gabriel lost Hans in a crush of people, and decided to try to see the paintings.

Since their days at the École, Didier had been painting a series of women from the point of view of their vaginas. Curly hair, fleshy legs, painted toes. Sometimes a penis coming toward the viewer, intent on entering the viewer's space. Then he began to experiment with the legs, the color, the background. It wasn't bad, in Gabriel's opinion. Technically a little facile, but Didier had been the workhorse, doggedly continuing with his oeuvre while everyone declared painting over. And now that painting had come back, here was Didier, ready. Gabriel understood why it would sell—the male artist painting from the woman's perspective. And, hung here against the backdrop of the tall white walls, it looked, well, it looked like real art. He stood back to try to create some distance between himself and the painting in front of him, to see it as a whole, when he felt a foot beneath his own.

"Excuse me." He turned to find a woman standing behind him. Her blond hair framed a face slightly older than his, skin taut across its prominent cheekbones. It took him a minute to place her. Lise. He had been so in love with her at school, consumed by thoughts of her. He loved her Frenchness, the unthinking way she was able to summon a check or ask if someone was using a chair without drawing stares or questions, when it felt to him that clearing his throat was announcing his foreignness.

Last he'd heard she was working as an assistant to Mikhail Ambrosine, a popular painter-turned-gallerist. And had she married? Yes, he'd heard that. Someone not French.

"It's okay, I have another foot." Lise smiled. "How are you, Gabi?"

Only his mother had ever called him that. When other people used the diminutive it usually annoyed him, but he was happy to hear the familiarity.

"Fine. Good." He kissed her on each cheek. Remembering his love for Lise amused him. It had to have been, what, six, seven years since he'd last seen her? Where did people go when they left your mind? When you no longer thought about them daily, weekly, yearly, at all? They ceased to exist for you, but yet their lives went on.

"How is it possible that in a city as small as Paris we don't run into each other?" Lise asked.

Gabriel shrugged. They moved in different circles, that was obvious by her expensive clothing: a black silk sheath that covered one shoulder. The exposed one was freckled and tiny. The dress hung down, skimming her breasts and hips and stopping just above the floor.

"Have you ever met my husband, Giancarlo? Gio, my old friend from school, Gabi." The man, who was in his early fifties, looked distracted and slightly bewildered. They shook hands and Gabriel saw that the man wore a diamond ring. Gio's eyes alit on the bar.

"What do you want? I'll go," Gabriel offered.

"Thanks," Gio said, with the gruff trace of an accent. "She'll have champagne. I'll have a bourbon."

Gabriel fought his way to the bar and found his bartender friend, who quickly filled three drinks. Hans was truly brilliant. Gabriel squeezed through the crowd to find Lise and her husband laughing with a dark-haired woman in a print wrap-around dress.

He handed the couple their drinks. "What would you like?" he asked the woman. Her features were sharp but attractive; she wore the kind of makeup that looked as though she wasn't wearing any makeup at all, an unseasonal glow.

"Are you the waiter?" she asked.

Gabriel blushed, and Lise introduced them. "This is Colette; she's at Tinsley's, you know, the famous auction house. Gabi was one of the best in our class."

It was interesting how living for so long in a foreign country had changed Gabriel. If they were conversing in his own language, he might have made a joke or asked a question about her job. But in French, while he could come up with the words, he would probably mangle the grammar. Anything he said would invite a question about his origins, or at least a confused smile while the person parsed his accent. So he said only, "Hello," kissing her on both cheeks.

Colette smiled, which made her nose crinkle upward fetchingly. She was darker than a typical Frenchwoman, with curly brown hair she'd pinned back into an unruly chignon.

Marie-Laure, another classmate with whom Gabriel shared studio space, approached Lise and gave her a hug. The women squealed in excitement to see each other, which left Gabriel and Colette standing awkwardly together. Gio was typing rapidly on his phone.

"So," Colette said. "You know Lise from the École?"

Gabriel nodded.

The woman stood as if she were smoking, her left hand across her body, her right hand held up in a peace sign, an imaginary cigarette between her fingers.

Gabriel struggled to think of something to say. "You work at Tinsley's," he finally sputtered. "What is your job?"

"Oh, it's mostly clerical, though, you know, I went to school in conservation and connoisseurship. We are merely an outpost of the New York house, arranging for European transportation and acquisition."

"Old art?" Gabriel said. It was a question, though he didn't phrase it with the long French interrogative.

"Mostly. Some contemporary, if it's well-known, though, you know most of the interesting stuff is coming out of developing countries, or America, not Europe so much. And so much is undisplayable junk, video, or ephemera."

Gabriel nodded. He had been a video artist, once upon a time. Colette looked bored. He could see her eyes darting around the crowd.

Lise and Marie-Laure rescued him. "It's like an École reunion!" Lise exclaimed.

"Because we're all hoping to meet de Treu," Marie-Laure said. She was dressed like a little girl, in knee socks and a pleated skirt.

"Or Cosimo de' Medici," Gabriel interjected. It came out more glumly than he'd planned, and as he said it he realized he was looking at Giancarlo.

Lise narrowed her eyes and took her husband's arm. "Well, I say, good for Didi." She raised her glass.

"To Didi," Marie-Laure echoed. Gabriel drained his glass. He was on his way to being very drunk.

"Colette, did Gabi tell you that he is a descendant of Connois?"

"No." Colette turned to him with renewed interest.

"Yes," Lise said. "He does fantastic imitations. Colette is a specialist in Impressionist painting. You've handled some Connoises, right?"

Colette nodded. "How fascinating."

Didier came upon the group and kissed everyone on both cheeks. "Thank you so much for coming," he said earnestly. He was sweating in his tuxedo jacket. "I really—it means so much to me." Gabriel wasn't sure if it was the lights or if Didier's eyes were moist. For some reason, perhaps because of nervousness, this tearing struck Gabriel as irresistibly funny. Involuntarily, he giggled, and an embarrassed silence descended on the group, graver for the noise around them.

"Well," Lise said. "We have to pay the babysitter, so . . ."

Everyone repeated the kisses to say good-bye, and congratulated Didier again. As Lise leaned into Gabriel, she whispered sternly, "Behave," like she was scolding a naughty child. He felt his face flush.

Colette placed a hand on his forearm. "Do you have a card?" she asked.

Gabriel shook his head.

"Here," she said, presenting him with the postcard of the show, "write down your number. I'd like to talk to you about Connois, if you don't mind." A strawberry-scented curl of hair fell in her face as she opened her small pocketbook.

He wrote down his cell number and she put the postcard in her purse, snapping it tightly and patting it to confirm it held something valuable. "I'll be in touch," she said.

Hans appeared. "Who was that?" he asked. "Pretty, for a Frenchwoman. And was that Lise?" Hans was drunk, slurring his words slightly. "She looks good," he said. Gabriel couldn't tell if he was smiling behind his beard. "Are we really in our fucking forties?"

Gabriel turned to him: "I would like to get blind, stinking drunk."

———

The next day, after slogging, dehydrated and irritated, through work, Gabriel made the trek to his studio. The space was cheap and illegal, so far out beyond the Périphérique that it almost didn't deserve the title "suburb." A friend from school had jury-rigged the place, pirating electricity and erecting crude walls of corrugated cardboard.

Gabriel nodded at Didier, who sat on a supermarket crate near the front door, smoking. Didier had been a part of his life since he arrived in France twenty-one years ago. They weren't friends exactly, but years of proximity had cultivated a mutual fondness. When Gabriel slipped on the ice outside Galeries Lafayette last winter and hit his head, they wouldn't let him leave the hospital unless someone came to get him. He called Didier, thanking him by taking him out for a beer.

If Gabriel hadn't seen Didier's finished canvases, he wouldn't have believed that Didier got anything done, so often did cigarettes interrupt his day. In fact, Gabriel thought that it would be fairer to say that painting interrupted his smoking. But it seemed to work for him. Gabriel wished, not for the first time, that he was a smoker too, so he'd have something ostensibly productive to do while avoiding painting.

The air had grown cold now that the sun had set, and Gabriel hugged his arms to his torso and shifted from foot to foot. Didier emerged from the darkness, pushing himself upright from his smoking squat.

"Hey," he said.

"Hey," Gabriel replied. He hadn't expected to see Didier in the studio. If it had been the day after his solo show, Gabriel would be lying in bed, or getting a massage. "Your show was really great."

"Thanks," Didier said hollowly.

"I'm surprised to see you here," Gabriel said. "I thought you would move out of the studio, you know, after the show."

"Not everything sold. What did sell, you know, the commission, materials. I mean, I'm not dirt poor anymore, but it's not like I'm buying a mansion on Avenue Foch or anything."

Gabriel was surprised that he and Didier were still peers. He had expected that Didier's show would enable real studio space, shows in other countries, attention for his previous work. But it seemed that Didier's brush with greatness was just that, a slight catch of the wrist, a fleeting touch. Gabriel should have known better than to be surprised, should have known that the art world never simply anoints royalty.

Didier pinched the end of his cigarette and threw it on the ground. "You look terrible."

"I have a hangover." Gabriel hugged himself tighter. "My work's going badly."

"Sorry, man. That sucks. I've been there. But, I mean, work through it. You'll have a show soon. It'll be your turn."

Gabriel frowned.

"Seriously, man. I mean, you won the student choice award at the École. You have massive talent. It'll happen for you. Hey, have you ever sent de Treu your slides? You know, he reps Gutierrez, he might like your stuff."

Gabriel was often compared to Gutierrez, a Spanish abstract imagist whose artwork bore nothing in common with Gabriel's.

"I'm not really ready," Gabriel said. "I'm transitioning." Gabriel never sent out his slides. He considered it akin to hawking his wares on a street corner.

"Come on, man. You gotta put yourself out there. Otherwise, it's like some previous century dream of poverty and burning canvas to stay warm. There's no noble artist anymore, no purity. There're just working artists, and that's us, so we work it."

Didier patted his pockets to make sure his lighter was secure. "I gotta head back in. Take care, man." He clapped Gabriel on the back twice and made his way inside.

Gabriel waited a minute, then followed. Inside, he wound around the maze of walls, the clip lights throwing harsh shadows. It was cold in the studio. Space heaters brought little warmth and tended to blow the electric lines. Fires were sometimes started in barrels, hobo style, but often smoked more than warmed, and tended to draw attention. Usually, the starving artists slaved away in the cold, wearing an unofficial uniform of scarves and fingerless gloves.

When Gabriel came to his area, it was dark and shadowed. A silhouette of a chair, the can of turpentine, a bouquet of brushes. He stood in the gloom for a moment and looked at his painting. He was painting large scale, much larger than he had at school. Édouard lent him stretchers; canvas was not too expensive; he mixed his own gesso. His paintings were Classical Realist, an evolution of the atelier method taught at the École. They usually showed public French spaces occupied by dozens of French figures who were not French: gypsies, Africans, Arabs.

After graduation, he thought he had left painting forever. In the rush of new technology, the increased digitalization of the world, he began a series of video installations. There was so much money at the end of the nineties that patrons practically gave him equipment and walls on which to project his art. He'd worked with a computer programmer, synchronizing screens and creating sound pieces to accompany them. But then everyone started manipulating video. His work became passé.

So he revisited his thesis, a series of canvases. They seemed to him now to show talent, a skill for color and composition, but they were also naïve, the work of someone who had yet to live in the real world. He was not embarrassed by them, but it was like looking at someone else's work.

Occasionally he could conjure up that young, idealistic person again, but only in the realm of memory, swift flashes of sentiment that left as quickly as they arrived. He had changed, yes. Had he grown?

He'd spent a year away from his studio. It made him anxious to hear the industry of all the others in the space. He drank more than he should have. His right motorcycle boot developed a hole that the Russian cobbler couldn't repair. And then one day he felt like painting again, and he went back to the studio, where nothing had changed, really, everyone still tossing paint at the wall or plastic in the mold, ending up with an anti-aesthetic, ugly and formless. He was rusty. He tried not to judge himself too harshly, but the inner critic was loud and unforgiving.

It took him six months to paint something halfway decent. Another year to perfect his canvas preparation technique (he liked a surface as smooth as poured resin, a process that required endless gesso and sandpaper).

Now Gabriel lined up his tubes of paint. He didn't feel like painting tonight. He felt like lying on a couch and watching an old John Wayne movie on television. He felt like sitting in his mother's kitchen watching her fry *morcilla*, hovering above the hearth like a medieval archangel. But he had no television (nor couch, for that matter) and his mother had been dead for a decade. He longed for a home, and that made him angry with himself. An artist thrived on imbalance, on the edge of deprivation, which made him strive for more. Comfort bred complacency. He leaned against the studio wall, which bowed under his meager weight. He straightened, steadied the wall.

This painting wasn't done, but he wasn't sure why. It was like a sentence left trailing off. It was like his French: fine, but not eloquent, not quite right. He was calling it *La Gare*, and it was simply the corner of a nonspecific railway station, a gypsy beggar and a woman having a nervous smoke. He was trying to work mostly with a gray palette, branching out into olives and mauves, but the subjects refused to blend adequately, almost like he had cut out and collaged separate paintings. There was something unfluid about his work. Gabriel's professor at the École had called it "brutal." The gallerist he'd convinced to pay a studio visit said it felt "unfiltered, diffuse." But it wasn't that. The canvas was somehow always present in his work. Like a helium balloon tethered to a chair, it was never able to transcend its medium.

When Gabriel was stuck, he liked to copy paintings in his sketch-

book. He opened the dog-eared coffee table book he'd bought off the
quai for ten euros at the end of a long, rainy day. A plate of Canaletto's
The Feast Day of St. Roch was most interesting because of the trio of
figures standing along the canal edge. Though blurry, there was a natu-
ralness to their poses; something had caught their eyes while they were
busy with other tasks. A man in robes, two women, one of whom was
carrying her shopping. Quickly, Gabriel got absorbed, picking up his
pencil and sketchbook. He sat on the high stool and began to draw. He
sketched the form of the man, his female neighbor next.

He hummed nearly silently, "The doge is coming, the doge is coming," to remember why the figures were staring at the palace, though
nothing was happening. "The doge is visiting. It is an important day, a
day to keep heads up and eyes bright. A day to shade foreheads to see
farther in the setting sun." Gabriel sketched a sharp shadow, a raised
flat hand. "The robes swirl in a sudden gust of wind. The sleeves of
the woman puff and undulate. She clutches her basket. She has purchased . . . a chicken and . . ."

His own preparatory sketches looked anemic, incomplete, yet this
one, in Canaletto's style, for Canaletto's painting, that had already
been long completed, was alive. The lines were fluid, like Canaletto's,
the hand sure, the graphite thick. This was not the way art was done.
This was backward, drawing sketches of museum pieces would get him
nowhere but the weekend swap at the *marché aux puces*.

Disgusted, Gabriel lit a piece of incense, aware that if Marie-Laure
were here, she'd yell over the partition. He felt constricted—roommates,
studio-mates, boss, even his fucking pants were too tight. Fuck motherfucking Canaletto.

Sure enough, Marie-Laure's tight soprano summited the corrugated
walls. "We agreed you wouldn't light that in here," she said. "You know
it bothers my lungs."

And yet the turpentine and oil paints and fixative are mountain air,
Gabriel thought. Out loud he said, "Sorry."

His phone vibrated. It was a text message, which he had to hold far
from his face to read the small letters. "What's up?" it read.

It took him several minutes to type out, "Who is this?" Why did
everyone think texting was so much faster than calling? He could not
get his phone to put in the correct accent marks.

"Colette :)"

Was that a sideways smiley face? Still, he sat up straighter. This was an interesting development.

"What are you up to?"

He tried to make his fingers hit the small keys, but he kept passing up letters and turning them into numbers. Without meaning to, he pressed call.

By the time he realized what he'd done it was too late. Colette answered on the fourth ring. She sounded out of breath.

"Hi," he said. "It's me."

"Hello?" Colette said. "Who's this?"

"Gabriel," he identified himself.

"Oh, hi!" she said. She was someplace loud. The gym? A restaurant? A train station? His left hand worried the seam of his jeans against his thigh.

Colette let the silence sit over the phone. She was obviously not going to help him. But why would she have contacted him if she didn't want to see him?

"Would you like to have dinner?" he asked.

"Sure," Colette answered quickly. "When?"

"Um, I don't know. Tonight?" Gabriel said. There was a silence. Gabriel closed his eyes, though it felt like it was brighter behind his lids. Why was he so awkward? Had it been so long since he'd asked someone out?

"Yeah, okay, sure. Where do you want to meet?"

Gabriel ran through a mental log of places he'd eaten before. They were few. The couscous place near school. That place he passed by on his way to the *métro*. Very French: candles and boars' heads and lots of silverware. Finally, he named a touristy brasserie where he'd never eaten.

Colette laughed. "You're hilarious."

Gabriel laughed as well, as though he'd meant to make a joke. "You decide."

She said, "La Tour de L'Oqueau," and named an address.

Gabriel hung up, elated. There was nothing to do to clean up, no paints to cover, no chemicals to dispose of. Just put the pencil back into the box and close the coffee table book. It was like Gabriel was never even there.

Elm

lm's colleague Ian had investigated the Attic and returned with some postcard-sized oils and accompanying drawings of the Hudson River School. Whittredge, not Elm's favorite, but still name enough to draw the Hudson River Rats out of the proverbial woodwork for the fall auctions. Elm asked Ian to do the legwork—confirm the provenance, send the pieces to the authenticator, investigate potential reserves. The Hudson River School was in a minor resurgence—there'd been a secondary exhibit at the Fogg that reacquainted the public with its existence.

It was only later that day that she realized she had not asked to see the paintings or drawings for herself. This lack of curiosity, she knew, was a symptom of the depression she'd been suffering since Ronan died. She stopped being interested in things not directly affecting her immediate circumstances. She'd lost all natural curiosity: What's behind that door? What did that person mean? How does wireless work? And here she was, a supposed expert, a presumed devotee, who sent the drawings directly to the lab, to science, when she probably could have told just by looking at them whether they were forged, misattributed, or the real McCoy.

Elm was a keen judge of drawings, etchings, lithographs, and all prints prior to the twentieth century. She wished she could trust Ian's eye, but they had both agreed, after a couple of martinis at the Algonquin Hotel one night, that Ian's talents lay in client relations—in selling or commissioning art, not appreciating it. He admired it, adored it even, loved being around it, took an aesthete's pleasure in viewing it. But he lacked that critical and ineluctable something that allowed a viewer to hear a painting speak—the "eye." Elm had it, a way of seeing through a painting or drawing, of gathering in an instant its myriad qualities, good or bad, and forming an almost infallible judgment. No amount of study or exposure could teach you the eye if you weren't born with it. And while it wasn't necessary to have the eye to work in art (many collectors, gallerists, and even some artists lacked it and were successful), it was essential for a director. Ian would grow and deepen, certainly, gain a greater store of knowledge from which to draw comparisons, but he would always be hobbled by his dead eye.

Elm's eye, on the other hand, had been honed since birth, growing up her whole life around Tinsley's with its revolving museum-like galleries. She looked at the drawings, let her gaze soften, and became, just for the moment, the artist himself. Apart from her acquired knowledge about paper, materials, subject matter, and style, she could effect this transubstantiation. That and her position at Tinsley's led to her acknowledged preeminence in the field.

Ian poked his head through her door, then came in and sat down without waiting for an invitation. "So, up near Columbia, right?" he said. It took Elm a minute to figure out he was talking about his visit to the Attic. "Picture one of those old buildings that has housed academics for the past couple hundred years. The lobby's marble has grooves between door and mailboxes and stairs. The elevator—unspeakable. I took the stairs, of course. Fifth floor. I knock. There's no answer. But I'd made an appointment with the caregiver. Finally, a shuffling noise, and the door creaks open, straight out of some Bela Lugosi film. This woman, one hundred years old, skin hanging off in folds, some nightmare of old age, answers the door and without speaking waves me in."

Here Ian paused for effect. Elm loved his stories the way Moira loved being read to at night. She wanted to hear them over and over again, revel in the inconsistencies, in their slight variations.

"So I walk into this apartment, and I swear it is unchanged from 1940. I half-expected to see Marlene Dietrich waltz in from stage right. Not only that, it hasn't been cleaned since then either. And piles and piles of stuff—newspapers, folders, advertisements, boxes, envelopes. Just like the those brothers . . . What's their names?"

"The Collyer brothers," Elm filled in. They were part of New York lore, the brothers who saved every newspaper for fifty years and then died inside their prison of newsprint.

"Right. Complete with the paths between piles from kitchen to bedroom to toilet."

"Just like the marble grooves in the lobby."

"Don't throw my storytelling inadequacies back at me. What, Homer never repeated an epithet?"

"Sorry," Elm said. She leaned forward and put her chin in her hands, pantomiming rapt attention. "Pray, continue."

"She still hasn't spoken to me, but we go into the bedroom, where a wan light is shining through the windows, illuminating the dust motes."

"Poetic," said Elm.

Ian ignored her. "And then she points to the drawings, which are in a Woolworth's shopping bag, circa, say, 1920. And I'm wondering if the bag is the artifact she wants us to appraise. So I take the gloves out of my pocket and lean over and remove the drawings—"

"That like an idiot I forgot to ask to see," said Elm, sighing.

"And they're beautiful. At least, I think they are considering there is no light in the room at all. So I tell her they are beautiful. And then she says to me, 'Young man, are you a homosexual?'" Ian did his best Katharine Hepburn accent, so that the word sounded like "homo-sucks-shell."

"What?" Elm burst out laughing.

"I know. So I'm imagining all these great responses, like, 'The guy I'm fucking thinks I am,' or, 'I prefer the term fudgepacker' or something. But I'm such a good boy that I just say, 'Yes, ma'am.' Then she looks up at me, and her eyes are all filmy with cataracts, and she says, 'My late husband was a homosexual.'"

"Wow, you wandered into some weird gothic novel or something."

"Then she turns around and hobbles out of the room. So I put the drawings back. Their archives, by the way, consist of two pieces of construction paper connected with a piece of tape so yellow it's merged with the paper."

"People like that don't deserve art." Elm breathed disapproval.

"Wait. This is the good part of the story. I follow her, and over the bed there's this painting. So I walk over and wipe the glass with the glove to see the attribution. There's a note. '*À Indira avec tout mon amour, René.*'"

"So she's gotten a little action from the love that dare not speak its name too?"

"No." Ian's voice rose with impatience. "Try to keep up, Elmira."

"Don't call me that. Seriously."

"René Magritte, my slow one. Indira Schmidt."

"No! *The* Indira Schmidt?"

"One and only."

"Oh, my God. That's amazing. She's still alive?"

"Apparently. Or, rather, barely. So I follow her into the kitchen, where she says to me, 'Young man, can you make me tea in the English manner?' So I say, 'One spoonful you think for each who will drink, and one for the pot, the best that we've got.'"

Elm looked at Ian uncomprehendingly. He said, "Grandmother was English. It's . . . never mind. Anyway, that seemed to convince her that I was somebody or something, because she sat me down and talked to me for, like, five hours. And here's the gist: Georg Schmidt was a poofter."

"Hardly news to the thousands of young men he 'took under his wing.'" Elm's fingers made quote marks in the air.

"She had the most amazing life, really. She told me all about escaping Austria, and hiding out in the French countryside, then walking to Belgium, which is where she met Magritte and had this torrid affair. I got the details. *All* the details."

"Eww."

"As you say. She's totally amazing. She said, 'My ceramics are on display at every major museum in the world. Well, every museum in the *civilized* world.'"

"That's priceless," said Elm. "You are the luckiest guy ever."

"Someone should write her biography."

"You should," Elm said. Her computer gurgled, signaling that she had an appointment coming up.

"I can't write," said Ian. "You should do it."

"In all my free time."

"The woman has an entire museum in there. She's saved everything—letters, *objets.*"

"Can you talk her into parting with some of it? Does she have children?"

"I don't know. No living ones anyway." Elm's heart lurched. Did they die young? How many did she have? "This is why I'm telling you this, Elm. This could be our focus, if you catch my drift."

"I do," Elm said. "Let me know when the drawings are back. You're seeing her again?"

"I'm bringing her croissants from some ancient bakery on the Lower East Side next week."

"You are truly the best." Elm grabbed her purse and kissed Ian on the top of his head.

"I hear that all the time," he replied.

———

Later that afternoon, there was a quiet knock on the door frame. Colette, from the French office, the one who had the annoying habit of tapping her pen during meetings. That woman was here so often she might as well be working in New York, Elm thought, and saving the company the airfare.

Colette was the type of woman other women disliked. She flirted with husbands out of habit, and picked lint off other women's shoulders. Elm also objected to her accent, flawless, just enough Gallic to make you ask where she was born and then exclaim "But you speak so beautifully" when she told you Chalon-sur-Saône. She had the most annoying habit of speaking English as though she had learned it from a grammar primer, but occasionally she'd pause and say, "How do you say? What's the word? For the scratch-the-sky?" So that you would say, "Oh, skyscraper," and she would show off the breathy giggle that Parisian women tittered so effortlessly. Elm spoke college French, but her accent was atrocious and the only vocabulary she remembered anymore was for eighteenth-century painting and drawing techniques. Colette also spoke too much in meetings. She was only a step above an administrative assistant, and yet because she had an art conservation and dealership degree from some fancy French *université* that only the top 5 percent of students qualified for, she felt as though she made up for her inexperience with credentials. Everyone else had an art history degree; only *she* was qualified in the business of art, at the age of all of thirty, if that. She stuck her nose in every department—offering suggestions to Eastern antiques, medieval painting, display ideas. *Be quiet and listen*, Elm wanted to tell her.

"Oh, you are just the person with whom I wanted to speak," Colette said. She made herself as comfortable as possible in her pencil skirt on the edge of Elm's desk. Elm noticed Colette's shoes had small bows that matched the trim on her suit. Colette cleared her throat and stared straight at Elm, her eyes narrowed and focused, somehow too shiny in the fluorescent light. Had she done something cosmetically to make them sparkle?

Elm was acutely conscious of being watched. A familiar feeling of worthlessness and exhaustion overtook her. She was sick of people's disapproval. She turned away from Colette's gaze and let herself look at Ronan's picture on her desk. Sometimes looking at him gave her peace, quelled the nameless feeling that wasn't as acute as grief or as chronic as depression.

He was, as he would remain forever, a little boy, eight years old. This was the last picture she had taken of him, one of the few from that vacation where he was alone in the frame, not clowning with Colin or fighting with his sister. He had the Tinsley avian nose, but Colin's coloring, his gray eyes and blond hair. He was a beautiful child, Elm thought. Was he beautiful to outsiders too? she wondered. She didn't know; she'd spent so much time staring at that face that it ceased to be a whole. Each part of him was a memory—the ancestral nose, the ears that stuck out just a little too much, the way Colin's did. His cheeks, ruddy after soccer in the cold; the hair that once got gum stuck in it which he had tried to hide with a hat for three days; the hairless torso, puffed with childhood; the mauve swimming trunks she'd bought him that he wanted to wear all the time, pockets turned out. In this picture, he was standing with his profile to the camera, his gaze out to sea. Elm resisted the temptation to see the wise forehead of the seer, tried not to imagine that he knew the water would swallow him. It was impossible. He was looking out to sea because there were diving boats heading in from the morning's expedition, and he couldn't wait to turn twelve so he could dive too. He knew nothing of the water's plans. No one did.

Colette said, "I have something for you."

"Oh?" Elm tried not to sound too interested.

"Yes," she said. "I have made a very interesting acquaintance." Colette studied her hand.

Two women: a portrait of nonchalance, Elm thought, captioning the moment. They could cut to the chase or they'd be here all afternoon, apathetically making small talk until dinner.

"Yes?" she prodded.

"A dealer."

"And . . ." Elm encouraged her.

"He has procured interesting pieces."

"Why are you telling me?"

Colette smiled sweetly, as innocently as she could. Her eyes opened wide as if to say, *Why would I not want to share good news with you?* She had curled the pieces of hair that escaped her bun into tightly obedient ringlets.

"Some of it is minor, but the sheer volume . . . *pof!*" She didn't so much exclaim as let breath leave her lips in that slightly aroused Gallic expression. "Vertu, Hogarth, Moreau . . . Good condition, slight mold but completely restorable."

"You've seen them?"

."Why, yes," Colette said. "I saw them and I said to myself, How exquisite, I must rush to tell Elmira."

"So I'm supposed to commission them for the auction."

"If you have half the eye they say you do, you can do nothing but."

"Please don't take this the wrong way, but I feel like there's a catch." She clarified: "Something you want from me."

Colette smiled. "I am a small fish playing with the bigs," she said. "No major auction has occurred in Paris since 1941, this is no secret." During World War II, Paris ceased to be the center of the art world, and it never recovered its status. Now London, New York, and Tokyo were the only places major events were held. Tinsley's Paris office, the "outpost," they called it, was more for letterhead than for actual business. It was located on the second floor of a Champs-Élysées building, nondescript, but in the correct Eighth Arrondissement. When they held their auctions, meager affairs—the good stuff always came to New York or London—they rented space nearby. It was not an ideal arrangement, but it had worked decently well for fifty years, and so, in true old-school business style, they left things as they were. Someone went over there once a month or so to see what was happening in the office. Really, it was an excuse to travel to Paris, which no one in the Tinsley upper echelon ever passed up.

Colette continued, "Perhaps you will remember that I helped you when there is an opportunity for an associate specialist position in New York? Or even senior specialist?"

Before Elm could change her face muscles to laugh the ludicrous cackle she wanted to, Colette was down the hall, leaving a strawberry scent in her wake.

"What was that scurrying noise I heard?" Ian stuck his head around Elm's door. "Was there an errant crumb to be gathered?"

"Colette wants me to recommend her for associate specialist in New York."

"Ahhh," Ian sighed. "That would be, unless I'm mistaken, a position I currently hold?"

"And that you will continue to hold. Don't worry. She's found some sort of treasure trove. She wants to plumb its depths."

"Don't mix metaphors, it's unseemly." He closed the door behind him and moved a pile of papers, then unbuttoned his jacket to sit on the low couch. "You know the photocopy room?" His knees were higher than his chest. Elm often forgot he was tall; he had a short man's willingness to please. The look on his face was one of worry.

"Yes," said Elm, impatient. "I am acquainted with the photocopy room. In fact, it doubles as the supply room, they tell me."

"Listen, Elm, this is serious. You know how you can hear the ladies' room from there?"

"You can?" Elm thought back to all the times she'd sat in a stall, bawling her eyes out.

"There's a vent. Anyway, Colette was in there, on the phone."

"Of course, your scrupulous honesty prevented you from listening."

"She wants my job, Elm."

"Since when do you speak French?"

"She was talking in English. To Joel. From transportation? You know she's fucking him."

"No, I didn't. I don't know anything around here." Elm tried to put a face to Joel from transportation, and came up with a hazy picture of a man with novelty facial hair. He was basically in charge of shipping, which required expertise in its own right, knowing the medium and its preferred way to travel, designing packaging for fragile items, and occasionally transporting the invaluable item personally. Elm had once flown on Air France with a Fabergé egg on her lap. She'd brought it with her to the bathroom, balancing the package on the small metal sink while she urinated.

Elm covered his hands with her own. "Don't worry," she said. "I'm a Tinsley, for chrissake. And as long as I'm here, you're here."

"Yes, okay, Elm, so what if you get moved to some ceremonial post dealing with midcentury African masks or something? And then you can't protect me. You have a family, another income. I can't be looking for new employment. Not now."

"That's not going to happen," Elm said. "You're valued even beyond me. I mean, you're a valuable employee. And don't be so sure about the two-income thing."

"What do you mean?"

"Colin said they're restructuring at Moore."

"What does that mean for you two?"

"No telling." Elm sighed. She knew Ian could see her worry. He knit his brow into a large V.

"We've got to get our acts together," Ian said. "We have to quit moping about." He stopped, realized what he said. Elm's heart lurched. Was her moping that obvious? Then: a flash of anger. She was just supposed to get over the death of her son? Her face must have registered her reaction because Ian immediately backtracked. "I mean, not that you're moping, or, I mean, you have something you can mope about. I didn't mean you at all, I meant me. I'm going to shut up now. Do you understand what I meant?"

"Yes." Elm nodded. She did understand. They needed to focus. Maybe that's what she needed, to concentrate on her work, and maybe then she could move into the next stage of grief, whatever that was. Each new wave felt like he died all over again. She suspected that it would always feel like this, that each year would bring merely innovation instead of diffusion.

"I'll take care of it," she said. This was her solution to everything; she volunteered to be in charge. She knew, of course, that not allowing anyone else to help was a pathology that only deepened her disconnect from the world. It entrenched her in a battle with the day; it alienated even her husband. She knew this, and yet she didn't know how not to feel this way, how to break the pattern.

Ian, however, was not going to let her. "We'll fix it, both of us." She wondered if he was pulling her back into the fold of humanity for her own good, or if he didn't trust her.

"How?" Suddenly, there were tears in her eyes. Frustrated tears, she thought. She'd never known how many different kinds of tears there were until Ronan died. Like a parody of the old saw about all the Eskimo words for snow—tears of frustration, of hurt, pain, anger, angst. And there were new tears to discover all the time, vast galaxies of hidden stars and satellites of pain that orbited into view.

Ian turned up his palms. "We'll think of something, sweetie. I didn't mean to upset you."

"You didn't," Elm said, wiping her eyes with a tissue. He hadn't, really. Tears like these didn't count.

Elm rubbed her eyes. "Do you think it's seemly for me to go home now?" she said. "I'm having . . . I'm really tired."

"Wait for me, we'll walk out together."

Elm turned off her computer and gathered the papers she was going to pretend to look over during the weekend. She spent the week dreading the weekend's aimlessness, and then she spent the weekend dreading work. She looked at her watch. She could pick up Moira from school instead of letting Wania do it. She could go shopping. She could crawl into bed and read a magazine. None of the options sounded appealing.

There was soft music playing in the elevator, the same Beethoven symphony that recycled constantly. Elm had written e-mails to the office manager on more than one occasion, begging him to put some Sibelius or Handel into the mix. She did get Handel: the "Hallelujah Chorus" at Christmastime on repeat. She sighed heavily. Ian put his arm around her.

They stepped into the elevator. "Do you have exciting weekend plans?" he asked.

Elm shook her head. "You? Hot date?"

"I don't know," he said. "I haven't gone online yet."

Elm laughed obediently. Ian paused. He was lonely, she knew, in a many-friends-no-partner way. She remembered that feeling of swinging trapezelike through her twenties. There was the net if you fell, but no one to link arms with midair. She should invite him over for dinner, or out for a drink, but she didn't feel like it. Didn't feel like coming up with witty jibes to match his zingers, to laugh at the jokes he inevitably made at his own expense. She would make it up to him another night.

He kissed Elm's cheek. She felt his breath, warm on her neck. His tenderness was so sweet, it was another unexpected thing that brought tears to her eyes. She didn't bother to wipe them; they wouldn't spill.

Gabriel

He walked past the restaurant once before checking the address and doubling back. What he'd heard as "La Tour de L'Oqueau" was actually El Toro Loco, a tapas place that was trying extremely hard to replicate some fantastic ideal of Spain. Tapas came from the north, País Vasco, and yet this place was a Southern Castilla of the previous century: dark wood, taxidermy, rustic tableware, and mustachioed waiters. Of course the featured beverage would be sangria. No one Gabriel knew drank sangria after age fifteen—cheap wine and 7UP guaranteed a headache. He opened the heavy door and waited for his eyes to adjust to the light. He imagined sitting at an ornate table for two with an open bottle of wine and an empty chair across from him. She might very well stand him up. She wouldn't mean to, but something might come up.

He began to plan for this contingency. He would pretend like he always dined alone. He'd drain the bottle of wine, order a few *pintxos*, and nonchalantly drop the cash on the table before leaving, trying to convince himself that adults did this—they dined alone. It was not pathetic. It was independent.

And then his pupils finally dilated and there she was, at a table near the entrance, head down and hair falling into her lap, bent over her phone.

"Hey," he said. She looked up and he felt his chest constrict. Her eyes sparkled. She had put on smoky eye makeup, à la Edie Sedgwick, and painted her lashes impossibly long. Had she done this for him?

"Hey," she said, sounding surprised, as if they'd just bumped into each other instead of arranging to meet here. She put her phone into her large leather bag, slumped at her feet like a cat.

Gabriel leaned forward to kiss her cheek and she politely presented each side to him. He sat and removed his leather jacket, then put it back on when he noticed that the other diners were dressed in button-down shirts.

There was a silence while Colette rearranged her silverware. "Is this place okay?" she asked. "I just thought of it while we were on the phone. My friend brings clients here sometimes and then we hung up and I thought, That's so stupid, bringing a Spaniard to a Spanish restaurant. It's bound not to be any good."

"It's fine." Gabriel smiled. "It's like home!" His voice lilted.

She frowned, not sure if he was being sarcastic. The waiter came by and handed Gabriel an enormous, leather-bound wine list. He chose a bottle at random, a Rioja that was neither the most expensive nor the least expensive.

"Very good, sir."

"How come you didn't talk to him in Spanish?" Colette asked.

"I think he's Albanian."

She looked at him expectantly, waiting for him to continue the conversation.

The bottle of wine arrived, interrupting their silence. The waiter showed Gabriel the bottle, and Gabriel bent close to it in the darkened restaurant, pretending the words meant something to him. They both watched the aproned man, neat mustache, biceps divulging a past life as a laborer or an athlete, insert the corkscrew and pull the cork out. It gave way with a satisfying *pop*. Gabriel saw with satisfaction that Colette jumped, just a little bit. Or flinched.

"To art." She raised her glass.

He took a sip. She swirled her wine inside the glass, her wrist moving barely perceptibly, but forcing the liquid into undulations against the sides, churning red waves.

He knew that if he tried to copy her effort, he would spill drops onto the white tablecloth that would haunt him for the rest of the meal, like spots behind his eyes after he'd unadvisedly looked at the sun.

Colette was talking now, and Gabriel was nodding, listening but not really hearing. She talked quickly and had a small endearing lisp that made it hard for him to understand the specifics of what she was talking about. Now, for example, he knew she was relating a story that was supposed to be unbelievable, he could tell by the way she paused dramatically to inhale, eyes wide and head bobbing as if to encourage belief. *No, really,* her eyes said, blinking rapidly.

She blew smoke away with the hand that was holding a cigarette, not clearing the air much at all. The lit butt followed her at all times, a firefly punctuating her sentences. Would she lose her charm when the smoking ban went into effect? Gabriel wondered. Or would it simply transfer to another expressive tic, like buttoning and unbuttoning a sweater, or worrying her clamshell telephone?

Tonight she wore more elaborate makeup—her eyelids had a sheen to them and her mouth was painted a bright red. The story finished in a burst of giggles, which Gabriel mimicked. He had gotten used to only half understanding his surroundings. He liked the remove his foreignness gave him. Sometimes, being outside of a culture was like having a one-way window into other people.

He was free to contemplate her in a way that was completely visual. What did her cheeks do when she inhaled? How did her shoulders react to a touch or a perceived slight? Examining a person became part of a narrative he continually constructed, that he always wanted to put in his paintings but emerged only in his drawings, his derivative drawings, his Connois and Canaletto homages. Someday, he would work that sense of completion into his real work, when the pendulum swung away from abstraction and confession/expression and back toward observation and the notion of the artist as a commentator on modern society.

"Do you want to order for me?" she asked. "I don't know what any of this is, anyway."

"Um, okay." Gabriel felt a quick, airless second of panic, then he settled. "Do you not like anything?" As soon as he said the sentence, he realized he'd said, "Don't you like anything?"

But Colette graciously or unconsciously ignored the fault and said, "I'm French. I eat whatever doesn't eat me first."

"So you trust me?"

"Implicitly," she said.

When the waiter came by their table Gabriel ordered paella for two, with *mariscos,* and a beet salad and some sausage and dates to start. The waiter took the menus and Colette sighed with relief; now there was room for her elbows.

He took a gulp of wine, feeling courage well up in him in inverse proportion to the sinking alcohol. He said, "You look beautiful."

She smiled, pursed her mouth as if to deflect the compliment. Then she sat back in her chair. "Where are you from in Spain?"

"Near Barcelona."

"Barthelona," she mimicked his accent. "Hmmm, I liked it there. It was . . . God, this will sound stupid. It was very Parisian." She laughed.

Gabriel smiled. "No, I see it," he said. "Large boulevards, old, parks, cafés . . ."

"Well, I meant more like, when you study art, you get an idea of a place. My idea of Barthelona—" She paused.

"Very good," he said.

"—was from Picasso and Dalí and Miró."

"Picasso was barely from here. There."

"I know," she said. "Which is why I should have expected that his Barcelona would look like Paris. But, I didn't."

"Have you always lived in Paris?"

"Oh, no," she said. "Can't you tell by my accent?" Gabriel shook his head. She continued, "You know Parisians, unless you're born here you might as well be from Mars. I'm from Chalon-sur-Saône. Do you know it?"

He shook his head again, contemplating her assessment of Parisians. So she too understood the continuing alienation of being a foreigner. Apparently her accent, which he couldn't hear, branded her as an outsider too. He wanted to take her hand, but resisted.

"Nobody does," she said. "It's completely without interest. My father owns a smoke shop." Colette pointed to her cigarette as if it were the natural result. She stubbed it out in the silver ashtray. It was an ingenious contraption that when lifted released the ash and the butt inside. "And what do your parents do?" she asked.

"My mother baked bread for the market, sold things," he said. "My father played the guitar. He died when I was young."

"Oh, I'm sorry," she said. She shook her arm; a tinkling cascade of bracelets fell to her wrist. "How, if you don't mind me asking?"

"No," he said. "It was strange. He died of mushroom poisoning."

"Seriously?" Colette asked.

Gabriel nodded, though his father had died of a heart attack. But he liked this story better. "He was very passionate about mushrooms, and he was never wrong when identifying them. I think someone tried to poison him."

"You're lying to me," Colette said, hitting his forearm.

The waiter deposited the appetizers in front of them. When Gabriel motioned that she should serve herself, Colette reached over and took exactly half of each.

She hummed approval. "This is delicious. Is this really what the food is like?"

"Sort of," Gabriel said. "I can't really explain it. It's all the same ingredients. It just has a taste that is different. Tomatoes taste different in Spain. So do beets."

"It's like going to a French restaurant in America," Colette said. "The food there is totally inedible. Have you spent much time in New York?"

"No," Gabriel admitted. "I don't travel much." In fact, he had never left Europe.

"I go for Tinsley's quite often," Colette said.

Before Gabriel could comment, the paella arrived and the waiter presented it to them before scraping the contents of the pan onto two plates, including the burned-crisp bottom layer of rice that Gabriel loved.

They ordered another bottle of wine. Colette's eyes grew glassy and her lips a tad floppy, stained from her drink. He wondered if she might go home with him, or he with her. A wave of longing overtook him that was so acute he nearly choked, and took a large swallow of wine to hide the frisson. A silence fell while they ate. He wanted to keep her here, at this table, buzzed with liquor, in a sort of suspended animation. He knew the spell would be broken, even as the waiter reappeared to take their plates, and so he ate slowly, excruciatingly slowly, as if he could somehow stall time and extend the moment.

He watched as she put down her fork to light another cigarette. She waved the smoke away from their table. Maybe it was the wine, but now he didn't find the silence uncomfortable. He wondered if she did. Should he say something? No, he decided. He was not going to make conversation for conversation's sake. That was what *bobos* did. Artists didn't have to conform to those conventions. It was one of the few perks.

She tapped her ash in the clever ashtray.

"I'm done," she announced, and pushed the half-full plate closer toward Gabriel. "Too much food for me!"

Gabriel finished his plate. Then he ate the rest of hers. No sense in letting it go to waste, and he was hungry. In fact, he felt empty.

When he finally set down his fork, she stubbed out her cigarette and, by lifting her head, summoned the waiter.

She demanded the check in the typical French way, which had the trappings of *politesse*—the conditional verb, the *s'il vous plaît*, the honorific *monsieur* that dripped of condescension. There were parts of French culture that he would never master. Spaniards asked for the check in full recognition that the waiter's job was to bring it, which implied neither servitude nor gratitude. No class wars were played out in restaurants.

Gabriel counted out the bills slowly, attempting to hide them under the table. It was easily the most expensive meal he'd ever eaten. Colette didn't offer to split it.

"We'll have coffee at my place," she said. "I don't live far."

They walked back along the Avenue de New York. When Colette slipped on a stone, tottering on her heels, Gabriel grabbed her arm and felt the give of her flesh. When you touched someone you were attracted to, why was it different from touching a stranger on the street? Was the difference in the touch itself, the pheromones that the other person gave off? Or was the excitement all in the mind—did the brain send signals to the arm hairs to tingle, the webs of the fingers to itch, the toes to curl?

They turned down a street he didn't know. She unlocked the front door, and without a word, without turning on the stairway light, she walked in front of him up the stairs.

Her apartment was an efficiency, tidy and compact. On her walls she had framed vintage Tinsley's catalog covers. There was a red velvet love seat and a bed. He sat on the love seat.

Colette turned on the electric kettle. Then she sat down next to him and turned her face to his. When her lips met his, Gabriel let her take the lead, keeping his hands on her hips.

The kettle clicked off and Colette pulled away. She spoke for the first time in minutes. "How do you take it?"

"With sugar."

As she was making the coffee, her phone rang. She answered it and began to chat, using so much slang and speaking so quickly that Gabriel had trouble understanding what she was saying. She was talking to a good friend, that much he knew, because she called the person *pote*, an old-fashioned word that meant "mate" or "buddy."

Still talking, she set a tray with coffee and biscotti down on the love seat and then went into the bathroom, closing the door behind her. Gabriel sipped at the coffee. Her voice went quiet. What was she talking about in there? Hadn't they come back to her place to screw? Gabriel felt suddenly confused by the evening. Had he completely misinterpreted her signals? He decided to wait until she came back, and then say a quick good-bye.

He'd finished his coffee by the time she emerged from the bathroom, wearing a black boned corset and high-cut lace panties. Gabriel was surprised at her aggression. Pleasantly surprised, and immediately aroused. He stood up and she steered them toward the bed, undressing him quickly, biting his nipples. Her silence was exciting. Once he was inside her he looked down and smoothed her hair back from her head. The intensity of his feeling surprised him. She didn't even blink, not for hours, it seemed like, and then he closed his eyes. Because he was embarrassed. Because that's what you were supposed to do when fucking. Because he was afraid.

The next day, after Gabriel had gone to work and put in a couple of hours at the studio, he stopped by Colette's. She was home, and dressed in a business suit that Gabriel thought made her look like a sexily stern airline attendant from the 1950s.

"Oh!" she said when she answered the door.

"I don't like the telephone," Gabriel said. "Is it okay?"

"Come in," Colette said. "Sorry it's such a mess in here."

Gabriel thought the words must have been a reflex because they'd both left together that morning. He realized he was still wearing the same clothes. He also realized he should have let a couple of days go by before he contacted Colette again. She made him unnaturally and uncharacteristically nervous. She was so obviously out of his league, intellectually, socially, aesthetically, that he wanted to make sure she had no time to think it over.

"You probably think I'm a strange person to appear on your doorstep." He leaned in to kiss her and she accepted the kiss on the lips. "I promise I'm not a . . ." He wasn't sure of the word and let the sentence trail off.

"I'm not worried," Colette said. "Let's go out to dinner."

Gabriel had to stop at an ATM in order to pay for the evening. In two nights, he spent as much on restaurants as he usually did the entire month for food. Dating was an expensive habit.

A week later, Gabriel, hoping to stem the hemorrhage of money that Colette's young professional lifestyle was costing him, packed a picnic and took her to the studio. She held his hand on the *métro*.

In his dark space she examined the paintings by peering at them closely, commenting on shading and color. Though she professed not to know much about contemporary art, she knew what she was talking about. She seemed most interested in his imitative sketches.

"This really looks like Canaletto! How did you do this?"

Gabriel shrugged.

"Do you have any Connois sketches?"

Gabriel dragged out the large sketchbook reluctantly. It was embarrassing, creating sketches in someone else's style. But she squealed with delight as she turned the pages.

Gabriel unpacked the food, and Colette looked with disgust at the dirty floor, even though she was only wearing jeans. Gabriel was sorry he didn't think to bring a sheet or a blanket. He borrowed a tarp from Marie-Laure's studio and they sat on that, the lamp on the table casting long shadows. Colette took small bites at the cheese and sausage he put out, though she drank much of the wine and smoked.

In the morning, the first thing she said when they woke in her apartment was: "I'd like you to meet my uncle." Gabriel was getting dressed, putting on last night's clothing, which, he realized, was the previous day's clothing as well. He had to go home and do some laundry.

"Well, I mean, it's a figure of speech," Colette said, lighting a cigarette. "He's not really my uncle. His and my mother's families were all refugees from Germany. They lived in the same village, I think. Our family came to France and his went to England, but they reconnected after the war."

"Refugees?"

Colette said, "If you're asking if I'm Jewish, not really, though technically, yes, I guess. Poor Maman. She married a destitute Christian and my grandparents disowned her. But they each gave her money secretly every month until they died and left her enough that she could leave my father. She lives in the Canary Islands now." Colette laughed. "We'll have dinner with my uncle tonight."

———

Gabriel met Colette at a restaurant in the Marais that he was unhappy to see was extremely expensive. There was almost no money left in his bank account, and the end of the month's payday was still a week away. He would have to deposit the check and deliver the rent to the landlord in cash as it was. And now he was going to be obligated to pay for three more meals. Colette had the habit of ordering fish, always one of the more expensive dishes on the menu, and he could not resist her excitement when she came across some appetizer they had to try. Once the entrées arrived, she merely picked at her food, so Gabriel had learned to order sparsely, counting on being able to eat the rest of her meal.

Inside, the maître d' led them to a private room in back where Gabriel saw there was a small dinner party.

Colette introduced him to her uncle, Augustus Klinman, an overweight Englishman with thinning hair. He extended his hand for Gabriel to shake, and despite its fleshiness, the grip was solid.

"Sorry we're late," Colette said.

"I'm afraid you've missed the first course, but I'll introduce you around," Klinman said. "Everyone, this is my niece Colette's boyfriend, Gabriel Connois, relation of Marcel Connois, of the École des Hiverains."

Everyone nodded, either in recognition of the name or in pretend recognition of it. It was interesting, but not surprising, that Colette had told her uncle about his ancestor. He wished, not for the first time, that he could be introduced on his own merit. But she called me her boyfriend, Gabriel thought.

Klinman continued, "This is an associate, Avram ben Hakim." A Middle Eastern–looking man in a dark suit nodded at Gabriel. "And the Bairds, and next to them the Schoenbergs. Do you know Patrice and Paulette Piclut? No? I'm surprised. They run a gallery in Canal St. Martin. *Very cool*," he added in English.

Colette kissed Patrice and Paulette and sat down. The waiter brought over an amuse bouche, some sort of dumpling in a spoon. Gabriel lifted it to his mouth and a spurt of hot liquid shot down his throat. He reached for his water glass, determined not to cough.

Colette said, "In fact, PP, you might be interested in Gabriel's work." She popped the dumpling in her mouth and chewed it naturally, swallowing without incident.

Patrice crossed his legs. He was wearing pale pink pants, exposing a skinny, sockless ankle. "It's not street art, is it? Because we are so over street art."

"Painting," Gabriel said. "I'm a painter."

Paulette nodded. "Painting is so retro it's new again."

Klinman addressed them, "When was painting out? Painting has always been in style."

"No," the person to Klinman's right said. "Have you been to the Biennale? It's been all conceptual for years."

"And Miami Basel is even worse. It was like being in Las Vegas. You've been to Vegas?" a woman with a strong American accent asked.

"I love Vegas," said Paulette. "I've never been there, but I know I'd love it."

"It's like a psychedelic experience," said ben Hakim. "Like what taking LSD was like."

"An artist, how nice. We only ever meet dealers, like art grows out of the ground," said a German woman.

"Better the ground than the ass," Gabriel said. There was a pause while everyone considered whether to be offended or amused. Gabriel's face turned bright red. He was so used to the accepted vulgarity of artists; he forgot that civilians had more refined sensibilities. But Colette saved him by giggling and then everyone laughed. He was proud of himself for making a joke. Maybe he fit in better than he thought he did.

Gabriel sat back to let the waiter replace his plate with one that held a piece of meat with a brown-red sauce on top of it. When everyone was served, the waiter announced, *"Filet mignon avec foie de volaille."*

Gabriel took a polite bite. The meat melted inside his mouth, and the sauce had a pleasing peaty flavor. "I don't think I've ever tasted anything like this," he whispered to Colette.

She stopped eating to take a sip of her wine. "So many things to try."

From the head of the table Klinman asked him, "So Connois was your relative?"

"He was a grandfather," Gabriel said in French, unsure of the exact word for a distant, yet direct, relative. "Of my mother."

"Ahhhh," the man sighed. "And your real name?" He raised an eyebrow.

"Does it matter?" Gabriel asked.

Klinman caught his eye and winked, which so disconcerted Gabriel that his fork slipped and he dropped poultry innards on his lap. He was not at all disappointed to hear Colette's delighted laugh, and see her napkin winging its way toward his crotch.

———

Édouard and his boyfriend took advantage of the "bridge" long weekend to fly to Corsica, leaving Gabriel to deal with the unlikely foot traffic or emergency in the gallery. Gabriel spent the day doodling, drawing geometric shapes on graph paper and shading them by shining a light from the left margin.

He heard the whoosh of air created by the opening of the door. There stood Klinman, dressed elegantly in a bespoke suit, carrying a hat and an umbrella, popping by from a previous century.

Gabriel stammered hello, and a thank-you for the dinner the night before. Gabriel had grown increasingly nervous as the meal wore on, partly from Colette's hand on his thigh and also because he was unsure of how the payment for the meal would take place. As it turned out, the waiter brought no bill, and no one took out a card or cash.

"Who paid?" he'd asked Colette on the way to her apartment.

"Oh, Augustus has an account there," she'd said.

Mr. Klinman smiled and strolled around the gallery, looking at the art on the walls. He grunted, a noise that betrayed no opinion.

Gabriel reverted to his canned speech. "Our stock is in prints and engravings. Monsieur Rosenzweig has a special fondness for the simple line. Can I show you anything in particular?"

Mr. Klinman looked baldly at Gabriel, while Gabriel tried to look indifferent. "You have a very good eye," Klinman said.

"Édouard picks out most of our work," Gabriel said. "Can I get you anything? Water, or a coffee?"

"Coffee," Klinman said. His French was nearly accentless.

He held out his raincoat and hat, so Gabriel took them and hung them up on a nearby coatrack. Gabriel ground coffee beans, scooped the grounds into the casing of the percolator, and screwed the top back on, placing it on a hotpad. The machine began to hiss and bubble.

They both stood waiting until the coffee was done. "Sugar?" Gabriel asked. The man nodded. Gabriel added one square with the small spoon. He handed it to Mr. Klinman.

"You are patient and you are precise." Mr. Klinman set down his cup. "Both are qualities I admire. And Colette tells me you are good. Very good."

Gabriel smiled. Mr. Klinman smiled back. Gabriel could play this game. He uttered what he called the "French hmmm," a sound that meant neither yes nor no, not invitation or rejection; rather, it was a volley: your turn. Gabriel waited for the man to continue.

Finally Mr. Klinman did. "As you may know," he said, "I am responsible for the artwork in many of Europe's finest luxury hotels."

Gabriel didn't know, but nodded.

"We are doing the new Andre Balazs. Eighty-six rooms. All will need art."

Gabriel nodded again. Was the man going to ask for some kind of bulk discount?

"What we would like," Mr. Klinman said, "is some Impressionist drawings, pastels, and watercolors. Landscapes, decrepit cathedrals, women by rocky seashores, you understand. Connois."

"We don't have inventory like that right now," Gabriel said. "I'm not sure that in his lifetime he even drew—"

"You misunderstand me," Mr. Klinman said. "I am not speaking of Connois the elder, but rather Connois the younger. You." He switched to the familiar pronoun.

"You want me to make you eighty-six drawings?" Gabriel must have misunderstood the number. French numbers were impossible, derived from some Gallic counting system that predated Arabic numerals.

The Englishman laughed, and then there was another awkward silence while Klinman rocked forward onto his toes and back onto his heels. His shoes were worn but well made and polished, the laces new, as if to imply that he had the means to purchase new shoes but loved these old ones, and felt secure enough to indulge that fondness. Gabriel fingered the callus on the inside of his left thumb.

"Let's say by the end of next week? One-half charcoal sketches, one-third those half-finished watercolors your great-great-grandfather liked so much—the landscapes with the sea, perhaps? A few still lifes, the old markets, a couple of pastels."

"Connois didn't paint still lifes," Gabriel said. "He was interested only in movement and light."

Klinman waved his hand in front of his face as though encouraging a bad odor to waft away. "People like still lifes, find them soothing . . ." He let the sentence trail off.

He reached into his breast pocket and removed a long leather wallet. "What shall we say, per drawing? I'll send over the paper I want you to use, to look like the nineteenth century."

"Umm, I don't know." Gabriel tried to put his hands in his pockets, but his pants were too tight. Instead he crossed his arms in front of his chest. His sweater felt itchy against his neck, little prickles of heat. He shouldn't have to make art for hire. It made him feel like he was prostituting his talent and training. But he desperately needed the money. Colette was proving to be a very expensive habit, one he wasn't yet ready to give up. He found himself thinking about her more often than he had about any woman in the past decade, so often that he was worried. "What did you have in mind?"

Klinman shook his head. "No. You name what you think your time is worth. I'll supply the paper; it's important that it looks authentic."

What was Gabriel's time worth? Figure a couple of hours per watercolor, some money for supplies: sketch paper, brushes, paints. Would he want them mounted? Matted? Gabriel's father, a minor musician who played guitar for weddings and baptisms, always told him to name a sum greater than what he expected to get. It gave the client negotiating room, made him feel like he was getting a bargain. But he should not ask for too much, for that would seem like stealing and the client would be suspicious and miserly.

"Fifty euros per sketch," he said. "Sixty-five for watercolors."

Mr. Klinman shook his head, a disappointed expression on his face. Gabriel felt a wave of embarrassment. Had he overvalued himself?

"If you do not think yourself significant, then no one will. Charge high when the client is willing to pay, and then deliver a product that exceeds satisfaction. I will pay you one hundred euros for the drawings and one-fifty for the watercolors, which will be unmistakably authentic

Connois *Père* when viewed from two meters. Here are five thousand euros. I will come back next Friday, is that all right?" Augustus handed him two banded stacks of bills.

Gabriel stared at the money in his hands. He had never held that great a sum at one time. The bills were new. Gabriel wet his lips. "Thank you, sir," he said.

"Augustus," he said. "Use the familiar. We are friends now." He took his jacket and hat.

"Augustus," Gabriel said. "Eighty-six drawings by next week is more than I can do. So quickly. If you want Connois."

Augustus turned, his lips pursed sourly. He sighed, exasperated. "Very well, then ring up your old classmates. Reconvene the École des Hiverains." As he turned, Gabriel thought he saw the man wink.

The door took the air with it when it closed. The papers thumbtacked to the cork that served as the backsplash to the desks lurched toward the door as if to follow Augustus Klinman out, then settled back flat again. Gabriel's desk was messy with yesterday's croissant crumbs and sticky notes stacked like layers of paint. Gabriel looked at the sketch he'd been doodling when the man had walked in. He took the bills and fanned them out over the paper so that the drawing was obscured. A much better source of light, these euros, than anything he could shade.

———

The École des Hiverains was an inside joke that had escaped its confinement. Marcel Connois, having immigrated to Paris in 1870 from Cataluña, found himself an unpopular second cousin to the more successful Impressionists and so had fled with his circle, which included Del Rio, Monlin, Ganedis (one of the few successful Greek painters of the time), and Imogeney, to the Lowlands, settling first in Belgium and then in the Netherlands, where their talents were appreciated among the lesser nobility. They continued to paint the sunny, arid landscapes of their homelands and the voluptuous women at fruit-filled feasts that characterized their repertoire. They were always cold in the north, wearing scarves, hats, and fingerless gloves even into summer and so gained the nickname Les Hiverains, or "the Winterers." The active years of the École were few. Monlin died of tuberculosis, Del Rio followed a carnival troupe to Capri where he lost a duel over a gypsy woman, and Ganedis returned home to his native island, where his mother's cooking still sat warming on the stove for him. Imogeney married a Flemish girl and worked as a portraitist to support his thirteen children. Only Connois survived the dissolution, installing himself back in Paris. Still he painted the Pyrenees, the orange groves, the fish markets of his home.

Gabriel's mother had owned one painting by her great-grandfather, a half-meter-square oil of the Costa Brava called *Febrer.* In it, the Mediterranean was an impossible blue, the color changing on the underside of each white-capped wave so that the effect was a mosaic of fractured sea, melting together as the water tumbled back into the roil. Gabriel had spent countless hours staring at the painting, the stiff points of hardened oil paint that revealed the exact motion of the brush. Connois was a meticulous painter; each dab of blue—almost transparent, stark cobalt, aquamarine, nearly glowing, or a navy so dark as to masquerade as black—intentionally rendered. The brushstrokes were visible, small whisks. Connois must have used only the smallest brushes; the canvas would have taken him months to complete.

Gabriel wanted to sell *Febrer* when his father's arthritis had set in and playing the guitar became nearly impossible. Gabriel's father was a proud man with a face that gravity had claimed. His eyes had sunken into the flesh of their sockets, jowls swollen like wet laundry. He continued to give music lessons, but by then they'd moved to the *pueblo,* abandoning their apartment in the city. They were poor, their neighbors poorer. Gabriel made some money selling his drawings to wealthy weekenders at the markets, and his mother began making pastries for special occasions, but still money was tight.

Gabriel must have suggested it a thousand times. Each time his father said it belonged to his mother and she said it was out of the question. After his father's fatal heart attack, Gabriel and his mother often went hungry. He found her crying one day in the kitchen, an empty bag of flour at her elbow. "We'll sell it," he said. "We'll sell it and this can be over."

His mother wiped her eyes. "This painting is a part of our family. Selling it would be like selling a child, or trading a grandparent."

"We know it so well," Gabriel said. "If we want to see it, we can remember it, exactly like it was."

"It's not the same." She shook her head. "I can't explain it to you. You are an artist. You have all the talent of your ancestor, and yet you don't see the value."

"It's because I'm an artist that I do see the value," Gabriel said. "It's a piece of cloth with some decorative oil. We need to eat. You should see the doctor. I need material to paint with. It's not like we'd destroy it. It'll just be on a different wall."

"There is sustenance more important than food." She crossed herself. Gabriel was rendered speechless by the illogic of faith.

When the scholarship letter arrived, Gabriel debated whether to tell his mother. He knew she would insist he go to France. It had been her dream to visit Paris, to see her great-grandfather's work hanging in the *musée*.

As he predicted, she was overjoyed. He had to stop her from packing his suitcase that very moment, and she insisted they open the bottle of French wine that she'd been saving since her wedding day. It was vinegar, but Gabriel drank it down. The alcohol moistened her eyes. "I know you have his talent," she said. "I hope that they will recognize it."

"My grandfather gave us the painting for our wedding. He had inherited it from his father. He was old then, and nearly sightless, but he came in a chair pushed by his young wife and he gave us *Febrer* and kissed my forehead. It was a love match, your father and me."

"I've heard this story," Gabriel said softly. The kitchen was lit low, one bare bulb. The cabinets he'd known for most of his life, the rustic chairs, the icon of baby Jesus that hung over the large farm sink, the chipping floor tile, were as familiar as the curve of his knee, the jut of his hip bone.

"And then we waited fourteen years for you. We had given up hope, though not faith." Gabriel rolled his eyes in anticipation of yet another retelling of the story. Each year on his birthday she forced him to go pray at the altar of the Virgin to celebrate the miracle of his birth.

She stood and untied her apron, framed by the light. She was lumpy and formless in her widow's dress, her ankles swelling over the tops of her shoes like overly leavened bread. Her hair in its braid had gone mostly white, and one eyelid drooped a bit. And yet he thought her beautiful, and hugged her from behind while she washed the plates, feeling the rolls of her stomach, and decided that his plan to deceive her was genius, not knavery.

He spent the summer in the converted woodshed, painting. Every morning he drank coffee in the kitchen, looking at *Febrer* while his mother kneaded dough for the pastries she would sell at the market. So

many coffees that he thought he would begin to convulse with caffein-
ated anxiety. When she left for the market, he took the painting into
the shed to study it closer, careful always to return it before she arrived
to make supper. Each evening it hung in the fading daylight, its varnish
reflecting back the staticky black and white of the television, tuned to
an American sitcom, his mother's laugh drowning in the dubbed laugh
track.

Then one day he took *Febrer* to his woodshed studio and turned it
over. He removed the nails from the frame and exposed the canvas.
Connois had painted two centimeters above what was visible through
the frame. He must have known the edges would be lost, and yet this
part of the painting was as worked as the rest. This was not an expression of meticulousness or perfectionism. It was simply a part of the
painting, regardless of whether or not anyone would see it, and deserved
the same level of care.

Gabriel pried the staples from the stretcher and the canvas sagged
with relief. He rolled it carefully, trying not to crack the paint, and placed
it in a tube he had stolen from the stationery store. Then he turned to
his painting, the one he had been working on all summer. It wasn't quite
dry; August's humidity stalled the oil, but it would work. He stretched
the canvas over the supports and hammered the staples back in. Then
he reframed the painting, careful to mimic the small space where the
frame's right angles didn't quite meet.

He was in the kitchen when his mother came home. "Gabriel," she
called. "Oh, there you are. Are you very hungry tonight?"

Gabriel shook his head. His insides were as agitated as though he
were traveling on the waves of the painting. Would she notice?

She set about the business of dinner, peeling potatoes and cutting
tomatoes to spread their innards on thick pieces of bread. Gabriel heard
the click of the salt container's top snapping open and closed, but his
gaze was fixated on the painting. He stared at it so long and intently that
the landscape ceased to resemble any recognizable vista and became a
jumble of intermingling colors and shapes. It was like a tangle of thread;
if he tried to follow one brushstroke or one color, he confused it with
another layer of pigment and texture.

"What's wrong with you?" his mother asked. "I think the woodshed
is not a good place for a studio. Too hot. And too much coffee; you're
dehydrated."

He turned his head to smile absently at her.

"*Febrer* changes for me as well." She served him potatoes. "Depending on my mood, I project onto it, almost like I am the painter. Today it looks shinier, more alive."

"I cleaned it," Gabriel said impulsively. "As a present to you before I leave. I cleaned the surface so it's like a new painting. Don't let anything touch it for a couple of weeks until the new varnish has a chance to dry."

Tears rimmed his mother's eyes. She said nothing. Not "Oh, thank you!" as he thought she would, nor "You shouldn't have bothered," nor "I'll miss you so much." He wondered if she knew, if she suspected. Impossible. It was a nearly perfect copy, and she would have noticed right off if it weren't exact. If he could fool her, she who knew the painting better than anyone in the world, then he was indeed as talented as she claimed he was, as the school in France thought he might be. He might even be as talented as his great-great-grandfather.

When he got to Paris, he approached Sotheby's with the canvas. He told the story truthfully, and was lucky enough to have arrived just as the art market was hitting its peak. Houses couldn't afford to be too thorough in checking provenances. The house verified the painting's age through forensic testing and *Febrer* was put up for auction in a group of minor Impressionists, under "École des Hiverains, artist unknown." It still sold for more money than Gabriel had expected. He sent his mother all of it, telling her he'd sold one of his paintings. In a sense, he had. The more he thought about it, the more he believed it himself, until it became as much a fundamental truth as the bitterness of coffee or the hot stink of the Parisian *métro*. He had sold his first Connois.

Elm

Mrs. Schmidt's drawings returned authenticated. Several times, minor copies (or forgeries, it was impossible to know) crossed Elm's desk. She could always tell—the lines lacked the natural progression, the logic of the artistic mind. Where an artist's charcoal would fly across the paper, gathering speed in the weave and bumps of the pulp, the copyist's was hesitant, looking back to check on its progress. The artist's work was freer; those who followed in his footsteps were always a step behind.

Even though clear forgeries were often obvious, people still tried to sneak them into auctions. Their provenances were sketchy—they were discovered in an attic or behind an old painting or in a flea market—or even nonexistent. The perspective was off, or the material was wrong, or it contained other anachronisms. Elm once saw smoke rising from an industrial chimney in the background of a Blavoin, even though the artist worked before the industrial revolution and lived, famously, secluded in the provinces. Terrified of horses, he traveled only on foot, and therefore never left his township, nestled in the foothills of the Alps, far from any such smoke. This willful disregard for scholarship offended Elm, even as she laughed at it. It was insulting that someone would think her that stupid, though she knew specialists and departmental directors often were. She had seen obvious misattributions (the euphemism for fakes) fool good eyes and wind up in private collections.

Elm was not supposed to voice her suspicions. First of all, it was bad for business. Too many items pulled from auctions because of suspect authenticity gave houses a reputation they didn't want. Second, it was bad to be the whistle-blower. Also, unless Elm had the opportunity to examine the drawing under the loupe, she really couldn't be sure. And, of course, if the purchaser enjoyed his "Brueghel" or his "Delacroix," who was she to rain on his parade? Still, pangs tugged at her heart when she saw small museums blow their acquisition budgets on inferior drawings. It was like watching the government build a bridge that she knew would fail.

Elm did a quick search in the Art Loss Registry. The database of stolen art was part of her due diligence, a hedge against liability if the pieces had been stolen. Nothing surfaced.

Elm wanted to meet the great Indira Schmidt, so she joined Ian and his croissants in a company car up to Columbia. Ian had described both the building and the woman perfectly. Mrs. Schmidt looked Elm up and down skeptically with rheumy eyes and let her into the apartment. Ian she kissed on the cheek, and as he straightened he winked at Elm.

The apartment was dark. The rays of sun that escaped from the velvet curtains blinded like spotlights instead of illuminating. The hallway carpet gave at each footstep. Elm noticed, as she walked slowly behind the old woman, that instead of family portraits, the pictures lining the entryway were all professional: Stieglitz, Leibovitz, Mann, Sherman. Not their controversial or iconic images, but recognizable nonetheless. In fact, Elm realized, there were no photos of family anywhere in the apartment.

Elm sat on a couch so low her knees were above her chin. She wondered if she'd be able to get out of it.

"That one's broken," Ian whispered at her, extending his hand to help her up. "Sit there." He pointed to a thronelike carved wood chair.

"Mrs. Schmidt," Elm began, "I'm a huge fan of your work. You know, I'm on the board of the New Jewish Institute, though I'm not myself Jewish. Your genius has—"

Mrs. Schmidt held up her hand in a "spare me" gesture. "This is not a case where the one I'm most fond of will get to sell my art, Mrs. Howells. When I am ready to part with it, the one who can offer me the most favorable terms will be my proxy, even if they are a one-armed ax murderer. You are here because I enjoy meeting new people. What can you tell me?"

"Beg your pardon?" Elm asked.

"I spent World War II in a hayloft in France," Mrs. Schmidt said. "I walked into Texas from Mexico. I once met Elvis Presley."

Elm began to say "Wow," then realized these were examples, not actual experiences. The sound that emerged was "Whoa."

"My family has land on this island off the coast of Connecticut," Elm began. She very rarely parted with this information. She was never invited to the island now that her mother was dead, and she felt it gave people the wrong impression of her. They imagined a silver spoon. But all the silver had long since been hocked. "We used to go there in the summers when I was a child. Dinners were formal for the adults, but the children were served in a separate dining room, Tater Tots and miniature hamburgers. Paradise. The summer I turned twelve I was dying to be let into the adults' room. The official age was thirteen, but I begged and begged, reminded them my birthday was coming up in October. Finally, on the last night, they let me. Mother gave me one of her old dresses to wear. It fit like a gunnysack. She put the necklace her mother had given her around my neck, an add-a-pearl necklace that no one ever added pearls to. She did my hair in a high bun and stuck a small sunflower into it, and I was convinced I was a grown-up.

"At dinner, we were served steak medallions and potatoes au gratin. I concentrated on not spilling. I had half a glass of wine. Then a nice man came around to shake hands and when he got to me I gave him the handshake my father had taught me, firm but not rough, look the person in the eyes. He had nice blue eyes, very bright, or maybe it was just the light in the lodge. He said to me, 'Lovely to meet you. What grade are you in?' I told him, 'Sixth grade.' Then I responded how my father always did. 'And what do you do?'

"The man laughed and my father laughed, and my mother turned bright red and clutched me to her. The man said, 'A little of this, a little of that. Nothing of any great importance.' And then he walked away. Later I learned he was President Reagan."

Mrs. Schmidt smiled, but Elm was unable to tell what the smile meant. Had she passed the test? Ian, who had heard the story many times before, nodded encouragingly. Without turning to him, Mrs. Schmidt said, "Young man, would you please run out and get some half-and-half? This milk that the woman brings me is too watery."

"I think I saw some in the refrigerator," Ian said. "I'll check the expiration."

"Young man," Mrs. Schmidt sighed, "I'm trying to get rid of you. Be a dear and run to the deli and get us some half-and-half. And go to the Korean one, not the Pakistani one."

Elm thought she saw Mrs. Schmidt wink at her. The woman was a web of tics; no wonder she was so thin. Ian shrugged and stood up. Elm could hear him as he banged into the piles of paper and bric-a-brac, beating his way to the front door.

Mrs. Schmidt lifted her teacup to her lips. It shook, but she managed a loud slurp before it spilled. The teacup banged loudly as it hit the saucer, and, before she knew what she was saying, Elm sputtered, "My son died."

"Oh," Mrs. Schmidt said.

"Do you remember the tsunami two years ago? We were on vacation in Thailand. He was next to me, and then he was gone."

"I'm sorry," Mrs. Schmidt said. A different old lady might have petted her arm and called her "dear," but Mrs. Schmidt just reached for a sugar cube and dropped it shakily into her tea.

Elm didn't know why she told Mrs. Schmidt about Ronan. There was comfort, somehow, in meeting people who didn't know about him. Elm was allowed to explain the story to them. She was allowed to say Ronan's name. It was a taboo word elsewhere where she had used up people's willingness to sit still for the story. Sometimes she felt like even Colin wanted to sweep him under the rug. Though he patiently reminisced with her, she could see the slight knit in his brow that meant he was annoyed. He missed Ronan as much as she did, but it brought him no relief to say Ronan's name. It didn't fester inside him the way it did in Elm.

But what if she had told Mrs. Schmidt merely to shock her? Had she said it to get the woman to like her? Elm was horrified that she'd used her son in this way. His death wasn't like the Ronald Reagan story; it was a sacred subject, and she had sullied it. She felt ashamed and put her head down, blinking back tears. What kind of mother was she? Elm knew the answer: she was the kind of mother who let her child die.

Intellectually, Elm knew that what happened wasn't her fault, that it was an act of God, whatever that meant. The phrase suggested a divine malevolence Elm wasn't sure she was comfortable with. She wished she remembered better her last few moments with Ronan. She was lying on the beach, half reading a magazine, half watching Colin play catch with

Ronan, and keepaway from Moira. Ronan still threw like a child, all jerky elbows and stiff hips. Moira ran back and forth between Colin and Ronan, screaming with frustration that the ball was above her head. Colin was laughing, but Elm could tell a tantrum was imminent.

Finally Ronan turned to her. "Mom, can you make her stop?" He knew that Elm was the disciplinarian in the family, and any grievances must be expressed to her. Elm remembered thinking that she just wanted to read the damn magazine. Couldn't the three of them play together for fifteen minutes without her?

She shaded her eyes. Moira's suit was riding up her bottom, while the top was completely askew. It had looked so cute on the rack, but now, with Moira wearing it, the bikini looked like an attempt to age her, even, possibly, to sexualize her. Tomorrow she would wear the one-piece.

"Moira!" she called. "Come fix your swimsuit." Moira reluctantly trotted toward her.

"Thank God," Ronan said. "Hey, Da!" and then Elm stopped paying attention. Why hadn't she paused there, cementing the scene in her memory. Why hadn't she called both her children to her? She fixed Moira's suit and took her up the beach behind the dune to pee, the sand so blindingly white that everything was filtered, hazy. Elm recalled being surprised when the beach abruptly ended in a row of palm trees; what stretched behind was dirt, reminding her of the empty scenery of a movie studio backlot. That's what had saved the two of them, the higher ground. Elm remembered screaming, covering her eyes as if watching a horror movie. Then, as the wall of water moved closer, she grabbed Moira.

She wasn't sure if she had passed out or if she had blocked the memory. The next thing she could piece together was that Moira was crying, screaming, the cut on her leg angry and bleeding. The water that had carried them into the trees that lined the shore receded just as quickly. All around her people were yelling, in pain, in search of loved ones . . . And she registered the fact that Colin was not with her. She prayed that he had grabbed Ronan the way that she had grabbed Moira. Or, rather, she hoped he had. She forgot to think about God. The moment she most needed to believe in all her life, and she didn't think about Him. And Ronan's death was proof, she believed, that God didn't exist. No God would take a child, just snatch him away with the claw of a wave.

The hospital was postapocalyptic—writhing bodies and shocked tourists, wailing Thais and overwhelmed hospital staff. Elm found gauze and peroxide and dressed Moira's wound herself. She poured the liquid onto her leg and Moira was reduced to infancy, screaming wordlessly, face red with anger. When they got back to Bangkok, and for three months afterward, Moira returned to wearing diapers, though she was close to four years old. It was not surprising, said the psychiatrist they consulted, and she would regain her lost maturity.

Colin was rushing through the wings, peering into every bed to see if he recognized the wounded. He almost ran into Elm before he grabbed her by the arms and looked into her eyes. They both realized that Ronan was gone, and Elm moaned slightly, a foreign high-pitched whine.

Then she joined him in a frantic search. They hitched a ride to another hospital and looked there. Moira fell asleep and grew heavy in Colin's arms. She woke up hungry at a third hospital, and Elm accepted God-knows-what that someone handed her to eat.

Bodies were piled up in a row alongside the elementary school. Elm refused to look. Colin let his eyes glaze over; he looked only at height until he saw someone about Ronan's size. Then he would look at the hair. Only if it was sandy blond, a little too long in back, would he look at the face. He didn't find Ronan.

Moira began to throw up and retched constantly all through the night. The next morning she looked pale and shrunken. Her skin was sagging and Elm could see she was dehydrated. Elm and Moira got in line for transport to Bangkok, a snake of dazed, disheveled tourists in bright sarongs. Most were barefoot; some wore a single sandal. All had mud in their hair, beneath their nails, streaked across their backs.

"I swear I will find him," Colin said. It was the first sentence he'd uttered in three days that didn't involve a description of Ronan or a directive to a stunned Elm. "I will bring him with me and we will meet you in Bangkok. Check in at the embassy and I'll find you there."

Inside the cargo plane, strangers huddled together for warmth. Moira had stopped throwing up, but now fluid was leaking from the other end in a consistency that reminded Elm of the meconium babies emit the first two days of their lives until their intestines are clean.

They were met by embassy officials and Elm slept for the first time in three nights, slumped in a chair with her head on Moira's hospital bed. She had no word from Colin.

Moira was in the hospital for two days receiving intravenous fluids and antibiotics. There were many worse off than she was. People were missing limbs; people had lacerations to their torsos and organs; people were in comas after having hit their heads. In the hotel room the embassy arranged for Elm to stay in, she sat in the bathtub and cried, rocking back and forth. It was like an organ had been torn from her body, and she found herself cradling a nonexistent hole in her abdomen. There was no air in her lungs; she couldn't breathe, and yet her heart kept beating, loudly, as if to mock her with its vitality.

During the day, Elm and Moira camped out in the waiting room at the embassy in Bangkok. There was coffee there, safe water, hard-boiled eggs, and Cheerios. Moira was eating solids again. Her face had regained its color and the pain in her leg was bothering her only intermittently.

One of the embassy officials had brought in his teenage daughter and her friends, who supervised the children, drawing and reading to them. The children, understanding the importance of the moment, were silent and obedient. So Elm was able to leave Moira, though the girl clung to her so desperately she had to pry Moira's hands from around her thigh when she went to meet the embassy official to start a file.

There was a box of Kleenex on the table between the armchairs that served as a makeshift intake station, but Elm didn't need it. She was too empty to cry, too anxious and worried. She felt continuously as though she were about to throw up, not nauseated, but as though her insides were going to revolt, to turn themselves inside out.

The man who interviewed her followed slavishly a sheet of questions, even when Elm had already answered them. Their conversation was taped. He was large for a Thai man, his hair cut close to his head, and Elm could see an old scar peeking through it from his scalp. His eyes were wrinkled from squinting into the sun.

He said that the fact that she'd heard nothing was because the Red Cross had only just arrived "on scene" and that "communication lines haven't been established." He gave her a list of items they would need in the event that they had to identify a body, and a pamphlet about surviving trauma. He handed her an application for a replacement passport. Then he directed her to the phone room, where she had fifteen minutes to call relatives in the States.

The list: copies of their passports, Social Security cards, dental records, hair for a DNA sample, a current photo, and a description of what the missing person was last seen wearing.

The only phone number she could remember was Ian's, because it spelled out "I-ROCK-U-4." She woke him up.

"Elm, thank God. You've no idea how worried—"

"He's missing," Elm said. Now the tears started to flow.

"Colin?"

"Ronan. He's gone, and I'm in Bangkok with Moira, and Colin's still looking . . ." Her words stuck in her mouth.

He calmed her down and promised to get copies of the passports she'd left in her files. He would scan the photo of the family on her desk and e-mail it. He would go to the apartment and make the super let him in and take Ronan's brush and toothbrush and DHL them overnight. He said he would call their dentist, and repeated back to her the number the Thai man had said to fax the records to. He would do that first thing in the morning.

Next to her a white guy with dreadlocks and faded hemp clothing cried, "Mommy," into the phone.

"Elm," Ian said. "Elm, are you there? You'll be okay, Elm. He'll be okay. He's probably with some Thai family in a village or something. There's no phone service there, right? He's probably fine."

"Probably," Elm said. She hung up.

———

In Indira's 1920s bathroom, Elm turned on the old taps to splash her face. When she emerged from the bathroom Ian had returned with the half-and-half, and the two of them were smoking Kools at the kitchen table.

"My girl will be here soon," Mrs. Schmidt said. "But if you want to poke around, I spend weekends at my studio on the island."

She meant Fire Island, Elm knew. There had been a profile in *The New Yorker* that detailed the delightful mess of the old house, down the beach from Frank O'Hara's, an easy row from Pollock and Krasner's house. But that had been a different time, and her famous neighbors were dead. Now artists stay-cationed at their studio apartments in the Bronx, unable to afford any sort of weekend getaway.

"You still design?" Elm asked.

"Unbelievable, but true," Mrs. Schmidt answered. She brought the cigarette to her lips and took a drag as it quivered. "I ask my assistant to draw a shape. He draws it in permanent marker on large paper, and I can see the outline. I make changes, then he makes a model. I can see it then with my hands. I can feel it. Is it sexy? Is it cool? Cool temperature, not the other."

Elm thought she understood. From just a piece of Ronan she could conjure up his entire existence, the smallest down on his back, the curve of his heel, the roughness of his elbows in winter. A piece of clothing could do it, a drawing he made, even a sock fallen behind a radiator that was retrieved years later. The part invokes the whole; there was a literary term for that. When she learned the term in college, it struck her that it described a phenomenon that she had experienced but been unable to express. It explained how pictures were fine, but a single Lego discovered in the box of crayons was a placeholder for an entire world. How a small toy could cause a pain so deep it felt like a hand was squeezing her heart, so insistent that it was impossible to imagine that she'd ever recover.

———

In the car on the way back to the office, Ian stretched his long legs out in front of him. "I think I'm in love," he said. "Don't you want to be like that when you get old?"

"Lonely and palsied?"

"No, you pessimist. Direct, no bullshit. 'I'm trying to get rid of you, young man.' Classic."

"I suppose," Elm said.

"Oh, Elm," Ian sighed. Elm could hear the slight note of irritation in his voice, even as he pretended he was only kidding. There was a silence. "We really should poke around in there." Ian affected a Slavic accent and caressed an imaginary crystal ball. "I see many weekend days of sifting through unimportant newspaper clippings in our future."

"Colin will love that."

"Tell him you're having an affair."

"He wouldn't believe me."

"Marriage," Ian scoffed. But, like the note of annoyance she heard earlier, she could see through to the underside of his statement, which admitted a certain envy.

Elm felt grateful that people envied her marriage. Elm even envied it a little; the marriage people thought she had, or the marriage she used to have. Colin was terrific: funny, fun-loving, loving. But she regretted the loss of their idealized existence. Ronan's death had taken a toll on their marriage. It made sense to her that many couples split up after tragedy; it certainly hadn't brought them closer together. Colin assumed the role of clown, desperately trying to cheer Elm up. She mourned for both of them. And then he would lash out at her when she didn't expect it, his grief bubbling over like soda in a shaken can. They would stay together, she didn't have doubts about that. But would they ever be close again? Elm felt like she was moving through a fog, that a vast misty plain separated her from everyone else. Ian's comments only made her more aware of the emergent distance.

"Listen," she said, changing the subject. "You would have loved the party we went to last week." Elm described the apartment, the artwork. "And some dealer named Relay who was sucking up like I was a free milkshake practically forced her card on me."

"I know her," Ian said. "Do you know she's Lacker's daughter?"

"Wait, Tom Lacker?" Elm asked. Tom Lacker owned an influential gallery on Fifty-seventh Street. The hipper downtown branch was on Twenty-fifth Street, and the superhip cousin was in Williamsburg, Brooklyn. He had all his bases covered, in other words. He was not about to miss a chance to represent an artist. Supposedly, young artists complained that showing with Lacker was like selling your soul to the devil. He fronted you money for supplies, rent, etc., but then you owed him everything. For life. It would make sense that the woman she met was his daughter. In fact, now that Elm thought about it, she had the same nervous laugh, waiting until you joined in to really titter, to make sure you agreed that something was funny.

"Mephistopheles himself. She is your friends' adviser?"

"I wouldn't say they're my friends," Elm said. "They're acquaintances of Colin's from the gym. Oh, and here's the really funny part. In the master bath, right over the Jacuzzi tub—pink marble, by the way—hangs this portrait of their dog, Dishy or something. Full oil, photo-realist. It's hilarious."

"*Avec* or *sans* bone?" Ian asked.

"And they're planning on cloning him," Elm said. "Some European company that clones people's pets. Is that not the most ridiculous thing you've ever heard?"

"Right up there with assless chaps, and squeeze-bottle cheese. Can they really clone him?"

Elm shrugged.

"I went to college with Relay. We were good friends then. Do you still have her card?"

"Not sure," Elm said. It had been her New Year's resolution several years ago to ask if anyone knew the person before Elm got catty about someone. She never quite mastered it.

The cab stopped suddenly as a pedestrian buried in a guidebook failed to notice the red light. "Fucking tourists," said the cabbie.

"Sometimes I hate New York," Ian said, with uncharacteristic vitriol.

––––––

When she got back to her desk there was a voice mail from Colin. He was whispering into the phone, speaking in mock code. "Shit is about to hit fan. Repeat, shit is about to hit fan. Ring my cell."

Elm dialed him. He picked up and said, "George! Grand, and you?"

"You'd make a terrible spy," Elm said.

"Yes, of course, George," he said. Elm wanted to let him know he was overplaying it, but let him continue. When he was out of his colleagues' earshot, he said, "Christ, Elmtree, you can cut it with a knife in there."

"What's going on?"

"Fuck if I know," he said. "Looks like the merger will keep most higher-ups, but provisionally, just until the FDA ruling. Look, Elm," he said, concerned by her silence. "We'll be fine, I promise. Don't worry."

"I won't," Elm said.

"Everything else okay?" he asked.

I don't know how to answer that, she thought. Nothing's okay. Nothing will ever be okay again. "Fine," she said.

"I'll give you details tonight. I'd best go back in. Love you."

Elm put her face in her hands. Maybe her cousin Greer was right. She could use some time off. She hadn't taken more than seven consecutive days since the month Ronan died, when she had started back at work, too soon by most people's standards. They didn't understand that home was unbearable, suffocating, each room a cubby of memories. If she was at work, there were eight hours a day she couldn't be lying in bed, remembering, mourning. Maybe during five minutes of the day she'd forget to think about him, and then a flood of guilt would overtake her even as she savored the relief of it, the lifting of the iron weight.

She searched her desk and briefcase for Relay's card to pass on to Ian. She was wearing the same trench coat she wore that night, but the pockets contained only gum wrappers and used tissues. Maybe she had put it in the pocket of the pants she was wearing? She'd sent them to the dry cleaner's with a stain on the right knee from falling guacamole. She could call the hostess. She supposed she should probably call her anyway, to thank her for the evening.

To her surprise, Ellen picked up the phone after the second ring. "Hello?" she said, breathless. Elm wondered if she was expecting a call. Maybe from her lover. Elm always imagined that people were having clandestine affairs, but usually there was some mundane reason for the erratic behavior, like a stomach virus, or a broken refrigerator. Elm thanked her for the party.

"Oh, of course. We're glad you could make it. Sorry, I'm waiting for a call from France. From the company that's cloning Dishoo?"

"That's really happening, huh?" Elm asked.

"That's what they say. We're paying for it anyway."

"How did it even occur . . . How did you find them?" Elm asked.

"My holistic health healer heard about it somewhere. They have a website."

Elm wrote down the URL, thinking that Colin would get a kick out of it. She remembered to ask for Relay's information before she hung up.

She took the phone number over to Ian's office before she lost it again. "You know, it occurs to me now, I thought she looked familiar," Elm said, pausing at the entrance to Ian's office. "Is it possible she's been to an auction?"

"I haven't seen her." Ian continued to look at his computer screen. Elm couldn't see what was requiring such rapt attention. "At school she was into modern dance, I think," Ian said, still not looking at Elm.

Elm stared at him, his profile sharp, his neck tucked neatly into his collar, his hair gelled to obedience. The computer screen threw off light that reflected off his high forehead. Suddenly, such a wave of loneliness overcame Elm that she thought she might faint from despair. He was shutting her out.

This was a recurring paranoia she'd felt since Ronan had died. In therapy, she had discovered that she felt he had rejected her, as silly as it sounded. That he had somehow chosen to perish in order to get away from her. Her psychiatrist had teased this out of her one day after she related the dream she'd had a million times, so cliché she dismissed it as embarrassingly banal and mainstream: she was returning from a journey to her childhood house and no one recognized her.

Knowing that this fear of abandonment was irrational did nothing to dispel it. So Elm had learned to at least acknowledge that what she was feeling was probably in her head, and to try to assemble evidence to the contrary. One, Ian loved her and was fiercely loyal. Two, she had done nothing to incur his annoyance. Three, he wasn't one to suffer in silence. When he was angry, you knew it. Ergo, whatever was bugging him was him, and not Elm.

"Well," she said. "I'll leave you to it."

"Bye," he said, waving.

Gabriel

As soon as Klinman left the gallery, Gabriel began to think about his new business opportunity. He could get Didier to help him; the man could do a passing Pissarro. Marie-Laure worked for hire too, he knew. Recently she had illustrated a children's book. Surely she'd be more interested in this work.

A team thus mentally assembled, Gabriel closed the gallery early. After he checked his various pockets for the money (he'd spread it out both to avoid losing it and because the wad was too big to fit into his tight pocket), he locked the door behind him and pulled down the grate. Paris was in the midst of a cold snap, its regular mist hanging heavy like a compress. Gabriel turned up his collar, but it did little to warm him. He arrived at his studio in the *banlieue* jumping up and down to shake the cold from his limbs. Both Marie-Laure and Didier were there, and he told them about Klinman's visit. Marie-Laure looked at him with such blatant gratitude that Gabriel was embarrassed.

"Who is this man?" asked Didier. "Our benefactor?"

"He's English," Gabriel said. "A dealer or collector or something."

"Who cares?" said Marie-Laure. "As far as I'm concerned, he's an angel from God sent to pay my rent." Marie-Laure's live-in boyfriend dabbled in heroin; he was always stealing money from her wallet and threatening to hurt her.

"Angels pay your rent?" Didier baited her.

Marie-Laure opened her mouth to answer, but Gabriel cut her off. "We have until next week only. The paper will arrive tomorrow."

The paper was delivered by messenger to Rosenzweig's the next day. It did look like nineteenth-century artist's paper, irregular and obviously not mass-produced. Gabriel took it to the studio, ready to hand it out, feeling a dry-mouthed panic. He was not used to being in charge. He was not a leader. He was an outsider, and this new role of cheerleader/ whip cracker was an unfamiliar fit. He didn't like being responsible, especially for other people's work. He liked to work alone, rely on no one, and certainly not flaky Didier or weepy Marie-Laure.

Today, Marie-Laure didn't complain as Gabriel lit incense, and did him the favor of turning her American pop music selections down low. Gabriel sat down at his table. He took out the sketch he had started the day before, planning to transfer it to Klinman's paper. Some of the elements weren't working. The perspective was not quite uniform. The clock tower in the background was elongated at the top, the point of view low to the ground. Yet the women's skirts were viewed from above. This inconsistency bothered Gabriel. He suspected this fussiness was related to the lack of spirit in his art, his preoccupation with structure at the expense of emotion. These kinds of imperfections further falsified the piece of art. Yet there was no time to obsess over details in his current assignment. It was all about production. Line them up, bang them out, pocket the cash.

Gabriel put on the old earphones that led to his Walkman. He was the only one he knew who still listened to cassettes, but that's how his music was recorded, and it wasn't like he had money to buy some fancy new digital music player. He pressed play and the familiar Spanish rap music blasted from the headset. Gabriel turned it down. He picked up his pencil. He was more excited about this project than he could remember being in a long while, perhaps since he had copied *Febrer*. But that hadn't been excitement; it was more like nervous apprehension.

He was happy that his work would be compensated for once, instead of merely criticized and shunted. He was guaranteed money for his art, even if it wasn't really his. He felt disappointed in himself; he had fallen into the trap of capitalism, into believing that an object was valuable only if it was monetarily valuable. But he lived within the culture, it was bound to have an effect on him.

Unsellable art was bad art. So according to the cognoscenti, Gabriel was making bad art. And by this same perverse logic, any art that sold was automatically good art, in direct proportion to its sale price. Who were these buffoons who decided what sold and what sat out in the soggy cold of the *marché aux puces*? Soulless men who, no matter how they tried, saw only Swiss francs and yuan in the brushstrokes of the masters. They would never understand Gabriel. It was futile to try. Rather, give them what they want—eighty-six pieces of art by next week.

He decided to get one of the pastels out of the way. Mediterranean blue was almost impossible to render without oil paints, but he could try. He layered on the pigment, swirling like he remembered the waves in *Febrer*. Then he completed the scene, a marketplace near the coast.

Almost without realizing it, he drew a large figure in the foreground. A woman, selling bread. It was his mother: the waistless apron, the plaits in her hair, her uneven eyes, one lid heavier than the other, always winking.

No time for nostalgia. An aesthetic assembly line; finish one, on to the next.

———

On Saturday Marie-Laure and Didier came to his studio. Gabriel, concentrating, didn't hear them approach until Didier tapped him on the back, startling him.

"Sorry, man," he said.

"What do you mean?" Gabriel rested his old-fashioned earphones around his neck.

Marie-Laure said, "We can't do it. Figure it takes us at least three hours for each one—"

"That's if they're shitty," Didier interrupted.

"And we can only work like max sixteen hours a day. So that's five per day, max, which is nearly impossible, and there's three of us and five days. And I promised my boyfriend that I'd do Sunday lunch with his family. Do the math."

"I can't," said Gabriel.

"I can't either," Didier said. "But I'm working my ass off and we're not going to finish."

"Yeah." Gabriel put down his brush. He hated watercolors. Something about them seemed so wishy-washy, so like a Sunday painter. The colors were too muted, the lines inexact. "So who should we get?"

"Hans?" Didier asked. Gabriel nodded. "I'll text him right now." Didier busied himself with his phone as he walked out of the room.

Marie-Laure said, "What about Antoine, on the end?"

"I don't know," Gabriel said. "I don't want the whole studio involved, you know?"

"Okay . . ." Marie-Laure said slowly. She clearly didn't know. She wasn't at all embarrassed, Gabriel realized. She didn't care that they were painting cheap knockoffs for money. But he did, and he didn't want it spread around. Nor did he want to be the rainmaker for the people in the studio. He didn't even really want Marie-Laure and Didier involved, to tell the truth.

"What happened to that Russian girl who went to school with us?" he asked.

"Back to Russia."

"What about Lise?"

"Lise Girard? I just saw her at Didier's show. Oh, wait, right, you were there. I can find her on the Internet," Marie-Laure offered.

"I'll do it," Gabriel said. Why hadn't he thought of her in the first place? "She's a good idea, right?"

Lise had been the expert draftsman (draftswoman?) in their circle. She had specialized in technical drawing; as a teenager she'd considered becoming an architect. During one of their first conversations, in a smoky bar full of American students near the Sorbonne, she told him that to her lines were clearer than words. She saw the world in charcoal and lead, every person, object, and place an outline, shaded, smeared, or cross-hatched into its third dimension.

"For example"—she picked a piece of tobacco from her lips using her pinkie and her thumb and flicked it away—"right now, in this bar? There are only curves and angles. I could close my eyes and sketch it."

"All I see is color," Gabriel said. "I look around and I see sweaters and jackets and hair and surface texture."

"Together, we would make a great painter." Lise laughed. Her front tooth was turned slightly inward, an imperfection that made her dearer to him, the way that flaws of unrequited love increase its indelibility.

Lise could render anything, in anyone's hand, practically effortlessly. Her room had been a shrine to the greats: she had sketches of hunters from the caves at Altamira, Fra Angelico studies, *Whistler's Mother* . . . the lines as sure and exact as if the masters had drawn them. It was part of her final project: a history of the male torso. By copying the style, if not the subject matter, of art history's most macho protagonists, she subverted their power somewhat, strengthening her own. Gabriel had thought it masterful, though by then he recognized that his judgment concerning Lise was somewhat suspect. Even now, he was motivated by wanting to see what her life was like so many years later.

Gabriel was not well versed in Internet searches; in fact, the entire world of the computer remained opaque to him. In that sense, he had the perfect job—Édouard's gallery was run as if they were living contemporarily with the old masters. Sales were recorded in double-entry ledgers. Occasionally, Édouard's bookkeeper would come by and grumble at the lack of Excel spreadsheets. If Gabriel wanted to use a computer, he had to go down the street to the seedy café and time his computer usage to the minute so as to avoid extra charges.

Now, confronted with Google's French home page, he typed in Lise's name. It returned more than fifty-five thousand hits. "Lise Girard" was a popular name. He clicked on images, and saw, among an elderly lawyer and a teenager in an inappropriate see-through dress, a tall blonde with a hiking pack on her back, mountains behind her dwarfing her. He clicked on the picture to make it bigger, but Facebook wanted him to join in order to see it. He didn't like the idea of his personal information being accessible to anyone and everyone. He knew this was silly—he had nothing to steal, and who would want the identity of a fucked-up Spanish artist who owed France Telecom two hundred euros?

What the hell, he thought, and went back to Google's home page to create a new e-mail address. Was it a good sign or a bad one that leshiverains@gmail.com wasn't yet taken? He signed himself up for Facebook, and by the time he was able to navigate back to the picture of what might have been Lise, he had gone over his fifteen minutes and would have to pay an extra five euros.

When he enlarged the picture he saw that it was indeed her. She had several photos up, including some with what Gabriel thought might be four or five children. It was hard to tell which were repeated in the various photos, so alike did they look. In the photos her eyes had gone starry with crow's-feet and her freckles had taken over a good portion of her nose. He hadn't noticed these flaws when he saw her at Didier's show; makeup had done its trick.

Had he gone through the same aging process? He was, granted, a bit lumpier than he had been. Not fat, but shaped differently, his belly developing a slackness that was sure to be a pouch should he ever stop drinking so much coffee and start eating regular meals.

He wrote her a short note saying that it was nice to see her at Didier's show, thanking her for introducing him to Colette, and letting her know there was money to be made; if she was interested, she should call him. He hated writing in French. He had never taken a formal French class, and the accent marks felt insurmountably arbitrary. *Circonflexe*, *grave*, *aigu;* it was like some strange superlanguage on top of the letters. He felt this way about French in general, and French people. He could understand the basics of conversations, of customs, of conventions, but there was always another level that he failed to grasp, people speaking over his head, looking down on him. But Paris wasn't really France. Paris was Paris—and it had become his home.

A small box popped up in the corner and there was Lise, virtually, telling him how glad she was to be back in touch, and, in fact, it was a particularly good time for her since her youngest was now in day care full-time. What was the project?

Gabriel looked at his watch. There was one minute until he had to pay for another quarter-hour session. He typed, "Can we just meet?"

"Sure," Lise responded. "Where?"

Gabriel replied with the first place that came to his head, their old haunt, the Biche Blanche.

———

The Biche Blanche had the advantage of being across the street from the École. It lacked charm and originality, but was convenient and inexpensive, and the waiters let students linger at tables long after others would have cleared their throats to get the squatters to leave.

The amazing thing about Paris in general, and its cafés in particular, was that they remained outside time. All had identical bistro tables in fake marble, the rounded wooden chairs that were comfortable for no ass. The same large blond Americans, trying to speak French with the pimpled French boys, the insouciant students, too bored even to take a drag from their burning cigarettes.

Lise was already there when he arrived, reading a large book at a window table. As he recognized her she lifted her head, waving vigorously, so that he smiled. She stood and gave him two kisses which were not really kisses but cheek contact. He noticed she didn't bother making the kissing noises, and he admired that about her. In the brief seconds their heads were touching, he noticed her lemongrass perfume.

At first they made small talk. Lise showed him pictures of her children—three, as it turned out—on a smartphone. She seemed very proud of the fact that she took care of the children with no outside help. Two days a week she worked at Ambrosine's gallery.

"It's good. I was actually managing the gallery before the kids. I used to think he was full of shit. He *is* full of shit, but he's a genius at recognizing color," Lise gushed. "You know how everyone always says color in my work is an afterthought? I think I finally get how important it is. Does that make sense?"

Without prompting, Lise began to tell him about other people they had gone to school with. Most of the names did not conjure up faces in Gabriel's memory, and some were completely unfamiliar. She was friends with them on the computer, she said, whatever she meant by that.

Then there was a silence. Gabriel had noticed, in their brief friendship, and during the briefer-still time they were lovers, Lise's way of asking few questions. At first he had assumed that she understood if he had anything important to say he would tell her, but he came to realize that she was not actually particularly interested in what he was doing or thinking.

What had he seen in her? he wondered. He mooned for more than a year, despondent when he saw her talking to men at parties, until she cornered him, said she could feel his eyes on her, and would he please stop it? Yes, they had spent one night together, but there was alcohol involved and it was just that once. Gabriel felt hollow inside, his pain so great that he stayed away from school altogether for two weeks. Why? he wondered now. She was just a girl, or rather, now a woman nearing middle age.

Lise smiled, accentuating the lines spreading from her eyes. "Now, what is this business proposition?"

Gabriel explained Klinman's visit.

"Sounds great!" Lise said.

Gabriel handed her an envelope full of euros and several sheets of Klinman's paper in a portfolio.

"Fantastic. I'm really excited." She made a show of opening the envelope and removing a bill to pay for their drinks. "I insist. I'll bring them to Rosenzweig's after work on Wednesday?"

"Or I could come by Ambrosine's." Gabriel thought it might be a bad idea to have his friends traipsing in to drop off portfolios. Édouard might get suspicious. Her face fell; quickly she recovered her smile. It occurred to Gabriel that she didn't want him there with his motorcycle boots and ratty secondhand clothing. He felt hot shame curl up into his face.

Lise said, "Could you come by the apartment? That might be easier."

The waiter took the bill away to make change.

"So I'm, um, painting again," Gabriel said.

"Painting! Oh, my God, I just told Ambro that everyone was going to return to painting after plastics. It was the only natural progression. Painting! Both Didier and you. I love being right. You know, I really liked your final project," Lise said. "I know you took a lot of—" She used a slang word that Gabriel didn't know.

"A lot of what?"

"People criticized it a lot."

Gabriel didn't know that was common knowledge. He always assumed that he was invisible to everyone else. If he wasn't in the room, he ceased to exist. A thousand times something he said came back to him, proving him wrong, but his self-deprecation resisted logic.

Hans had called him repressed. That was what his adviser LeFevre had said about his work too. The same day, as if in chorus. He'd argued with Hans—Gabriel had fucked both women and men, he said. He'd had sex on boats, on the beach, with strangers, in chicken coops. Hans said that it was perfectly possible to have repressed sex with both sexes at once, with hermaphrodites and dwarves and Amazons. It was emotional unconstraint he was talking about. Any asshole could do anything with his body if he was high enough. It took true courage to love the person you were sticking it in.

And then Gabriel had gone back to his studio, where he had an appointment with his adviser. LeFevre had stood with his hands on his ample hips and frowned before turning to Gabriel and saying, "The subject matter may be daring, but the line is repressed, censured." And Gabriel had balled his hands into fists, his too-long nails leaving crescent indents in his palms.

Now Gabriel quoted out loud: "'Gabriel Connois's work, though technically proficient, is devoid of any recognizable individual style.'"

"Well, that was really petty, in my opinion. Your work was beautiful, organic. I don't know what happened to aesthetics, but I think they count for something."

"Thanks." Gabriel was embarrassed. He began to wonder if the waiter had thought the large bill was his to keep. "I liked your project too."

"You're sweet." She touched his arm.

Finally the waiter tossed the silver tray containing the change down on the table. Lise gathered up all the large coins, sliding them into her jacket pocket. She had never removed her gray coat, and when she leaned back, it retained the shape of her hunched shoulders. "I'll see you next week then," she said.

Gabriel stood up to follow her out, but she was quicker than he, and was out the door before he wove his way through the tables. As he walked toward the *métro*, he thought about what Lise had said about his work being beautiful. She meant: beautiful, but not profound. His adviser had offered a similar criticism. "It's not that you're not talented," he'd said. "It's patently obvious that you are. You wouldn't be here if you weren't. There's just not that spark. There's no passion in your work. There's competence, originality even, but no inspiration, no voice. I think you'll find it—I hope you will. Your talent is too big not to, but so far you haven't reached that place."

"And I am supposed to reach this 'voice' how?" Gabriel had asked, to his surprise and embarrassment, near tears for the first time in years.

"I don't know," LeFevre said. "Think about what moves you. What frightens you. Access the place you don't want to go."

"So now you're a psychiatrist."

"That's exactly the kind of defensive attitude that is apparent on your canvases. I've taken you as far as I can."

Asshole, thought Gabriel now. All that French psychobabble. If LeFevre didn't like the work, why didn't he just say so? Gabriel had been so proud of his final series of canvases, a pictorial essay on the travels of water. The paintings had turned out rather more conceptual than he would have expected his "research" to produce, but he was commenting on color and reflection, and no one seemed to understand that.

And then video. No one really knew how to judge it, and he gained a foothold in the community without really understanding what he wanted to accomplish, now that he looked back on it. He was still obsessed with color, with the screen as canvas. He loved the graininess of the images—exactly what he was trying to get away from with his glass-smooth canvases now. He also loved the space between the images, found that to be the place where he felt most comfortable. Then he just . . . lost interest. When everyone moved to solid sculpture (plastic, resin), he moved on to film, making Super 8 reels and blowing up the negatives as stills, drawing on them. A sentence in *Paris Match* about his work in a group show called it "more interesting than its surrounding pieces." Not exactly a rave, but it could have been worse, coming from that critic, known as a poison pen.

And now he was back to painting, as though he had returned to the beginning of his career. He was reconvening schoolmates to create the camaraderie that didn't exist the first time around. It felt like starting over.

———

Gabriel looked at the address Lise had written down for him. He had never really been to the neighborhood known only by its victory-arch landmark: La Défense. The streets were cleaner here, wider. No *clochards* begged for change; tourists were absent. The boulevard was filled with midrange prix fixe bistros, punctuated by an authentic-looking Japanese restaurant and an upscale Chinese noodle shop.

He should have brought his *Paris de Poche*. He wasn't sure where to find the street, and surely none of the upper-class mothers pushing their prams would answer him, dressed as he was. He went back down into the *métro* to look up the street on the map.

As he walked, he wondered what Lise's life must be like. He hadn't quite guessed she'd be living such a bourgeois existence. How could you go from studying art at France's most prestigious school to living this far outside the action? She had fallen victim, then, to the vicissitudes and trappings of success. That made sense. The fancy phone, the job at Ambrosine's. It all fit into a neat little *bobo* package. Maybe she wasn't embarrassed by him. Maybe she wanted him to come to her apartment to seduce her, to get a little excitement of the art world that her life now lacked.

There was an elevator attendant. That was rich; someone whose job was to press buttons all day. The cage rose slowly to the seventh floor. The attendant bowed as he held the door open. Gabriel stepped onto the landing and pulled the knocker on Lise's front door, letting it fall back to its cradle.

A very small person answered the door. He was blond like Lise, with streaks of Nutella on his face. Behind him loud children's music was playing: synthesizer piano and high-pitched melodies. A small white dog turned circles, yipping excitedly.

"Hello," Gabriel said.

"Maman!" the child yelled.

Lise came around the corner, wiping her hands on her jeans. "Hey, Gabi, this is . . . Oh, for . . . Look at this." She grabbed the little boy's face and turned his head toward the door. "There are fingerprints on the door. Geraldine was just here. Go get a towel."

The little boy ran off. Lise shook her head. "Come in, Gabi. I'm sorry if the place is a mess." She used the slang word for mess: *bordel*, the same word that had so confused him when he first arrived in France and couldn't figure out why everyone claimed to live in a whorehouse. The living room was spacious, a thousand shades of white, and smelled sweetly chemically of new paint. The furniture was modern *alto disegno*—Noguchi tables, Eames chairs, a Nelson Home desk, a Mies van der Rohe bench, as if she'd received a bulk discount at a modernist design store.

Reading his face, Lise laughed a little. "Giancarlo's father was a design instructor at Iuav in Venice. He collected pieces. . . . Don't make fun."

"I wasn't," Gabriel said. "This is amazing." He walked toward the window; the apartment looked over the Boulevard Maurice Barrès for a full view of the Bois de Boulogne. The white dog panted at his feet, pink tongue hanging too long out of its mouth. Gabriel toed it away with his shoe.

"Well?" Lise turned on a lamp next to the sofa. "Would you like coffee? I'll make some."

Gabriel nodded and Lise disappeared into the kitchen. He looked around the room. A dining table, flat-screen television with hidden wires, an intricately pocketed coffee table. He opened one of the drawers to find a remarkable remote-control collection. There were photos on the mantel of the vestigial fireplace. Gabriel crept closer to look at them.

Lise's family at Euro Disney, at Chamonix, at someone's house in the country. Gaggles of children piled in laps, smiling at the camera. Lise at someone's wedding: A sister? A cousin? Early teenage years, dressed in a long, flowing pink gauze dress, arms folded, shoulders hunched forward to hide nascent breasts, hair straggly. Lise and Giancarlo at a scenic overlook, maybe somewhere in Italy, Lise's face tanned, her chest freckly, and her nose beginning to peel, Giancarlo looking off behind the photographer with a surprised and pleased expression, as though he were seeing someone he knew unexpectedly.

Gabriel felt like a detective on an American television show. He was looking for a problem, something off, a Photoshop mistake that would reveal the entire hoax. But he knew he would find nothing. Lise had real photos of her childhood, trips, birthdays, etc. Gabriel had only his memories and one photograph, the low-quality colors fading into oranges and reds, of his parents posed stiffly on their wedding day. That was it. The sum total of his past: one kitschy photo and a gaggle of memories. And his name. Maybe talent, if he had any.

Lise reappeared with a plastic tray that Gabriel recognized as IKEA circa 2001. He could hear the cars outside honking as they entered the intersection, the horns muted through the windows. Lise went over and opened one slightly, hooking the handles together so the panes wouldn't bang. The horns immediately got louder, drowning out the cloying baby music, and a cold breeze blew in, smelling faintly of fish.

In another room a child began to cry. "Be right back," Lise said.

There was no sugar, so Gabriel put three small disks of sugar substitute into his coffee and sipped it. It was too sweet, sickening. He debated sneaking into the kitchen to pour it out, but in front of him, staring at him, was the same little person who had opened the door.

"Who are you?" he asked.

"I'm Gabi," he said. "An old friend of your mother's."

"You talk funny. Are you foreign?"

Gabriel nodded and tried not to be offended. Now that he had a chance to examine the child, he wasn't sure it was a boy after all. He'd had so little experience with children that he wasn't sure how to tell how old they were, or what it was appropriate to talk to them about. Plus, it always felt odd that someone who had lived in France—lived on the planet—fewer years than he should speak the language with much greater fluency.

"Which foreign?"

"I'm Spanish."

"My father's Italian." The child picked at the fringe on a throw blanket.

"I know."

Gabriel shifted uncomfortably. The conversation appeared to have hit a dead end.

"But you don't talk as weird as he does." Gabriel felt a silly flush of pride. Why was he in competition with Giancarlo? To live in this suburban aerie working a soulless job and raising some brats?

Lise came back into the room carrying a parcel wrapped expertly in brown paper. "Here they are," she said. "Do you want to look at them? Oh, you're talking to Gabi?" She held another child on her hip. This one's face was wet with tears, and he/she was making small hiccup noises. Lise balanced the package on a chair.

"He talks funny like Papa."

"Maybe you talk funny? Did you ever think about that?" She smiled and bent to tickle the child's ribs. It giggled and ran out of the room.

"My six-year-old," Lise explained.

Gabriel knew he was supposed to say something like "So cute" or "How precious," but he wasn't sure how to do so without revealing that he didn't know the child's gender, so he just smiled.

"I'll look," he said.

He unwrapped her package. The drawings were good, remarkable likenesses of Ganedis, his soft lines, his domestic subjects. There were the requisite charcoal still lifes, and a gouache of the child he'd just been talking to wearing a yellow dress and holding the small white dog.

"Coffee's no good?" Lise asked. She slid the child down her leg and it landed on its feet, rubbing its face into the back of her knee.

"I put too many sugars in," Gabriel said.

"Oh, yeah, I forgot to warn you. Saccharine. I'll get you another one."

"It's okay," Gabriel said. "I should get going."

"Thanks for coming by. I'm sorry it's so chaotic here. You must think my life is hugely boring. That's because it is." She sat down and the baby climbed up her, sitting on her lap and burying its face into her neck. She instinctively hugged it and began to rock. What would it be like, Gabriel wondered suddenly, to have something love you that much? He felt an urge to join them in an embrace.

As he left her apartment, with its overpriced furniture and the small fingerprints on the preposterous white walls, Gabriel felt he should pity Lise for what she had become. And yet she seemed so at home in her world, far more content than he was in his. And while she could dabble in his world, work in an art gallery, create just enough to call herself an artist, he would be as lost in hers as if he'd been asked to join a troupe of circus acrobats. He was completely unsuited for a life of convention, unable to imitate it, let alone desire it.

He'd lost Lise, that was patently obvious. And she was not the only one. A phenomenon he'd noticed on the far side of forty was his growing disdain for all his former friends. So many of them had made such boring conventional choices: marriage, children. Most were no longer making art; one had gone to law school, another worked for some sort of graphic design firm. He remembered the long nights, drinking red wine from a screw-top bottle that stained everyone's teeth red, being told by neighbors to shut the fuck up for chrissake, talking about art like characters out of *La Bohème*. When was the last time he had a real meaningful conversation about art? Or anything more substantive than who was showing where and what vitamins everyone was taking? If this was what it meant to be middle-aged, then Gabriel vowed to forgo it.

———

On Friday, Klinman met Gabriel at the gallery before it opened. Gabriel spread out the best of the art he and his École had drawn on Édouard's light table. Édouard never came in before ten, so he and Klinman had an hour or so to go over them. Though Klinman's expression remained stoic, Gabriel could tell by the way his eyes crinkled in the creases that the drawings, watercolors, and pastels were satisfactory. Gabriel's shoulders opened up and he stood straighter.

Klinman looked at the drawings carefully. He lingered approvingly over the pastel Gabriel was proud of, but then he turned to the next drawing and saw Gabriel's mother repeated in a sketch. "This is the same woman, in both drawings."

"Sometimes Connois drew from the same models."

Klinman nodded. He also paused over Lise's gouache of her child with that yippy white dog. He pointed.

"Ganedis," Gabriel said.

Klinman nodded his approval. At the bottom of the pile, Gabriel had included his take on a Piranesi arch as well as a Canaletto plaza scene.

"What are these?" Klinman asked.

"Oh." Gabriel was slightly embarrassed. "There were a few extra sheets of paper, and because they were so beautiful, I drew on them. It's not the style you asked for, but it was so pretty. . . ." Gabriel was scared. Klinman's expression was of rapt concentration on the drawings.

"Might you be free on Sunday?" Klinman asked. "I have an idea. I would like you to come for a drink."

He wrote down an address in the Marais.

"What time should Colette and I be there?"

"Not Colette. Just you," Klinman said. He took the art, placed it carefully in the portfolio, and left without saying good-bye.

———

The bar Klinman had chosen was attempting to mimic a living room. It was decorated with low, ornate sofas, purple velvet worn through, and embroidered armchairs. Mirrors and candelabra adorned the walls. Klinman ordered a scotch, so Gabriel ordered one too. He was unused to the taste; he took large, infrequent gulps while Klinman sipped daintily. He was hungry, but didn't want to order something to eat. It was sure to be expensive and tiny.

Klinman was appraising him, looking him up and down. Gabriel was dressed inappropriately for the occasion, as usual. Though they were in the Marais, ground zero for hipsters and artists (wealthy hipsters, successful artists), everyone else seemed to be wearing couture while Gabriel was sporting thrift-store chic. He was the only one without a jacket in the bar, and certainly the only one wearing shit kickers instead of loafers.

Klinman's clothes, on the other hand, came straight from the set of a 1940s film, a three-piece pin-striped suit that clung to him like he'd recently outgrown it, his barrel chest swelling beneath the fabric.

"So where in Spain are you from?" Klinman asked in Spanish.

"How many languages do you speak?" Gabriel responded in Spanish, taken aback. The scotch was warming in his stomach and the room had taken on sepia tones, reflecting off the mirrors and ormolu.

Klinman laughed. He reverted to French. "My Spanish is terrible, rusty. But I am good at two things." He let his head fall back, searching the ceiling for words and then staring again at Gabriel. "No, three. I am good at communicating. Languages, *puf*, they just make sense to me. I am good at judging character. And I know art. My grandfather was a portrait painter to the aristocracy before they took his life. I inherited his eye, though not his talent. You, it seems, have inherited both."

Gabriel shook his head. "I hoped that by now I would be better."

"Paris." Klinman pronounced the city the English way. "What is Paris? And now they say it's all about Berlin. Tomorrow it'll be about somewhere else. At some point it will be someone else's turn, besides Europe. You, Monsieur Connois, have a choice."

Klinman stopped speaking. He removed a cigarette from a silver holder and offered it to Gabriel, who shook his head. With affected slowness, he removed a lighter from his breast pocket. It looked heavy, in the shape of a lion whose mouth emitted fire. Its eyes were stones. Emeralds? Topaz? Glass? Klinman took another sip of his drink and then a long drag on the cigarette.

"I have high blood pressure," he said. "I allow myself two a day. You don't smoke?"

Gabriel shrugged. Klinman nodded his head. "Hmmm," he said, as though this revealed something important about Gabriel.

There was a long pause. "Your choice, señor, is the following: make art, or make money. Maybe you will make money with art. Not likely. Maybe you will make art with money. More likely. It's up to you."

"I don't understand." Gabriel wasn't sure if he wasn't following the thread or if the man was not making sense.

"You are dating Colette. She likes fancy restaurants. And maybe you'll fall in love with her, and will want to make French babies. French babies wear couture, have you not noticed? They eat organic vegetables. Not inexpensive." Klinman opened his wallet and threw a few euros down on the table. "Come, I have something to show you."

Gabriel had a brief moment of fear that Klinman was going to take him somewhere and expose himself. That had happened to him once, with a gallery owner, right after he got to Paris. The man actually said, "Would you like to see my etchings?" And Gabriel had followed him into the back room, where the man turned around, fly open, half-erect cock waving. But Klinman's interest seemed solely artistic and avuncular.

They wove through the Marais, cutting across the Rue Bourgeois. The shops here were chic; their front bay windows abutted the tiny sidewalk, displaying mannequins that suggested figures rather than imitated them. Whimsical children's furniture, a store devoted only to men's cravats, heavy modern jewelry. Above the stores were the minuscule apartments of the old quarter, slanted floors and hallway bathrooms. Some were still occupied by elderly Jews who had returned after the war. The smaller side streets sold kosher food, hid yeshivas. From some second-story windows emanated Sephardic music, plaintive Moroccan wailing. Some of the other apartments held squatters: artists more interested in the bohemian lifestyle than in art. If they were real artists, they would live outside the city, as Gabriel did, in a rented room, with a separate studio. And the Marais was also the new place for wealthy Americans ("new money," Édouard called it, using the English words).

They turned left onto a small side street and were in the garment district. The sidewalks were wider here, but no less crowded. Though the racks of clothing seemed to part for Klinman, they closed back up immediately, so that to follow him Gabriel kept having to dodge mobile wardrobes and cudgels of cloth.

Finally, Klinman ducked into a large courtyard. Flagstones surrounded a fountain in the middle, where the wan light drifted down from the cloudy sky. The fountain had obviously been functional rather than decorative at one time. The spray rose and then dripped down a symmetrical spindle with a wide base.

"This is my office. Paris office," Klinman said, waving at the *portière*. He led them straight across the courtyard and pulled a set of antique-looking keys from his pocket. He unlocked the door and stepped inside, hurrying to turn off an alarm on the far wall. When he flipped the lights, they were thrown back in time.

The room looked as if it were transplanted from a nineteenth-century men's club. The furniture was all burgundy leather, redolent of cigar smoke. A low mahogany table had been remade to double as a lightbox. Heavy brocade curtains suggested windows, but no light was in evidence.

"Have a seat," Klinman said. "Put on these gloves."

Gabriel felt a flutter of nervous excitement. Whatever the man was about to show him would be important. The setting demanded some sort of unveiling. When Klinman left the room and all was silent, Gabriel could hear the hum of dehumidifiers.

Klinman returned with a large portfolio. He set it on a desk and unzipped it. As soon as he stepped forward, holding the paper with his gloved fingertips, Gabriel knew what he was looking at.

It was a small square of paper, probably not more than thirty centimeters, and it held three drawings. The first was a barely rendered face. The lines were exact, if they didn't quite connect. A young man's face, an aquiline nose, an erect neck, and a sensitive gaze. Here was youth, but a youth that was concerned: Wounded by the past? Worried about the future? Melancholic? Pensive? Beneath this was a more detailed study. A hand gloved in heavy leather. Gabriel was sure it had some sort of name. A falconry glove? But no, then it would extend up the forearm, and this glove ended at the disembodied wrist. It held its mate, which was limp, sagging, though it maintained the memory of the form of the fingers that had just been inside it. The third sketch was a ruffled, high-collared Renaissance shirt, just a neck. It was a play of shadow, the ruffles suggested by shading rather than line.

It was obviously a study for Titian's *Man with a Glove;* the final canvas hung in the Louvre and Gabriel had seen it a dozen times. A sketch for a work this important was like looking into the artist's atelier, or even into his brain. Here was how he worked out his precise lines, the faces that registered age, pain, pleasure. Here was the nascent expressive hand so naturally curved and lifelike—an entire portrait boiled down to the placement of one finger, one empty leather finger.

Carefully, Klinman turned the drawing over. On the back was the ornate mark of its original dealer, which Gabriel didn't recognize. Also, through the light, Gabriel could see the embossed watermark—the paper had been handmade and signed by its maker. These two marks served to authenticate the drawing. This was a real Titian. The master had drawn this himself.

"Stunning, isn't it?" Klinman asked. "People think of dealers as tooth pullers, but we are just as moved by beauty as the next person. We unite beauty with others who appreciate it."

Cold air blew on Gabriel's neck. He felt feverish, and his back was clammy.

Klinman showed him a succession of significant studies by little-known Renaissance painters, rococo practitioners, and Mannerists. He had an impressive collection. Some came in their original frames. All the while he talked to Gabriel about his profession.

"This drawing I found in a *marché aux puces*. It does happen sometimes. I was looking for something else entirely when I came across this Piranesi. The seller had no idea what it was. He had dated it correctly, but he missed the classic Piranesi hand, the subject matter that is unmistakably his piazzas."

The afternoon wore on. Gabriel put his head close to each of the drawings, so close he could smell the peaty mold and the fragrant pulp. The smell reminded him of the woodshed where he had painted the Connois all those summers ago, the same dense, rotting earth. He looked at the lines, the hesitations, the fluidities, the places the master pressed down harder and where the line was fainter, fatter, thinner, darker, grayer.

Then Klinman pulled out a sheet of blank paper. It was old; not quite as old as the others, but meaty, like paper produced with care.

"Care to venture a guess as to who this is?"

Gabriel felt confused, intoxicated, like he'd been breathing in turpentine for days. He looked up at Klinman.

"Come on. You can guess. You've gotten every artist right all afternoon, even Chassériau imitating Ingres. You can identify this artist. Try."

Gabriel motioned for Klinman to put the page on the light table. It was definitely blank. Klinman was playing some kind of joke on him. The paper had some glue on the edges; it had been pasted into a book, but it had never been drawn on. Faintly, in the top left corner, Gabriel saw the traces of a pencil: £50. He looked up. "Fifty pounds? The paper belonged to someone famous?"

Klinman chuckled, though he did it kindly so that it wasn't exactly at Gabriel's expense. "No, no," he said. "That's how much the paper was worth. Before I discovered it was a Connois sketch."

Realization dawned on Gabriel like extremities thawing after coming inside from the cold. "A Connois? You want me to draw on this?"

"It is already drawn." Klinman stared at him, his face close to Gabriel's. "Do you not see the Spanish marketplace?"

Gabriel nodded, though he didn't exactly see it. Klinman continued, "It looks perhaps like a sketch for *Víspera de Fiesta*, but not exactly like

it. You can see here—" Klinman gestured at a spot on the page that was
no different than any other. "Instead of the gypsy selling the fruit, there
is a small boy. And there are touches of his other paintings; the clouds
from *La Baia*, this rooster."

The paper was beautiful: handmade, pulpy. Gabriel could see
how it would absorb the ink and then reject it, making an inimitable
smooth line. You couldn't find paper like this just anywhere. It was a
work of art in its own right. Drawing on such a piece would be like
opening a five-hundred-euro bottle of wine, or staying at the Ritz—a
once-in-a-lifetime experience. Suddenly, Gabriel felt such a strong
desire to draw on the paper that he didn't recognize himself. He felt his
hands itching to grab the paper off the light table, to run away with it
and make it his. The desire was almost sexual, the raw hunger of it.

Klinman leaned back. "You understand me now?"

Gabriel licked his lips, chapped from the cold air. "I think so, yes."

"You can restore the drawing, then? Return it to its intended state?"

"Yes," Gabriel said. He was thirsty; he wished Klinman had offered
him a drink, though no real art lover would let liquid anywhere near
these treasures.

"Well, then, we will make each other very happy, I suppose." Klinman lifted the paper by its corner. Gabriel's mind was already spinning
ideas. Klinman put the page inside a cardboard portfolio, then put that
in turn into a faux-leather briefcase. "Should be safe like that," he said.
"You take your time."

The *métro* could not come fast enough. Gabriel gripped the briefcase
in both hands, holding it in front of him like a schoolboy. He longed to
take the paper out and examine it, even here in the station, but he knew
that would invite disaster. He felt like he'd won an award, like he'd been
singled out as special. For the past decade nothing—no woman, no
grant, no group show—had produced anything other than anemic con-
tentment. But now he felt like he had arriving in France years ago with
the Connois tucked in his suitcase, his acceptance letter in his shoulder
bag, the same exhilaration, the same sense of optimism, of possibility
that had eluded him for the past few years as his work failed to impress
his professors, colleagues, and gallerists. He'd let them toss him aside
like potato peelings, but no longer. He would show them what he could
do, what they all overlooked.

Elm

On a rainy Friday, a week before she gave birth to Moira, Elm took Ronan to the Morgan Library & Museum. "Is that the house one?" he asked. She wasn't sure if he was talking about the Frick or the Morgan.

They rode in the first car of the 6 train, so that Ronan could pretend he was driving it. "If we're going to Thirty-sixth Street," Elm said, "where do we get off the train?"

"Thirty-third," he said, as though anyone on the planet could answer such a simple question. He was turning an imaginary steering wheel, yelling out the stops when they slowed. The subway car found it cute; people were laughing behind her as she held his belt buckle while he tried to peer out the window. Elm couldn't lift him anymore.

A black man in a doorman's uniform came over and, without asking, picked Ronan up so he could see out. Elm was startled—a sudden rush of adrenaline made her extend her arm as though she might snatch him back—but the man was totally benign, just trying to help, and Ronan squealed with delight.

After Forty-second Street Ronan said, "We get off here," to the man, and he set him down.

Elm took Ronan's hand in the crowded station as they moved slowly up the stairs. The baby was heavy, resting on her pelvis, and picking up her legs was difficult. She had woken up that morning with swollen ankles. The only shoes that fit were her sneakers.

Ronan's hand was slightly sticky while hers was sweaty. They walked down Thirty-fifth Street. Usually she let him walk on his own, but today he held her hand the entire way. He walked slightly behind her, as though afraid she'd fall down.

In the museum, she found him a children's guide to the exhibition "From Bruegel to Rubens: Netherlandish and Flemish Drawings," and gave him the first item to find within the intricate drawings, a dog with a curly tail. He stood far back so he could see them. Elm had come to study the exhibit, a sort of continuing education session, which she had left until the last minute, but instead she watched Ronan taking his task so seriously. She could read the triumph on his face when he found the dog, rushing back to tell her, almost running into a middle-aged Italian couple. "I got it!" he screamed, and when Elm put her finger to her lips he whispered it again.

"Now you have to find a horse," she said, and he resumed his scrutiny. Elm stood in front of Cossiers's portrait of his son Guiliellemus. The nose was too large for the small head, but Cossiers had exactly captured the child as his attention was drawn to something else, that moment between focus and excitement that she loved to watch in her own child. Moira kicked inside her and Elm rubbed the spot.

"Babies, babies, everywhere," Ronan said next to her, reciting a children's book. "There"— he pointed to the drawing—"and there"— pointing to her belly.

"That's right," she said.

"Girls," he observed.

"Actually," Elm said, "that's a picture of a boy with long hair."

One of his pant legs was tucked into his sock, and it was time for a haircut. Knowing it was likely the last time they'd spend real time together before the new baby was born, and knowing that everything would change, she held him to her and clung, perhaps a bit too tightly.

"Ow, Mom, she kicked me," he said, pulling away.

"You two are fighting already?" She had felt it too, a little foot wedged between them.

"I just hope she likes trains," he said, sighing.

"Me too," Elm said.

———

She was staring at what would have been a window if she'd had a decent office; she answered the phone only half-paying attention. "Young lady," the voice on the line said, "I am Indira Schmidt."

The name triggered a memory of her afternoon sobbing in the woman's living room.

"Young lady," the woman said. "I would like you to come over."

"Now?" Elm asked.

"Whenever it is convenient for you. I have something to show you."

"It's difficult right now," Elm said. "Maybe Ian, the young man that was with me before, can come take a look?"

"It is for your eyes only," Indira said. "Is that dramatic enough? I want your opinion. If I had wanted that young man's, I would have called him."

Elm sighed. "How about I come by after work tonight?" She considered. She would have to get across town and then up to Columbia. She was committing herself to at least an hour commute each way, though it wasn't more than a couple of miles.

"That would be fine," Indira said. "I'll expect you then."

As Elm waited for Indira to answer the door, she noticed a dead cockroach. She wondered why cockroaches always died feet up, and how they managed to do so. The welcome mat was frayed on the edges. She rang the bell again, heard it loudly on the other side. Was it possible that Indira wasn't home? That she had forgotten? That she couldn't hear the bell? Dead? Elm considered what to do if Indira didn't answer the door. Ring the next-door neighbor's bell, she decided, and ask them to call the super. Elm was imagining the conversation with the super when the door's chain began to rattle.

Indira seemed more resigned to see her than happy. She drew back the door slowly and grimaced. Elm was immediately infused with anger. She had come all the way across town for this woman. The least Indira could do was acknowledge her effort.

Indira's apartment looked even darker than it had before, if that were possible. The heavy curtains were still shut tight.

"I'm sorry," Indira said, as she limped down the hallway. "Some days are not so good, and this is one of those days." She collapsed into an armchair, out of breath.

Elm's anger melted into pity and guilt. "Can I get you something?" she asked.

Indira waved her off, her hand crooked like a skeleton in the air. Elm sat down in the armchair opposite her. Between them stood a footed table, a dingy lace runner just slightly larger than the tabletop's circumference resting on top. There sat an ashtray, its sole contents a dead fly, curled into itself. "Do you know about my family?" Indira asked.

"The Holocaust, isn't that right?" Elm said. She placed her hands in her lap, sat up straight.

"Yes. I was married. They do not know that." Elm wasn't sure who "they" were. "He was taken almost immediately: Jew, Communist, student."

Elm wasn't sure what to say. She took advantage of the brief pause to say she was sorry.

Again, the skeletal hand. "I am telling you this for a reason. You'll have to trust me. This is not just the ramblings of an old woman. No, it *is* the ramblings of an old woman, but one who is coming to a point. Young lady, can you please bring me that box there by the lamp?"

Elm stood and picked up a small curio box. It was plain, the top held by a latch. Elm wondered what was inside it. A broach of some kind that she wanted to show Elm? A portrait on a napkin by Picasso? Indira took the box and opened it. Elm couldn't see inside it as Indira moved her hands. Then she brought out a small cigarette and a lighter.

She placed the cigarette in her mouth and handed Elm the lighter. It was antique, and it took Elm two or three tries before she got it to light. When the cigarette caught, Elm realized Indira was smoking pot, and she had to fight to stifle a laugh.

"Laugh, laugh," Indira said. "It's funny to see an old lady get high. I will join you in laughing in a minute." She took a drag and held it in. Then she flicked it into the ashtray. Indira held out the joint to Elm. "Do you smoke?"

Elm shook her head. "I have other bad habits."

"I know it's silly, but I turned ninety and thought, what the hell, might as well, and now I keep Columbia's pot dealers in business."

Indira stubbed out the joint in the ashtray on the side table. Elm now saw that what she had thought was a fly was actually a piece of ash.

"I have been criticized," she said, "because my work is not political. It doesn't reference the Holocaust. Why should it? Art is about beauty and balance, nature, and by nature I mean God. If I want to make a statement I use my mouth. We leave politics for the politicians and historians to make up whatever they want."

Elm stared at Indira's profile. Her face was turned toward the painting above the sofa, an abstract that Elm didn't recognize. But Elm could see that her gaze was soft; she was looking elsewhere.

"I lived the politics. I don't have to be reminded." Indira paused, but Elm sensed she wasn't supposed to speak. "I had friends in France, and when the Nazis took Jacob my friends insisted I come. When it looked like France would be occupied, they arranged for a U.S. visa, impossible to get at that point, but my friends were . . . important. I say this because it explains why it happened. I met him when I attended a state dinner at the White House. He talked to me in German, and he understood. And he wasn't like the others. His guilt was quiet, like mine. He emigrated. He didn't have to walk across the Alps or hide in chicken feed or get smuggled out like contraband. He was smart, and he hated himself for it. That was the connection. I've never told anyone, but now he's dead."

Elm wasn't sure who Indira meant. She wondered if the woman wasn't a little off. "Who?" she asked softly.

Indira looked at her as though she had just asked her own name. "Blatzenger, of course."

"Nixon's guy?" Elm knew Blitz-Blatz, as everyone called him, had had many affairs, but she hadn't known that Indira was one of his conquests.

"I attended a state dinner at the White House. That's where I met him. We were together for twenty years, until his death."

"I didn't know," Elm said.

"No one does," Indira said. "We were very careful. Toward the end it was an affair without the physical, but we believed in the same God, passionately."

"Wow," Elm said, realizing as she said it how ugly and inadequate the word sounded. How American.

"There is one more piece that I haven't shown you. One more. I was supposed to meet him in the Netherlands, but there was a crisis. During the cold war there was always a crisis, and his trip was cut short. Still, he bought this for me, a Connois pastel."

"I would love to see it," Elm said.

"It's there." Indira pointed but her fingers were so crooked it was impossible to tell which way.

Elm noticed that behind the dining table, leaning against the dark, stained wallpaper, was a large square, undoubtedly a frame, covered by a dropcloth that had the same stained dark green color as the wallpaper, camouflaging it.

"I had it brought up from the storage unit."

Elm walked to the other side of the room. She felt like a magician's assistant; when she pulled off the cloth, what would be underneath? She was dizzy, not like she was going to be sick or fall over, but as if the room had become untethered and she was floating above it, looking down on the scene from on high. She wondered if the secondhand pot smoke was going to her head.

She put her hands on the dropcloth and it felt damp, or cold. She felt a stab of worry—if it had been stored like this there would be little of it left. Carefully she pulled the cloth off.

It took her eyes a second to adjust. The lighting conditions were far from ideal, dull gray diluted further by the heavy curtains and the dust, but quickly the bright colors resolved into a market scene, the swirling texture became stalls, baskets, a dog. The background was a dull blue, the flat light off the dusty ground as it fell away to the sea. Elm remembered light like this from her backpacking days in Europe, when she still thought she was going to be a painter, how drastically the light shifted once you went inland enough that the ocean fell away from view, that the sparkling off the water was absorbed into the dirt and no longer shimmered, but rather made the vista murky, like looking through unwashed windows.

It was amazing, that Connois could do this with mere pastels. Here was that same blue, almost gray in places, aqua in others. There were the typical market stalls, an oddly shaped dog. This pastel featured an older woman, face lined, one eye slightly lazy or palsied, a strange detail that she registered.

"It's *Mercat*," Indira said.

"Excuse me?" Elm asked.

"*Mercat*, 'market' in Catalan. The title."

Elm remembered vaguely, from art history class, that there were several inventories of group shows of the Hiverains, advertisements and handbills, for paintings, pastels, watercolors, and drawings that had since been lost. Some of these, as described in newspaper accounts of the time, had been masterworks. Elm remembered this because of the sense of loss she had felt when she read about it. Like the library at Alexandria, burned, and all the knowledge it contained destroyed. She had just been dumped by a sophomore-year love (sophomore year, for some reason, had been full of heartbreak), and the idea of these paintings, spoken about so admiringly in the newspaper, and even in a letter written by Édouard Vuillard to his Parisian gallery, felt unbearably tragic.

Could this be one of those lost pieces? Possibly, she supposed. She pulled it away from the wall. The frame was new, but that didn't mean anything. "It's beautiful," she said. "He must have cared about you very much."

Indira made a grunting noise that may have been agreement, derision, or just clearing her throat.

"Do you have the bill of sale? A certificate of authentication?"

Indira shook her head. "It was for me," she said, "not for resale. But sentimentality will only feed you so long, yes? Before you get too old. So sell it with the rest. I have no children; that way I can live to be one hundred and afford to have young male nurses wave palm fronds to cool me."

Elm felt a quick stab of pity. She didn't usually consider herself lucky compared to other people. Indira's loneliness, though, made her suddenly grateful, for Colin, for Moira, and even for getting to live with Ronan for the short time he was here. It felt strange, like the first sting of lust in a newly pubescent teenager, foreign but not bad necessarily.

"Why not display it?" Elm set the frame carefully back up against the wall and sat down across from Indira.

"It hurt, to look at it, especially after he died," she said. "I put it away and didn't think about it until the other drawings . . ."

"Do you know where he got it?" Elm asked. She didn't want to seem pushy, but unless the provenance was solid, it would be hard to get its maximum value.

"He bought it in a gallery, he said."

"Any more surprises lurking in your storage unit?" Elm asked.

Indira smiled. "I don't think so. But, then, an old lady's memory is not what it used to be, so you never know what will turn up, do you?"

Elm wasn't sure if she was teasing or not. She felt like there was a joke being played on her, like the time she was sure that Colin had planned her a surprise party for her fortieth birthday a couple of months before Ronan died, and she spent hours getting ready each morning for the two weeks surrounding her birthday, just in case (it was her pet peeve that everyone knew about surprise parties except the guest of honor, who then appeared in every photo in what was potentially the worst outfit in her closet on a terrible hair day). But when on the big day Colin presented her with a pair of earrings, a babysitter, and a nice dinner not too far from their apartment, she finally relaxed. How had she thought him capable of deceit, even for her own benefit? A full week later when they went for their regular date-night dinner, all her nice clothes were at the dry cleaner's, so she threw on a pair of slacks from the previous decade (pleats, a little snug in the hips), and put her hair up in a ponytail. Sure enough, when she walked into their local pizza joint, forty people yelled *"Surprise"* and the flashes lit.

Was it possible that Indira didn't know she was storing major masterpieces, even though she was an artist herself? It was illogical, considering the woman still lived alone and seemed to forget nothing at all. Elm looked at her; she was wearing foundation. Foundation that exactly matched her skin tone, none of the clownlike myopic mess many older women adopted.

Elm considered: Pastels lurked in a murky space between drawing and painting. As the Hiverains were theoretically Impressionist, Elm wondered if she shouldn't notify Claudio in nineteenth-century painting. But the Impressionists always filled their "quota" and Elm needed the boost. She decided that if it came back authenticated she would enter it in an auction under her supervision. Indira was a respected artist; surely that was provenance enough.

Indira stared back, waiting for Elm to challenge her. Elm opened her mouth to speak, but Indira's foamy eyes wandered past Elm, unable to focus on her face, and Elm saw that she was indeed old and frail, blind as a newborn, incapable of guile.

———

Elm spent too long in the shower, and was late to drop Moira off, which made her late for her doctor's appointment. She calculated—the office was ten blocks downtown. She could walk it in fifteen minutes, or she could grab a cab. But a cab down Second Avenue at this time of day could be a disaster, plus she would either have to catch one going uptown and go around the block or walk crosstown, which would eat up time. She decided to walk, and arrived overheated and frazzled. She stripped and put on the flimsy gown and then sat, increasingly frustrated at the passing time, in the chilly exam room with its view of a brick wall.

Finally the doctor came in. Elm had changed ob-gyns in the wake of Ronan's death; she just couldn't imagine explaining to her former doctor what had happened. When Dr. Hong took her history, she asked how many times Elm had been pregnant. "I have one child," she answered.

Dr. Hong didn't speak much during the exam, for which Elm was grateful. She hated having to make small talk with doctors. The nurse was silent as well. Soft music drifted in from a different office. Below, a truck backed up shrilly.

"Well," Dr. Hong said, "everything looks fine."

Elm had waited until the last moment. She and Colin hadn't discussed it any further, but she said, "I was thinking about having another child." Elm wasn't sure if it was her imagination or if she saw the nurse raise her eyebrows. Dr. Hong looked at her chart again. "Well," she said, slowly. "I won't lie. You're almost forty-three. You're still getting regular periods?"

"Yes," Elm said. They weren't regular, necessarily, but they were not infrequent.

"There are two things we can do," Dr. Hong said, resting her clipboard on her hip. "First, we test your FSH level, your follicle-stimulating hormone."

Elm felt her annoyance rise. She wasn't stupid, and yet doctors always explained biology as though she were completely uneducated, as though they were reading from a book about talking to patients. "Right, on day three," she said.

"Yes. So you can come back in. Additionally, I'd perform a transvaginal ultrasound, that's an ultrasound of your uterus."

Elm's patience ended. "Yes, I know what my vagina is."

The doctor continued as though Elm hadn't interrupted. "We do an antral follicle count where we, well, we count the follicles. That's a pretty good indication of fertility. Would you like me to do that now?"

"Yes, please," Elm said. She lay back down, her heart racing. Please, she begged silently, please let there be follicles. She tensed as the ultrasound wand entered her, and Dr. Hong pressed lightly on her abdomen. "Okay, three right," she said to the nurse, placing her hand on the other side. "And four left."

She removed the wand and took off the protective condom, placing it and her gloves in the bin. She immediately washed her hands. Elm sat up, nails thrumming on her thighs.

"I'll be honest, Ms. Howells," Dr. Hong said. Elm looked at her, her eyebrows so thin, barely visible. "I counted only three follicles on the right and four on the left. That's consistent with poor ovarian reserve."

Elm felt the nervousness evacuate her body. It was replaced by nausea, the precursor to a wave of grief. "So I'll have to take a fertility drug."

"Well," Dr. Hong said. Elm thought that if the woman said "well" one more time she might throttle her with her stethoscope. "The fertility drugs stimulate the follicles. If there's nothing to stimulate, then it won't really work. You're not a good candidate."

"What about IVF?" Elm demanded.

"In vitro has the same problem," Dr. Hong said. "I won't tell you absolutely not, because you hear these stories about spontaneous pregnancies, but it appears very unlikely."

"How unlikely?"

"With these follicle levels there's a less than one percent chance of spontaneous conception," Dr. Hong said. "I'm very sorry."

Elm fought the lump that was condensing in her throat. "I see."

"I'll send you to a specialist, to do more tests," Dr. Hong said. She made a note on Elm's chart. "I'm sure you'll want to exhaust all the options. And we do have the best-ranked fertility clinic here in the hospital."

Elm had stopped listening. She made a mental inventory of her clothing—pants, trouser socks, blouse, belt. Don't forget your sunglasses, she reminded herself. Don't forget to fix that bra strap that was bothering you this morning. She didn't dare look at herself in the mirror above the sink, sure that her reflection would make her cry.

She charged her copay and left the office, walking to the East River. The air had switched directions; coming off the water it was cool, almost sharp, and she let it blow her hair back as she walked. She imagined that it blew right through her, getting rid of all the liquid that troubled her: her blood, which kept her heart pumping and aching, and the tears, which were threatening now.

She held back until she got to her office, then closed the door and collapsed on the small couch sobbing like she hadn't since Ronan's funeral. It felt, in that moment, equally as painful, as wrenching, as the day she said good-bye to her son. This was it, then, no more children. No sibling for Moira, no feeling of fluttering kicks in her belly, no first steps, first words, first haircuts. From now on, only lasts.

The phone rang, a conference call that required none of Elm's attention. She hit mute and put the phone on speaker while she worked on the breathing exercises her doctor had shown her to help her calm down. Soon her breath and chest regained their rhythm, and only the occasional sharp intake betrayed the magnitude of her disappointment. Next to her phone was the notepad with the web address of the cloning center. All week the website had been calling to her, and Elm had tried to ignore it, but as she half-listened to the phone, she traced the URL bold, then serifed. She drew a box around it, stars, vines snaking up the side of the page. And then she could deny herself no longer. She told herself it was out of curiosity that she typed in the address. It would be a laugh, as Colin would say. It took awhile to load, and Elm puffed her cheeks out with impatience. She threw a quick look toward the door of her office. Not that there was anything for people to be suspicious about. She wasn't doing anything wrong. She was looking at a website, not porn, and there were plenty of people who looked at porn on the job. This was a scientific website, sort of.

Pictures formed in horizontal stripes. The top was monochromatic: sky, wall, and then the beginnings of heads, the round edges of cells, of letters. The background was a light robin's egg blue, patterned with faint fleur-de-lis. Finally, the page paused, then refreshed itself, forming fully.

The Institut Indépendant de la Recherche sur la Réplication Génétique had spent a lot of money on its website. There was a picture of a sheep—Dolly, presumably—and the "camera" swooped into her mouth and down into her DNA spiral, which replicated itself in a new frame, twirling independently. Clicking on either strand brought you to the home page, a slideshow of happy smiling people. Elm clicked on the Union Jack, which took her to a menu.

"About us: We are a group of physicians and researchers dedicated to exploring the exciting new field of genetic replication since 1997. With the highest regard for ethical considerations, we are discovering the ways in which science can help us live fuller, better lives. Have you been devastated by the loss of a loved one? DNA replication may be the answer to your problems. All consultations are kept strictly confidential and thus we are forbidden to present testimonials. However, our clientele include diplomats, moguls, CEOs, royalty, and other important world figures."

"Devastated by the loss of a loved one." The phrase struck Elm as particularly apt. She was devastated; utterly laid to waste. She had to admit she was impressed. The introduction, stilted though it was, took exactly the right tone. It was sympathetic without being sentimental, informative without providing detail, and reassuringly professional.

She turned to the other pages, which were not translated, but she could read French decently, and with the help of the diagrams she could tell they were explanations of the various types of cloning or the mechanisms used. One involved, apparently, removing the anchovy from a cocktail olive. Others involved volleys of arrows emanating from an eyeball, a snake fighting with a beach ball, and two M&M's fused together. Another page was FAQs, this one translated into English. *Do you replicate from nonanimal subjects?* "The Charter of Fundamental Rights of the European Union prohibits the genetic replication of humans. For an explanation of the implications of this regulatory policy, please contact us." Elm paused. What did that mean? It sounded like it might be possible to clone human beings, like the legalese meant the opposite of what it said. At the bottom was a Paris phone number and a disclaimer: "We regret that we are unable to respond to electronic mail inquiries."

Elm was disappointed. This site was not the comedy she had predicted. It didn't have cartoon dancing sheep or pseudoscientific mumbo jumbo. Instead, it looked like a real medical establishment. And Elm knew that if she even remotely believed that it was possible to bring Ronan back, or to re-create him, the thought would obsess her. The conference call demanded her attention. She unmuted it, thanked the participants, and ended the call.

She stared at the same particle (of food? of lint?) that had been there for months, too close to the corner to be sucked up by the vacuum. Colin would not feel the same way. Though agnostic, he called himself a spiritualist. "Twelve years of having the nuns beat it into you, some of it has to stick." What happened to Ronan, according to Colin, was no one's fault, not theirs, not God's. It was just a cruel twist of destiny. It was fate.

"That makes you a fatalist," she had said. Colin had shrugged.

He would not want to explore bizarre and probably illegal ways to reincarnate their son. It was ridiculous. Elm wouldn't be able to tell anyone, if it happened. She imagined herself as she was nine years ago, pregnant with Ronan, swollen, her belly drawing her hands to it like a magnet. She would have to say that it was a new baby.

This was insane. This was magical thinking, something her grief counselor had told her to watch out for. "It's not that it's harmful," her therapist had said. "But it's unproductive, backward. It doesn't help you move forward."

Elm had experienced this minor psychosis in small ways. There were signs that Ronan was attempting to communicate with her from the beyond: sticks arranged in an R shape on the playground, subliminal messages encoded in television commercials and billboards, certain precocious statements by Moira. Elm was even temporarily convinced that Ronan's ghost was visiting his sister at night. All those, she saw now, were signs of the early stages of grief. She hadn't experienced them in a while.

When the experts referred to grief as a cycle, they neglected to mention its vortex effect. It was more like a series of concentric circles, and she was merely orbiting around again, returning to the early stages, like aftershocks that do more damage than the earthquakes themselves.

The institute's website felt like an indulgence, like napping at the office, or eating a brownie while dieting. She knew she shouldn't, but the gratification was so intense that she couldn't stop herself. She clicked through the various pages again, stopping at the illustrations of the technical process. Elm had a solid grounding in chemistry, necessary for an art history Ph.D. with a concentration in restoration. But she rarely used her scientific training for anything other than helping Moira build a volcano for the science fair. The cloning process was beyond her powers of comprehension.

Colin would probably understand it. He'd picked up a fair amount of biology at his job; holding his own at medical conferences and extolling the benefits of Moore's drugs required a working knowledge of biochemical processes. But Elm knew she couldn't ask him. He knew her too well, knew the way her mind spun, and he would divine that she was interested in cloning for reasons that exceeded mere curiosity.

Elm pictured Ronan's pink face when they brought him home from the hospital. He had been overdue, and his skin was wrinkly and peeling like a tiny bird. What would they name a clone? They couldn't call it Ronan.

A tease, Elm thought. A crock of shit. She felt stupid for even looking at the site. Were they going to bring Ronan back from the dead?

With their magic potions, their "patented scientific process"? Who fell for this? The same people who actually thought they were helping a Nigerian prince or the Russian czarina in response to an e-mail request.

Was it possible that this site intrigued her because she was secretly interested in cloning Ronan? It was ridiculous, science fiction. She went back to the FAQ section; she imagined Colin asking her: Wouldn't it result in defects? Wasn't it dangerous for the mother? Was it ethical? Was it legal?

Most of the ethical arguments seemed to hinge on the slippery-slope philosophy. First *you* start cloning, and then what? This didn't apply to her, Elm thought. She didn't want to make a clone assembly line; she wanted her child. She wasn't fiddling with nature; she was replacing what nature had stolen from her. There were no larger implications of her actions. She just wanted her little boy back, with all his imperfections intact—his stubbornness, his slightly awkward run, his teeth that would inevitably need braces.

And couldn't she do a better job raising him this time, having raised two children already? She knew that he was allergic to cherries, that he didn't like chocolate ice cream, that he would be bad at soccer but excellent at baseball. He had had trouble spelling; she could start him earlier. Elm felt a small hope begin to flutter, a minor lessening of the contraction that was her grief. If she could just hold him again, for a minute, it was worth any amount of money. Surely Colin had to see that.

Before she knew what she was doing, she had the phone in her hands and was dialing an international number. For kicks, she told herself. Just to see. The phone rang in that non-American click that always screamed to her: "Expensive call! Don't talk too long!" Then she realized that it was evening in Paris—likely no one would answer the phone and she could put this nonsense behind her. She was surprised when a voice greeted her in rapid French.

"*Bonjour,*" said Elm in her college French. "*Je voudrais de l'information, s'il vous plaît.*"

"You are American?" The voice was clogged with accent. "I have someone to speak to you."

Elm was transferred. The phone played generic hold music until a man answered. Hang up, Elm told herself. This was ridiculous. Just hang up.

"You are the American woman who would like information?" He was French too, but his English was smooth, fluent.

"Yes, I was wondering—"

"Excuse me, but on the phone we speak in generalities, yes?"

"Of course," Elm said. "I'm so sorry." She felt as though she were investigating a crime, pretending to be someone she was not in order to glean information.

"You are a member of a government agency?" he asked.

"No," she said.

"You must by law identify yourself if you are a member of a government agency. It is both EU and American law." Was that true? Elm wondered. Or was that just something people got from the movies?

"I'm just a citizen," she said.

"And you are calling from your home?" he recited.

"My place of business." Elm began to worry. She hadn't realized what she was doing. She was just calling out of harmless curiosity. She didn't want to start an international incident. "Look," she said. "Maybe I should hang up."

"I suggest the same thing," said the man. "You give me a number at your home and I will call you this evening so we can both talk freely."

Elm said, "I don't think . . . I mean . . ."

"Madame," the man said. "If you will permit. You obviously called here for a reason. You were curious. You might as well satisfy that curiosity. There is reason for subterfuge, but only because there are those who would impede the progress of science. You are seeking information. There is still nothing wrong with that, even with your Patriot Act. Am I not correct?"

"Yes," Elm said. She began to breathe faster. She felt a horrible sinking in the pit of her stomach; she realized she had made a terrible mistake that was going to reverberate for longer than she had anticipated. What had she started in motion?

She gave him her name and phone number and replaced the headset in the cradle.

She hit her home key and was immediately returned to a cached version of Tinsley's site: brocade tapestry background, the trademark photo of her great-grandfather in Egypt next to an enormous amphora, links to departments. She stared at the page and permitted herself a small fantasy in which she walked out of a new clinic somewhere on the outskirts of Paris holding Ronan's hand. But no, she corrected her reverie. He would be a baby. She revised the vision, holding him in her arms, remembering his wrinkled, red hands, the skinny legs that looked too big for his body, the slightly smushed head. Then she shook her head as if to get rid of the image, just as someone walked by her office door. Elm rolled her head on her neck, pretending to be stretching a kink, and not rebooting her mind.

Elm was supposed to be writing a press release, but she was unable to concentrate. Her heart beat fast, anticipating bad news. It was barely noon. Too early for lunch.

Sometimes looking at prints brought fresh language to her cortex, loosened her tongue enough to find new-sounding synonyms for *important, major, chef d'ouevre,* etc., so she headed down to the print room. She got off the elevator on the mezzanine. She would take the grand staircase, see what was happening on the floor. Emerging from the elevator, she had to appreciate, though it was not to her taste, the new entry, designed by a celebrity architect. The mezzanine floated above the main floor, turning what once had been a cavernous hull, like a high school gym, into a display place for hanging, appreciating, and admiring art.

The mezzanine walkway (or the mezzie, as facilities called it) extended from one side of the building to the other, but was only ten feet wide, so that views of the downstairs were not only unavoidable but the focus. Sculptures, or *objets,* were sometimes displayed here, but often the space was left intentionally bare. Today facilities had set out small pedestals at regular intervals, but they remained as yet artless, so that the walkway looked like a conceptual graveyard, or the control deck for a spaceship.

The main space was four stories tall, and the front wall of windows extended all the way to the top, their steel supports nearly invisible. The usual East Side traffic of nannies and children paraded by, and the normal array of large delivery trucks was blocking traffic. She stood with her hands on the railing and looked down over the first floor. It could have been the lobby of any enterprise: dark marble floors, receptionists, post-9/11 security measures (less ridiculous than in most businesses when the building's museum-quality contents on any given day could exceed the gross national product of medium-sized nations). But at Tinsley's, the air, filtered through the purification system and the tempered glass, was different. It was entitled, cultured. No one walked with the slumped posture of those beaten down by the cruelty of the corporate world, its ladders and pernicious chutes, its denizens who toiled merely for the paycheck to feed the family, to pay the credit card debt, to get the health insurance. Instead, in the art world, there was a tacit rule that everyone was doing exactly what he had always hoped he'd be doing. The fiction stated that proximity to the world's most beautiful objects was a privilege, and there was a slight pity for everyone else who didn't get to do this fantastic job.

In this environment, which Elm's great-grandfather had purposefully cultivated via mandatory monthly all-company meetings-cum-lectures, and a refashioned annual picnic that was more of a gala, including the receptionists, facilities, and the janitorial staff, complaints were not only prohibited but smacked of ingratitude and, frankly, the same uncomprehending troglodism that marked the noncultured. Part of the elitism of Tinsley's was the culture of secrecy, the mystery of fine art, of its aesthetic possibilities and its inherent value. Yes, one could point to artistic mastery—beautiful composition, or a startling use of color, an elegant line—or the provenance of an *objet* (Queen Elizabeth's ivory fan, Edgar Allan Poe's cloisonné snuff case)—but the best pieces had their own allure, unspoken and magnetic. Part of the value, though, required that no one mention the emperor's new clothes, for fear of driving down prices or the perceived importance of a work. Therefore, it was wise to play up the aura of mystery surrounding fine art, and this secrecy spread to all facets of the industry. The auction house hid minimum reserves, obfuscated provenances, kept buyers anonymous. Dealers buying for clients sometimes phoned in their bids from the auction room itself, adding an unnecessary layer of intrigue. Rarely were the numbers published, and no one would have dreamed of asking. The less anyone knew the better. And so Elm often felt like she was working inside a burlap sack—light filtered in, but not enough to see by.

She made her way across the mezzie and down the utility stairs to the basement. The corridor was long and painted a glowing white so that the hallway looked like a cinematic version of an endless existential hell. The corridors were monitored by video cameras that downloaded the activity to remote servers in India. Doors along this expanse of hallway were marked only with numbers, either for security's sake or to propitiate the secrecy gods. Elm punched in her code to the third one, marked 4357, and the green light above the combination pad clicked, granting her access.

Inside, the dim light was such a contrast to the overlit hallway that Elm stopped automatically at the entrance, waiting for her eyes to adjust. Finally, the shelf materialized, traversing three walls, a complicated three-dimensional lightbox. Standing at the one in the far corner was a thin figure poring over a drawing with a loupe, a stack of others at her elbow.

Elm identified the woman before she even looked up. "Hello, El-MEE-ra," Colette purred. Elm had to admit that her name sounded better with a French emphasis than with the American "El-MY-ruh."

"I didn't know you were back in town." Elm tried to sound chipper. Colette smiled in response.

"Whatcha doing?" Elm asked.

"Familiarizing myself with our inventory. What are *you* doing?" Colette asked. Elm wasn't sure if her tone could be described as hostile or French.

"Making sure everything's how I left it." She was unable to disguise the antipathy in her voice. Colette continued to smile. The woman enjoyed sport; intrigue, not art, Elm thought. This was what the art world was coming to. Dealers who acted like businessmen and businessmen who acted like dealers. No wonder Elm's numbers weren't what Greer had hoped.

"Where's . . ." Elm snapped her fingers, grasping at the intern's name.

"Franz?" Colette said. "I sent him out for coffee." She turned back to the drawing she was examining.

"He's not bringing it in here," Elm said. It was unthinkable to let liquid anywhere near these drawings.

Colette didn't even look up and yet that feline smile was unmistakable, mirthless. "I will meet him in fifteen minutes."

"Ahhh," Elm said. She put on a pair of white gloves from the basket close to the door. They were scratchy on the inside; she disliked wearing them. She couldn't feel the drawing, which was, for her, as much a part of identifying it as looking at it. She stepped over and took the top three drawings from Colette's pile. The first was by Delacroix, undated, unsigned. It was an apparent study, for *Christ on the Lake of Gennesaret,* of an oarsman, muscled back to the viewer. It was beautiful, and Elm's heart had sped when she first saw it in the ornate public conference room. The seller was getting divorced (a common, if sad, method by which many drawings and paintings came to sale), and needed to sell his collection as part of the settlement. He was a small man, emotional when handing over the drawings, which he held by their edges like photographs in danger of being smudged. His few strands of hair were combed in concentric circles on the top of his head, and when he looked down to say good-bye to his Delacroix, Elm could see the delicate flakes of dandruff woven like cotton in a bird's nest.

This was the kind of sale Elm loved. Not that she was glad to profit off someone's disintegrating marriage, but she rejoiced to see others who felt the same connection to the art that she did. This man was selling more than a ripe investment, more than a decoration. He was selling something that was as close to his heart as his wife must once have been. He had lived with the art, loved it, saw in it the accomplishments of mankind, the sensuousness of nature, the artist's raw talent and unique vision. That's what would ultimately separate Elm and this man from the Colettes and the Greers of the world: art could still bring Elm to tears.

It was truly beautiful. She would be sad to see it at auction, but, then, she knew she would secretly root for it as its lot came up. She often grew attached, rejoicing when a piece fetched a higher price than expected, flushed with pride as though she had drawn it herself.

Elm put it aside, assigning adjectives to it for the catalog entry: *paramount, influential, emblematic.* She watched Colette, who had returned to her loupe, minutely peruse a drawing. This was not the way to examine something, Elm thought. You hold it away from you, judge it as a whole, not scrutinize each individual stroke of the quill or pencil. Unless you were trying to authenticate it. Then you might look for telling details.

The two women stared in silence. Colette straightened and said, "You have not contacted Monsieur Klinman."

"I'm so sorry, I've been busy," Elm said.

"Well," Colette said, reminding Elm of her high school French teacher, whose disappointment when Elm didn't complete her homework hurt worse than the F she'd receive for the assignment. "Unfortunately, the drawings I mentioned have been dispersed, but he has acquired other artists: Canaletto, Piranesi, some contemporaries of the Impressionists. I will forward you the PDFs. I think you will like what you see."

Elm said, "I'll take a look."

"Well," Colette said, after a pause. "I'll say good-bye."

Before Colette left the room, she rolled her skirt up and put on another coat of lipstick, smoothing her hair in its bun. The sight of her primping disgusted Elm. Her willingness to use sex to further her ambition, the strength of that ambition, reminded Elm that she had entered a different age. An age where having children was no longer possible. The light, when Colette closed the door, was an odd brown shade, nearly ochre, thrown up either from the play of light against the dark carpet or, more likely, from the palimpsestic echoes of the brown wash lingering in Elm's visual cortex.

———

By the time Elm got back to her office, Colette had sent the PDFs from her contact, Augustus Klinman. Did she forgo her coffee with Franz? Elm wondered. She opened up the file.

The images were actually quite interesting. The first seemed to be a Piranesi. The subject matter was typical Piranesi—blueprintlike attention to architectural detail. An arch, in ruins, with Romans strolling nearby. And the line was spontaneous in the manner of a study for an etching. And certainly, the wash and ink, the exaggerated shading, and the lack of interest in nature all suggested that the famous artist had created this with his own hand.

There was also a gouache by that artist who was a contemporary of Connois, that Greek guy, what was his name? Elm could never remember. It was of a little girl, a bow in her hair, petting a white dog whose tongue lolled out of its mouth, giving it a rather dumb appearance.

The third was by Connois, a market scene, a sketch that looked to be a finished drawing in its own right, which was curious, because Elm wasn't aware that Connois ever finished his drawings. Two Connoises so close together—Indira's pastel and now this sketch? How strange, their popping up like toadstools. But, then, coincidence was commonplace, and this was rather lovely.

Klinman's web page said he dealt primarily in eighteenth- and nineteenth-century pieces, especially French, Italian, and Flemish artists, maintaining offices in London and Paris. Working in conjunction with museums, restorers, and master framers, he presented the art in its best possible condition.

Other Google entries quoted Klinman in articles about stolen Nazi art, specifically the faking of provenances. "Ruthless dealers and incompetent experts abound, sadly, in the art world. The temptation to verify that which is not verifiable is strong." "Art stolen by the Nazis should be returned to the family of the original owner whenever possible. When not possible, the families should be compensated. Descendants of murderers should not be allowed to profit from their grandparents' marauding."

Another entry was a press release announcing the highest price ever paid for a Raphael sketch, $48 million, sold via Sotheby's in London by a family who wanted to be known only through their representative: Augustus Klinman. The purchaser's name was also kept anonymous.

The uneasy feeling that started the second she dialed the clinic hadn't subsided all day. It remained through the rest of the afternoon, following her on the bus up First Avenue, to the grocery store, and home, where she was distracted.

Colin was involved in his own drama. "It won't be inked for thirty days, the deal," he said tersely in response to her automatic *How was your day?* "I don't want to discuss it before then."

"Fine," Elm said. She slammed the door to the microwave. She was planning on telling him about her visit with Dr. Hong, but his hostility made her want to keep it to herself.

Moira must have sensed the tension. She refused to eat the spaghetti Elm made for her, and then, after Elm microwaved some chicken fingers, refused to eat the middles, or even touch the single stalk of broccoli alongside them.

"Just eat it," Colin said with uncharacteristic harshness. Moira sat up as straight as if he'd thrown a glass of water in her face. She began to cry. Elm frowned at him. She picked Moira up and carried her to the bathroom for her bath. Moira began to cry louder, in a whining, overtired way that grated on Elm.

"Please, Moira," she said. Then: "Don't you dare kick me. You love baths." She tried to strip her daughter, who had turned her body to stone in protest. Finally, she wrestled Moira into the bath still wearing underwear and a T-shirt.

"Mom! You forgot to take this off. Now it's all wet," she said with an accusatory and slightly teenage inflection. She removed her shirt in disgust.

Elm sat on the closed toilet while Moira splashed and sang. She both hoped the man from the institute would call her back and dreaded that call. She rubbed her eyes, worried again that she was going crazy. Crazy like those people with the dog. Would a sane person believe her son could be cloned? The dog's name popped into her mind, Dishoo, and got stuck like song lyrics. She repeated it as a mantra: Dishoo, Dishoo, Dishoo, Dishoo.

"Mom?" Moira interrupted her reverie. "Can we get a cat?"

"No," Elm said.

"You didn't even say maybe, or we'll see."

"That's because there's not the slightest glimmer of hope that we'll get a cat."

"But why?" Moira whined. Elm wondered if Moira was entering one of those phases through which Elm wished she could fast-forward.

For a while, in a bathroom humor phase, Moira had finished every sentence with "in your butt." As in, "Where's your jacket?" "In your butt." "How was school?" "In your butt." Elm wasn't sure if she should say something or just let Moira get over it. In the end she decided to ignore it and it wore off within the week.

It was terrible, she knew, to compare children, but Ronan hadn't been this difficult. She recognized that she was looking back at the experience, and the past was always gossamer and preferable to an uncomfortable present. Maybe she'd been more involved then. She remembered looking at him in the bath and thinking, I created this. His smooth small arms pushed a rubber duck around, creating small swirls of water. "Duh-key," he said slowly, his first word after "Mama" and "Dada." He grabbed her hand, wanting her to touch it too; he always wanted her to share his experiences, as if to maintain the closeness they had when he was part of her body. "Duh-key."

She'd been finishing up her dissertation then; really it was all finished except for the formatting, and she was home with him constantly. Everything he did was miraculous and amazing to her, because he was her first. Then Moira came and did the exact same miraculous things at nearly the same rate (or faster) and Elm simply couldn't muster the same enthusiasm.

Her guilt was so repressed—she couldn't bear even to think about her children in this manner. But the truth was that Ronan had been *her* child, while Moira was Colin's. Colin had had little to do with Ronan's first months—the processes by which he might have bonded with the infant were opaque to him, plus it was a particularly busy time at work. Colin would stare at Ronan, the baby's legs windmilling while Colin changed his diaper, as if he were looking at an exhibit in a museum. Maybe Elm had made it difficult for him to spend time with Ronan; she was so protective. By the time Moira was born, the bond between Ronan and Elm had been cemented, and babies were a known quantity: Colin wouldn't inadvertently drop her, or do some irrevocable damage with his neophyte parenting skills. Since then Moira had been Daddy's little girl.

While Elm never speculated or wished that Ronan had survived and Moira had been taken from them, she did admit to her psychiatrist that she felt it wasn't fair that "her child" had been taken, while "Colin's child" remained. She refused to elaborate on this line of thought, though Dr. Schultz had prodded and pried. Some things said in the throes of grief should not be reuttered.

Now she asked Moira, "Do you miss your brother?"

"Yes," Moira answered automatically. She rang out a washcloth over her head and blinked to get the water out of her eyes.

"Do you remember him?" she asked, leaning forward.

"Yup," Moira said. "His name was Ronan and he died in the su-mommy."

"Tsunami. But do you remember anything else?"

Moira thought. "Umm, no?" she asked, not sure if this was the right answer to Elm's question.

Elm sat back. She wouldn't be able to get a straight answer out of a kindergartner. Today Moira might not remember, tomorrow she would, twenty years from now, who knew?

"Time to get out, Mo," Elm said, smiling to prevent tears.

"Noooo," Moira wailed.

"Yes, come on, the water's cold." She reached in to pick Moira up under her arms. Moira began to squirm.

"Careful, Mo, you're slippery."

Moira splashed Elm with her feet.

"Goddammit, Moira. Can you just please for once behave?" And Elm, surprising herself, began to cry.

Moira was immediately contrite. "I'm sorry, Mommy. I didn't mean it." *I didn't mean it* was child talk for *Now that I'm in trouble I wish I hadn't done it.* But still Elm cried, out of frustration, exhaustion, residual grief.

Moira was not as upset as another child might have been; she'd seen her parents cry innumerable times—so much there couldn't possibly be any liquid left in their eyes, their bodies. They should be sacks of skin like dehydrated cartoon characters.

Elm sat back down on the toilet, and Moira wrapped her towel around herself, then hugged her mother around the middle. "It's okay, Mom," she said. "I remember Ronan. I promise."

———

The phone rang twice before Elm picked it up, though it was next to her. She had told Colin she was expecting a call from overseas. "Is anyone awake in Europe?" he asked.

"Asia," she said.

She walked into the bedroom with the phone to her ear, waiting to say hello until she was out of Colin's earshot.

"Ms. Howells?" said the voice. Had she given her name? Elm wondered.

"Yes," she said.

"I am glad we can speak further. You are interested in seeing Ronan again, am I right?"

His name, so unexpected, took her breath away. She gasped. "How did—?"

"The Internet, Madame, is a powerful tool. There is much information about you; for instance, that you took *Inside the Slidy Diner* out of the public library on Ninety-sixth Street last weekend."

"That's a little disturbing."

"That's the world we live in," the voice said. He seemed willing to make small talk, speaking rhythmically, hypnotically. "We live in technology. There is no reason to fight the inevitable; it is dissecting clouds."

"This seems completely unbelievable," Elm said.

"Yes, there is a lot of misinformation about what we do. When I first began here, it seemed like a science fiction story. But I assure you, it is very real."

"I thought we were still many years away from . . . doing what you do."

"Governments have an interest in disseminating false information," he said.

"I'm really not a conspiracy theorist," Elm said. "What possible reason would the government have for suppressing science?"

"You think the government doesn't keep science from the public? What about the dangers of Vioxx? What about the syphilis experiment with the Negroes of the South? What about how cigarettes aren't addictive? Even now, they are claiming that the lung problems the people of 9/11 are having are not the result of breathing that air. Ha!" he scoffed. "You should feel surprised your government ever tells you the truth."

Elm sat silent, chastised. This was stupid, she thought. This was a joke that had gone on too long. This was crazy. This was abnormal.

"The next step, Madame, is for you to come to Paris to tour our facility and to submit to medical examination, if you want to be the host."

It took Elm a moment to parse this information. If she wanted to carry the baby. "I'm told, my doctor said, I don't really have any eggs. Follicles. Active ones." Elm could barely get the words out.

"It's very easy to get donated ova." Elm was astonished. He didn't seem remotely worried about her infertility. A donor egg, of course. If they were removing the nucleus, all the genetic information, what did it matter where the raw materials came from?

"Madame?" the man asked into the silent phone.

"I don't know if I can come to Paris, fly three thousand miles to meet—"

"With all due respect, Madame, the process is not inexpensive. Consider the trip a holiday, a deposit on the ultimate benefit."

Elm supposed he was right. The process must be tens of thousands of dollars. In comparison, a long weekend to the City of Light was pocket change.

"Perhaps it could be coupled with a business venture?" he asked. "I see you travel to the Continent not infrequently."

Elm nodded, alone in the bedroom, until she realized that he was obviously looking at a record of her transatlantic travels, which made her shiver.

"Shall we say in two weeks?" he asked. "We can arrange flights and a nearby hotel, transportation from the airport to our facility."

"I'd feel better if I could be on my own," Elm said, imagining an international kidnapping scandal.

"As you wish," the man said graciously. "You may e-mail to let us know when you'll be arriving, and we will send a car for you. Our location is within an hour of Paris."

Elm hung up the phone, and tried to stop imagining herself getting off the plane, being whisked away in a limousine to some estate with voluptuous nurses and sterile Swiss hospital beds. Maybe she should look at it the way she used to encourage herself to look at dating: as a social experiment, with an anthropologist's permanent interest and detachment. Then she could laugh about it, about going to a secret medical facility in France. She wandered back out into the living room. Colin was sipping from a scotch.

"I have to go to Paris," she said. "For work," she added, realizing the detail was more suspicious than its omission. Tell him, her conscience urged. Tell him you went to the doctor and you have poor follicle reserve and then there was this website . . . Don't, it said. Check it out first. If it's real, then you can discuss it. She made a bargain with herself. If he remembered her doctor's appointment, if he asked her about it, about her day, about anything at all, she would tell him. She waited anxiously for him to respond.

"Hmmm," he said. The light from the television fell unflatteringly across the stubble on his chin, giving him a pallor that puttied his soft features.

Gabriel

Gabriel's roommates, curiously, were all out. He lived with a gaggle of Scandinavian students who were completing degrees, or avoiding the completion of degrees, in various subjects. Two in particular were studious, often sitting at their communal desk until early in the morning. The walls were so thin in the flat that he could hear the computer keys clacking at night.

The apartment had once been a garment factory, and the landlord got a tax incentive for renting to students. It was one room cordoned off by makeshift walls. The kitchen/living room was furnished with found furniture; when sat on the sofa gave a sigh and belched dust.

Gabriel took out the paper to examine it. It was dotted with wormholes, as all old paper was. The holes would soak up his ink and betray the fact that though the paper was of the proper age, the drawing was not.

Gabriel silently thanked his first-year drawing instructor at the École. He had insisted the students prepare their rag paper à la the old masters. Gabriel had learned to make ink, to size paper evenly.

He mixed gelatin and hot water. While it dissolved, he emptied the boxes that were stacked on his floor. Here they were: his notes from those sessions with the professor. He continued to paw through the boxes. Gabriel had spent hours in the rain visiting various Chinese herbalists until he found the jet-black ink he was looking for. He overwatered it, so he mixed it with gum arabic. It had been labor-intensive; Gabriel had cursed him. At four a.m., stoned nearly unconscious, he was shaking a mustard jar of turpentine and walnut oil. Now, leaking into the box below it, but still useable, the old mustard jar was full of ink. He was in business.

He took a wide brush and spent more time cleaning it than usual, meticulously paring each bristle, trimming the ones that seemed to point in errant directions. He was ready.

The sizing would determine how authentic the drawing looked. He knew he could draw like his ancestor, but if the sizing was uneven, darker in patches or streaked, then the forgery would be obvious. He took a deep breath, steadied his hand, and bathed the paper in glue. The professor had explained that artists should relax their wrists when sizing paper.

"It is like you are on a swing," the professor had said. "No, it is like you are pushing your lover on a swing, back and forth, with care and force equally." Gabriel found that the French compared most things to sex. Spanish analogies mostly had to do with food or body functions.

The sizing complete, Gabriel took the page into his room; it would take a few hours to dry. He went back into the kitchen and cleaned the brush again. Then he dumped the rest of the sizing out into the garbage and scrubbed the bowl. He was probably being too clean. His room-mates would be suspicious of the washed dishes and the wiped counters. So he made himself a coffee, making sure to let some grounds linger.

Sitting in his kitchen, listening to the sound of the coffee bubbling and waiting for the paper to dry, he remembered being a first-year student. His first few months in Paris were simultaneously exciting and disorienting, tinged with worry for his mother—justified, as it turned out, as she was diagnosed just a few months later. She didn't tell him, didn't want to worry him, until the very end, and he went to see her, taking the bus twenty-six straight hours until he was at her bedside holding her hand.

They'd brought her home from the hospital, and the neighbors, who were as much an extended family as any he knew, had arranged for a hospital bed to be placed in the kitchen, so she wouldn't have to climb stairs. As it was, she never left the bed again. He sat with her and petted her hand, smoothed the hair off her dry, shrunken forehead. She had always been plump, but in her last days she was as thin as a paintbrush, brittle and desiccated. He gave her sips of water through a straw, fed her ice.

She stopped eating two days after he got there and lived for three more. He sold all of her possessions and earned just enough to bury her and pay his rent for a year. The copied Connois he gave to neighbors before he returned to France. He wasn't sorry to have left it there; it would have been a constant reminder of his duplicity.

Would the *pueblo* feel different to him now? Look different? Smell different? It felt strange to think of a Spain without his mother in it. The world would never again taste her *croquetas* or the bread she baked and sold at market. He had not gone back since then because he had no money, nor anyone to visit. If he didn't return, then his mother was still alive, still in her kitchen. Spain was like a photograph, perpetually frozen in his memory.

He missed his mother. He sighed, finally able to put a name to the knot of anxiety in his stomach. He was lonely and scared that he might disappear from this life and no one would remember him. An image came to him unbidden of Lise's child burying his face in Gabriel's neck. The fantasy was so strong he could even feel the moist heat, smell his baby odor. And then it was Lise in his arms, her body pressed close to his, her heartbeat sounding on his chest. She was telling him she was there, would always be there. His eyes suddenly welled with tears, and he lay back on his bed and stared at the juncture where the plasterboard wall met the old tin ceiling until the urge to sob had passed.

———

He drew in his studio with his headphones on. There was nothing suspicious about his actions. He just had to make sure that no one from the studio would later recognize the drawing as his. But artists deserved the stereotype of being notoriously self-centered; he doubted anyone would even see his drawing, so involved were they in their own work.

It was a disaster. His lines were hesitant, as if the value of the page weighed his hand down, made it sluggish, scared. And it didn't feel like modern paper. It was unexpectedly rough and yet pillowy, like drawing on a piece of toilet paper. The ink was blotchy, alternately thick and reed-thin where he was unable to adequately control the nib. Gabriel wished he'd thought to bring alcohol to the studio. He wondered if Marie-Laure had any. He hadn't heard her complain, so she was most likely not working tonight. He could just sneak into her space, grab a nip, replace it the following day. Or maybe he just needed to clear his head.

Outside, it was raining, but he didn't go back in. How would he explain his failure to Klinman, who would be angry with him for ruining the paper? He was furious with himself, as usual. He'd fucked up again.

———

He snuck out of Édouard's early the following day, complaining of a stomachache. He did have one; his innards were tied in knots with the knowledge that Klinman might murder him. He had to go back to his studio to retrieve the failed drawing. Then he had a five p.m. appointment with Lise for a tour of Ambrosine's. His earlier fear that she was embarrassed to have him come to the gallery proved to be unwarranted. Gabriel found that was often the case; he imagined that people were embarrassed by him, disliked him, designed elaborate schemes to get rid of him. Only afterward did he realize that not only did people not think of him in that way, but most often, no one was thinking about him at all. He was glad he had been wrong about Lise's intentions, if not about her bourgeois life. He was glad to have her as a friend.

Few were the artists who had their own studios that doubled as storefronts. Among these elite, even fewer had the staying power of Ambrosine. He had capitalized on his real estate and fame to serve as a high-end market for contemporary art. But not the avant-garde post-postmodern installations that interested Gabriel. Rather, he was a purveyor of big names, little talent, like Damien Hirst, Jeff Koons, Tracey Emins. Gabriel felt simultaneously envious and dismissive of these sellouts. He knew, even as he looked down on them, that he would trade places with them in a heartbeat. It had become his habit recently to check biographies for birth dates. More often than not, those written about in art magazines or shown in the windows of Marais galleries were younger than he.

At Ambrosine, the ubiquitous Cy Twombly was showing. In the window hung a colossal canvas. It was several shades of pale blue, from cyan to titanium to cadet, each seamlessly integrated with white swirls descending the canvas like streaming tears. Something looked strange to Gabriel—the light reflecting off the window? —but then he realized the painting was done in acrylics. He nearly laughed out loud. Acrylics were the fingerpaints of the art world, the medium of Sunday river painters and rich American art vacationers. Of course, when someone as great as Twombly used them, they were ironic, but to everyone else they were cheap, easily manipulated, and somehow too shiny and artificial. They looked ephemeral compared to the aristocratic authority of oils, with their distinct linseed smell and blunted peaks. You had to really layer on acrylics to get them to have the texture of oils. Of course, Gabriel did not fail to notice the discreet red dot in the lower-right-hand corner of the description. Someone had bought this shit.

Inside the gallery an improbably androgynous assistant sat behind a long glass desk bereft of anything other than a keyboard. He/she was peering down into the table, and it took a minute for Gabriel to realize the monitor was embedded in the glass. He cleared his throat.

The androgyne made no sign of acknowledgment. Gabriel cleared his throat again, louder.

"May I help you, *monsieur*?" There was a long pause between *you* and *monsieur*, emphasizing that the asker was not sure if he deserved the honorific.

"I'm looking for Lise Girard."

The man—Gabriel now saw an Adam's apple—waved his hand in a gesture of incomprehension or dismissal.

"We are not a missing persons bureau," the man said. He swept his hair out of his eyes with one hand.

"I'm not looking for her," Gabriel said. He had chosen the wrong word. "I have . . . an appointment." He wondered how much jail time he would do for slashing a Twombly canvas. Or slashing a supercilious Ambrosine intern.

Without altering his scowl, the intern picked up a thin silver phone from under the desk. He could hear it ring in the bowels of the gallery. Lise came out, clicking fast in her high heels. She wore a pencil skirt, and he could see, even though she was thin, the traces of her three pregnancies in her belly.

"Thanks, Claude," she said, motioning Gabriel to follow her into a small, windowless office. It was crowded with catalogs, all up the walls and stacked on the floor.

"What's in there?" She pointed to his makeshift portfolio.

"Nothing," Gabriel said. "Something I'm delivering."

"For Rosenzweig? Can I see? What is it?"

"I don't want to unpack it."

"Come on," Lise said. She reached around him to grab the briefcase from his hand. "Show me. I'll have one of the peons wrap it back up better than this Naugahyde folder."

Before he could protest, she had the briefcase in her hands and, gloves on, was unzipping it. She placed the disastrous drawing on a flat table in her office, the only noncovered surface, and inhaled. She tilted a lamp to shine the light directly on the drawing and leaned so that her face was inches away from the page, examining the ink.

Gabriel sucked in his breath. He was sure she was debating how best to put the delicate question. It was obviously drawn in his own hand, inexpertly at that. He let himself smile a bit as he enjoyed her obvious discomfort, imagining her mind spinning through the possibilities: Édouard had been duped; Gabriel had been duped, had tried to fake a drawing.

When she straightened up, she was not smiling. "Amazing," she said. "It's fascinating to see the changes from sketch to painting, isn't it? I mean, I recognize the theme, the composition, certain elements, from . . . what's that one Connois called? With the market?"

Lise paused. Gabriel did not answer her. He was shocked. Did she really not see that the sketch was a fake? Was she so gullible or superficial that she didn't see the hesitation in the lines, the disproportion in the figures? Or did people really expect so little of sketches that they were willing to assume any mistakes would be smoothed over in oil paint? Maybe she was teasing him, trying to see if he would correct her. "*Víspera de Fiesta,*" he said, finally.

"The other one," she said. "With the old woman."

"*La Vieja*? There's no old woman in this one."

"Yes, but"—Lise grabbed a pencil and pointed the nonsharpened end at the paper—"see the triangular composition, with the kiosk pole as the top. And then the inverted triangle just below it with the barrels and the hay bales? Classic Connois, isn't it?"

Gabriel nodded. Now that she made the point he could see how other Connois paintings must have influenced him. And even a little Canaletto in the exaggerated pleats. Lise didn't see his hodgepodge of styles?

"It's so great to deal in older drawings. Sometimes I get so fed up with contemporary posing, you know?" She picked up the phone and pressed the intercom. "Hi, can you send someone to my office to wrap something?" To Gabriel she said, "Are you insured for this sort of thing?"

He shook his head, as much in wonder as in answer. She really believed this was a Connois sketch? He had always respected Lise, her eye. She babbled, yes, but in between volleys of nothingness she often had insightful opinions about work. If he had her fooled, maybe he hadn't done such a bad job after all. Or maybe a bad job was good enough.

"Come on," she said. "I'll show you the goods."

They began in the showroom of the all-white gallery. The paintings were so large that only one fit per wall. In a small room off the main hall was a second show, a cartoonist who collaged pieces of glossy magazines. The characters depicted life in French slums, with old women calling out obscene swears and young men smoking hand-rolled cigarettes. They stared in silence. Finally, Lise spoke.

"It's funny," she continued, "working for Ambrosine, I thought I would get really jaded, you know, like I wouldn't care anymore about art."

"But . . ." he provided.

"But, I kind of enjoy it more, spending time with it. Like, take Damien Hirst. I get him. Finally. I see what all the fuss is about."

Gabriel fought the urge to cackle. Of all the contemporary posers who seemed to have charmed the establishment, Damien Hirst seemed the most vile, mercenary, talentless of the bunch. His vivisections, rotting inartistically; the pomp with which he unveiled each readymade was laughable. And the aestheticism of the influence of mortality? Really, were people still painting ideas? Inserting themselves into their artwork? Gabriel abhorred the cult of personality surrounding contemporary art. But he couldn't say this. Not to Lise. Not in French. He was slightly amazed that he had never seen her willingness to be a part of the masses before, her desire for acceptance into the canon.

His package came back wrapped expertly and nondescriptly, separate from the briefcase, which now looked even cheaper in comparison.

As if to confirm his condemnation of her *bobo* ways, she ended their awkward silence by saying, "Shit. I have to go pick up the little one from the *crèche*. Walk with me? It's just over the Seine."

Gabriel had a quick flash of reverie of being in Lise's all-white apartment, children hanging off him like rats in some horror movie. What if that had been his life? He would have fucking committed suicide.

"I can't," Gabriel said. "The client is waiting."

Lise kissed him on both cheeks and headed off toward the Île St.-Louis. Gabriel was actually traveling that way as well, but he set off in the opposite direction. He'd had enough of the art establishment, with its poor taste and gullibility, for one day.

———

When Gabriel rang Klinman's bell, the *portière* eyed him suspiciously. Gabriel held up the package, signifying official business, trying to exude more confidence than he felt. Why did it matter what the building's caretaker thought? It reminded him of the failure he was carrying. He did not look forward to having to explain to Klinman what happened.

Inside the apartment, Klinman was sharing a coffee with a man Gabriel didn't know. When he came in, Klinman rose, but the man remained seated. Beneath his pants, which had a large, purposefully tailored cuff, Gabriel could see the outlines of sock garters. The man, though obviously in his early fifties, had a full head of chestnut hair cut and styled in the manner more suitable for the 1940s than for today. In fact, his whole demeanor, the gentle manner with which he held his coffee cup, his wide-legged yet demure seated position, suggested another era.

The air in the room was charged. Klinman was tense; Gabriel could tell by the tight pull of his shoulders, the creases around his smile. "Gabriel, hello. Mr. Schnell"—he turned to the seated man, pulling Gabriel to him—"this is the young man I was telling you about." He introduced them in German: "Gabriel, Mr. Tobias Schnell."

"Pleased to meet you," Gabriel said in French.

The man nodded. He scratched his small chin and Gabriel spotted his large, jeweled watch. "Gabriel, you've fetched the sketch from my apartment, have you?" Klinman asked.

"Monsieur speaks French?" Gabriel asked.

"I understand," Schnell said.

Gabriel pursed his lips. He had no idea who this man was, but he needed to tell Klinman that the Connois sketch was an utter failure that should never see the light of day. "Mr. Klinman," Gabriel started. "May I see you alone for a minute before I show the sketch?"

"I think Mr. Schnell is in a hurry," Klinman said, looking nervously over at the man, who seemed to have settled deeper into his chair. He did not look like a man with pressing obligations.

"There's a small problem," Gabriel said. "With the sketch."

"Not a serious one, I hope," Klinman said, smiling.

"It doesn't really look like a Connois," Gabriel said. "Not exactly."

Klinman laughed. "I think that's for the expert to decide, don't you?" He turned to Schnell and said something rapidly in German. The man laughed also, at Gabriel's expense, he suspected.

Fine. Fuck it. He had tried to warn Klinman. He unwrapped the adeptly packaged drawing and arranged it on the easel that had been set up for this purpose.

Now Schnell rose. He put down his coffee cup and took a plastic capsule out of his breast pocket. He removed a folded pair of reading glasses and stepped toward the drawing, moving his head in circles around the drawing as if stretching his neck. In a couple of places, a shoulder that Gabriel hadn't gotten quite right, a chicken whose neck seemed too long for its body, he paused and stared, his eyeballs flashing back and forth. Then he focused on the signature.

Gabriel had started out by signing the drawing because it was the part he felt most confident with. He had practiced Connois's signature so many times that it was almost as natural as his own signature, and nearly indistinguishable from the master's. Signing got him in the mood to paint as someone else. Like a method actor, he found he was a better mimic when he inhabited the character of the artist he was imitating. To draw like Connois he had to *be* Connois, and the physical statement of that was signing a drawing that hadn't yet been started, but was somehow, in a trick of time, looping itself, already complete.

Klinman gripped Gabriel by the shoulder, his fingers digging into the bones. Gabriel didn't dare ask him to stop.

"He is right," Schnell said finally in French, breaking the silence. "This is not Connois."

Gabriel didn't dare look at Klinman; instead he stared at his shoes, tried to line up the toes even with the edge of the wooden floor slats.

The man continued in German, and Gabriel lost the thread, hearing only the French cognates: "signature . . . École . . . paper . . ." Klinman's grip on his shoulder relaxed, and when Gabriel dared to look up, he was smiling genuinely.

"Did you understand that?" he asked.

"No," Gabriel admitted.

"Mr. Schnell said—"

"Tobias," said the man, who was now all courtesy and warmth.

Klinman bowed his head in thanks. He gestured to Schnell, clearly not comfortable referring to him by his first name: "—said that the drawing was indeed not by Connois's hand, but that the style is very like his, the period is appropriate, and the signature undoubtedly the master's. He concludes, then, that the drawing is by one of the school of the Hiverains, and attributes it to a disciple, signed by the teacher Connois himself. Herr Schnell—Tobias"—he emphasized the first name—"is the foremost German authority on nineteenth-century French schools."

Gabriel was shocked. This hesitant piece of shit was going to be accepted into the pantheon of drawings? He felt he should really say something, admit that the work was by his own hand and not one of the master's pupils. But what should he say? That Klinman was a liar? That the so-called expert was an idiot? That some scrawny starving artist with a chip on his shoulder knew the real score? Don't be an idiot, he told himself. It's not like Klinman and he were fooling some unsuspecting neophyte. This man, who was supposed to be an authority, couldn't even recognize a terrible fake. Gabriel had no obligation to divulge the truth, he decided.

The men conversed in German while Gabriel studied his drawing again. He supposed, in the strong but diffuse lighting, the lines seemed more graceful. The men concluded their conversation, which ended with a discussion of dates, or times. Tobias Schnell ignored him; he shook Klinman's hand in that stiff Germanic way before Klinman walked him to the door.

When he returned, Klinman was grinning. "Well, that went well!"

"What was that?" Gabriel asked.

"We have placed your work in an auction."

"I don't understand." Gabriel sat down.

"There's nothing to understand. That man is an authority."

"And he's putting it in an auction as authentic?"

"It *is* authentic, Gabriel," Klinman said patiently. "It's an original work in the style of Connois. That's exactly what the expert determined it to be. The picture doesn't lie. What he sees in it is his business."

"I suppose."

"Don't *suppose,* be *sure.*" Klinman began to pace in front of the drawing. "Think about it, Gabriel. What is the real value of this piece? Some pulped rags, a little ink. Its value is subjective, as all aesthetics are. Why should it be valueless if one person drew it and worth millions if another did? The picture didn't change."

"I did a terrible job," Gabriel said softly.

"There's room for improvement, yes. Don't be so glum. You'll make us a lot of money with your talents."

"How much money?"

"Ah, now we get down to business," Klinman said. "How does five thousand euros sound?"

"I want thirty-five percent," Gabriel said.

"It might not sell for years. It may never sell at all. No, you should be recompensed now. And please don't give me that look. I found the paper and the expert. How about seventy-five hundred? It will be in cash."

"I want ten thousand."

"You drive a hard bargain," Klinman said, extending his hand for Gabriel to shake. "Shall we go to dinner?"

Gabriel nodded glumly. He still felt irrationally guilty. Everything Klinman had said made sense. Hadn't people overlooked him just because he was Spanish? Because he didn't know how to manipulate the right people? Art should be judged on its own merits, but that wasn't the world they lived in. Hadn't being on the planet for forty-two years taught him anything? But he had just earned ten thousand euros, more than he'd ever made on all his art put together. Ten thousand euros was several months of salary at Rosenzweig's gallery.

He followed Klinman out the door, past the still-disapproving eye of the *portière,* who scowled equally at Klinman. Maybe that was just her default expression.

He called Colette to see if she wanted to join them, but there was no answer. In the restaurant, a nice bistro on the Rue des Ecouffes, Klinman ordered them a bottle of wine, and the *menu fixe.* When their salads came—frisée with lardons for Gabriel, a pâté terrine for Klinman—Gabriel finally asked him: "Where will you say you got the drawing from?"

"That," he said, wiping his mouth, "requires a story, which I will tell you over coffee."

After their main course, Klinman sat back and pulled a cigarette from his breast pocket. "My story . . ." He paused to drop a sugar cube into his cappuccino. Then he lit his cigarette, puffing occasionally as he spoke. "I'm German. And Jewish. My family escaped just before the war was starting, through Switzerland to Italy, then on a boat to China. I was born in China and we lived there for four years. When the visa came for England we settled in Leeds. That's where I grew up. Did Colette tell you all this? No?

"My parents' passion was art. Their apartment had paintings and drawings hung so closely together they said it looked like a frame store rather than a living room. When the war started they hid their art with friends, they buried it in vaults or tried to trade it for favors. Others had their art seized by the Nazis.

"Some of it was kept by the local families, impossible to claim after the war ended. Some of it was taken by looters. Some the Nazis hung in regional offices. At one point, they even found canvases that Goering tried to hide in a cave. Barbarians."

Klinman paused for a long inhalation. He held the smoke inside his cheeks, savoring it. Gabriel was not sure if he was referring to the Nazis' callous disregard for human life or to their ignorant neglect of art. He thought he could see where this line of argument would take them.

"In short, there is a lot of art out there that is still floating about, waiting to be reclaimed."

Gabriel said, "So you fake the provenances."

"I do not like the word *fake*. *Fake* makes it sound as though there were something real that the fake is imitating. This is not the case."

Klinman leaned forward so close to Gabriel's face that he could smell the thick coffee and the deep tobacco on his breath. "It was ours. It was ours and they stole it. This is just squaring the deal."

"Well," Gabriel said. "Wouldn't returning the real paintings to their true owners or descendants really . . . square the deal?"

Klinman chuckled condescendingly. "Say you borrow twenty euros from someone. Then you pay them back. Does it have to be the same twenty euros? Of course not. You spent that twenty euros. It's a different bill that serves the same purpose."

Gabriel nodded. This reasoning did make sense, in a certain way.

Of course, it wasn't a perfect analogy: money, after all, just stood for something. There was no value inherent in the particular piece of paper, so they were interchangeable. Art, however, was not a substitute for something else. It was itself.

Gabriel felt light-headed, the blood gone to his stomach digesting his large meal. "I don't know," he said. "It just seems a little bit . . . unethical? Illegal? Deceiving people like this?"

Klinman put out his cigarette. "I deal with some of the most important curators and dealers in the world. They have everything to lose by dealing with me and nothing to gain. Except exceptional art. Gabriel, I like you for the same reason all older men like younger men. I see myself in you. Your heritage has been taken from you. You have the goods, obviously." Klinman waved his hand, palm up, stating the obvious. "Why won't they let you use them? Why do you spend all day pushing papers for that poof Édouard? What works of Michelangelo might we lack now if he had to, I don't know, tote water instead of being patronized by the Medicis? If they are going to try to keep you down, then you employ any means necessary to pick yourself back up, yes?"

Klinman's voice was rising. People in the emptying restaurant were staring. "I didn't mean to offend you," Gabriel said.

"Of course you didn't," Klinman said. "I know. I shouldn't get so worked up. But when I see bogus bourgeois morality, invented precisely to restrain people, prohibiting creativity and progress, I get upset."

Klinman paid for lunch and they stepped outside. While they were eating, it had grown overcast. Rain looked imminent. A cold breeze had picked up. Klinman turned the collar of his suit jacket up to cradle his neck. He handed Gabriel a thousand-euro bill. Gabriel had never seen one before. "We'll work out the rest of the payments later. I'm off." He shook Gabriel's hand, and before Gabriel could reply, Klinman had turned his back and was walking away briskly.

Gabriel was certain he'd offended Klinman. He hadn't meant to. He liked the man, respected him, and needed the money the man would provide. He just didn't like making money off others' ignorance.

He called Colette; again, no answer. She was probably out for lunch. She liked her independence, appointments he didn't know about, "girls' nights" where she and her friends dressed up and went dancing. Gabriel was racked with jealousy on those nights, managing to convince himself that she was picking up men. Sometimes he found the thought erotic, even as he lay awake thinking about how much he wanted to be with her.

Suddenly, he was getting what he wanted—money, respect. So why did he feel rather like he'd been rejected yet again, from a fellowship or grant. *Don't be stupid,* he thought, and went to spend his newfound wealth, but he discovered that a thousand-euro bill is not money that can be spent. He had to go to a bank to get change to buy an umbrella for the rain that was starting to fall.

———

When Gabriel emerged from the *métro* near his studio the rain was steady, thick gooey drops that seemed to hang in the air and then explode upon contact with the ground. Outside the front door, under the awning, sat Didier and Hans, a half-empty bottle of rum at their feet. In the gray light, Hans looked older; the lines around his eyes had increased. Did that mean Gabriel looked older too?

"Hey," Didier said. "We're celebrating. Join us."

"What's the occasion?" Gabriel pulled up a crate and sat down with them. He accepted the bottle offered to him and took a swig. The liquor made him feel like it was raining inside his gut as well as outside.

"It's Friday," Hans said. "We made it to Friday."

"Thursday, I think, actually," Gabriel said.

"Reason enough for me. Happy Thursday," said Didier, and took a large swig, wiping his mouth on his paint-splattered sleeve. "But actually, we are celebrating that Brigitte's pregnant."

Gabriel received the news just as he tilted the bottle back. He lowered it while gulping. "Seriously?"

"Yeah, wild, right?" Hans nodded emphatically.

Didier said, "I asked him if he knew who the father was."

Hans ignored him. "Aren't you going to congratulate me?"

"Of course, sorry. No one . . . I didn't think . . . Did you mean . . . ? Congratulations," he finally said. He handed the bottle back.

"They're not even married and the old lady wants his art out of the house," Didier said, laughing.

"The fumes." Hans shrugged. "So I took a space here."

"Wow, a kid."

Hans said, "You look like you're smelling shit. It's not a bad thing. We're really excited."

"Sorry," Gabriel said.

Didier pulled a joint out of his cigarette carton. "This requires a little hash."

Gabriel felt the liquor spreading its warmth. He hadn't realized how much he missed this camaraderie, how good it felt to be talking, drinking, laughing.

Didier sparked his lighter and breathed in deeply. "So you'll have to quit this shit once the baby's born, huh?"

"Don't see why I should." Hans took his turn.

Before Gabriel could stop himself, he giggled, clapping a hand to his mouth to stanch it too late. The two men looked at each other and laughed, and then paused and laughed again. Gabriel took the joint and breathed deeply. The smoke traveled through him, a gritty hurt.

"I don't know, man," Hans said, breaking a silence. "It's going to be weird, being a father."

"Hmmm," Gabriel said. Didier examined the end of his shoelace.

"My father was such an asshole, you know? I barely knew the guy. Bavarian and cold, like . . . like . . ."

"Yesterday's weiner schnitzel," Didier provided. Hans glared at him.

"I only went to his funeral for my mom's sake."

"Hmmm," Gabriel said again. He thought about his own father's funeral. His mother, weeping copiously, leaning on the employees of the funeral home for support. And Gabriel in a suit too short for his long legs, embarrassed for a thousand different reasons, wanting to feel sadder than he did, but mostly angry.

Without thinking, Gabriel asked, "If you guys could fuck over the art establishment, would you?"

"Yes," they both answered at once.

"What if it was kind of illegal?"

"Are you thinking of something in particular?" Didier upturned the bottle and shook it over his mouth to get the last few drops.

"No, it was just, like, a question."

Hans looked at him curiously.

"Not that shit we did for the hotel guy?" asked Didier.

"No, it's just . . . forget it," Gabriel said, shaking his head violently, as if clearing water from his ears.

"No, what?" Didier said.

"You brought it up," Hans said.

"Fine." Gabriel paused. "I was reading about this guy who forged old master paintings."

"The Italian guy?" Didier asked.

"I think he was English," Gabriel said.

"I heard about him," Hans said. "Hepburn or Stubborn, or something. Didn't he go to jail?"

"He forged paintings and made them look old and then sold them. They're all over museum collections."

Didier said, "Did he claim they were Rembrandts or whatever?"

"I don't think so," said Gabriel. "I think he just brought them into auction houses."

Hans said, "They decide who painted it."

"He just copied a painting and everyone thought it was a real Rembrandt?" Didier still didn't get it.

"No," Gabriel said. "He didn't copy anything. It was an original painting, but in the style of the master."

"Wasn't that the guy who snuck into the Tate and planted a false catalog, or doctored the records with an X-Acto knife and some school glue?" Hans asked.

Didier brushed ash off his lap. "If those fucking bastards are too stupid to tell a Rembrandt from their assholes, then I think they deserve to get taken."

"Very fancy, coming from someone who's showing at de Treu."

"Exactly my point," Didier said. "They have shit for brains."

Hans shook his head. His hair flopped into his eye, and he brushed it back, using his fingers as a comb. "Intent to deceive is deception."

Gabriel and Didier looked at him. Didier said, "The whole art world is completely fucked up. It rewards youth because it's novel; it rewards simple art because it's palatable and it discriminates against innovation. It's almost our duty to infiltrate and expose the hypocrisies."

"That's a really juvenile justification," Hans said. "That's like pulling the fire alarm at school."

"How is that like pulling the fire alarm?" Didier's voice rose. He was getting angry.

"Lashing out at authority figures because you're frustrated with the establishment." The stubble from Hans's beard showed in relief in the light cast by the entryway as he leaned forward.

Gabriel remained silent, watching the two men. This was how he thought he'd feel in art school. Slightly stymied by the language, more stymied by the sheer education and intellectualism of his peers. But as it turned out, art school was actively anti-intellectual. Emotions were privileged. If you overthought your art, you weren't naturally talented. But then you were supposed to come up with some sort of artist statement that, through the gobbledygook of art-speak, would shed light on the intellectual process behind the art that you were supposed to create *without* intellectual process. No one's French was that good, not even Flaubert's.

But here he was, eavesdropping on a conversation he'd started about ethics and creation of art, and he felt like it was pretentious and a waste of time. Maybe the hash was making him feel impatient, but the theoretical argument seemed more like posturing to him. Hans was justifying his conventional, moral life, and Didier was trying to attack him for it. It was the same old shit, with art as the weapon.

"Who said anything about lashing out? It's like a war. No one has any moral high ground." The conversation was getting increasingly heated.

Gabriel stood up, brushing his pants down his thighs. "I'm going in. Congratulations again."

"Thanks." Hans waved absently. He turned back to Didier. Then Gabriel realized they weren't angry with each other. This was a debate, friendly and substance-fueled. Nothing was at stake. As he entered his studio and the voices receded behind him, he was struck again by his ability to feel shut out, even from a conversation he himself instigated.

There are decisions, Gabriel mused, that can change your life. And often those decisions are both spontaneous and ill considered. He had made a joke at a dinner party. And he had done a favor for his girlfriend's uncle. Several favors, actually. And, from the nadir to which his life had descended—artistic slavery, intense professional jealousy, wasted potential—he rose suddenly to exultant heights.

Klinman had given him a dozen more sheets of period paper, and Gabriel had filled them with Piranesis, Canalettos, and Connoises in exchange for several thousand euros. He had gotten good at being almost nonchalant with the paper, not worrying he would smudge a line, or betray too much Connois the younger and not enough Connois the elder. He drew market scenes, Italian squares, his childhood kitchen, the buildings on the Île St.-Louis. His bedroom had turned into a veritable sizing factory—rare was the evening when there was not a piece of paper drying.

When Colette made one of her frequent trips to New York, he missed her with an intensity that worried him, one that he was not sure was reciprocal. He examined his ardency like a lump found suddenly under his armpit, with concern. He usually found women irritating, but that might have been because he tended to date the young École students and graduates, who found his experience alluring. Ultimately, the relationships ended in tears when the women realized Gabriel had no interest in deepening the commitment. These young bohemians, who professed to enjoy having someone to go see openings with, to walk in the Tuileries on Sunday afternoons, to fuck every few days to mutual satisfaction, were really just biding their time until marriage. He simply wasn't built for relationships. He met people, spent time with them, gradually there was a mutual loss of interest and he moved on. Some took longer to try his patience. Some he couldn't get away from fast enough. But to live with someone, on purpose, to start sharing toothpaste and finances and friends, seemed boring at best.

Gabriel knew his avoidance of deep relationships probably revealed something dysfunctional about him. But what if it wasn't pathological? What if this was just the way he was wired? He didn't feel unhappy. He didn't feel lonely—not often—even when he celebrated his fortieth birthday by himself at the studio. He was poor, but that was a choice he'd made a long time ago. Shouldn't there be people in the world who shunned convention, congenitally, to balance out those who wanted monogamy and offspring? What if he was a loner by DNA? The irony, he did not fail to recognize, was that he voiced these thoughts to no one, and so there was no one to provide the counterargument, if such a thing existed.

He went reluctantly back to his shared apartment, which was where he was when Patrice Piclut phoned him. It took him a minute to place the name, and then he remembered: the gallery owner at Klinman's dinner party. Patrice wanted to pay a studio visit. Would Gabriel be around tomorrow?

Gabriel got to the studio earlier than he ever had, rearranging canvases to look like he'd been hard at work, like he'd always been hard at work, on his own paintings. He used his elbow to sweep the pencil shavings off the work table onto the floor, then shooed them to the corner with his foot. He took all the crusted cans of dried-out paint, some with preserved bugs, some with science-worthy dust and mold specimens, to the communal sink, where he let them clatter and left them.

Sure enough, like clockwork, Marie-Laure stuck her head into his studio minutes later. "Um, about the sink?"

Gabriel fought the urge to tell her to go fuck herself. It sounded so great in French: *Aller se faire foutre.* Instead he said, "I can't talk to you right now. I'm waiting for a studio visit from the Picluts."

Marie-Laure stuck her chin out in disbelief. "*The* Picluts?"

"Yes," he said nonchalantly. "I met them at dinner a couple of months ago. They want to come see my work."

"Would they want to come next door?" Marie-Laure pointed with her brush to her studio space.

Gabriel shrugged, and Marie-Laure scurried back into her studio, where he heard her similarly straightening.

He adjusted his lights. He leaned on his table. He stood by the large wall. He paced. He went to the front door to look. He went back inside. Finally he realized he couldn't just stand there, and busied himself with a modern miniature, which kept him sharpening his pencil every thirty to forty seconds. He decided to draw the Louvre, in imitation of the thousands of small frontispieces of the *palais*. But his drawing depicted the shimmering glass of the new, horrific entrance that obscured the original square. Mitterrand had already committed architectural murder by the time Gabriel moved to Paris.

There was a polite knock on the door. Patrice stepped into the studio, followed by Paulette, who was carrying an enormous purse. She was on the phone and she smiled before turning her back to Gabriel.

Patrice stood for a long time in front of each of Gabriel's eight pieces. His face betrayed no emotion, but he seemed utterly enthralled, scratching at the small goatee under his lip as if in parody of thinking. Finally Paulette got off the phone and stood beside him in silence. They moved together from piece to piece, shifting as if by wordless signal.

Patrice turned to him. "I love most of all the incongruity of your images."

"Absolutely," Paulette echoed. "The juxtaposition of unlikely elements is echoed by your choice of color. Were you consciously commenting on the state of French immigration?"

"Um," Gabriel said. Had he been? Had he been painting his own *carte de séjour* visa status?

"It's really fantastic," Patrice said. "How many of you work out here?"

"About ten," Gabriel said. "It's really cheap."

"And hard to find. Like a geode," Paulette said.

"I'd offer you a coffee, but . . ." Gabriel let the thought trail off.

Patrice began to speak but Paulette cut him off. "No, we're on a really tight schedule. Thank you so much. This has been a real pleasure."

"A pleasure," Patrice echoed.

And they were gone. Almost immediately, Marie-Laure appeared in the doorway. "They seemed to really like it."

"It was all art-language bullshit," Gabriel said. He couldn't look at her face.

"Yes, but it was convincing art-language bullshit," Marie-Laure said.

———

The phone call came a few days later, while Gabriel was walking home from the *métro*. Patrice, on speakerphone with Paulette, offering him a solo show. Would September work? They were going to have a series of shows on immigrant artists. Gabriel was so excited he forgot to be angry that yet again he was exoticized for his nationality.

Patrice said, "We especially liked the market scenes."

"What market scenes?"

"The ones that are reminiscent of Connois's scenes, but with a contemporary irony that modern life cannot escape."

Gabriel wondered if his French was failing him.

"We didn't see many of them," Paulette continued. "Maybe one, or two. But we think that's your strongest work. They need a little finishing."

"Finish them while thinking of your relative, freezing up there in the Low Countries, missing his homeland the way you surely miss yours," Patrice said.

Realization came over Gabriel slowly, like the delay of warm air as it blows out a subway grate. "You want Connois."

"We want your originals, yes, but ones which echo your ancestor. I'm so glad you understand me. I don't speak the language of artists, only the language of art appreciators. It is a tremendous failing, I know." Patrice sounded actually pained. Paulette tittered in the background.

"Why don't you come by the space next week?" Paulette asked. "You can see the current show and we can talk over the plans."

"Sure," Gabriel said. "Thanks. Of course. Thanks so much."

Gabriel sat on a bench built in a circle around a plane tree. On the other side, an old woman was feeding the pigeons that swarmed her feet out of a Monoprix bag. Whenever they got too close, she kicked them away.

A show. At a real gallery. Not famous like Ambrosine or de Treu, but maybe even better because it was a gallery that was cooler, that showcased up-and-comers. Could you be an up-and-comer at forty-two? He hoped so, because he was certainly not an already-there, and the only other option was a has-been.

But they didn't want him. They wanted Connois. Fuck Connois, Gabriel thought. It was possible that his ancestor had ruined his life. Had made him want to be a painter, had made him forge *Febrer*, had set him on the path that led him to Klinman.

He should tell the Picluts to *aller se faire foutre*. If they didn't want him, his art, then they could find someone else. Let someone else take their direction, be their little bitch.

The woman behind him kicked her legs and pigeons fluttered over to Gabriel. He stamped his foot to make them scatter.

On the other hand, a show was a show. This could really launch him. Maybe what Patrice and Paulette were doing was curating, shaping his work, editing it. Maybe it didn't matter that it wasn't his original vision.

The woman shooed the pigeons over toward Gabriel. He shooed them back.

———

Gabriel went directly to Colette's, stopping only to buy the cheapest champagne he could find.

"Well, hello!" Colette said, glimpsing the bottle.

"I got a call from the Picluts today. They want to give me a show there."

"I know!" said Colette. "Isn't that fantastic?"

"You know? How do you know?"

"My uncle said they were going to call you. Apparently, he really likes you, to set you up with them that way."

"To set me up?"

"I mean, to put you in contact."

Gabriel hid inside his champagne flute. Had Klinman put them up to this? Why?

His thoughts must have shown on his face, because Colette put an arm on his. "They love your work. They'd have to. Every show figures in a gallery's reputation. They wouldn't risk that. Not for anyone."

"Do you know how long the gallery has been open?"

"Three years, I think."

"And how long have they been married?" Gabriel asked.

"Who?"

"The Picluts."

"They're siblings."

"They are?" Gabriel was sure they were married. "I thought they were together."

"That's gross. No, they're siblings." Gabriel thought about how they shared telepathic communication, how Patrice put his hand lovingly on Paulette's back. How had he confused that with romantic love? "Silly," Colette said. She yawned. "I'm jet-lagged."

"Oh, right, how was your trip?"

"Good. I saw the most beautiful Delacroix." Colette drained her glass and refilled it, sipping quickly before it fizzed over the side. "It's upsetting. These people in New York, these Americans, they don't appreciate what they have."

"I appreciate what I have," Gabriel said, taking Colette's free hand. Colette patted his cheek and said in English, "So cute."

―――――

The gallery space was exactly how he had imagined it would be. In fact, he thought he'd been in the space in another incarnation. Was it possible that it had been a punk club in the nineties? It was the perfect location for an up-and-coming gallery. Not so trendy that the rents were high, but trendy enough that *centre-ville* Parisians would feel safe sojourning there, and receive a taste of adventure while doing so.

Though small and low-ceilinged, the gallery had a nice flow to it, with plenty of interior walls and new track lighting. Colette came with him, standing so close to him as he paced the room, he could smell her strawberry shampoo.

She asked Paulette and Patrice a number of practical questions, and they had an animated discussion conducted so rapidly, with so many numbers, that Gabriel couldn't follow it. It seemed almost like an argument.

But Gabriel trusted Colette. It had been so long since someone had been his advocate. It felt odd, improbable, yet Gabriel and Colette seemed to share a certain practicality that made Gabriel feel that as long as his and Colette's interests were aligned—or at least, not competing—he could count on her.

He smiled as Paulette opened a bottle of champagne, and signed the contract willingly. When they clinked glasses, Colette's bubbled up and over the rim and she brought it quickly to her mouth to save it. "Now, that's talent," Patrice said.

———

After work, still nursing one of the more vicious and perseverant hangovers he'd ever experienced (he swore never to drink champagne again), Gabriel shuffled home and got into bed, contemplating his luck. Could it be that it had finally changed? He permitted himself a fantasy in which he was the toast of Paris. He wore a tuxedo, a satin pocket square, shirt partway unbuttoned. Around him was a cast of characters like in *Breakfast at Tiffany's*. Women in beehive hairdos with long cigarette filters and men with highball glasses. The setting, though, was modern: a view of the Parisian skyline (from *in* Paris? his common sense asked him. Yes, a view of Paris from Paris). The lighting was perfect for his art and for people watching. Still fantasizing, he looked at the walls. His drawings were professionally mounted and framed. It took him a minute to realize that what he was admiring in the fantasy as his own were the forgeries he'd drawn for Klinman.

He sat up in bed and turned on the light, embarrassed. Could he really have thought that he achieved this show on his own merit? For all his posturing about his supposed talent and the art world's prejudice, it was entirely possible that his work was inferior. Plus, he had to reflect that the happiest and most fulfilled he'd felt in years was when he worked for Klinman. To produce so exactingly the work of a master created a greater sense of satisfaction than when he finished his own work. Was that because the drawings were accepted so enthusiastically? Obviously, praise was powerful motivation. And money. Maybe this show was what he needed to get the same commendations for himself. After all, being an art world darling was about opportunity, exposure.

A thought: Klinman set up the show. But, again, why? So that Gabriel would stay happy and continue to forge his pictures like a good little boy? Should he accept this charity? Should he feel offended? It was hardly life-changing, a small gallery in the Fourteenth on a low-rent block with two-euro wine and stale crackers at the *vernissage*.

Or maybe Colette had arranged for the show. Or Édouard. Or even, for all he knew, Didier. The possibilities were endless, and all pointed to the fact that regardless of who prodded the gallery to offer him a show, and regardless of the fact that a solo show was the first step to a career of any kind, Gabriel could only see the offer as further proof that he would never amount to anything. He turned off the light, rolled over, and pulled the covers up over his head, willing himself to sleep.

———

Gabriel took great pride in announcing to Édouard that he would no longer be working at the Rosenzweig Gallery in order to prepare for his solo show. Édouard didn't look impressed, nor did he seem upset to hear that his employee would be leaving him. There were a dozen recent grads who would be glad to take his place. Édouard insisted that he stay two weeks to train a new hire, but Gabriel refused. Only then did Édouard show emotion. They fought, and it escalated to the point where Gabriel told Édouard exactly what he thought of him and his gallery. Édouard responded in kind, hurtling insults that sounded just like the characteristics about himself that Gabriel already knew and hated: his attitude, his intractability, the suspicion that if he hadn't made it in the art world by now he never would.

But going to the studio at ten the next morning, Gabriel was elated. This was what an artist did, got up, drank oodles of coffee, and hit the studio early. He practically sauntered from the *métro*. He was not the first one there; Marie-Laure was an early riser. Still, Gabriel felt virtuous, pumped from caffeine.

Over the weekend, Gabriel had cleaned out his area in the studio, considering canvases and putting aside those he could re-gesso and paint over. He made a list of possible titles for his show. But after stretching two canvases and priming them, he was at a loss as to what to paint. It might help if he had a theme for his show. But he couldn't really develop a theme until he'd painted something. A vicious circle. He paced; he ran out of batteries in his tape player and switched their places to eke out a bit more power. Then he went outside.

Didier was having a cigarette. "How's it going?"

"Oh, you know," Gabriel said.

"Christ, when I first found out about my show," Didier continued, "I couldn't do anything. It's like all my ideas had been sucked out of my head. Do you feel like that?"

"No," Gabriel lied. "I'm painting like they will cut my arms off tomorrow."

"Nice image," Didier said. "Lucky. It took me like a month to settle down and produce. You got a title yet?"

"Still thinking," Gabriel said.

"Don't think too hard," Didier warned. "Thinking makes for bad art."

———

Lise was impressed by Gabriel's sudden success. She was full of questions. He did not tell her about having to tailor his paintings to the Picluts' requests, because he knew she would disapprove. She would wrinkle up her little French nose and scold him like a child. Why was he compromising himself that way? Why had he been true to his art all these years, only to sell out now? What did that make him?

Gabriel was aware of her arguments, because he was making them himself. Why should it matter to him what she thought, this artist-turned-housewife? Except it did.

Sitting in a café near Ambrosine's, Lise had dedicated her lunch break to brainstorming a title for his show with him. They were talking about Gabriel's interests, how alienation was always a theme in his works, and they discussed the possibility of the title *aliénation*, then two words in English, *alien nation*, and they laughed that they were filming a sci-fi movie. Then it came to Lise. She had to write it down so Gabriel could see the wordplay. *"Dé/placement, Dé/plaisir."*

"'Dis/placement, Dis/pleasure.' I'm happy," he blurted out. He blushed. He was happy that Lise was his friend, happy to be having a show at last.

Lise laughed. "I'm happy too."

When he told Colette the title, she scoffed. "It sounds like some sort of Derridean circle jerk."

"Well, I like it," Gabriel said.

"You would."

He was sleeping poorly, partly because he was often at Colette's and her bed was lumpy. She also generated so much heat when she slept that he awoke sweaty and breathless. Every night he had anxiety nightmares.

One night he dreamed that his painting had made the cover of *Art Forum,* only to realize, to his horror, that he had copied the *Mona Lisa.* He awoke panting.

"What is it? Tell me." Colette stroked his back as Gabriel fought to regain his breath.

"Am I doing the wrong thing?" he asked her.

"I don't understand what you mean."

"I feel like . . . I feel like I'm pretending to be someone else."

"Because you're accepting direction?"

"I guess." He turned to her. "Doesn't it seem strange that they want to capitalize on my connection to Connois?"

"Why?" Colette lay back down on the bed. Her breasts pointed opposite ways, like contradictory directional arrows. "I mean, you exploit it."

"Yeah, but. Wait, I do?"

Colette laughed. "You have his name, though it's not your true name. You like to sketch like him, I've noticed."

Gabriel froze: was it possible she knew about the work he did for her uncle? But Colette continued on. "Just do what they want. Now is not the time for principles. You don't catch flies with vinegar."

Part Two

Summer 2007

Elm felt such a surge of relief as the wheels lifted off the ground that she sighed more heavily than she meant to and felt her seatmate bristle in annoyance. She loved her family, but escaping from them, even for a couple of days, lifted a tremendous burden. She felt she was never doing enough. When she expressed to Colin, lost in his own anxious space, that she worried about her efforts as a wife and mother, he looked at her as though she were speaking a language he didn't understand.

"That is so New York, to worry about these things," he said. "You're a terrific wife and a fantastic mother and a terrible cook. All my girl-friends say so." He nuzzled her. "I don't understand why you worry like this when there's real stuff to worry about, like aliens and serial killers." He was being nice, but he wasn't saying the right words. What were those words? Some form of assurance that she didn't let her son die, that everyone forgave her for letting her son die.

New York fell away, replaced by a blue that was either ocean or cloud cover. She was flying business class; she reclined and sipped at her not-terrible wine.

It had been a fight to get to go on this trip alone. Ian had wanted to come, even offering to pay his own way, claiming not to have been to Paris in *ages*. She had laughed like he made some ridiculous joke, but she would have been blind not to see the hurt in his eyes. Then Colin had suggested she take Moira with her. "She's never been to France, Elm." Elm wondered if he needed a break as much as she did. "I'll be working too much," she answered. "I'd have to find a sitter."

Colette had, if unintentionally, helped Elm out. Needing to see Klinman's stock was the perfect excuse to take a trip to Paris. Ordinarily, it was the dealer who came to the auction house, but Elm agreed with the man's assessment that he didn't want the works traveling unnecessarily; each minute they spent out of prime archival conditions was a year off their lives. It would be dangerous to ship them to New York. Easier to ship Elm to Paris. No one would ever have to know her real impetus.

But here she was finally, unencumbered. She made it uneventfully through customs, dragging her overnight bag with a few clothes and a couple of reference books. The taxi driver seemed surprised that she was staying on the Left Bank instead of the Champs-Élysées. Klinman too had been surprised, as had the mystery man at the clinic; apparently only backpackers tried to recapture the dirty glamour of the 1960s. She checked into her room; the hotel had no elevator so she climbed the two sets of carpeted stairs with a baggage porter in tow. She tipped him one euro, which he received silently so that she had no clue if she'd tipped him appropriately.

The small room was decorated in a faux Louis XIV style, lots of ormolu and brocade, but the window, when she pulled the curtain, looked out onto the back side of the Luxembourg Gardens. Across the patchy green she could see the busy Boulevard Saint-Michel.

She hadn't visited Paris since Ronan died. But though he'd never been to Paris, the city reminded her of him; it was the site of Elm's first solo trip after becoming a mother. He was a little over fourteen months, and she'd insisted that Colin put him on the phone every evening though he didn't understand that the voice coming through the receiver was hers. "Yes, he misses you," Colin said. "No, I haven't fed him refined sugar. Wait—is Guinness refined sugar?"

Paris bustled beneath her, the snarl of traffic heading up the boulevard haphazardly like a group of beetles, the high-pitched claxons of hooting taxis. Here was a city where she knew no one, where no one knew she'd been Ronan's mother. This feeling was simultaneously thrilling and devastating. She could be free. She was not under examination as a woman who had lost a child. The flipside of being where no one knew about Ronan was the feeling that all traces of him had been erased from the collective unconscious. She wanted to tell people on the street, "I had a son," just so there would be some recognition of him. She tried to insert him into her memories of Paris: the smoky cabaret where the fat Frenchman stroked the older lady's hair, some of which fell out in clumps between his thick fingers; the brushed-clean streets and the whir of the machines as they sprayed water into the gutters. Ronan would have delighted as the fountain went off in front of the Centre Pompidou, or at least, a young version would have. An older version would have enjoyed the Bateaux Mouches, or a tour of the sewers and catacombs. But all these fake memories were like a reel of movie pastiches. She would have to live without Ronan for the weekend, except for the DNA samples she'd brought: the hairbrush she'd kept from Thailand, and a baby tooth retrieved from a plastic box that Ronan had insisted they keep his teeth in once he realized that the Tooth Fairy didn't exist.

She stood at the window in her room until night fell and it was a decent hour to venture out for dinner. She had with her Pedrocco's book on Canaletto; with a decent Bordeaux she could try to make the evening pleasant. But even as she thought this she knew she was only going through the motions of a person visiting Paris. She was playing the role of "Elm" and simply waiting until she could shed her cover and visit the clinic. The knowledge simmered underneath her skin. She felt elated; the strange lack of jet lag was like a turbo boost of energy. She remembered a bistro not too far from the hotel. It had changed names, but the decor and the menu remained the same (did bistro menus ever change?), and they sat her at a table by the window so she could watch the people go by. The waiter patiently suffered through her nervous babbling in inferior French, her debate about whether to order steak tartare, and her eventual decision to have the roast chicken, because, she added, no one roasted chicken better than the French. The waiter took the menu and bowed slightly. Elm wondered if she'd said what she thought she'd said. She often made mistakes in French that were hilarious and sexual—commenting on the length of dicks outside the opera, or talking about how her grandfather liked to hunt twats.

She read up on Canaletto by candlelight, having trouble focusing after the carafe of wine. Whenever she caught herself thinking about the clinic, she corralled herself. She was afraid that if she let her guard down everyone in Paris would see the nakedness of her desire. She ordered a decaf coffee and a *tarte tatin* for dessert. Then, like someone had flipped a power switch, her jet lag caught up with her. She paid the bill with a Visa card, which the waiter ran through a handheld machine tableside, printing out her receipt immediately. When he pulled her chair out as she stood up, she had the feeling that, like Ronan, she didn't exist here, that she might disappear on the way to her hotel and it would be like she had never been here at all. She checked that the hair and tooth were still where she left them in the room safe before donning her eyeshade and falling asleep.

———

Augustus Klinman was not the man she supposed he'd be. She was expecting a typical Englishman—thinning hair, scarecrow body stuffed into an ill-fitting, obviously expensive suit. Instead, when the man approached her in the lobby of the George V hotel and extended his hand, she was faced with a hairy-knuckled, hirsute, overweight, well-tailored surprise, though she had the expensive suit right. He shook her hand like an American, forcefully.

"Ms. Howells," he said.

"Mr. Klinman." She allowed her arm to be pumped.

"I'm very pleased to meet you," he said. "Won't you come upstairs?"

The elevator attendant looked at his gloved hands discreetly. Oddly, Colette had not asked to accompany her to see the drawings. That saved Elm the trouble of explaining that she wanted to see them on her own, that is, without Colette. The less she saw Colette the better.

Klinman had taken a suite on one of the upper floors. It was decorated in what Elm recognized as an attempt at Empire-style homage to Josephine and Napoleon. Heavy velvet curtains were tied back to offer a view of the Eiffel Tower, or part of it; the city was covered in its typical fog. Some of the *objets* decorating the room, while not fantastic examples, were period-correct, Elm knew. On the coffee table near the sofa, a small, covered urn sat uselessly, throwing shadows from the lamp on the glass. Bronze winged figures perched on marble-plated pedestals, and cherubic babies frolicked on painted canvases.

Klinman offered her a drink. Though it was only noon, Elm accepted a glass of wine. She was nervous and had the paranoid thought that she was being drawn into some sort of trap. She had even left a note in her hotel room saying where she was going. Having Klinman appear opposite her expectations didn't help. She crossed and uncrossed her legs. The sofa was too deep; she couldn't get comfortable.

"So," he said. "I appreciate that you came all the way to Paris to meet with me."

"My pleasure," she said. "I had other business, and Colette had such good things to say about you."

"I am sorry that I could not receive you in my office, but it's undergoing renovations. And the French take their time with these things." Elm smiled politely.

"I am originally German, Ms. Howells. My family is Jewish; we narrowly missed Auschwitz."

"I'm sorry," Elm said. The wine was too sweet, but she had another sip. Why was he telling her this?

"That is why I am able to do what I do. There are individuals in England and in Germany who will still only do business with those whom they trust."

"I don't blame them," Elm said. "There are a lot of unscrupulous people out there." She smiled, but Klinman remained deadly serious.

"People have wondered, sometimes. Out of jealousy? Innate suspicion? I don't know. But I can tell you that these drawings are new to the market."

Elm's eyebrows rose in surprise. New to the market? Most deceased artists' catalogues raisonnés were long complete. It was rare that another drawing would be added to the oeuvre. Several at once would be strange.

"May I take a look?" she asked.

He nodded and took back the wineglass, placing it on the bar. He handed her a pair of gloves, donned a pair himself, and zipped open a case Elm had not noticed behind the chair. She got up and hurriedly drew the gauze undercurtains so the light would not damage the drawings.

She approached the table, the whirr of excitement building. She loved this part of the job, the sense of discovery that accompanied looking at truly fine art. And she wouldn't lie: she loved the power. She determined what was authentic or fake, important or disposable, decorative or museum-worthy.

He laid the first drawing on the table. A typical Canaletto *veduta*, it showed a palazzo in architectural detail, with some extra flourishes that were clearly added by the artist, who often moved or added obstacles to suit his compositions. She noticed the gently swaying shadows and how the woman who was standing in front of the palazzo holding a basket mimicked that curve. The clouds were in a light wash, slightly sepia-toned, either from age or from original intent. She held it up gingerly. The watermark was appropriate. She couldn't remember the firm off the top of her head, but she was sure she'd seen it before. The paper was handmade, the grains haphazard and the remnants of the pulp visible. Occasional wormholes dotted the page, with some mold spots. Period paper, then.

Her heart began to beat quicker. She could hear her own breathing. Maybe she was excited to be holding such an important piece of work. But that couldn't be it. She had held much more important works, works that held significance for her personally, without such an extreme reaction. Maybe she was anxious about tomorrow.

She studied the lines. The drawing had Canaletto's sure hand, his talent for perspective that wasn't exactly as nature (or man) built monuments, but made sense to the naked eye. She took Klinman's proffered loupe and looked more closely at the wormholes. The ink hadn't bled into them, meaning that the holes were made after the drawing was complete, not before. Otherwise excellent fakes often had this telltale sign; the forger had drawn over the old paper, but the ink had betrayed him.

Mentally, she classified where in Canaletto's oeuvre this work might fall. She recognized the street in Rome from her stay there in graduate school. It was not exactly as she remembered it, but that was possibly a fault of her memory, or of Canaletto's. Sure enough, faintly underneath the ink lines she saw the barest remnants of chalk and red pencil where he had sketched the outlines before returning to his studio.

Elm considered, watching the curtains sway with the forced air blown out beneath them. It could be from one of Canaletto's atelier. By the end of his life, he had quite a production line going. But the scene was from a *veduta* earlier in his life, when he was still sketching primarily on commission. And it wasn't a pastiche. Too often, imitators of a master (whether forgers or hobbyists) amalgamated all of a master's styles into one piece, the visual equivalent of overembellishing a lie. This piece had remarkable restraint. It had to be a Canaletto. And yet . . .

She put the picture down, willing her face not to betray any emotion. She felt the barest pinch of a headache, the constriction of her lungs. Her head told her that this was an authentic work. She had been trained by both the academy and personal experience to be an expert. She needed four hands to list the reasons this was definitely a Canaletto original and didn't have a single reason to doubt herself except that her body seemed to be signaling her to trust instinct over reason.

"Hmmm," she said, noncommittally. "The others?"

"Another Canaletto," he said. It was from the same papermaker, which made sense. It showed a bit of water, a rare Canaletto subject, a gondola in the distant background, rowed by just the suggestion of a gondolier.

He stood by her, a respectful distance, his hands clasped in front of him, rocking on his toes. He looked at the ground so as not to make her nervous. He did everything a dealer was supposed to do.

When he showed her the Piranesi, the word *no* rose up in her like a belch. She managed to quell it before it escaped her lips. An odd reaction to what was by all accounts a beautiful drawing.

What, she asked herself, was that voice responding to? She realized it was responding to her assumption that this drawing was by Piranesi. Her reptilian brain was telling her that her first impression had been not quite right. It was this inner voice, this eye, that made Elm a superior attributer. Unfortunately, attribution was only half of a department head's job. She forced herself to focus. The paper and materials were period-appropriate, no mass-produced postindustrial concoctions. The intricacy of the drawing suggested that it was a finished work, as opposed to a sketch for a copperplate engraving. However, the scene was one she recognized from *View of the Arch of Constantine* which meant it would most likely have been rendered as a practice for a definitive later work. But Piranesi was famous for etching straight onto the plate, drawing on his draftsman skills and prodigious memory for the details. It was not inconceivable that he would sketch out his plans for an etching beforehand, but all the extant studies attributed to Piranesi were crude outlines, lacking the inspiration and aestheticism of the finished product.

Similarly, its unity of style disturbed her. Piranesi's theories on the development of human civilization and pastiche's important role in that development, especially in the artistic realm, were well publicized. He liked to mash up various line strengths, tones, improvisations, and impressions. This drawing adhered to a rather rigorous Baroque temperament. She would have to examine it further against a previously authenticated Piranesi, or against a facsimile of *View of the Arch of Con-*

stantine, but if she had to decide right now, she would say it belonged to one of Piranesi's followers, his École, or an acolyte. This uncertainty would not stop her from placing the piece in the auction, but it would be reflected in how the drawing was listed in the catalog and in its final price. This should not be listed as Giovanni Battista Piranesi.

"And now for the Hiverains."

She hovered over the first drawing, let a holistic impression fill her before focusing on any detail. It was a Connois, undoubtedly. A sketch, unsigned. Sketches came in four versions, Elm always thought. Important artist, important sketch, like, say, a study for a Rembrandt self-portrait; important artist, uninteresting sketch, like Tintoretto's doodles, or ten incomplete versions of a hand by Rembrandt; fascinating sketches by arguably more minor artists, or artists in the atelier; and dogs' heads by no one you've ever heard of. Interestingly, the first and third sold best at auction. No one wanted an anatomy lesson to hang on their living room wall, even if it was by Fra Lippo Lippi.

She picked up the paper carefully and held it up to the wan light. It had the right texture for nineteenth-century paper, pulpy and uneven, meaty. This first sketch impressed her. Connois was an artist's artist, but this was beautiful, a work of art that stood among the best examples of Les Hiverains. It was a close study of a woman's face. Elm examined the lines, following the artist's hand in the process of laying the ink on the page. The lines were fluid, graceful. Even the thatching in the background was smooth and consistent. The woman's face was complicated: one of her eyes was smaller; in the other one, a cataract was just beginning to form. Her nose had a broken bump, while her hair peeked out from her scarf. The lines radiating from the corners of her eyes betrayed a lifetime spent outdoors.

Perhaps it was the years of practice she'd had in searching out every face for the familiar features of Ronan. Perhaps she was simply well trained in her profession. She thought she recognized the woman in the drawing. It was the same woman who appeared in Indira's Connois with the uneven eyes; most artists would correct a defect like that when drawing, either consciously or for aesthetics' sake. But Connois had not. How strange, that this woman would appear suddenly in two previously unknown pieces of art. It was possibly simply a coincidence; Elm could think of explanations, but the fact that she had to make excuses for the art set off warning bells.

Attempting to maintain her poker face, she looked at the other two drawings. Now she was certain; they were too perfect. The watermarks were all different, which would be surprising considering that artists usually found a paper they liked and stuck with it. Also, they were all "typical" Connois scenes, the dry landscapes, the marketplaces, the wild dogs and peasants. Too typical. Connois drew these every day. It was hard to imagine that he would need to sketch them out in such detail at this point in his career. Composition, yes; new elements, yes; but a barking dog would have been second nature.

The artist, whoever he or she was, must have seen Indira's *Mercat* when the auction was announced. The image appeared widely in all the art blogs. He must have taken that as inspiration. By the time she came to the little girl with a dog she'd seen in PDF form, her suspicions were impossible to dismiss. These were most likely forgeries. The question was, did Klinman know, or was he being duped? Did he draw these himself, or was there a separate artist in on the scam?

She tried to maintain her composure. "What are the provenances like?" she asked.

"These were in the families of German Jews with trading and import concerns," he said. "Never sold. They were stolen during the war. The descendants finally got them back when the court case was settled in England last year. Now there are too many descendants to split them up, so they are taking them to market."

Elm turned the first drawing over. There was no mark indicating it had ever been sold at auction, but there was a faint pencil inscription, "Exhibit C," in the lower-right-hand corner.

"I could verify this?"

"Of course, Madame," he said. "They were among items recovered from a cave outside Berlin. The suit was brought by many families. I don't believe the results were made public. The German government likes to keep these things quiet—they make a big fanfare about reparations, but they don't disclose the details."

"A cave?" Elm asked.

"Archivally controlled of course. The Nazis were barbaric only when it came to humans. With art they were as careful as surgeons. And, of course, there was jewelry and *objets* too. The Jewish community was not poor. I myself had the opportunity to examine many of the items—I was a plaintiff in the case, though I probably shouldn't disclose that.

These are not my drawings, rest assured. In fact, none of the valuables recovered belonged to my family, as far as we could ascertain, but the take was really quite beautiful."

Elm wasn't sure exactly of the appropriate response. Should she apologize? Express sympathy? She asked to examine the paperwork, and he handed her a binder, each document in a plastic protective sheath. Sworn, notarized statements from German and Austrian Jews. Narratives of discovery: a hidden safe, the opening of a vault in Switzerland, the death of an old man posing as a Gentile. A blurry photograph of a Weimar Republic family around a dinner table in front of what may or may not have been the third sketch of women digging on the beach. Certificates of authenticity from the experts at Sotheby's in London and the curator of drawings from the Louvre, a man Elm had met over the years. Maybe not sufficient for a museum acquisition, but enough for an auction, or a private sale.

Elm looked at Klinman. He met her gaze. She tried to imagine what he might look like if he were actively deceiving her, but he was inscrutable, open, inviting her questions and smiling around the eyes hopefully, a bit desperately, as if he needed her to take these drawings off his hands, a burden that he was tired of shouldering. He was an excellent actor. She was shocked by his audacity, and too afraid to call him on it in this strange, secluded hotel room.

"Your sellers are anonymous?"

"They do not have the means with which to insure these drawings at the moment. It's best if their names are not available."

That made sense. Many people didn't want others to know what kind of treasures they were keeping in their modest two-bedroom flats. The art may be worth a fortune, but it doesn't help pay rent or put food on the table until it goes to auction.

Elm should just accept them, she thought. No one else would suspect their origins; no one else had the eye. She should be thrilled. She should be exhilarated. The next auction would go well; Greer would be happy; she'd prove she deserved her position. But something felt wrong. Why was it, she wondered, that sensations were always felt in your torso? Occasionally knees knocked and palms sweated, but everything else felt like a punch to the stomach, a knife in the belly, a tug at the heart.

"Let me make a few phone calls," she said. "I'll let you know soon." She would send him an e-mail in a day or two, thanking him politely but saying that she didn't think they were right for the house at this time, and wishing him luck in his endeavors.

"Please do," Klinman said. "Some of my clients are very old, and need medical help as well as closure, as you Americans say."

The hallway was brightly lit in contrast with the darkened room, and Elm had to blink when she stepped out. Klinman shut the door behind her softly, barely allowing it to click.

———

The inside of the Mercedes was upholstered in white leather, which Elm found ostentatious until it melted around her body as she sat in it. The backseat contained a folder of information to thumb through while the uniformed driver twisted and curved his way out of Paris. He barely spoke to her, only asking if the temperature was all right, and if she wanted music or silence, which increased her nervousness. Then he told her to look at her feet for the cooler if she wanted water while en route. It would take them about forty-five minutes, he said. He did not ask her if it was her first time in Paris, or comment on how lucky she was with the weather.

She fidgeted. If she crossed her legs, she slid at each turn across the white leather, but her feet weren't comfortable on the pristinely uphol-stered floor. She opened the folder. The literature was specific. It dia-grammed how the clone would be produced (*engendered* was the word they used). There was a sheet of paper on what to expect for the mother with a list of medications to take, and an additional sheet for the father. Elm noticed that neither had any of the clinic's contact information. She was abruptly terrified. She put one hand on top of the other to stop their shaking. When that didn't work, she tucked both under her thighs until they were numb from lack of circulation.

She sat back and looked out the window to calm herself. She opened it a crack to get some air and the driver immediately turned the fan on so that cold air blew on her shins. They were in the suburbs now. The housing projects rose from the ground, broken windows like corn cobs missing kernels. Men sat on the benches in playgrounds, the old ones resting their hands on their canes, the younger ones performing calisthenics. The few women Elm saw were wearing dark robes and long veils that hid their faces. She knew the outskirts of Paris were mostly Muslim, but she didn't expect to feel like she'd traveled to Yemen. She didn't think that the buildings would look so much like Detroit. Or, rather, if she was honest, like *Escape from New York*.

And then, just as suddenly, the projects ended and a field began. The scenery turned rural—a few stone farmhouses, an old barn. Some were obviously second homes whose manicured English lawns and in-ground pools betrayed their owners' wealth, while others were occupied by farmers. The small gardens were staked out back, tomato plants just beginning to climb. Occasionally, they passed through a small town, the houses built right up to the road, dating from before the invention of cars. Her driver sped through these towns, and Elm bobbed with the turns, attempting to avoid an open shutter or a leaning broom she was sure they were going to hit. As they drove by curtains ruffled, and Elm got a split-second glimpse into someone's life—a woman washing a baby in a large sink, a teenager talking on a telephone, an old man napping in a reclining chair—before they were out of the small town and back in the fields.

Elm thought the driver was deliberately trying to disorient her so that she wouldn't be able to find her way back to the clinic. He needn't have bothered. Elm's sense of direction was so poor she often relied on Moira to remember where they were going. Or they could have blindfolded her and gone directly, saved everyone some time.

They circled a roundabout and headed down a long dirt road that had recently been graded. When they got to a fence, seemingly in the middle of a field, the driver leaned out the window and swiped a card. The gate swung in. Only once they were inside did she see the guard station.

The clinic was smaller than she'd expected, and newer, though built to look like an old house. Two columns held up the front entryway and five pale stone steps led to an ornate door with decorative wrought iron. They drove counterclockwise around the circular driveway.

A man opened the door and held out a hand to help her out of the car. "Your voyage was fine, Madame?"

"Thanks," Elm said. He closed the door behind her and the car drove away before Elm could thank the driver, say good-bye, or debate tipping him.

"This way, Madame," the man said, gesturing with his hand up the stairs. When Elm reached the last step the large door opened.

While she waited for her eyes to adjust to the darkness within, she found herself questioning what she was doing there. Really, it was all very silly, a gothic novel. Now all that remained was for Count Dracula to approach her from behind and ask her if she wanted to stay for dinner.

Instead, a small man wearing khakis and a polo shirt appeared at her right. "Ms. Howells," he said. "So nice to meet you. I am Michel. We spoke on the telephone?"

She recognized the voice from their brief conversation. His accent sounded less pronounced in person, and he had a warm smile. His face was angular, his body compact.

"You would like to freshen up, after the journey? You are not experiencing vertigo?"

Elm shook her head. "I don't get carsick, luckily," she said. "I wouldn't mind freshening up though, thank you."

He pointed to a door along the hallway and Elm went in and closed it behind her. A powder room, wallpapered with violets, a pedestal sink, and a toilet paper stand. Elm sat down on the closed toilet lid and put her head in her hands. What was she doing here? She was embarrassed and frightened. She could no longer pretend she was here for a joke, or out of curiosity. She couldn't even relate the story afterward, in a "look what stupid thing I did" way. Traveling across an ocean on a lark wasn't funny. It was obsessive, pathetic. Crazy.

Her heart was pounding; French espresso was much stronger than coffee at home, and she felt a knot of anxiety. She went to the bathroom, then washed her hands and face in the sink. The soap was lavender, a scent her mother used. She'd washed all her makeup off, she realized, so she applied some lipstick, which just drew attention to her unshadowed eyes and unblushed cheeks.

Outside, she found Michel conversing softly with another man. He looked up at her as she came out. "Mattieu will get you a beverage. Would you like a coffee?"

"No, thank you," Elm said. "Just some water."

"Why don't we go to my office?" Michel said, using one arm around her back to herd her down the hallway. Their steps echoed on the marble. On the walls, Elm noticed a sort of fabric wallpaper that reminded her of the tapestries she'd seen hanging in castles in the Loire. The gothic novel, the castle in France, James Bond films: her mind was trying to make sense of this place, to render the unfamiliar recognizable.

The office was sparsely furnished, a large desk polished to mirror-like shininess and a large Aeron chair. In front there was a seating area with two suede chairs and a small table between them. Michel gestured to one and sat in the other.

"So," Michel said.

Elm smiled. Out the window she could see the round driveway she'd just come from. She looked at the windows—unbarred. Other than these two men, she'd seen no signs of life. She had expected . . . She didn't know. Pregnant women walking around, two-headed goats, identical Labradors. Not silence.

"Are you all right?" Michel asked.

Elm tried to reassure him, but then a lump in her throat rose faster than the words, and suddenly she was crying.

Michel reached over and handed her a box of tissues. Then he took her hand in his. Elm had not held hands with anyone besides Moira in years. Colin didn't like public displays of affection, and said it was difficult to walk attached to someone. Elm didn't really like them either. They seemed boastful. And yet, here was this stranger, holding her hand while she cried for no reason. Or, rather, for the same reason she always cried.

Michel said nothing. His hand was cool; it didn't squeeze. "I'm sorry," Elm said. She wanted to pull her hand away, but she didn't know how to do it without being rude.

"There is nothing to be sorry about," he said. "People come here and they tell me that they feel silly, or desperate or embarrassed. They're worried that we are taking advantage of their grief. I assure you, that is not the case. You should not feel embarrassed, any more than you would feel looking for a medical answer to a medical condition. And do not be afraid to hope. There is a very good chance we can return your son to you. But if we can't, you have tried everything in your power, exhausted every option, you see?"

Elm nodded, taking back her hand. She wiped her eyes. The tissue came back with deep black smudges from what was left of her mascara. She crumpled it into a ball and held it in her free fist.

"I wasn't expecting . . . this," she said. "I thought it would be a hospital, or a sanatorium or something. I didn't expect a mansion."

"We house the laboratory in an addition in back," he said. "And the in vitro is routine—it can be done at the office of any doctor. And then you have a normal pregnancy."

"I just thought it would be sort of like a farm, with animals? My friend . . . her dog—"

"We have another site for nonhuman subjects," Michel said, with such an earnestness that Elm smiled. "Maybe you'd like to tour the facilities?"

They stood and walked into the hallway. At the end, a sharp corner revealed glass doors secured with a fingerprinting panel. Michel put his second finger on the pad and said his name in a loud voice. The doors swung inward, revealing a small lab about the size of a high school science room and decorated somewhat similarly, with petri dishes and microscopes. Inside, two people were standing in front of what looked like a microwave oven, watching something inside whir and whistle. They smiled at Elm and said nothing. Michel led her to another door, which revealed an examining room with a table and stirrups. Behind a wall was a small operating theater, tidy and silent.

"And that is all," Michel said. "You'll never see any other guests here. And if you decide to go ahead, we will meet only once more."

They walked back into Michel's office. The space between the blinds projected a rectangular patch of light on the floor.

"You have questions?" Michel asked. He walked around the desk to sit down, motioning that Elm do the same in one of the two brown leather club chairs that faced it.

"I was wondering about . . . compensation."

"Our fee structure is outlined here." Michel handed her a sheet. "The total fee is $250,000. We ask that you make a down payment of forty percent. Another forty percent is due when we successfully replicate the DNA, and the third payment of $50,000 is due upon implantation. All of these deposits are nonrefundable. We can make no guarantees about the outcome of each of the parts of the proceedings. If a certain part of the process is unsuccessful and you would like to try again, and we consider it within our medical power to rectify the problem, then an additional $25,000 is required to retry that step. Is that clear?"

Elm took a deep breath. Where would she get that kind of money? "I'm not sure . . ."

"Say you decided to go ahead. You give me $100,000 as soon as possible, and the DNA sample. My lab retrieves the DNA and grows several cells to retrieve the DNA nucleus. You, meanwhile, take an estrogen receptor modulator to prepare yourself for egg retrieval. This is easy to order from Mexico or Canada. You will come to see us in about two months, at which point you will pay an additional $100,000 and we will retrieve your eggs. Wait, I remember in your file that you have poor ovarian reserve. Very well, we get a donor egg. That will add an additional $20,000 to the price, and increases the chance the egg won't implant, but only very slightly. Then you pay the remaining $50,000 and we implant the egg. Voilà."

"What kinds of things can go wrong?" Elm asked.

Michel blew air out of his cheeks in a way that reminded Elm of Colette, making a *poof* sound to indicate that many problems might occur. "Well," he said. "It has happened that the artifacts fail to produce a valid sample that we can extract DNA from. Sometimes, for reasons unknown, the cells fail to reproduce when implanted into an egg. Then there are the risks associated with IVF—that the egg won't implant, that the woman will have an ectopic pregnancy. And there are the associated risks of pregnancy—risk of genetic mutation, risk of cells that divide unevenly. There's also the possibility, though we've never seen it, of identical twins."

He sat back and crossed his legs. "I should tell you too that there is a higher instance of miscarriage among cloned fetuses. We're not sure why. And a higher risk of genetic malformations. Of course, you can choose to terminate any fetus that shows these signs. However, what you might have heard about the genes being improperly expressed is nonsense. We simply changed the medium for growth and the cells mature normally."

Elm shook her head. "What kind of elevated risk of genetic malformations?"

"We estimate it to be twice as high as a regular pregnancy, which is still fairly low. There is only the normal risk of pregnancy to the woman."

Elm shifted. "What about, I've read, I mean, that there are diseases that . . ."

"The risks I outlined are the only ones we have seen. Will your husband be participating?"

"I haven't talked to him about it," Elm admitted.

"We each grieve differently," Michel said. "I do not pretend to get involved in marriage negotiations, but we will need to discuss what you will want to do."

"How come you can do this and no one else can?" Elm asked.

"You think no one else can clone?" he said. "That we are somehow light-years ahead of other governments and private institutions? No." He shook his head. "The technology is there. They are afraid."

There was a small silence while Elm stifled her desire to question the man's bravery. She was reminded of Colin's joke: "The pharmaceutical companies cured the common cold years ago but haven't released the cure to the public because it will cut down on cold remedy profits." There was something about the doctor's attitude that irked her; his self-righteousness. She supposed, though, that you would have to believe deeply in the rightness of your cause to ignore its ethical and legal implications.

"What about the law?" she asked.

Michel shrugged. "They know about us; they have to. But who would bring charges, and for what? Every government agency claims this is the jurisdiction of another. In any event, you would mostly likely be unimpeachable—you are living in a different country. And how would they prove that it was a clone? I wouldn't worry. That said, it would of course be in your best interest to keep the information a secret. . . ." He slowed his voice down so that Elm understood it was a veiled threat, and she was back in the gothic novel from earlier. Her hesitation must have shown on her face, because Michel drew in a deep breath to continue.

"Yes, it's against the law, but so are many other things we do daily that we don't consider crimes: walking against the streetlight, for example, or not reporting the money we pay the babysitter on our income taxes. These are crimes without victims. The legal prohibition against cloning hinges on the fear of its abuse. Because the potential for abuse is there, people have thrown the baby out with the bathwater, pardon the expression. Consider this: Do you think it is a crime to want your child back? Who does it hurt when we succeed? I think you'll come to the same conclusion I did."

Elm thought. His argument made logical sense, but it was the logic of the criminal. Still, Elm imagined herself holding Ronan again, his blind eyes closed while his puckered mouth sought out her breast through her shirt. She would give anything, anything, to be able to watch him retrace his path, to outlive his eight-year-old self, to hit ten, then enter high school, to go to college, get married, have children of his own. As his mother, she owed him this chance. As his mother, she deserved it too.

"How does the payment work? How do I get the money to you?"

"You're buying an oil portrait of the deceased," Michel smiled. "On installment. And you will get the oil painting as well. I'm afraid it won't be very good."

"I might even get a tax write-off," Elm said, attempting humor.

"So," Michel stood up. "Do you need time to consider?"

"No," Elm said, surprising herself. She felt a strong sense of relief at having made the decision she wanted to all along. She knew she would try. She had to. Why even pretend to hesitate?

Michel smiled widely. "I'm so glad," he said. "From the pictures I saw online he is a fine, handsome boy. I'm glad we'll be able to give you some comfort."

"I brought you . . . what you need," Elm said. She reached into her purse and took out the envelope with Ronan's DNA samples. She had to force herself to hand them over, these pieces of her son. And it seemed impossible that this envelope would re-create Ronan, that this doctor had the gift of necromancy. And yet, she clung to the hope that he did.

"I don't have the cash. I'll need to . . . move some things around."

Michel accepted the envelope. "I'll get Pierre to drive you back. When you send in the first installment, we will let you know if the DNA extraction is successful. Then we can talk about the next step."

As the driver wound back through the small towns of the rural countryside, Elm's relief began to take on a more anxious edge. Where was she supposed to get the money? She could cash in her 401(k), but that would cover only the down payment. Even if she were somehow able to convince Colin that this was a good idea, they would be able to scrape together maybe fifty thousand dollars. They could sell the apartment, she guessed. She clenched and unclenched her fists until the car dropped her off back at the hotel.

There was one other way to get money, but it seemed so farfetched that Elm couldn't even consider it. Or could she? Presumably, she could do it on the sly. And it wasn't illegal, exactly. Not the most moral decision, but a victimless crime, like the cloning. And then the decision felt inevitable, a force moving with the laws of nature propelling it forward. It was desperate, yes, but she was desperate. Consideration to decision lasted a surprisingly short time. When she got back to the hotel, she didn't even put her purse down before she took out the card and dialed the number Augustus Klinman had given her.

"I have a proposition," she said.

———

Colin spent more than a minute unlocking the door. It was after ten p.m. Elm sat on the couch watching a *Law and Order* episode she'd already seen. She'd been back from Paris for two weeks, but had somehow never found the proper time, or adequate words, to tell him the details of her trip.

He stumbled a bit on the entry rug before he noticed Elm looking at him. "I'm sorry," he said. "I should have rung. Were you worried?"

Elm could hear the descending chords in the background, signaling a change of scene. Was the jury back in? Was there a development at the precinct? She fought the urge to turn her attention back to the television.

"I've had the longest fecking day," he said, throwing his jacket on the chair and kicking off his shoes. He came around to sit next to Elm, taking her feet in his lap. She hadn't changed since coming home from work, and her feet were still stockinged. She wiggled her toes but he didn't rub them.

He smelled faintly of alcohol and sweat; tired, stale sweat, like being in an airless meeting all day, which was probably what he had been doing before he went to a bar, either alone or with people from work. She didn't care that he drank, only that it was an activity he embarked on without her. It was another distancing factor.

"What happened?" she asked. *Guilty,* the foreman said. The television defendant burst into tears, mouthing, *Why? Why?* at the startled jury. The credits began to scroll on the right of a split screen. The other half plugged the nightly news.

"Can we talk about it in the morning?" he asked, turning to her. His face was so forlorn, so utterly exhausted, that it reminded her of the morning he had arrived in Bangkok, soulless and failed.

"Okay," she said. Then a pause. "No, you have to tell me now."

"It's not bad," he said. "Can we leave it, Elm? Need a kip. A little pissed, I am. I'll look in on the beanbag?"

"Just let her sleep," Elm said. "Tell her you looked in on her and she slept through it."

In the early morning, Elm woke up to the sound of Colin peeing long into the toilet, and then the hinge of the medicine cabinet where he was probably taking something for a headache. Then she heard the whir of the electric toothbrush.

The bed began to grow cold. Elm stretched, and suddenly, she wanted Colin. "Come back to bed," she called.

"In a minute," he said. "I want to shower."

This was marriage, then, she thought. Sublimated desire, delayed gratification. She had thought marriage would fulfill some of these needs, emotional as well as sexual, that having a permanent partner would end her loneliness, her frustration, her anxiety. But no, she often had to wait as long for release as when she was single, when she waited for her girlfriends to get off work so they could meet for a drink, spend the evening identifying then flirting with a stranger, making out with him outside the bar before giving him a fake number and slipping away in a taxi.

He came to her smelling of soap and shampoo, and a little like deodorant, a bouquet of artificial scents. She surprised herself by attacking him. Usually, their morning lovemaking was leisurely and half-asleep. He typically started it, and often she could catch a few more minutes of shut-eye afterward. Not so this morning. She bit his ears, held his arms down while she straddled him, then insisted on a position they didn't normally use.

Afterward, she pulled the sheet around her. It was still early. Moira wouldn't stir for another thirty minutes. She felt better—less frustrated, but still anxious.

"Now you'll tell me," she said.

"What?" he asked. He was dozing again, his eyes half-closed.

"What was bothering you yesterday."

"Oh," he said. "Al resigned."

"What?" Elm was shocked. Al had been Colin's boss for ten years. He had been at the company for nearly twenty.

"He just quit?" she asked.

"Pretty much," Colin said, stretching. "He said he didn't want to work under that admin."

"That's insane," Elm said. She twisted around to face Colin. "What's he going to do?"

Colin said, "Fuck if I know. His noncompete clause means he won't be working in the pharmaceutical industry, at least." Colin closed his eyes again, avoiding looking at her.

"Colin," Elm said. "What does that mean for you?"

"I"—he paused—"no longer have an advocate. Which means that possibly I no longer have a job."

"What?"

"Or, maybe they'll promote me. I can't really say at the moment."

"How can you be so . . ." Elm searched for the right word. "Nonchalant? This is your future. You have a noncompete agreement too."

"I'm not in a tizzy, Cabbage, because it's not something I have any control over at the moment."

"What do you mean? Don't call me Cabbage. I hate vegetable endearments. We need to plan or something. Did Al really resign? For good? Irreparably?"

"Afraid so. Elm, we just have to wait. Don't you think I'm bloody worried too?"

Elm's secret chafed like an itch, like an inflammation of the conscience. This would be the time to tell Colin. She could pretend she was joking, see what his reaction would be. And then he would stop her, because, of course, someone needed to talk her out of this insanity. Because she was thinking about it as something she'd already done. Or rather, something that the person who was inside her body had done. She felt so removed from herself that her hands were things of wonder, her knees foreign.

She should tell him now. Now, she urged herself. But it would be so easy to pretend that she hadn't purposely stopped taking the pill, that it had simply failed. And then they wouldn't have to have that conversation, the one where he voiced all the nagging worries she was pushing down into her subconscious, the uncomfortable distance that arose whenever they talked about Ronan, like the topic was a furnace grate that blasted hot air when opened.

Colin was already out of bed and in his boxers. "I'll get Moira up for school," he said.

———

Relay Lacker operated her art-consulting business from a small office in Midtown, but suggested an upscale restaurant near Tinsley's on the Upper East Side when Elm invited her to lunch.

Elm ordered the least stomach-turning thing on the menu, but even as her Cobb salad arrived she knew she wouldn't be able to eat it. She pushed it around with her fork while they made small talk.

"So," Elm said, hiding half of an egg under a large piece of lettuce where it wouldn't stare at her. "I've asked you to lunch because I would like to discuss some business."

"I'm all ears," Relay said. She smiled, and Elm caught just a glimpse of a gap between her teeth and gums. She'd had porcelain veneers put on. Elm didn't know anyone who had done that, and she wanted to ask her about it, but it didn't seem appropriate.

"I have available these drawings for sale, really beautiful pieces. A Piranesi, two Canalettos, a couple of Connoises, Ganedis, or at least from their schools, new to the market."

"Ooh," Relay said. She leaned forward on her elbows. "I don't know the last artist."

"I was wondering if your private clients might like to take a look at them."

Relay sat up. "Mostly they're interested in modern art, but . . . Why wouldn't you put them up for auction at Tinsley's?"

Elm chose her words carefully. "Their provenances are sort of slim. Art owned by Jews, stolen by the Nazis and recently recovered. Their sale goes toward reparations for the families, you know, the ones who survived."

Relay furrowed her brow. "So you don't want them for Tinsley's, but you want to foist them off on me?"

Elm laughed, though Relay was close to the truth. "It's not like that. I just can't verify the ownership to the extent that the house demands. But they're really beautiful pieces, and the cause, so to speak, is good."

"What kind of a financial arrangement would you be looking for?"

Elm had planned out what she was prepared to offer, but she pretended to consider. "How about we split the twenty percent commission?"

Relay nodded.

"And, my name stays out of it," Elm said. "That's really important. Obviously, I'm not supposed to deal privately, but I really want to see these pieces end up in good hands."

"So I'll deal directly with the sellers," Relay said.

"Well, actually, me, and I'll deal with the Englishman who is selling them on behalf of the owners. They want to remain anonymous."

"Okay . . ." Relay dragged the word out, the thinking evident in her pause. She seemed about to ask a question, then thought better of it. "Yeah, that works. Send me the PDFs." Relay held out her hand for Elm to shake, an odd formality that amused Elm.

When the check came, Relay insisted on paying, even though Elm had invited her to lunch. "Because you're bringing me business, that's why," she said.

This had been so easy, Elm thought. Why had she thought it would be impossible to sell Klinman's drawings? She didn't even have to pay for lunch.

———

Relay called her the following week and left Elm a voice mail saying she thought she had a buyer for a couple of the drawings. Elm called her back.

"I think you know them? You were at their party? The people with, you know, the dog?" Relay had the unfortunate habit on the phone of raising her voice at the end of each sentence so that each statement sounded uncertain.

Elm looked at her fingernails, feigning nonchalance, even over the telephone. "Super," she said.

"They want the old woman? And the beach scene?"

"Great."

"They offered $175,000 for both."

Elm sat up straighter. She did some quick math: 80 percent to Klinman and his clients, the remaining 20 percent split between Relay and Elm. That would come to $17,500. "That's a little low," she said.

"I know." Relay sighed as though they were discussing a common evil, like traffic or losing sports teams. "But they were concerned about the certificates, the provenance not being so great, you know? Resale and all that. They're investors, not collectors." Relay lowered her voice, confiding in Elm.

"I'll have to consult the seller," Elm said, swiveling her chair back to face her desk. She didn't know if Klinman would take it. They had hoped to sell them for $100,000 each. But if the sums she was receiving were smaller she would attract less attention.

As she hung up she considered too that she wasn't sure where Relay's loyalties belonged. Of course, she'd want to negotiate the best deal to earn her commission, but maybe she had a side deal going with the collectors, or "investors," as she called them. Maybe she wanted to get them a deal so they'd use her more. Maybe . . . maybe . . . it was impossible to tell.

Elm knew she did not have a criminal mind. The entire business made her queasy. Plus she knew these people. She'd been in their home. She had assumed the buyers would be unknown, at least to her. This made it more personal. Real criminal masterminds (at least in the movies) were free from anxiety. They slept dreamlessly at night. Meanwhile, Elm was lucky if she got two straight hours.

The worst-case scenario, she decided. I'll think of the worst-case scenario and then I'll feel better. She imagined herself pregnant, behind bars. Fired, bankrupt from an extended lawsuit. And still she didn't regret her decision to clone Ronan. That must mean something, surely.

She wondered where Klinman got them. How far back did the forgery go? To the Holocaust survivors? Did they even exist? Had Klinman commissioned the art or was he being manipulated?

She sent Klinman a brief message asking him to call her. Then she was sorry she had done so from the office. That would increase her liability. She made a mental note to buy one of those calling cards next time. She was getting better at this. Pretty soon she'd sleep through the night.

Part Three

Fall 2007

Elm

Elm tripped over a cable that hadn't yet been taped to the carpet. She caught the edge of a chair, banging her elbow in the process.

"Watch out, Mrs. Howells," one of the facilities guys said. "You okay? We don't want you to sue." He laughed; she wouldn't sue her own family. Still, she heard a little derision in his voice.

"I'm fine. Can't get rid of me that easy." She looked at the empty room, numbered chairs at the ready, red carpets vacuumed neatly. In this room her fate would be decided.

She walked to the front to check on the catalogs. "They're almost all gone," the receptionist said. "Don't worry." She pressed on her earpiece to receive a call.

Elm took a catalog, though she had plenty at her desk. She paced back across the floor and went up to the mezzanine gallery. There they were on display, in a row like solitaire cards: Indira's *Mercat* and her other treasures, alongside the rest of the items to be sold. Elm felt the old thrill of seeing her pieces come to auction. When she had made her first acquisitions, she felt almost like the artist. The power she had over the drawings was enormous. She decided their reserve, how they'd be listed in the catalog, where they would hang, what part of the mailing list might be interested. Then she waited anxiously in the back of the auction room for the lots to be called, as nervous as a pianist at her first recital.

The day waned, the hour of the auction approaching, Elm's anxiety mounting. Her first few auctions had been heady, then Elm settled into the routine and began almost to dread them. They seemed to be the worst part of her job. Procuring and curating works was worthwhile, noble, even. But selling them, and to the highest bidder, no less, seemed lacking in respect. So she had stopped thinking of the auctions as mercenary affairs and instead began to view that part of her job as a necessary evil. She put her head down and did what she was supposed to do. And then Ronan died and it all seemed even more like a shadow puppet show, like something someone else was doing.

The room was filling up, some of the regular characters—George de Marie Bosque, the drawing collector; the man whose name she could never remember who wrote that blog artsnob.com; and a curator from a nascent Impressionist art museum. He'd come in before the auction, explaining that he wanted to add to the already impressive collection donated by its founders, the Lees, wealthy Asian Americans. There were some dealers and art advisers, and a celebrity she recognized as being from one of those forensic television shows. Relay was there too.

Elm stood off in the wings. From there she had a clear view of the mounting platform as well as the audience. She waited until 7:00, then 7:05, when the auctioneer called for attention. The room was about two-thirds filled. Three auction agents were on phones at the side of the room, taking requests from anonymous bidders or those who could not be present at the auction. Usually these were Russians, eager to spend their new wealth. Though they especially liked contemporary pieces, they occasionally spent vast amounts of cash on important older items.

The platform spun slowly, and the first drawing was displayed. A Woodridge that Indira had consigned garnered an appreciative murmur from the crowd. Elm's bladder clenched. The auctioneer announced the minimum of $120,000, and the bidding began. The curator from the Lee museum raised his paddle. The auctioneer acknowledged him by name. Then a severe-suited woman Elm didn't recognize pushed the bid to $130,000. An older man, shirt slightly wrinkled and jacket shiny, raised again. Elm saw he had missed a spot shaving, a small patch of dark near his chin. She'd noticed that about older men; they had a neglected air, like the damp pages of an old book. No one to oversee their ablutions.

Elm wasn't sure how she felt about the auctioneer, Petr Hoosman, a Dutchman who wore patriotic orange ties every day. He had come to the auction house as an accountant, but was quickly encouraged to enroll in the auctioneer education department. Unlike a typical lackadaisical Tinsley auctioneer, he had his own gregarious, untraditional patter. He recognized important auction attendees, studying pictures of bidders and price lists before the auction, but never let on that he prepared obsessively. His shoes bordered on boat wear, and his sunglasses were eternally in his breast pocket. He had studiously floppy hair in the early Beatles style and was attractive, with high cheekbones and a lopsided dimple. Ian had had an enormous crush on him for a year, though no one was ever able to figure out his sexual preferences. He flirted indiscriminately with young and old, men and women (dogs, even), and after Elm had declared him asexual, Ian had corrected her: "Omnisexual."

"What's that?"

"Kind of like pansexual, you know, but instead of having desire for all types of sexual experiences, omnis just use sex, or the threat of it, to get what they want."

They were having a martini lunch, an occasional ritual on slow Fridays. She leaned over and sipped her full drink. "I guess," Elm said. She had had a bit of a crush on Petr too, the harmless fluttering she associated with the second decade of marriage. Just enough to make coming to work interesting, but nothing she would ever act on. She called these crushes "ab rollers," mostly futile exercise to keep the flirt muscle tight.

"Plus, I saw him in the bathroom"—Ian leaned closer, a sign that he was about to make a vulgar statement—"and, shall we say, it's all bluster."

"I thought you weren't supposed to look at each other in there."

"I snuck a peek."

"Are we talking gherkin, Fruit Roll-Up, or Second Avenue Deli pickle?"

"What's a Fruit Roll-Up?"

Elm sighed. Sometimes Ian's youth was tiresome. "A snack. . . . It doesn't matter."

"Normal, I guess, small size." Ian cast his eyes about the room, looking for a comparable object. "Um, like if you rolled up that cell phone."

Elm nodded, though she had no idea what this would look like. After that discussion, though, her ardor for Petr had waned to a trickle then dried up completely.

Now, though, she could see Petr's appeal, and the way both sexes responded to him. The attendees were beginning to relax: shoulders slumped, legs slack. There were genuine smiles appearing on the faces of bidders, not just grimaces of concentration. Petr had been a good hire, had shaken up the image of staid Tinsley's and injected it with a bit of youth and iconoclasm.

The bidding reached its estimated $135,000. Lee's representative bid again, and the bidding stalled at $140,000. Then a new bidder at the back of the room raised her paddle, and Petr squinted into the lights to see her. He must not have known who she was, a certain blow to his ego. A dark horse, bidding the price up to $145,000. Petr acknowledged her as the "woman in the blue suit toward the back."

Then Relay raised her paddle for $150,000. This was a bit uncouth. No one liked a buyer to sweep in at the end of a bid. Elm found herself silently critiquing Relay's outfit—Ann Taylor Petites for sure, pearls as accessories. Were you allowed to wear pearls without irony anymore?

Apparently, Petr knew her, because he supplied her name on the first bid. But Elm guessed that as a Lacker, Relay had been around art royalty since she could be relied on not to drool on it.

Between volleys, Relay hunched over, leaning on her elbows. She bid by raising the paddle high, like a cat springing to action. When Petr awarded her the drawing, at $207,500, Relay looked estatic, beaming like a child who finally got the pony she'd been begging for.

Then Indira's *Mercat*, the crown of Elm's contribution to the auction, made its appearance. The audience gasped. It was indeed beautiful; the texture of the pastel glinted in the stage lights. The woman's eye, the dog's tail, the blue sky, the scales of the fish for sale glistening. It was a magnificent lighting display and Elm was proud at having orchestrated the arrangement with facilities. If she'd left it up to them, they'd have just shined a fluorescent bulb straight at it like they were interrogating a prisoner.

The woman in the blue suit who bid on the first sketch raised her paddle, and now Petr, who had learned her name in the interim (his staff was nothing if not competent and swift, delivering updates into his earpiece), called her Mrs. Kostlestein and then shortened it to Mrs. K in subsequent acknowledgments like he'd known her for years.

The piece, which had been on reserve for $750,000 and expected to fetch as much as $850,000, managed to reach $900,000 before being awarded to the woman in the blue suit. Elm let herself hope, near the end, that it would reach seven digits, that magical threshold that would really make people stand up and take notice. But bidding had petered out, and Elm tried to remember that it had done well, better than she'd expected.

Elm smiled. Finally, she let herself relax, and realized she had been worrying a hangnail on her index finger and a bright spot of blood had formed. She stuck her finger in her mouth to stanch it. She looked up and could see Greer staring down at the proceedings from the private room. Ian winked at her from across the room, smiling widely. It was his victory too.

Other lots came up and were purchased. Two mediocre Callebaut sketches didn't make their reserve. Indira's esoteric postcard oils sold to a miniature fetishist. Then, though it seemed that no time at all had passed, all the lots had been presented. The auction was over.

Elm called Indira as soon as she got back to her desk. "Good news!"

"It sold well, then?" Indira tried to rein herself in, but the anxiety sounded in her voice, which rose squeakily at the end of the sentence. Elm wondered what she needed the money for. Medical bills? A debt?

"Very . . . $900,000."

"Oh, that's wonderful!" Indira sounded, like Elm, more relieved than happy.

"You'll collect about $550,000 when all is said and done," Elm half-apologized, though she had been careful to explain the terms to Indira in front of her lawyer to make sure she understood. Though Indira was a famous artist, she was still an Attic and had to be treated like one. "Plus the Woodridge and the oils."

Elm went back to her office to shut down her computer and collect her purse. An e-mail had arrived from Greer, asking her to lunch the following day. Elm sneered at it. *Now* he wanted to be a relative, now that she'd had some success. She left it in her in-box. Let him sweat it a little.

Ian stood in her doorway. "Grab a drink?" he asked.

"Can't," Elm answered. "I haven't been home in years, it feels like."

Ian smiled, the ends of his mouth turning up disingenuously. "All right. We'll celebrate another time. It was smashing, wasn't it?"

"Smashing?"

"I'm trying it out," Ian said. "What do you think?"

"I don't know," Elm said, standing and reaching for her purse.

"Gnarly auction, dude." Ian led the way to the elevator.

"Did I see your friend there?"

"Who, Relay? Yeah. We had a chance to catch up. It was nice." Ian leaned over and pushed the elevator call button, then looked at something down the hall.

"What?" Elm asked.

"Hmmm? I didn't say anything." Ian flashed her the same smile he gave the really dumb cashier at Starbucks who always charged him for an au lait instead of a latte. The smile that actually meant its opposite.

"What's wrong?" Elm asked.

"Not a thing." Ian put his arm in front of the elevator door, making sure it stayed open for Elm. "Have a lovely evening."

———

For two weeks Elm had been giving herself shots of Lupron and estradiol/progesterone in the bathroom after Colin left for work. She hid the medication with the stinky cheese in the refrigerator, one place she felt confident Colin would not look, as he hated any kind of blue cheese, claimed its smell of decay upset him and that it made no sense to eat anything rotten. He was irritable. He wouldn't tell Elm what was going on at work, which would have worried her in the past. But she wasn't paying the slightest bit of attention to her husband, occupied instead with deceiving him.

She blamed her inattention on hormones. She felt swollen, perpetually about to get her period, a little crampy, and so, so tired. Her ass was sore from her inept poking with the needle, and she had flashes of anger at Colin because he wasn't sharing this with her, wasn't helping her through this time, wasn't giving her the injections himself, then rubbing the pain out of the flesh with the heel of his hand.

Intermittently, she was subsumed in an enveloping heat. She fanned herself and undid another button on her too-tight shirt. The side effects of the fertility medication made her a teenager again—mood swings and breast tenderness. She had almost thrown a coffee cup at Colin the previous morning when he ate the last piece of raisin toast.

Elm hadn't anticipated that seducing her husband would be so difficult. She had a very small window, she realized, to pretend to get pregnant before she flew back to France. Michel had given her explicit instructions when he called to tell her they'd successfully extracted and replicated DNA from the samples she'd left with him.

She asked Wania to stay overnight with Moira and booked a fancy dinner and a hotel room in Midtown. But though it was Friday, Colin got stuck at work and didn't make it back to the city until after nine p.m.

When he walked in, Elm and Wania were watching television. Moira lay in her pajamas in a sleeping bag on the living room floor.

"Hi," Colin said sheepishly.

"Hello," Wania whispered. "The baby's asleep."

"Not a baby," Moira mumbled, barely conscious.

"Then let's go sleep in your big girl bed," Elm said, ignoring Colin's hello. "Wania can take you."

Moira was too tired to argue. Wania lifted her up and carried her down the hall.

"I'm fucking knackered," Colin said, falling onto the couch, not bothering even to set down his briefcase. "And we missed dinner."

"Well, I ate," Elm snapped. "Pizza with Wania and Moira."

"I'm so sorry," Colin said. "I know you went to a lot of trouble."

"Yeah, well . . ." Elm focused on the television.

"Is this *Finding Nemo*?"

"It's oddly compelling," Elm said. "Even the five-hundred-and-first time."

There was a silence that lasted so long Elm wondered if Colin had fallen asleep. "Can we go, still, to the hotel?" she asked.

"Ummm," Colin considered. "Okay. I'll just shower, then."

"No," Elm said. "Shower there. I'll help you."

Colin smiled tightly in a way that showed more politeness than interest. He stood and went over to the table where the leftover pizza was oozing onto the cardboard box. He rolled up a piece and shoved the whole thing into his mouth, chewing as he went down the hall to the bedroom.

Elm peeked into Moira's room. Wania was lying in the trundle, reading a gossip magazine. "We're going now," she said.

Wania nodded. "Okay. Have a good time, then."

Elm paused. She suddenly had an overwhelming desire to confide everything to Wania, to hear her calm, lilting acceptance. She was outside of Elm's world, and Elm wanted Wania to take her in her arms the way she did Moira when the little girl was upset about something. This was a skill Elm had never mastered, the art of comforting. She felt how inept she was at it every time Moira attempted to seek solace. But the desire to tell Wania that she was attempting to get pregnant with

Ronan's clone faded just as quickly as it had arisen, and Elm realized how stupid it would sound. When she had the baby, if she had the baby, she could never tell anyone who he really was. Ever.

When Elm walked into the bedroom, Colin had changed from his suit into a pair of jeans and a collared shirt. She walked over to him, sorry for being so cold to him earlier. She hugged him to her and heard him sigh heavily, felt his breath hot on her neck. He pulled away. "I—" he started.

Elm said, "Let's just go."

She checked them into the hotel while Colin waited just behind her. Once in the minuscule room he flopped down on the bed facefirst. "I should shower," he mumbled, sounding much like Moira's sleepy insistence.

Elm lay down next to him on the bed. "I miss you," she said.

He rolled over; his eyes remained closed. "I miss you too. Work's been . . . I don't know if I can take it any longer, Elm."

Elm didn't say anything. He couldn't quit now. They'd need the money, especially after she'd raided their accounts to pay Michel.

"It's bad, Elm." He pulled his knees to his chest, fetal style. "I haven't told you because, well, it's not that I don't want you to worry, rather . . . it's proprietary, but more than that, it's just that it's borderline, well, fuck, it's . . . it's one of those things it's better not to know."

"Okay . . ." Elm stretched the word out. She didn't really understand what he was saying. She knew it was important. She knew she should pay attention, but she was so singularly focused on her goal that she was having trouble concentrating.

"They might call me in to testify," he said.

Elm drew in a sharp breath. Had she really been paying so little attention that Colin had done something illegal? Hidden evidence of a drug trial that would require the drug to be pulled from the market? Had he embezzled funds, or helped someone embezzle them?

"Could you be charged with something?" Elm asked. She permitted herself a horrible fantasy image of being a single mother with an imprisoned husband, asking Wania to move into the apartment so she could care for Moira and the new Ronan full-time while Elm worked her ass off to make ends meet. Then Greer Tinsley would really have something to hold against her.

"God, no. Elm!" Colin opened his eyes and looked at her incredulously. "What are you thinking? No, I'm not a criminal. It's my department that's in trouble, not me. For chrissakes!" He was offended.

"Sorry," Elm said. She decided to pretend that she'd been joking. She smiled and his face softened.

Colin was so earnestly honest. When they wrote their vows for their wedding, he insisted on including an honesty clause—it was that important to him. And here she was not only deceiving him but forcing him to abet her. She had been hoping, she realized, that he would confess to having committed some crime, or at least an indiscretion. She also saw, equally as surprisingly, that her recurring worry that he was having an affair was her desire to see him humbled by a poor decision or a regret, the same way she was every day of her existence. She felt relieved that he might be capable of deceit as well. She understood then that she would never tell him about Ronan, that she would always have to keep it a secret until their graves. Her chest collapsed with the weight of it.

"I'll go shower. Then we can talk more," Colin said.

She watched him sit up from her position on the bed. He took off his shoes and placed them next to the nightstand, a gesture of neatness he never managed at home. Then he pulled his button-down over his head. He was still thin, but doughy in a way that he hadn't been when she married him. He had a small belly, which bulged over the belt of his pants, and his chest was fleshy with sparse hair. He turned away from her—residual shyness, after all these years?—and took off his pants. He walked in his boxers to the bathroom and closed the door. She could hear him pee, then the rush of the shower.

She took off her skirt and top as well. She'd bought new lingerie for this excursion, black lace with small red bows. When he emerged with the towel wrapped around his waist, he uttered a caricatured fake whistle in appreciation. Then he pulled back the covers and dropped the towel, revealing the same boxer shorts.

He lay down and Elm scooted toward him, putting her leg up over him and rubbing her mouth against his neck. He sighed and did not stir.

"Elm," he said, craning his neck back, "would you be angry if we didn't . . ."

"No," she said, a little too brightly.

He didn't catch the disingenuousness in her voice; he murmured, "Thanks, grand," and fell asleep.

Elm turned over onto her back and put her arm over her eyes. She felt tears start and clenched her teeth to hold them back. Why was she crying? How was it possible to feel so lonely with your husband of over a decade snoring softly beside you?

It was a big decision, choosing to lie. And she had done it so cavalierly. This must be what adulterers felt—caught up in the moment and hit by the magnitude of their duplicity. She felt almost sorry for cheaters at that moment. Certainly their pain was worse than that of the faithful spouse who suspects nothing.

She had known, though, that of the two of them she would be the one to betray. A friend of hers from college had made the astute comment, wise before her years, that in each relationship there was one who loved more than the other, the belover and the beloved. It was easier in medieval times, she said, when the roles were defined, the inequality accepted. Now it was among our neo-romantic myths that love should be equally distributed, like communal wealth.

In Elm's first real relationship, she had been the belover. She had loved Jason so intensely that she told herself it didn't matter if his love was less ardent, less pressing. She would have sacrificed anything for him. And when he broke up with her (kindly, he was always kind), his flaw was that he didn't love her enough, and she swore she'd never be the one to give more than she got again. When Colin came into her life, and loved her with a passion equal to that she'd felt for Jason, she found herself in the position she considered correct. She loved him, very much, and she liked him too. But there was something about his love for her—patient, completely unconditional—that Elm knew her love for him couldn't match. And here was the proof. She was willing to risk her marriage on a science experiment.

In the morning, Colin woke her up by pressing an erection into her back and they made love. In the moment, Elm was able to convince herself that this act was creating Ronan; this merging of bodies and souls in this Midtown hotel was sparking the life that would soon grow inside her. But as she lay there while Colin ordered Continental breakfast, wondering aloud as he did each time they stayed in a hotel about why it was called Continental breakfast since no one he knew from the Continent ever ate like that, not even those German wankers, Elm reminded herself that she was taking hormones to sync her cycle with the egg donor's, and that as much as she wanted to believe that they could re-create Ronan by themselves, it was science that would ultimately provide them with the son that nature had taken away. Colin looked at her and smiled in such an innocent and unadulteratedly happy way that she was almost able to forgive herself.

————

On the plane from JFK, Elm sat with her head against the window, holding a James Patterson novel she'd bought in the airport. She watched the ground recede and then the clouds bounce off the wing. A drop of water formed on the window, rolled across its plastic surface, and flew off into the expanse of air. Elm was startled when land appeared three hours later, but then remembered that the fastest way to Europe was to fly north and east before turning south again. So that large island would be Greenland, or Nova Scotia. Then she fell asleep and woke, unrested, to the smell of baked croissants coming from the first-class section of the plane. Cruel, to do that to economy passengers. Self-moving freight, she heard they were called by airline staff. Such contempt we all have for our clients, she thought.

Elm had liquidated all the stocks she could, sold her Magritte sketch to a private collector, and emptied her 401(k) (with penalties), but she still needed to come up with $150,000. So far, her deal with Relay had earned her $30,000. She was contemplating taking out a home equity loan, if she could manage to do so online so Colin wouldn't know about it. Of course, by tax time, he would. But by then she'd be pregnant. She knew she was digging herself into a hole, but she wanted this so badly that she would endure a prison sentence, torture, to have the opportunity to see Ronan one more time. If he could just come home once, after playing baseball in Central Park, and she could smell the outdoors on his hair, the mowed grass and the slightly sweet scent of child perspiration, fragrant, not sour like adult sweat, she would give anything.

Calm down, she told herself, knowing that her hope might be too strong, that it was possible she would need two or three implantations before she got pregnant. Where she would come up with that extra money was beyond her. Maybe she would start stealing art, she joked to herself. At least she knew what was worth stealing.

Tinsley's had arrested and prosecuted an employee two years ago.

He was a new hire, working within the transportation department, and someone reported him walking off with a tiny Giacometti sculpture. He claimed he had removed it by accident and then, when he discovered his mistake, was going to return it the next day, a lame enough story that Elm almost believed him—surely a lie would be better constructed. Security grew tighter after that. All employee bags were searched, even, oddly, on the way into the building.

They served the breakfast, tasteless melon balls and chewy rolls with butter and sugared jelly. She looked down at the Parisian outskirts as the plane descended, trying to see the clinic, but all the large houses looked alike from this height.

She stayed in the same hotel. They gave her a room overlooking an air shaft, and she considered complaining but then decided it would be quieter and darker than if she were facing the avenue. She left her bag on the bed and went out, walking along the Seine, passing Australians and Germans (most French knew better than to take the scenic route).

The Seine wasn't really water, in Elm's opinion. There was nothing about it that was riverlike. At most, it was an excuse for historic bridges, a way to maintain the vista of the opposite bank. No one walked along it, no barges trawled, no commerce was conducted, and it never rippled. Yet it was probably one of the most famous rivers in the world. In front of her, a dog stopped to pee, looking at her. The urine, green against the stones, shiny like antifreeze, slinked down the pavement toward the water.

She had lunch in a cute little square with a fountain in its center. She was early; the seating area was almost empty and the waiters were crowded together like bored pigeons. She ordered an omelet with salad and sipped water while she waited for it to arrive. Her anxiety turned to hunger and she nibbled on bread.

Tomorrow at this time she would be at the clinic. There would be a syringe there with the few cells that were almost Ronan and she would climb up onto the table and put her feet in the stirrups and then pray for implantation.

Her eggs arrived, and the symbolism of what she'd ordered struck her. She put down her fork and drank more water to quell the gag reflex.

She took the *métro* back up to the Seventh and bought a ticket for the Musée Rodin, one of her favorite museums in Paris. She had always loved Rodin; she had taken her first sculpture class because of him. But sculpture was so technical—the clay models, the covering with wax to make the negative mold, the pouring of the metal and then the melting of the wax, the conduits that had to be scraped. It was impossible for her to understand the negative space, that she was making the inverse of what the final product needed to be, and that's how she understood that she wasn't really an artist.

After she entered, she went straight to the garden. The grounds were well manicured, but dead in spots where people had tromped on the grass (FORBIDDEN, the signs warned, but the command was unenforceable). Neatly spaced bushes marked the edge of the gravel path. Her shoes chopped noisily on the gravel—she wanted to be quiet and yet her footsteps were so loud, so regular, like a deafening heartbeat.

She stood in front of the *Bourgeois de Calais* and looked at their faces, wondered how Rodin was able to convey their expressions so precisely through all those various stages of the casting. She put her hands in her pocket and found a sticky note. "Very Important," she had written, with nothing else. What had been so important, she wondered, and wasn't it funny how time made lint out of importance?

She left without looking at any of the other sculptures, not even *The Gossips,* her favorite Camille Claudel work. She had loved the movie they made out of her life, the romantic way in which she seduced and served as muse to Rodin, and then went mad. *The Gossips* she loved because of its title in French, *Les Causeuses,* which was both onomatopoetic and slightly vulgar, and because of the way the women leaned into one another. It explored the erotic nature of female friendships, a comfort in sharing their bodies, brushing one another's hair, touching hands, hugging. The sculpture always made her feel sad that she didn't have intimate female friends, that she rarely experienced this kind of closeness devoid of sex, the wonderful ease of sameness.

———

Again the mysterious car, again the circuitous route, again the deserted grounds. Elm's anxiety seemed to move up her body, like a cloud of warm air, starting in her restless legs and ending up a metallic taste in her mouth. When she contemplated what she was about to do, she felt like she had entered an alternate reality.

The car stopped at the large house and the porter opened her door.

Once inside, a woman in her early twenties, hair pulled back into a messy bun, lab coat open to reveal a blouse and black pants, shook her hand, introducing herself as Catherine.

She put her hand on Elm's shoulder, steering her toward the wing of the mansion opposite the labs she'd seen earlier. They walked down a long hall. Tapestries hung on the wall, geometric and vegetable patterns. At each column a plaster bust stared dully out. Elm recognized them as copies of Greek Kori, standard-issue. "We have rules that we ask that you respect, for the security, you know. If you encounter another client, which should not occur, please, you will not look at her or talk to her. She will do the same."

"Are there others?"

Catherine didn't answer. "This is yours." She reached past Elm and opened the door.

Inside was a spacious room. A four-poster bed stood against the far wall, so high there was a small step stool next to it. The wallpaper had tiny fleur-de-lis in stripes, the curtains were velvet. Elm crossed to the opposite end of the dark room. There was a secretary desk, a phone with no buttons. In the fireplace, ashes shifted. Elm reached next to the window and pulled the cord to open the drapes. The windows were shuttered except for the top third. Light flooded in, but she couldn't see out.

"You'll find the . . . um . . . to open for air," Catherine said, demonstrating the lever that tilted the window out. "It's not for viewing, you know."

Elm sighed. She was, actually, trapped. She panicked for a moment: What if she died? What would Colin and Moira do?

Her face must have blanched, because Catherine laid a reassuring hand on her forearm. "You look scared," she said. "Don't worry. I know it seems like cinema here, but it is a very normal place. We just have security, for obvious reasons. You will very much enjoy it, I think. Most women do. A vacation! Here you have the television with cable international, and a computer." She pointed to the rolltop desk. "We ask you use our computer because we have a special server. The same with the cell phone. You pick up the phone and tell us the number and we will call it. It's all protection!" She smiled, showing a gap between her front teeth.

"You have the refrigerator here, and fruit and also cheese," she continued. "Here is the menu for the food. If you want something special, let us know with advance, okay?"

"Sure," Elm said. She felt her lower lip tremble.

"*Awww, pauvre petite,*" Catherine said. "*Viens, je t'embrasse,*" and she pulled Elm into her bony shoulder for a practiced hug. Elm let herself be held for a moment, then withdrew, rubbing her eyes.

"I tell them to bring your bag, yes?" Catherine smiled. She patted Elm on the shoulders and shut the door softly behind her.

Elm went to sit on the bed and had to use the stool to climb onto it. Her feet dangled. She leaned back and found that the canopy above the bed had been painted. It was a Baroque scene of cherubs and nymphs, not one style or time in particular. Oddly, this made her laugh, this ignorant parody of art. Relax, she told herself. You're just getting in vitro fertilization. It was practically a hobby in New York.

Someone knocked at the door. "Excuse, Madame." The porter was back with her overnight bag, which he placed on a valet near the desk. "Thank you."

Elm stood up. Should she tip him? This wasn't a hotel. . . . Before she could decide he'd left. She opened the suitcase. Someone had obviously been through it and wanted her to know it. The clothes had been refolded, much better than she'd folded them herself.

Elm supposed they had to check everyone. After all, she could be a journalist, or a government agent. How were they supposed to know? Except that they seemed to know everything.

She laughed at herself. "They." Like some spy organization or an evil empire. When the phone next to her bed rang, she had unpacked and was watching a show on a nature channel in French about African elephants. The narrator was speaking too fast for her to understand, but the camera told the story: elephants have families, trek long distances, get killed by poachers, mourn their dead.

"Bonjour, Madame Howells." The voice on the other end pronounced it "ow-ELS." "You are installing all right?"

"Yes, very comfortable, thanks." She recognized Michel's voice.

"We would like to perform an ultrasound, to look, yes? I will have someone come for you in five minutes, all right? There is a robe in your armoire."

Elm was about to answer but he hung up. She put on the robe and continued to watch television until she heard the soft knock.

"Hello!" Catherine said brightly. "Let's?"

She followed Catherine back down the residential hall, the busts still staring eyelessly at her. Then they passed the office where Elm had met with the doctor and turned down the corridor that led to the lab.

Inside, Michel was laying out instruments. He turned to shake hands with Elm. He had cut his hair since Elm had seen him. It was too short now, sticking up, freshly mowed, the gray more prevalent. Elm thought it made him look older, less attractive. Probably better for his line of work. He didn't wear a ring, she saw, but he was European and about to perform a gynecological procedure, two very good excuses for no jewelry.

"Before we start, you have questions?"

"Yes," Elm said. She climbed onto the table. Rather than regular doctor's office stirrups, she saw that they were lined with sheepskin. There was a blanket behind her. Everything was designed for comfort and luxury. "The embryo is ready?"

"We have grown a two-day blastocyst and a four-day. Whichever looks more promising tomorrow we will choose." The doctor smiled. He turned on the screen behind him and pulled the stool closer.

"If you're using donor sperm and a donor egg, how are you sure that what you're getting is a cl— You know, a copy and not a fertilized egg?"

The doctor laughed. "Please lie back," he said. "We remove the nucleus and replace it with your son's genetic material. The egg is just the casing, the sperm just the signal to start replicating. Like planting and watering a seed."

He hadn't really answered her question, and she was still puzzling out the plant metaphor, but before she could speak he announced: "I'm putting the wand inside now." Elm felt the push then the ache of the intrusion. "This looks good," he said. "Looks fine. Excellent. You have had two children before?"

Elm nodded. "And we got pregnant after just thinking about having kids."

He removed the wand. "Tomorrow we will implant. You will be in a twilight sleep, so it should not feel painful. There is just a catheter we place in your uterus. Now we give you special low-alkaline food, injection . . ." He turned to Catherine and spoke rapidly in French. She nodded and took notes.

"Try to relax. I know it will be hard, but try. You do meditation?"

Elm shook her head. She had trouble sitting still for a pedicure.

"Well, try. Deep breaths, calming thoughts, you know. I see you tomorrow." He extended a hand to shake.

"Come, I'll take you back," Catherine said, helping her off the table.

There was no way that Elm was going to sleep that night. The best she could do was to sip the tea they'd given her (something herbal, calming, womb-preparing) and watch the fire they'd lit. She thought about Ronan, something she rarely let herself do consciously.

She remembered the obstetrician putting him in her arms. Then she realized what she was remembering was the video they'd made of his birth, Colin's scrubbed hands waving in front of the camera, Ronan's furrowed face. Were they supposed to be that small? she had wondered. That squishy and wrinkly? She wanted to rub some of the gore off him, but she wasn't sure she was supposed to. In fact, she had no idea what to do, so she just held him to her chest. In the video her face was hilarious—white and confused, her mouth pursed in a cartoonish expression of bewilderment. And then the nurses took him from her and she felt the absence of his small weight like a punch to the gut.

Now a memory that was a real memory, sitting on a bench in Central Park and nursing him. Her uterus contracted in a way that was almost sexual, and she pulled the blanket she was using to cover her breast over her head as well, so she could watch him suckle and no one could see her. That same bench a couple of years later, watching Ronan play in the disgusting sandbox, planning how best to disinfect him and listening to the mothers complain about their sex lives. She thought so much then about snacks. She was always planning the most insignificant activities: laundry, dinner, baths . . .

A dinner where he threw his chicken at her, and she swept him up roughly and shoved him in the crib, slamming the door on his angry cries. His face when he saw Moira for the first time, the mixture of wonder and curiosity and jealousy. He touched her tentatively, amid Elm's admonitions: "Gentle touches, Ronan. Gentle touches." Then he touched Elm's stomach, amazed at the no-longer-taut skin.

On the sofa, Elm making dinner, Ronan reading to his sister from *Thomas the Tank Engine*. He was making up the words, "picture reading," but had most of it memorized, even the questions that Elm used to ask them all the time: Which one is Thomas? Why do you think he's smiling? Who can find the blue engine?

The images of Thailand, Ronan turning his nose up at a whole fish, refusing to wear his green swim trunks, putting Moira's Dora shirt on for a joke, being dwarfed under Colin's sun hat, excited to go fishing the next day.

And then it was morning.

———

The implantation didn't feel like anything. Like a vaginal exam. There was no moment of eureka or a pop or ping. She'd always thought that was a fallacy anyway, and that women who claimed to have known instantly at the moment of conception were just feeling nostalgic, the hormones planting a false memory.

"*Et voilà,*" the doctor had said, sounding so French that Elm giggled. Probably her nerves. Or the Valium they'd given her. She felt like she was dreaming this scene, like she was above her body looking down, and had the feeling that she could control the events if she could only focus on them. As they wheeled her back to her room with strict instructions to lie down for the rest of the day, it seemed so right that she couldn't believe she had ever contemplated *not* doing it.

She waited for the Valium to wear off to see if she would change her mind, but if anything, the logic had cemented itself while she was floating in psychotropic-land. If she was pregnant, if this was indeed her chance to redeem herself, to prove that she could take care of her son, then she owed it to him to do this. She had no other option.

Gabriel

September was a busy time in Paris. France woke up from the slumber of August, the government offices reluctantly opening their doors, teachers shuffling to work, professionals stretching out the morning kinks. Gabriel watched everyone scuttle about on important business.

He was supposed to have spent the month of August painting, but instead had fiddled about with making antique drawings, doing research, and scouring antique and bric-a-brac stores for old pastels, paints, and palettes to make drawings for Klinman. He needed the money. He had joined Colette for a week at her mother's house in Tenerife, an expensive plane ticket, and his first real vacation. It was such a relief to speak Spanish, to be in charge. He felt swollen with masculinity, ordering for Colette, translating for her, trading proprietary looks with other men at her little ass in her bikini. But when they returned home, he found all sorts of reasons to avoid his studio. He just didn't feel like working in his own style. When he searched for ideas, his mind was blank. When he looked at colors he found no inspiration. And yet the Connoises kept flowing as though he were channeling the old man himself. He had to hurry to finish his own canvases for his show.

He had to hand it to Paulette and Patrice, the Galerie Piclut put on an excellent show. The paintings were hung with care. The postcards showed real design savvy, a reproduction of *Après-midi au Supermarché* in full color, with an appropriately vintage Figueiredo font. Gabriel had eked out fourteen canvases in the end, and after the third, he started to have fun. Connois's tropes were, as it turned out, exactly the kinds of locations that Gabriel had occupied since he moved to France. Tweaking them for a modern audience, with his own flourishes, created a visual pun that also commented on immigration and culture clash. Yes, all this was devised for the artist statement, written by Paulette, but somehow it seemed he'd been thinking about just this melding of styles and ideas all along.

"*Dé/placement, Dé/plaisir*" opened on a Thursday, and Gabriel was sweating profusely in his black T-shirt an hour beforehand. The lights were very bright, and he was up on a ladder adjusting one so that it didn't hit the slick surface of the oil and reflect back into viewers' eyes. If there were viewers.

He had gotten lucky. An item in mylittleparis.com highlighting the neighborhood had come out that Monday. Galerie Piclut was mentioned as one of the up-and-coming cool spots to catch emerging artists. He did pause for a moment to sigh that he was still considered "emerging" at forty-two. But he hoped the article would spur some foot traffic.

Climbing down now and surveying his work, a momentary twinge that it was not exactly his own pained him. He would not have chosen this subject matter (two paintings set in a Grand Prix supermarket; another at the airport; a couple of send-ups of Parisian street scenes, colorful African-print caftans and head wraps worn by the Senegalese; a dead pigeon, an empty wine bottle, and a pair of discarded panties as a still life). But his own choices had never netted him a show.

People like a story. A locksmith who makes chairs out of keys. An amputee who paints footraces. A flamboyant gay man who pees on his canvases and calls it art. And Gabriel had a good story.

As the show's opening had approached he felt alternately elated and full of dread. He was sure Patrice and Paulette would cancel his show. But they seemed as enthusiastic as ever. Probably everyone would see right through the blatant pandering that was now covering the gallery's walls. But maybe a few would sell. Maybe a few would sell to important collectors and Gabriel's career would finally be launched.

He turned to help Patrice and Paulette and their intern put out cheese and wine. The smell of the melting cheese made his stomach roil and he stepped outside for a moment. The streets were bustling with people coming home from work, young people, like him. Only he wasn't so young anymore. Artists, jugglers, dancers, designers. Could the world hold this many creative types? Could it support them all?

The first several guests were friends of the Picluts, middle-aged, gray-haired men and overly made-up women tottering on high heels. They shook his hand and commented asininely on the art. "Oh, the light!" "I love the use of red here. So deft." And, Gabriel cringed to hear, "I see the Connois influence. Is that cultivated on your part or innate?"

More and more people arrived until there was a veritable crowd. He made his way to the bar and downed his second glass of red wine. He knew he should eat something. The room was getting warmer and he started to feel a bit tipsy. But the cheese plate was picked over and someone had eaten all the grapes.

Marie-Laure was kissing his cheeks. Then her boyfriend was kissing them. He was touched that she had come. She squeezed his arm and said how much she admired the work, how far his style had come and how happy she was for him. She looked genuine. "I was supposed to tell you that Hans couldn't come. Something about his wife and a cough. But I think it's really rude that Didier isn't here. We went to *his* show."

Gabriel was formulating an answer when he saw Colette and Lise walk in together. They were a study in contrasts, Lise white-blond and Colette dark, elbows hooked conspiratorially so that Gabriel gave an involuntary smile to see them together.

"Super!" Colette gave him a kiss. "But wait, I told them not to hang that there. Excuse me." She marched off to see the Picluts, leaving Gabriel with Lise.

"I'm so proud of you," she said, squeezing his hand. He smiled again. "You did it." Her approval, her praise, was like a jolt of caffeine. He wanted to talk to her, to take her in his arms and hug her with joy, but there were more people, tapping his shoulder to get his attention, and he was pulled away before he could thank her. The room was crowded now. Paulette grabbed his arm and pulled him over to *Après-midi au Supermarché no. 1*. "Look! I'm putting a dot!" The dot was yellow, which meant someone had put a hold on it (red would have meant a purchase). Someone had actually put down money as a deposit on his work.

An old man came through the door, leaning heavily on the arm of his young friend. For a second, Gabriel thought it might be his old adviser LeFevre from the École, but that would have been impossible. The man was surely dead by now. He felt his cheeks flush. He would have been embarrassed to show him his work. How disappointed LeFevre would have been at this pandering.

"So much talent," someone said next to him; Gabriel heard it from

LeFevre's mouth—a sad lamentation that he'd done nothing with it. But it was a woman wearing a pearl and diamond necklace, obviously slumming in the new hip part of town. And she was saying it positively, and Patrice was behind him; Gabriel said obediently, "You're too kind. Thank you so much."

"No, thank *you*," the woman said, and Gabriel realized that a month ago this would have made him laugh.

Marie-Laure was in front of him again. "It's too crowded; we're taking off." The taciturn boyfriend kissed his cheeks again.

At some point the evening tipped and the numbers began to get smaller until finally the only ones in attendance were the art students hovering near the wine and Colette.

"Look!" Paulette said. "One red dot!"

"That's not bad," Patrice said.

"It's the smaller one, isn't it?" Gabriel asked.

"Still," Patrice said.

"Congratulations." Paulette refilled his wineglass.

———

What was he supposed to do the next day? He went to the studio. His space seemed larger emptied of work. He sat down in the folding chair and stared at the splatter patterns on the floor. He didn't really feel like working. It was like going jogging the day after running a marathon. His artist muscles were tired.

He decided to straighten up his studio. Some of his brushes could use a good washing, not the quick rinse he usually gave them. He set them in turpentine to soak. And maybe he should paint the walls again. He could go out and buy white paint. With the advance from the "red dot."

Marie-Laure stuck her head in to congratulate him. "Great show. Fantastic. I think that art blog guy was there."

"Which art blog guy?"

"He calls himself Sir Veille. Get it? Like surveillance?"

Gabriel didn't get it. That is, he got the surveillance part but didn't understand what the double entendre was. "What does he write?"

"A blog. An art blog."

"Oh," Gabriel said. He wasn't actually sure what that was.

"On the Internet?" Marie-Laure raised her voice; his confusion must have registered on his face. "The thing on the computer?"

"Oh, yeah, that. I just didn't understand your accent." Gabriel recalled that these online diaries were gaining in importance. In some circles they already outstripped professional art critics.

"Anyway, that's a good sign."

"Unless he hated it," Gabriel said.

"All press is good press," Marie-Laure said.

"Baudelaire?"

"I don't know who said it." Marie-Laure missed his sarcasm. She went back into her studio.

Just sketch, he told himself. Get lead on paper. He opened his sketchbook and hovered over the page. Don't analyze, he thought, just sketch. Why did he even care what critics thought? They were all failed artists.

A half hour later he looked at what he'd done. He'd drawn his shoe. But it was unmistakably a shoe in the style of Brueghel. The same hatching, the same stiff lines. He ripped the page up, disgusted. He couldn't even sketch like himself anymore. He was simply a cipher, a sponge, sopping up others' styles.

Gabriel went outside to walk while the brushes soaked. Didier was smoking a cigarette. "Man, I am so sorry I didn't make it to the opening," he said. He looked sheepish, crinkling the corners of his mouth in concern. "I had the worst day, and I just couldn't . . . I mean . . ."

"Don't worry," Gabriel said. "It was too crowded anyway."

"I feel awful. I mean, you came to mine. I promise to go look at it this week."

"Hey, don't worry," Gabriel said. Then it struck him. Had Didier not come because he was jealous, the same way Gabriel had contemplated not attending Didier's show last spring? Was it possible that Gabriel had achieved enough success to inspire envy? The thought made him smile.

That afternoon, he went to the Internet café and paid his five euros to log on. He tried to type in various versions of what he had heard Marie-Laure say, but he didn't find the art blog. Finally, he asked the teenager next to him how to find something when you don't know the name.

The kid looked at him with undisguised disdain. His hair framed his head like yarn on a doll, and he flicked his head back to get it out of his eyes. "What do you mean?"

Gabriel explained himself as best he could, and the kid got up and began to type on his keyboard. Within seconds, Sir Veille's page was up.

"Thanks," Gabriel said.

"Where are you from?" the boy asked.

"Spain."

"Don't you want to go home?"

Gabriel shrugged. "Why?"

The boy shrugged back. Something in his gesture was mocking, but Gabriel turned to his screen.

Nothing about the opening. Why had he listened to Marie-Laure? He was angry at himself for being disappointed. Sir Veille was a part of the same establishment that had shunted him aside for years. Why should this blogger be any different? He hated that he still craved acceptance.

A couple of days later, Marie-Laure burst into his studio. "Here! I printed it out for you. It's good. Well, mostly."

She handed Gabriel a piece of paper. "What is this?" he asked.

"A review. Of your show. By Sir Veille."

"Oh. I'll read it later."

"What?" Marie-Laure said. "That's ridiculous. Read it now."

Gabriel had trouble making out the small print in the dim light. "Can you read it?" he said. "I have a headache."

"'Swimming down Canal Saint-Martin the other night, I stopped in for free booze at Galerie Piclut. The cheese was decidedly low-quality, and there were stems that suggested that once there might have been grapes, now long gobbled by hungry students. It has always seemed uncouth to me (and for this you can thank my mother) to take grapes and leave the stems. Break off the stem and take it with you!

"'Oh, right, the art. The artist, skinny and sweaty, is a descendant of Marcel Connois of the École des Hiverains. Yes, *that* Connois. But this grandchild is an École des Beaux Arts graduate. Swarthy, sexy, all the usual stereotypes. He's riffed on his relative's style, painting marketplaces and still lifes and playing with light, but with an ironic twist. Street scenes become African markets, sun shining refracted off dark black skin. Boats on water are barges carrying fruit. There's a decent use of color and an obvious flair for satire (if not for a sense of humor. The paintings seem sometimes to not get their own joke). Mostly it appears to be an attempt by a foreigner to claim Paris, which is the subject of the art itself. Whether this goal is worthy of artistic inquiry is up for debate, but the artist does succeed in carving out his own space in the city. Overall, worthwhile if you're in the neighborhood, to get a glimpse of contemporary Connois.' "

Marie-Laure let her hands fall to her sides.

"That's good?" Gabriel asked.

"It sounded better the first time I read it," she admitted. "But he called it worthwhile."

"If you're in the neighborhood."

"Lots of people go to that *arrondissement*," Marie-Laure said brightly. She handed him the page and left.

Gabriel held it far from his eyes and squinted, reading it again. He hadn't caught it the first time, but one line stood out. "The artist does succeed in carving out his own space in the city." He couldn't help but feel proud. Finally, Gabriel owned Paris.

———

Gabriel sat in Colette's apartment. He was mostly living there, though Colette was in New York nearly half the month. Gabriel felt like he was living on a movie set, the views fake and the props hollow. It was still hot, and Gabriel sat on the love seat, watching Colette's small television. He picked up the top catalog from the large pile Colette used to form a side table. He fanned himself, then saw that it was a Tinsley's catalog from last spring. He began to flip through it.

He thumbed through glossy pages of antique bric-a-brac. Most of what they auctioned wasn't even art. It was artisanry, not at all the same thing. So he flipped to the index in the back. Automatically, he looked for Connois's name and there it was. For sale was *Mercat*, a pastel.

Gabriel's heart pounded loudly in his ears. He felt caught suddenly, like in a dream of being chased and then arrested by the police for an unspecified crime that he knew he'd committed. He turned quickly to the page. The pastel was not reproduced. Instead there was a square that said "Image not available." He read the description next to the entry: "Marcel Connois, 1825–1889. *Mercat* (*Market*). Signed by the artist. Pastel on paper. Provenance: Acquired directly from the artist by the family of the present owner. Literature: *Connois's Flights of Fancy*, 1901, described." The dimensions were listed in the ridiculous American measuring system; he wasn't able to tell if the painting was his or not. The reserve was 750,000 euros. For something Gabriel did. For something Klinman paid him 10,000 euros to do.

Gabriel threw the catalog down and slumped in his chair. He permitted himself a brief fantasy in which he went back in time to New York and burst in on the auction, announcing the hoax. There would be cinematic gasps, followed by newspaper articles, then international recognition.

"Fuck!" he swore out loud. The art world was stupid, insipid, without taste, and he still wanted its approval. No, he corrected himself, not its approval, its money. It wasn't fucking fair that some artists got plucked to fame. He wasn't asking for much. A nice studio, with light. The occasional vacation. He'd been living in France for nearly twenty years now. Well, existing, anyway. He wanted to be successful. He wanted to make enough money off his art that he could paint/create full-time. His art, not his personality, or his ancestry. Bullshit, he told himself. He had changed his style to suit a gallery. He had forged his ancestor's work, passed it off as original. God only knows what happened to it then. So what artistic standards was he supposed to be upholding?

His whole life was based on a principle he abhorred. He wanted to win a game he didn't believe in playing. No wonder he had spent the past fifteen years angry and depressed. Who wouldn't be when faced with the gaping abyss of existence? His happiness at his success of the last few months was the result of a grand coincidence that acted like some kind of numbing drug, so that he was in a fog of complacency.

He went to the studio, but felt his fury grow, speeding through his veins. He spent a few hours banging around cans of solvent.

"What are you doing?" Marie-Laure asked.

"Trying not to kill someone," Gabriel answered. This admission fueled his rage, and Marie-Laure scurried away. He heard footsteps and then Hans stood in the doorway.

"What's up, man?" he asked. "Did you threaten to kill Marie-Laure?"

"Those fucking sons of whores," he said.

"Who?"

"No one. I'm just . . ."

"Hey, man, chill out. What happened?"

"Nothing." Gabriel couldn't hide the irritation in his voice. "Everyone gets something from me. Everyone but me."

"Is this about me not coming to the show? My old lady had bronchitis."

"Never mind." Gabriel headed for the door. Hans blocked him and the two men played a game of chicken. At the last second, Hans stepped back. Gabriel's shoulder brushed him as he stormed out.

He tried to fuel his rage all the way to Klinman's. It took more than an hour, and there was a point at which the *métro* had a transfer with his line. He considered just going home. But then he saw a pair of shoes, expensive, handmade. They were on the feet of a woman sitting near him. The heels were tremendously high, the leather shiny. At the end of the shoe, a pedicured foot poked its toes out. Her ankles were slim in the French way—he wondered often how they held women up, calves so thin he could wrap his hand around one.

Finally he looked up at her face. She drew her arms in and after a couple of seconds stood up to go across the car and sit with her back to him.

This snub reignited his anger. He willed the train to travel faster and leaped out the doors at Klinman's stop before they had fully opened.

It occurred to him that Klinman might not be there, and he wondered what he would do if that were the case. He took the stairs two at a time instead of waiting for the elevator, arriving at Klinman's door breathing hard.

The door was open, the lock turned so that it wouldn't close all the way. He heard noise coming from inside the apartment, soft music, voices. He pushed the door.

The apartment had a large table in its center that Gabriel hadn't noticed before. Seated at it were about a dozen people, who stopped in the middle of their conversations to stare at his entrance.

"Ahh, Gabriel," Klinman said, standing up. "So glad you could make it." As though he had been invited and was merely tardy.

Gabriel had a speech planned. He opened his mouth to begin the recitation when the focus of all those pairs of eyes made him turn red.

"I need to speak to you," Gabriel said.

"Would you like a drink?" Klinman nodded at a uniformed waiter who approached Gabriel until his angry look made the waiter shrink away. "All right, then, we can go in here. I won't be a minute," he said to his guests.

He led Gabriel to a room off the salon. It was a bedroom, smaller than Gabriel would have guessed. In contrast to the dark, clubby main room, it was bright and minimalist. A platform bed with no headboard and a midcentury modern dresser. Blackout shades and an upholstered chair. There was no nightstand, but two sconces perched above the pillows, protruding from the wall on spider arms.

Klinman made no move to sit down. He set his drink on a small doily on the dresser and folded his arms. "What do you—"

"No, you listen." Gabriel pointed a finger at Klinman. It was dirty from his messing about in the studio and seemed to diminish his authority. He also hadn't noticed how tall Klinman was. His courage and anger began to ebb. Still, he had come for a reason.

"That's it," he said. "I'm done forging your pictures. You're making money, everyone is making money off of me. And I'm not making shit."

"Please don't raise your voice, I have guests. You *are* making money, I'll remind you. But all right, if you don't want to work anymore, that's fine. I can find someone else."

A siren called out, getting louder as it passed the building, then quieting again. "Just try," Gabriel said. "I'd like to see you find someone who can do Connois like I can."

"I'm sure there is no one," Klinman said, "but there are others who can do others."

Klinman's nonchalance surprised Gabriel. He had expected the man to apologize, offer more money. Then he would have the opportunity to refuse him. Gabriel had even entertained a scenario in which he got to punch Klinman. But here was a reaction that he hadn't planned for. He saw now he should have.

"Ha," he scoffed. "Try to find others when the police are after you!"

Klinman stared at him. Gabriel had rendered him speechless.

"I have evidence," Gabriel said. Which he didn't. Why had it not occurred to him to get evidence? "The German expert, he'll support me."

Klinman's stare began to change. Soon he was smiling widely at Gabriel, a look of derision rather than mirth. "You're going to report me to the police?" he said. "Rich." His smile emitted a sound that might have been a cackle. "Hilarious. The German expert will support you? I doubt that very much, since he is my business associate." He was laughing for real now, and Gabriel felt his ears go hot with embarrassment. Of course Schnell had been in on it. His drawing wouldn't have fooled a real expert. Gabriel had no reply.

"Turn me in," Klinman said, suddenly serious, "and it is you who will be sketching other prisoners' assholes. That I can promise you. Now, would you like to stay for dinner? We can have someone pull up a chair and make you a plate," he said, giving Gabriel a chance to respond.

Gabriel said nothing, unable to make his mind work out the words of protest in French. Klinman was all politeness now. Gabriel was a favorite nephew and not an attempted blackmailer. Gabriel shook his head. Finally, he understood his role. He was the rube, in way over his head.

Klinman shook his head sadly. "If you'll excuse me, then, my guests."

Gabriel could hear Klinman's voice in the big room, but couldn't make out the words. The guests laughed. He stood in Klinman's bedroom. The man was right. Gabriel was expendable. How could he not have seen that?

He sat on Klinman's low bed. The mattress was thin; he could feel the planks of the bed frame beneath it. He had never understood why rich people so liked the hard Asian way of sleeping. He preferred to sleep like Louis XIV, in a featherbed so soft he might be suffocated. He hoped he'd suffocate. This was just another reminder of the gulf between him and the rest of the world. The rest of the successful world.

———

His bank account was practically empty and Klinman hadn't called him in weeks. Gabriel regretted his outburst, but all his calls to Klinman went unreturned. When he asked Colette if she'd seen her uncle, she treated the question like a joke. "What, you like him more than you like me?" She had been distant, increasing her evenings out with the girls (he hoped this was true, that she was not lying to him about who she was out with) and telling him she needed some space. Reluctantly, Gabriel spent more nights at his shared flat, staring at the textured ceiling. It was all turning to shit. He was still poor and The Man was still rich.

Really, what was Klinman doing that he couldn't do himself? Providing period paper. That couldn't be that hard to come by. Yes, Klinman had the contacts to dispose of the drawings, but what would stop

Gabriel from entering any gallery in town and concocting some story about how he'd found this in the closet of his aunt (who was titled, of course; French people love royalty)? What would he need to strike out on his own? Appropriately old paper, a good backstory. Fuck it. He was going solo.

On the banks of the Seine the kiosks of rare-book sellers would certainly have some early- to mid-nineteenth-century paper. He could just buy an old book of prints and either split the paper or cut out the page glued to the cover. He had done that before, in *liceo*, taking the precious sheets of good, thick (though modern) paper and soaking them to peel them apart, splicing them into multiple sheets. He had also taken art books from the university library and liberated their back pages or the odd blank page left over from uneven pagination. Occasionally, he checked out a book and someone had already removed the page. He was not the only paper thief in town.

The *quais* were mostly deserted and the men sat in the shade of the linden trees fanning themselves. He stopped to take money out of the bank. He passed the postcard vendor and the LP stand and stood in front of a kiosk of larger folios that looked of appropriate age. Gabriel pretended to be interested in a vintage edition of Molière. Its spine was leather, revealing lighter beige suede inside. It looked like craquelure on an old oil painting. He opened the volume. The paper was ticklishly soft. But that wasn't what he was looking for. Too small, too yellowed. He put the book back and nonchalantly moved over to the larger books. He took one out, a loosely bound collection of botanical prints from 1863. The pages held smooth engravings, glued or partially glued to just the sort of old paper he needed. The man behind the kiosk eyed him suspiciously. Gabriel held his breath. He didn't need for the man to see him getting excited about a book; that would drive up the price.

"You're interested in botany?" the man asked.

"Hmmm," Gabriel said noncommittally. "I'm looking for something more . . ." He tried to think of something he could be looking for instead, but the word didn't come to him in French or Spanish. "I don't know how to say it." He smiled sheepishly. "But maybe this is okay. How much does it cost?"

"The price is on the inner cover." The man reached a thin arm over the mound of books to grab the prints from Gabriel. "One hundred euros."

Gabriel shook his head. "Sixty," he said, repeating the French number in his mind to make sure.

The man scoffed. "Ninety is the best I can do. They're original prints. Beautiful."

"And how long have you had this book?" Gabriel asked. "Maybe you are looking to get rid of it. Seventy-five."

"Eighty."

"Fine." Gabriel handed the man four twenties. "Do you have a bag?"

The man sighed, annoyed. He handed him a plastic Monoprix bag and Gabriel gingerly put the book inside, tucking the whole package into his messenger bag.

When he got home, Gabriel put a pot of water on to boil. He opened the botanical volume and, with an X-Acto knife, cut off the back cover. Then he held the board over the pot of water, tapping his foot.

He stood over the pot for forty-five minutes, his bladder growing full. But he didn't dare put the cardboard down to go to the toilet. The glue was almost fully softened. Finally he judged it ready. He sat down at the table, and carefully, so carefully, pulled the paper from its cardboard backing. He laid it facedown on the linoleum. Then he took a blunt butter knife and scraped off all remnants of glue. Now he let himself use the bathroom.

After sizing it and replenishing his period ink stash, Gabriel let the paper dry for twenty-four hours. Then he took it to the studio and drew on it. His finished Connois looked not half bad, if he said so himself. He had managed to draw the local market at his house in Spain from memory. His mother made an appearance in the drawing, toward the back, selling her bread. He gave the other market vendors wry expressions, as was Connois's custom, and made sure to sketch the figures with great detail, leaving the kiosks and wares only suggested. Concerned mostly with anatomy and expression, Connois rarely bothered to finish the nonhuman details, even in the final paintings. It was what separated him from the Impressionists who were his contemporaries—their canvases tended to be uniform, whatever their style. It was also, Gabriel suspected, why Degas was a name that even the uninitiated knew while Connois was known only to aficionados and academics.

———

Christie's was located in a rather unassuming building on Avenue Matignon off the Champs-Élysées. From the outside, the building looked like another one of the antique stores that characterized the neighborhood. Its two street-front windows were cluttered with antique furniture and mediocre nineteenth-century oils.

Gabriel pulled the door open, hanging his weight on it, and paused while his eyes adjusted to the interior. He made out a grand carpeted staircase, with a Baroque mural at the first landing. The first-floor ceilings were low and the room was filled with sandstone pillars holding up archways that blocked his entrance. There was no art hanging in the entryway, just a couple of glass cases highlighting recent auctions. The lavish rooms he'd heard about, the huge salesroom with its expensive carpets and textured wallpaper, must be on higher floors. The difference between this space and Ambrosine's was as stark as if they existed in two different countries, in two different time periods. Ambrosine's was white light; Christie's small archways threw off forbidding shadows. Ambrosine's was pulsing with energy; Christie's was languorous.

At a polished desk sat a receptionist who might have been eighty, dressed impeccably in a vintage pea-green suit with oversized pearlescent buttons. Her hair was sprayed into a large gray helmet, and her hands, when they replaced the telephone in its cradle, were covered in age spots.

"How may I help you today?" she asked.

Gabriel hadn't thought in advance what to say, and the French came out convoluted. "I am a Spanish, relative of Connois from the École des Hiverains, and I have a drawing to possibly sell."

"With whom do you have an appointment?" the woman asked, her French careful and slow now that she knew he was not French.

"An appointment?" Gabriel said.

"Ahh," the woman sighed, as though Gabriel had just admitted to her that he had wet his pants.

There was a long silence while they both waited for the other to speak. Finally they both spoke at once. "Please, you first," Gabriel said.

"I was going to ask you what kind of a drawing, so that we can make an appointment with the correct person."

"Um, it's a drawing, by Connois. A sketch of a marketplace."

"Yes," the woman said. "You'll forgive me if I'm not familiar with the artist."

"A contemporary of the Impressionists."

"All right, then you'll want to speak with Jean-Georges Tombale."

"Okay," Gabriel said. "Jean-Georges Tombale."

"I'll just ring him now," the woman said, "since you're here. When might be a convenient time for you to meet him?"

"Um, whenever."

The woman picked up the phone and pressed three numbers. "What did you say your name was, dear?" she asked.

"Gabriel Connois."

"Ah!" the woman gave a gasp of surprise, or recognition, or simply Gallic enthusiasm. She spoke quickly into the receiver, then turned to Gabriel. "You are in luck. Monsieur Tombale is available to see you now."

She placed her hands on the desk and heaved herself to a standing position. Despite her age, she wore small heels. Slowly, she waddled toward the staircase, and Gabriel feared she would have to ascend it. But she veered left and opened a door at the back of the room. She gestured down the sterile hallway.

Gabriel followed her directions, past a small conference room and a large area with cubicles. There was a small, balding head peeking out of one of the doors. "Monsieur Connois?" it asked.

Tombale introduced himself and invited Gabriel to sit. The office felt precarious; its shelves were overflowing with large coffee table books, most with colored flags sticking out of them. In between, catalogs of Christie's and other firms were curling with age, also marked up. There was no computer. This man did all his research by looking at reproductions of previous works. No wonder he was as stooped as a dowager.

"I have a drawing," Gabriel said. "It's been in my family for years, because, well, Connois was my great-great-grandfather."

"May I see it?" The man's hands trembled. A small spot of croissant stuck to the stubble above his lip.

Gabriel took it out of its portfolio. In the harsh fluorescent light of the office it looked yellow, the ink an anemic gray.

"Come, we'll take it to the viewing room."

They went back to the conference room Gabriel had passed. Here the light was better. There was a small clerestory window.

First the man held it up to the light, admiring the watermark. Gabriel studied him. In the light, the small wisps of hair left on the top of his head stood up straight, waving like seaweed in a current. His hands were flaky, and Gabriel fought a shiver of repulsion.

Tombale turned the drawing over, looking for a dealer's mark that wasn't there. Gabriel hadn't thought of inventing one, but now he breathed a sigh of relief that he hadn't—the man could have easily looked up its history in his catalog. Absence wasn't proof, but presence of the wrong element would be a red flag.

"It's never been sold before," Gabriel said.

The man turned the drawing around again slowly. He put it down on the table and stood up above it. Then he took out a magnifying glass and examined the drawing in sectors. During what must have been fifteen minutes, his face registered no expression whatsoever. Even more amazingly, the croissant flake held steady to his lip.

Finally, he sat back down. "Bah," he let out a Gallic sigh. "Well, it's very good, and the paper is authentic."

Gabriel realized he'd been holding his breath.

"But I can't be sure if it's a Connois original. Without a provenance, I will have to compare it with other Connois sketches. This will take time."

Gabriel's face must have shown his disappointment. His rent was due, and he didn't have money to pay it.

"You were expecting cash on delivery? Monsieur, we are not a Chinese takeout restaurant." Tombale looked Gabriel over with obvious disdain, settling on his shoes, the soles of which were held to the body by electrical tape.

Gabriel saw then that he should have dressed up. Looking like a desperate artist wasn't going to convince this established dealer that he had a treasure in his attic.

"This is a beautiful drawing," Monsieur Tombale continued, sounding to Gabriel's ears like his thesis adviser. "But we simply cannot take it on without further investigation. There have been so many nineteenth-century drawings of late. Too many."

Gabriel stood up, and though he wanted to snatch the drawing out of the man's grasp, he resisted. He waited for the dealer to pack the drawing up, then shook the man's dry, scaly hand, thanking him for his time. He walked quickly out, ignoring the ancient receptionist. On the street he stood in the gray light, fists clenched. Why had he thought he could sell it to Christie's? He should have started more modestly. It had been so easy to get rid of *Febrer*. But that was twenty years ago. Now everyone was much more savvy; now databases were accessible with the click of a mouse, without having to search through archives. Dating methods had become less expensive and more accurate. Maybe Klinman was right—he did need his help. He was the talent, yes, but Klinman understood the way the world worked. Gabriel was incompetent at anything that didn't have to do with art, and even, possibly, incompetent at art.

———

Gabriel quickened his step. He held an imaginary conversation with Klinman where the man laughed at him for showing up, in jeans and sneakers, no less, with an unauthenticated drawing at one of France's most important auction houses and attempting, on the spot, to have one of its experts declare it sellable.

And now the drawing was tainted. Tombale wouldn't soon forget it. Gabriel wasn't going to be able to sell it without a provenance, and if it came up for auction with a fabricated story Tombale would be suspicious. The drawing was now not even worth the paper it was drawn on. Gabriel could have sold it blank for more money.

He felt like crumpling it up and tossing it into the Seine, but he had affection for the drawing. He passed a bar and went in to order a panaché. A girl's drink, but one he still enjoyed. He didn't want to get drunk. He wanted to think.

Above the bar, instead of the polished mirror typical of a neighborhood café, there was a boar's head. *Sanglier.* He remembered the word, the way some bizarre French words—*huissier* (bailiff), *etalon* (studhorse)—seemed to glue themselves to his memory while more common ones—like the ones for "broom" and "great-great-grandfather"—remained forever out of reach. The bar was an odd sight, slightly foreboding. And then, looking around, he saw many other taxidermied game animals presiding over the few tables.

The bartender noted his interest. "I like to hunt, at my house in the country. Do you hunt?"

Gabriel shook his head.

"And my wife's uncle stuffs the animals. He does an excellent job. If you ever have something you need preserved, let us know. All these specimens are for sale."

"Who wants a dead animal in their house?" Gabriel asked, before he could stop himself.

"Not my wife," the man answered. "That's why they're here. But lots of people like the look. It reminds them of grand old hunting lodges." The man wiped the already pristine bar with a rag. A couple walked in and sat at a table. The woman held up two fingers—they wanted coffee. The bartender nodded, but before he turned to the espresso maker, he said to Gabriel, "People want to pretend they have nice things, that their family name is more important than it really is."

Gabriel reflected that his case was just the opposite. His name was illustrious; he himself was not. His name connoted great art; he did not. But perhaps the drawing wasn't a total loss. Maybe he'd gone to the wrong expert. An antiques dealer might like the drawing simply because of its age, and might appreciate it for its aesthetics, as opposed to where it came from. In a way, this could be a purer form of art appreciation. Then the drawing would no longer be pretending to be what it was not, but rather proclaiming proudly what it was.

Gabriel paid for his drink and took the *métro* up to the *marché aux puces* at Clignancourt. He haggled for and purchased the gaudiest nineteenth-century frame he could find, and then took his purchase home, where he mounted his drawing on matte paper and renailed the frame shut. He then lined the back with butcher paper, and the next day went to the Left Bank dressed in a pair of wool pants and a button-down shirt borrowed from one of the Scandinavians. The first store he went into offered him 150 euros for the framed drawing. The entire transaction was completed in less than ten minutes.

When Gabriel added up his hours of work and the cost of the materials, he was better off sorting paper clips at Édouard's. He couldn't help but feel angry, at himself, at Klinman, at Paris, at the art world that conspired to keep him out. He was destined to be exploited, and he returned to his studio out in the suburbs to sit cross-legged on the floor examining splats of paint that had hardened into small shiny pieces, impenetrable as a Pollock splatter, and nowhere near as valuable.

Part Four

Winter 2008

Elm

t was the strangest feeling. She would be fine. Hungry, tired, but fine. And then the world would turn upside down and that horrible feeling of her insides revolting, the organs contracting violently to expel the poison within, would take hold. She rarely made it to the bathroom, just looked for the nearest receptacle, sometimes missing even that.

Tired didn't even begin to describe it. She'd heard people say they'd overdone it, but she had never really understood the feeling. However, with this pregnancy exhaustion would overwhelm her. Even her elbows felt bushed. She actually sat down on the floor of the crosstown bus (she wasn't showing so no one offered her a seat) and rested her head on her bent knees until an elderly woman put a cool hand on her shoulder, asking, "Are you all right, dear?"

At home, watching her retch from the safety of the bathroom door, Moira asked, "What's wrong, Mommy?"

"I think I have the flu," she answered.

"Poor Mommy." Moira rubbed Elm's forehead the way Colin did when Moira was sick. Her hands were sticky with something—what had she snuck from the kitchen?

Elm and Colin had never spoken about what was happening with his job. It seemed like in the past weeks they had been living in shifts—they were never awake and without Moira. Elm was avoiding him, and wondered if he was avoiding her. What scared her was not that she didn't know what was going on but that she had forgotten to be worried about it.

She longed to confide her secret to someone—Ian would be ideal, but she knew she couldn't tell anyone. Her fantasies now involved pretzels and confession—sodium and some lessening of the burden.

———

It was after eleven as Elm turned the key in the front door and tiptoed gratuitously into the living room. After years of New York living, her family could sleep through fire drills, earthquakes, alien invasions. She set her purse down on the kitchen table and took off her shoes.

Thirsty, she took a container of orange juice out of the refrigerator and stood there drinking it from the carton. Then she became aware of movement behind her. She spun around guiltily, spilling some orange juice down the front of her shirt.

"Hey," Colin said. His hair was comically disheveled. "How'd it go?"

"Fine. I hate those things." Part of Elm's duties as a board member of the New Jewish Institute consisted of glad-handing donors at galas that often ended late. She reached in for a piece of cold pizza. It had gone pale and slack, and Elm wondered what it was that made mozzarella look like dead flesh after refrigeration. How often did they eat pizza? Would it stunt Moira's growth, being raised only on breaded chicken and tomato sauce? Would it hurt the fetus? She put it back down. "Why don't you go back to bed?"

Colin turned obediently and sleepwalked back to the room. When Elm went into the bedroom, though, she could feel that Colin was awake, more so than he'd been a couple of minutes ago.

Elm pretended not to notice and took off her suit, hanging it carefully in the closet and then putting on her nightgown. She climbed into bed backward, trying not to wake him, but he rolled over toward her, not touching her. "How'd it go?"

"You asked me that already."

"No, I didn't."

"It was good."

"Brilliant."

There was a pause.

"Elm?" Colin asked. He pitched his voice high. It contained concern and seriousness.

"Hmmm," Elm said, answering but not encouraging. She was tired. She wanted to sleep.

"Are we all right, then?"

"Of course." Even to herself Elm sounded disingenuous. She tried to change the subject. "Moira go to bed without fuss?"

"I mean . . ." Colin ignored her. "I just feel . . ." he trailed off.

Elm felt a sense of panic invade her again, welling up like an undulation of nausea. Without thinking, she said, "I'm pregnant."

Colin sat up quickly. "Really?" He put a hand on her upper arm. She rolled over to face him.

"Yup," she said. She watched his face break into a wide smile. Even in the dark she could see that his excitement was unfeigned.

"God, Elm, that's . . . great, fantastic, stupendous! When? How do you . . . ? Which?" He was unable to spit out an entire question.

"I think about four weeks," she said. "I took two at-home tests."

"Elm, I'm so happy. This is what we wanted. Wait, is it?"

"Of course," she said. "How can you ask that?" She sat up then too, genuinely injured. Had she really been so hostile these past weeks?

"I'm just . . . I hope the timing is all right. When do you think? I mean, with my work . . ." He began to babble, a sign that he was nervous. Now she laid a hand on his thigh.

"June, I think." She didn't think. She knew. "I'll go to the doctor in a couple of weeks. What do you mean, the timing?"

"I'm just worried about work, is all. Don't mind me. I'm so excited. Do you think it's a boy or a girl?" He put a hand on the small bulge of Elm's stomach where the skin was slack and a roll of fat had accumulated.

"Who knows?" Elm said.

———

There are holes in a marriage, Elm thought, periods of time for which if you were drawing a graph of marital compatibility there would be an absence of data. These dispersals are gradual, like not noticing that someone you see every day is getting fat until you are apart from them and return to find a different person from the one you left. It finally dawned on Elm that she and Colin had been gradually wandering in different directions. When she got married, Elm thought, as all brides do, that it was Colin and Elm against the world. She had assumed there'd be secrets, but from others, not between them, or if there were they would be minor: hiding chocolate in a stash, not necessarily telling him that someone had tried to pick her up at the gym. She had never imagined the need to keep a secret from him and found it incredibly difficult.

The urge was upon her nearly constantly to tell him, not only because she wanted to unburden herself but because it felt like an itch, a continuous low-level irritation, a desire to blurt out what she was thinking. She began to censor herself, and the effort was so great that she cut down on what she was saying to Colin, and then eliminated all but the most essential conversations: What do you want for dinner? Can you take Moira to ballet on Saturday?

From there, she imagined, it would be but a short leap until she found herself emotionally estranged from her husband. And then he would crave intimacy and find it elsewhere. Cheating now seemed inevitable, the end of the divergent paths she and Colin were taking.

It might have helped if Colin had put a stop to the estrangement that wasn't really an estrangement, but he was worried about his job (they had extended the merger period another three months, and whatever investigation was ongoing was moving glacially, but it felt like a stay of execution, not a pardon). She could see him searching for words with which to engage her. Recently, she had ceased to cede him any emotion. No matter what he said she would reply vacantly as though humoring a pestering child. A couple of times he said things that would have pissed her off just a couple of months before, but she had barely acknowledged that he spoke, let alone risen to the bait.

Elm had seen this in her own parents. Fighting, they'd at least declared their commitment to hating each other. When they quieted, finally, toward the end of Elm's adolescence, she knew the marriage was over. They remained together, inhabiting two separate sections of the same house. Elm saw the same vacant cohabitation looming in her own marriage. She vowed to herself that she would break this pattern, clenching her fists to seal the promise.

———

Moira looked adorable dressed as a Trojan for the kindergarten reenactment of the *Aeneid*.

"Typical posh New York school," Colin had scoffed, "forcing kindergartners to perform a book I wasn't even aware of until university." Still, he was there in the front row with the other parents digitally recording the play. Oddly, the still cameras were the larger instruments, with lenses better suited to shooting football for *Sports Illustrated* rather than elementary school thespians in a small church basement. The video cameras, on the other hand, were so small as to be nearly invisible, nestled in the palms of hands.

Elm sat toward the back with her friend Patty, who had a daughter Moira's age. Elm was overheated, as she so often was these days, fanning herself with the program. Patty had a second daughter, eighteen months old, who kept squirming on her lap, shrieking when Patty refused to let her down. "Be quiet," Patty kept saying, waving a teething ring in front of her, like she was coaxing a seal to do a trick. Elm looked at them, irritated. She had forgotten that toddlers were so willful, unable to say what they wanted or to make logical decisions. Ronan had jumped off the sofa at twenty-one months and hit his head on the ottoman. When he stopped crying, Elm left him for a moment to go throw the ice pack in the sink and he was up on the sofa, leaping again.

The piano music started and the shower curtain parted to reveal a dozen five-year-olds dressed in togas. The teacher stood to the side, her back to the audience. Elm struggled to pick out Moira, but it was difficult even to tell genders apart. And then she saw a child on the end whose unruly hair must be her daughter's. She waved, though Moira didn't wave back. She was concentrating on following the teacher's choreography. Hands went up, hands went down, hands went up, and the children began to sing, something high-pitched and unintelligible. Five children came forward to form a front line and they held hands, spreading out. Then Moira's row came through from behind, ducking under the joined arms. Then the process reversed and Moira's line went back through the hands. She bumped into someone on her way backward and got confused, spinning in circles until the teacher pointed where she should be.

Patty was laughing, bouncing her daughter on her lap.

"They're really cute," Elm said.

"Cleo has suddenly developed a mouth on her like a sailor," Patty said. "I think she's getting it from the nanny. It's not bad words, really, just, like, a bad attitude."

"Does it come with eye rolling? Sometimes I say something so stupid that Moira can barely deign to roll her eyes."

"God, they're such teenagers already. . . . Hey, are you expecting?"

Elm blushed. "Yes, how did you . . . ?"

"You keep fanning yourself. The last time I was that hot I was pregnant."

"Yeah. I'm eleven weeks."

"Congratulations!" Patty said. She wrapped her arms around her baby to clap at the end of the first number.

"We're not really telling anyone yet, so . . . I'm getting a CVS next week. I figured after that . . ."

So far Elm felt completely different than she had during her other pregnancies. She hadn't even known she was pregnant until her sixth week the first time, and when she found out she'd had more energy than she could ever remember having.

Michel had explained to her in his slithering accent. "The embryo is the same, but your body's reaction to it cannot be predicted. You are how old now, forty-three? It is not the same, having a baby at thirty-four and forty-three. Also you maybe eat now differently? Different stress? All these affect the reaction to the pregnancy. You can only expect the same result, not the same process."

She had had to switch OBs again, and she pretended to this one that she'd just gotten new insurance and was having trouble getting her previous medical records transferred. He, of course, suspected nothing. "Seems healthy," he said. Elm always wondered if it took practice to be able to speak to someone while your hand was inside her, but all doctors seemed to take it in stride, commenting about the weather or summer camp with their finger up her vagina or palpating her breasts. Maybe it was a course they took, and Elm giggled to think of a classroom full of young med students chatting while patients tried not to move under their fingers.

Michel had insisted on the slightly risky CVS procedure, though her own gynecologist left it up to her. "Really, it's your choice. You know the risk statistics, though they're lower than the national average in New York and even lower in our practice." How like New Yorkers, Elm thought, to consider themselves in a different data category than the rest of the United States. "But you are over thirty-five, so it is indicated." Michel, meanwhile, had said that there was evidence, "anecdotal, not scientific," of increased genetic mutations in clones. Diseases that hadn't occurred to Elm, like Fragile X and DiGeorge syndrome, which occur in utero after conception as cells replicate.

Patty said, "My lips are sealed. Are you going to find out the sex?"

"We're not sure. Appointment is on Wednesday and we're still fighting about it."

"Who's for and who's against?"

"Me, both sides, actually," Elm said. "I can't decide for the life of me." Colin didn't want to find out, but he left the decision up to her. Elm was worried that if she didn't pretend to find out the sex, she would have trouble remembering to refer to the baby as both he and she.

"My husband refused to find out if Gina was a boy or a girl," Patty said. "I had to keep it from him for, like, four months. Whenever he pissed me off I threatened to tell."

Elm smiled, but her anxiety mounted. All she could think about was the amount of paperwork on her desk, and when and how to tell everyone she was expecting. She tapped her foot on the floor in time to the music to hide her frustration.

They went out for ice cream afterward at the parlor that was every kid's dream: ruffles and hats and oversized parfait glasses filled with sugar-added candied fruits and sauces. Elm had one bite and had to put down her spoon, putting her hand to her mouth in case it came back up. She was confused. With Ronan and Moira she couldn't get enough of ice cream; for a while it was the only thing she could stomach. Colin gave her a puzzled look when he saw she'd pushed the dish away. He said nothing, though; they were out with Patty and her family as well as another friend of Moira's and his parents and stepparents and -siblings. Elm slid her sundae over to him and he finished it.

Moira fell asleep in the taxi on the way home, and Colin carried her into her room. Elm stayed in the bathroom, willing the nausea to stop. How was it possible that she was still feeling nauseated? Colin came in and said, "Moira asked for you."

"Tell her I'll be in in a second."

"Are you all right?"

"I think so," Elm said. She sat on the edge of the tub and rested her head in her hands. After a few minutes she walked back into the kitchen. She poured herself a glass of seltzer and drank it slowly, standing at the counter. She heard Colin close the door to Moira's room and walk into the kitchen behind her.

He took the glass from her hand and sipped. She experienced a flash of annoyance. The familiar gesture felt like an example of his lack of consideration for her. Of course, he didn't know what she was going through.

"Elm," he said. "I have to tell you something."

She froze, her heart stopping for a second, like being on an airplane as it suddenly drops. She couldn't help but feel that this would be something catastrophic, something that they would never recover from. He would tell her a secret of the same magnitude as the one she was keeping. He was usually so silly. He had been serious only once, when he had proposed to her, and she had thought that he was going to break up with her. She admitted to herself now that even fourteen years later she wasn't really able to read him.

"What?" she breathed.

"It's about work," he said. "I haven't been completely honest with you. Or with anyone, really."

"Did you . . . Have you lost your job?" Elm was surprised at the way her voice sounded: distant, unperturbed. It was like listening to a watery recording.

"Not yet." Colin sat at the table. "Can we sit down?"

"Okay," Elm said. She slumped into a chair and forced herself to look at him. He wore an expression of anguish, his face contorted by concern and anxiety. It was still the face she knew, nose slightly askew and a little too big for his face, the eyes close-set with nearly blond lashes. She recognized something of Ronan in his face and it would therefore never be the face of a stranger, no matter what happened between them.

"Federal regulators came by," he said. "They're issuing subpoenas next week."

"So you'll have to testify."

"Yes . . ." He strung the word out. "I'm in a spot. Before he left, Al maybe wasn't quite as forthcoming as he could have been. There were studies and he withheld some of the less positive data. It's something pharma does all the time; it's sort of a tacit agreement between the companies and the FDA. You've heard me say a million times that if we had to wait for FDA approval on everything, we still wouldn't have a polio vaccine. I know it sounds like I'm justifying," he said, cutting off the gurgle that was the start of a protest from Elm. "But really it's true. If this country had fucking national health care . . ." He broke off.

"So they asked me, the regulators, and I told them a . . . softened version of the truth. Now that I'm subpoenaed I'm going to have to come clean." He paused. "I could be charged."

Elm stuck her chin forward in disbelief. "Have you talked to Clint?" she asked. "What does he say to do?"

"I haven't spoken with him yet," Colin said. "This all happened Friday. But I have a call in to him to talk about the legal. . . . I wanted to talk to you first, Elm. I hope this isn't . . ." He physically reached into the air to look for a word.

Elm provided nothing. "What if you stuck to your story?" she asked.

Colin shook his head. "It'll be under oath. Besides"—he paused—"I think it will all come out, once it's upended."

It was just like him, Elm thought, to give the ethical reason for truth before the more practical one. This was one of the things about Colin she felt was so simultaneously endearing and infuriating, his insistence on living by principles in one of the most corrupt industries on the planet. That was what she had fallen for, his scrupulous adherence to the way he saw the world, its potential rather than its actuality.

This was the time, she knew. If she was going to tell him about the baby, this was the time right here. He was vulnerable. He had admitted a mistake; she could admit one too and they would be even. It would never again be this easy. "Colin," she began.

"I'm so sorry, Elm. I don't think . . . I didn't think . . ." He grabbed her hands in his and lowered his face. She felt the warmth of his tears.

Her decision to tell him dissolved. She of all people knew what it was like to fuck up and feel guilty about it. And here was a case in which he had fucked up royally, so royally that it was possible, though not likely, Elm knew, that there would be major repercussions. If he cooperated now, nobody would bother prosecuting him. Still, Elm pictured herself enormously pregnant, taking the train to Sing Sing and waiting for visiting hours in a room with greasy handprints on the Plexiglas dividers. She freed one hand and put it on his head, ruffling his hair. She felt a wave of love, and a sense of relief remembering that he too was fallible, that mistakes and misjudgments were the hallmarks of humanity.

"It's okay," she said. "It's all right. We all make mistakes." We all lie, she could have added.

That night Colin wrapped himself around her in bed and slept with his hand on her stomach. She lay still, sleepless but comfortable, watching the lights travel across the ceiling and wishing she'd had the courage to admit her own secret. She could be sleeping now like Colin, soundly and righteously, instead of willing her breathing to be rhythmic, focusing on moving air in and out of her lungs to match her husband.

She realized that her opportunity for unburdening herself had passed. Now it was too late and she could never tell him, never tell anyone. The weight of this knowledge pressed on her and she rolled over, letting Colin's hand slip over her hip to rest on the empty sheet between them.

———

Ian looked at her quizzically across the table. "You're pregnant, admit it. Or admit that you've joined some weird cult. Otherwise there is no excuse for not ordering a martini."

"What if I'm just not in the mood?" Elm asked.

"Impossible," Ian said. "Admit the state of your uterus, or I'm ordering you a kamikaze and you're chugging it."

"Okay, okay, I'll admit it, I'm pregnant."

"Aha!" Ian said. "Congratulations!" But his voice was hollow. "How long have you known?"

So the lack of inflection was jealousy at being left out of the loop. "I couldn't tell at work yet."

"So I'm just work to you?" Ian sat back and grinned goofily, but Elm could tell that he was genuinely hurt.

"That's right. You're a rung on my ladder to success."

"Stepped on, again!" Ian flung the back of his hand to his forehead.

Elm wondered if that's how easy it was, if that's what would put everything back to normal. She had dreaded telling him for weeks, worried about his reaction and his ability to keep it a secret. She didn't want him to make a big scene, to turn it into a cause for boisterous celebration. He was prone to making everything into a big production, and Elm just wasn't ready.

Wasn't that the way of it, she mused. You worry so much about something and put it off and then it turns out not to be worth even a third of the anxiety. And then something you didn't think would be important turns out to be a bigger deal than you thought, worthy of concern and strategy.

They toasted with seltzer water and Elm let herself smile, just a little, from the inside, instead of out of sheer muscular will. And then her chicken sandwich with garlic mayonnaise and roasted red peppers looked delicious and she ate it as if she hadn't eaten in weeks. They even indulged in a chocolate soufflé.

After the CVS she spent a tense two days in bed waiting for the cramping and spotting to stop. They did, and the report came back: a boy (*quelle surprise*) and a clean bill of health. Elm let out a long exhale. The next hurdle was twenty-five weeks, the limit of viability, and then she could relax a bit, although not fully until week thirty-four, when he'd be full-term, but then not really until his actual birth, and even then not until he was past SIDS age, and then he'd be into skateboarding and rock climbing like Ronan. Who was she kidding? She would worry for the rest of her life.

Colin said nothing further about the situation at work. He said he didn't want to worry her, and there had been a stay of execution while the investigators untangled some jumble of cords in other departments. Colin said he was doing nothing at work all day, playing Scrabble online with some insomniacs in New Zealand, reorganizing his files, exchanging jokes with coworkers in the canteen.

"It's horrible, Elm," he said. "Like it's obvious that we're going to starve so we'll have to eat someone and we don't know who it is. The fat guys are especially afraid," he joked.

She scheduled a meeting with Greer for the following week. Everyone had to know she was pregnant, though. With this third pregnancy her abdominal muscles just gave up, stretching in anticipation of her growing belly. She was pinning her pants shut by the sixth week, and now, in her twelfth week, she was wearing full maternity gear.

She purposefully scheduled her appointment for the afternoon, when she knew that the sun streaming in Greer's office window wouldn't blind her. But she needn't have worried. The day was overcast, gray like canvas had been laid outside the window. She sat down and attempted to make small talk. Was Greer going to the family estate in August?

"Yes, we're all going up there. The kids are each bringing some monstrous friend. The mosquitoes have been unbearable these last couple of years."

"They were always bad," she said. "Down by the boathouse?"

"I suppose they were. And it's really gotten hot. We've had to put air-conditioning in all the cottages. The main house is insufferable."

Elm remembered many nights on the screened-in sleeping porch, praying for breezes and hoping her bed partners (there were always piles of cousins) wouldn't move any closer, sweat pooling in any concavity. But she gave a sympathetic grunt.

"And, well, there's this situation there, but I'll tell you later." He was doing it again, piquing her curiosity by bringing up something and then delaying telling her. It would probably be something completely uninteresting, but now she wanted to know. She knew he wouldn't give her the satisfaction of telling her, so she didn't give him the satisfaction of showing her curiosity. A silence descended.

"So," Greer said. "To what do I owe the honor of this meeting?"

"You may already know," Elm said, "but I'm expecting again."

"That's great!" Greer said. "I'm sure you must be very happy after . . ."

Elm's face flushed. It absolutely infuriated her when people tried to suggest that someone could ever replace Ronan. But of course, she had replaced him.

"Can I ask you when you're due, as a relative, not as a boss. I'm not sure I'm allowed to ask that legally, except as a cousin."

"June," she said.

"That's when we're ramping up for fall."

Elm nodded. What was she supposed to do about it? It wasn't like some sort of vacation she could postpone to a more advantageous time. "We're always busy."

"I suppose June's as good a time as any." Greer sighed. He jiggled his mouse and looked at something on his screen. This was WASP for "time to leave." "You'll work up until the date, yes?"

Elm stood up. "Unless doctors tell me otherwise." She smiled. "Thanks for your consideration, Greer." She sounded like the close of a business letter, but if he detected something less than genuine in her tone, he didn't respond.

————

The e-mails of congratulations started pouring in. Having a baby was slightly more interesting in New York, where almost everyone, it seemed, had some sort of journey toward parenthood, either to China or Ethiopia or via infertility treatments. What Elm had been through was everyone's worst nightmare, and now they wanted to believe it could be erased. Also, while everyone had been unable to help Elm, to share in her grief, they might be able to make up that lapse now, by celebrating the happy occasion. Elm had to insist on only one baby shower.

And then came the censorious looks. Elm had forgotten that when you're pregnant you're public property. People touch your stomach without asking, even when any visible roundness might be an accumulation of fat rather than the swell of fertility. Because you are a vessel that is carrying the Future of the World, your every move is scrutinized: Should you really be eating that? Sugar in pregnancy can lead to gestational diabetes, which can lead to obesity in the infant's later life. That Diet Coke has caffeine! Phenylalanine can be neurotoxic to developing fetuses. Elm began to eat lunch in her office. She hid her diet Sprite in a Vitaminwater bottle.

It was really happening. It wasn't just in her mind; people were starting to cede seats to her on the subway, smile at her on the street. Moira loved to lie on her, cooing baby talk to her belly button, drawing circles around it with her fingers.

Colin's reaction Elm found more puzzling. He swung from the extreme solicitousness he showed during her pregnancy with Ronan (he scolded her for overexertion for merely bending to tie her shoes) to his laissez-faire "I've done this before" nonchalance with Moira (she'd nearly had her daughter at home, waiting for Colin to finish up his phone calls and take a shower). Sometimes he was gallantry incarnate, propping her feet with pillows, offering to take out the trash, letting her watch the dance competition television show that was her guilty pleasure. Other times he barely seemed to notice her. His snoring, which in addition to being annoying and a source of complaint was also a comfort to Elm, began to change. It grew erratic, staccato. Elm wondered if she was sending him mixed signals, excited and scared in such a complicated way that he was unable to understand how he was supposed to feel.

In early February, Ian showed up at her office door. Elm was snarfing an egg salad sandwich on white bread, shoving it down her maw before anyone came in to comment on fat content or salmonella. She held up a hand while she swallowed.

"Have you seen?" he asked.

"What?" Elm asked.

"Turn your computer on. Google Indira Schmidt."

Elm did, and read:

Reuters, Paris, France—February 4, 2008. French police, in cooperation with United Kingdom law enforcement, today arrested Augustus Klinman, who holds a U.K. passport. Klinman, 66, is accused of creating and selling forged paintings and drawings for personal profit.

"Mr. Klinman has raised vast sums of money by selling fraudulent art," said the head of regional Interpol, Sevier Becard, in a statement made today in Paris.

"He was able to perpetrate these acts by claiming that the pieces were found after the Nazi regime fell, and the works' owners were either deceased or unable to be identified. While it appears he has indeed shared some of the profit with other families of survivors, this Robin Hood is still a criminal."

Tobias Schnell, a spokesperson for Holocaust Survivors for Reparation of Stolen Art—a nonprofit organization dedicated to uniting Holocaust survivors and descendants with their families' art—reached at his home in Frankfurt, Germany, said, "It is unfortunate that a criminal is using the tragedy of the Holocaust for personal profit. Those of us who deal with art stolen by the Nazi regime aim only to return it to its rightful owners or their heirs."

The Nazis looted many homes in France, Austria, Germany, and Holland. Hitler and Goering, his commanding officer, took many of Europe's greatest works for their own personal collections (and a planned Führermuseum). Other art that was considered "degenerate" was destroyed. Still more was injured beyond repair during bombings.

In 1946, the Monument Men, a group of American art lovers, found a trove of masterpieces in a cave in the Jura region of France. Since then, the idea that works by such artists as Rembrandt, Ingres, Picasso, Vermeer, and others might be hidden in cellars has captured popular imagination.

"There is definitely art out there that has yet to be returned to its owners, or is still unidentified in a hiding place since forgotten," Schnell confirmed. "But to use it to perpetrate fraud is unconscionable."

Even when art is authenticated, its owners are difficult to determine, as records didn't exist or were destroyed. "This makes it exceedingly difficult to reunite art with its owners," Schnell said.

Klinman, whose extended family perished in 1943 in Bergen-Belsen, was born in China and grew up in Leeds, England. He is unmarried and has no children. His lawyers made this statement: "These allegations are completely false. Augustus Klinman has done nothing illegal, and it is unfortunate that anti-Semitism so persists in this day and age that people are quick to condemn before evidence is presented."

Police officials claim that Klinman had the art, mostly drawings, forged in Paris, though he seems to have had several international victims and clients. According to officials, who have yet to interview her, the internationally known ceramicist Indira Schmidt is a person of interest in this case.

Klinman's arrest follows an intensive multiyear investigation into international art forgery rings in Europe.

Elm stared at the screen in disbelief. Klinman arrested? Indira a person of interest? Indira was innocent; she had to be innocent. But if she were a person of interest, sooner or later the investigators would come and speak to her about the drawings and paintings Tinsley's sold on Indira's behalf in the spring auction. At the very least it would cast doubt on the legitimacy of the drawings' attribution. Elm could be implicated in the conspiracy as well. And if they found out about the drawings she sold with Relay . . .

She could do this. She'd had months of practice. "Wow," she said. "That's a scandal." Her mind spun. Elm thought to herself: What do I need? Wallet, keys, phone.

"But her pieces last spring in the auction. The provenances were good, right?" Ian looked at her expectantly.

"Hmmm," Elm breathed. They were decidedly not good. Flimsy, really. *Mercat* was given to her before the war and she kept it behind the sofa all those years? It threw everything into doubt. "I have to go," Elm said. "I have a prenatal appointment."

"That must be wonderful, to see the baby moving on the sonogram," Ian said.

"Yes, it is." Elm shut down her computer. Did Ian not see that Elm was hurrying, putting on her jacket, gathering her briefcase? "Can you hold down the fort?"

Ian spread his hands wide across the desk, bolting it to the floor. It was a quick gesture that would have been corny had anyone else done it, but he was fast enough to remove his hands to seem like he was parodying the type of person who would make such a stupid joke, even as he made it. "You're in a meeting," he said. "All afternoon."

"You're a peach."

"Did you just call me a peach?" he called after her down the hall. "The PC term is 'apricot-challenged.'"

Elm

The cab ride took forever. The driver went across the park and then up Riverside, but the street was blocked off for some reason and he had to go around all the way to Columbus and then back over. Elm tried to call Colette—she had brought Klinman to Elm's attention, maybe she knew something about this—but there was no answer. Elm was buzzed into the building without speaking to anyone, and rode the piss-smelling elevator up to Indira's apartment, willing it to go faster, even as she wanted to postpone what she knew would be a confrontation.

It took the old woman several minutes to answer the door, during which time Elm's bladder filled. She found that with this pregnancy, her urges to urinate were more frequent and more urgent. When the door opened, Elm said, "I need to use your bathroom."

"Go right ahead," Indira said.

Elm peed and washed her hands. When she came out of the bathroom, Indira was sitting in her armchair smoking a joint.

Elm said, "Can you please not smoke that? I'm expecting."

"That's good," Indira said, letting out another fragrant breath. "It's nice that now even older women can conceive."

Elm flushed. You have no idea, she wanted to say, what science has wrought in this body. "I read the article."

"I thought you would," Indira said. "And now you want to know what I know. What I knew."

"Right."

"Sit," Indira said.

"I'd rather stand."

Indira shrugged, indifferent. There was a long silence.

"Well?" Elm asked.

"Well what? Ask. I will answer."

"Do you know Augustus Klinman?"

"That is complicated. Yes, I have met the man. He spoke a few years ago at a symposium about stolen art that has found a home in the United States. No, I have never dealt with him professionally."

"Then why did the paper say that you're a person of interest?"

"Maybe he dropped my name to exonerate himself. How should I know? Maybe he believes I'm an authority? Because I'm an artist?" Indira stared off dreamily out the window, her eyes cloudy with cataracts. It must have been a habit; she couldn't possibly see anything. Maybe the light was refreshing. Something in Elm softened. Indira was just a little old lady. Even if she had committed a crime, she could hardly be held responsible at her age. Elm sat in the armchair across from her.

"What about the drawings I sold for you?" Elm said. "Those were authentic, right?"

"How should I know?" Indira asked with exaggerated innocence. "You're supposed to be the expert."

Elm stiffened. She sat up straight. She saw that she had been played and was breathless, as though the baby had suddenly begun pressing on her lungs. "You knew they were fake?"

"I don't know what I have or had lying around here. My memory isn't what it was."

Elm felt her rage expand. She stood up, clenching her fists. She wanted to hit an octogenarian genius ceramicist, and she didn't feel bad about it. She wanted to slap Indira's wrinkled smile, stub the joint out into her neck. "How dare you?" she sputtered.

Indira said nothing.

"This jeopardizes my career. Not to mention . . . if anyone suspects I knew, I could go to jail. You play this 'little old lady' routine, but you're smart and you're wily and you don't care who gets hurt."

Indira continued to stare out the window.

Elm said, "I'm turning you in. I'm leaving here right now and going to the police, or the FBI or whoever. Someone at Tinsley's will know whom to contact. I can't believe I trusted you. I told you about Ronan, for chrissakes." At the mention of his name, Elm began to cry, angry sobs of frustration.

Indira waited until Elm calmed down, passing her a box of tissues. "The police are not an option," Indira said, finally. "And you know that. You know that because you too have done what I did."

"I never knowingly—"

"Stop," Indira said. "I don't say this to criticize, only to make clear to you what happens when the truth comes out. During the war, my parents, it is not so surprising, they were taken to the camps and because they were old they were killed. My brother was put to work digging graves. He was strong; he survived the war, long enough to send a letter to our home, which I received years later. But he never made it back home. Did he die? Was he killed? Did he kill himself? It is not known. My sister-in-law I saw for the last time in a propaganda film. She was pregnant, not before the war, but during, which means that the father was most likely not my brother. In the film she is drawing at an arts-and-crafts table. The camera pans quickly, but you can see on the paper her drawing of a house. Only, it's not just a house, it's a *Shin*, the twenty-second letter of the Hebrew alphabet. The filmmakers wouldn't have known; that's how it slipped through, this symbol of resistance. Her name was on a manifest of the gassed. I don't know if she ever gave birth. My cousins, my twin aunts, uncles, all taken. How do we get back what was taken from us? Some things are irreplaceable. Others are not. You, of all people, know the difference. I can see from your body that you do."

Elm felt a knot of worry. Could she know about Ronan? Impossible.

"Your friend Klinman has sent you drawings that I'm told wouldn't fool an old blind woman. You, in turn, have given them to a dealer, who has placed them prominently in the city. She will not be happy to discover that these are fakes."

Elm sat; her legs weren't strong enough to support her. A prickling rose up her neck, an eerie feeling of slowly being electrocuted.

How could she not have seen this coming? It was too good to be true, the drawings arriving just as she needed them. Too good to be true always meant its opposite: not true, not good.

She opened her mouth to speak, but couldn't decide what to say. She wanted to smack the joint from the woman's mouth, and the violence of the urge scared her; it seemed so unlike her, so unlike who she used to be. Instead, she grabbed the antimacassar on the arm of the chair and squeezed it.

"Were you? Did you . . . think of this?"

"No, dear." Indira chuckled. "At this stage, my mind gets fuzzy if I think more than two steps ahead. I make tea and by the time I've gotten the milk out I forget what I wanted. It's a blessing, honestly. The future is always the present."

"But who involved me?" Elm asked. "Who got me into this?"

Indira took another long puff on her joint, looking like nothing so much as the caterpillar from Moira's *Alice in Wonderland* DVD. "You did."

———

During the cab ride home from Indira's, Elm rubbed her belly and tried not to cry. She made it to the elevator in her building before putting her head to the mirrored wall to sob, her breath made shorter by Ronan's constriction of her lungs. What the fuck had she done?

It was still early, and Wania hadn't yet picked up Moira from school. She had ballet this afternoon and wouldn't get home until after six. Colin wouldn't be back until seven or eight. That gave Elm three hours to get herself together.

She lay on her bed. There must be a way she could salvage this. What if she said nothing, stayed on at Tinsley's? The auction house was sure to come under scrutiny during an investigation. Auction houses always claimed that any illegal behavior was simply one bad seed, acting alone. At best, the house would receive bad press, a hit they could not afford in this climate. Elm would be thrown under the bus.

She would resign. Admit herself duped and clear out her desk. Ian would probably never speak to her again, but he'd be all right. He'd ingratiate himself to her successor the same way he charmed everyone else.

And that successor would probably be Colette. Why hadn't she seen it? Colette had brought her to Klinman. She was probably part of the whole thing. Hell, maybe she even orchestrated it. And she was seemingly blameless—nothing linked Colette to Klinman to Tinsley's. The only link there was Elm.

What had made Elm think she was capable of this kind of scheming? Elm couldn't even play tic-tac-toe, and she had fashioned herself a role as a duplicitous con artist. Someone should have stopped her. If she had confided in anyone. Why hadn't she told her husband? She didn't trust him anymore, she realized. Their grieving had taken different directions, made them peer at each other through new eyes as the other took a course that the partner disapproved of. She had forgiven him for losing their son as much as she'd forgiven herself, but she still wondered: What if he had grabbed Ronan when the wave hit? What if he had reacted faster, had more presence of mind? It was different from blame, it was disappointment, and she knew he could sense it.

She would just have to tell him about Indira. But then she would have to tell him about Relay. And then about Ronan. Was there a way to leave that out? The secret was a cluster of tin cans strapped to a fender, banging and clanging wherever she went. Not telling had become a full-time job. The literature from the clinic should have warned her about this. Colin would never forgive her if she told him. He would leave her, whether for the deceit or the cloning or both. She knew him well enough to know this about him.

What if they proved she knew the drawings were fake? Would she go to jail? She was fucked. Fucked fucked fucked. But at least she had Ronan, and in a few months he'd be with her again, and she could be in jail or in hell, for all she cared, as long as she got to hold him in her arms again.

———

"Ian," Elm called as he was leaving the break room, a mug in his hands.

"Hello, dahling," he said. "Exciting plans for Presidents' Day?"

"I have to talk to you," she said. Her voice cracked, even as she tried to keep her face neutral.

Ian paled. "Are you okay? Is the baby . . . ?"

"No, it's fine. It's about work," she said. She felt a flood of relief. No one was hurt. No one was sick. Her baby was fine. The rest was all inconvenience. "Let's go to the Cockroach."

"Okay . . ." Ian dragged the word out. "Can you give me a preview?"

Elm shook her head. "Meet you there in five minutes. No, ten. I have to pee, for a change."

The Cockroach was their name for The Coach House diner around the corner. It was disgusting, but it had the advantage of good acoustics and the fact that no one from Tinsley's would be caught dead there.

She found him in "their" booth, pushing his spoon around a bowl of oatmeal with raisins.

"This is gross," he said.

"I'll eat it." He pushed it across the table to her. She took a bite. It was gross, but food was fuel to her now; she was simply refilling the gas tank.

"I'm dying here," Ian said. He tried to cross his leg under the table but was too tall. "You have to tell me what's wrong."

"Okay," Elm said. "Promise you won't be angry."

"I don't promise beforehand," Ian said. "I've been hurt too many times."

"Then promise to *try* not to be angry."

"Okay, fine, get on with it."

"I, uh, think that Indira Schmidt gave us forged pieces."

"What? That's impossible. We had them authenticated."

Elm shrugged.

Ian said, "But it's not your fault. Fakes get put through all the time."

"But ethically, they shouldn't."

"Ethically," he echoed. They sat in silence for a moment. "What else?" Ian asked.

"What do you mean?"

"I mean, what else is there for you to tell me?"

"That's it." Elm held her palms open to show that there was nothing up her sleeve.

"Uh-uh." Ian shook his head. "I don't believe you. You don't look empty."

"I don't look what? Look, Ian, I already told you that I think I may be in trouble, possibly even with the police, and definitely with my job, at a time when my husband's about to lose his and I'm pregnant."

Ian drummed his fingers on the table, impatient. His other hand played with a package of Sweet'N Low.

"What about Relay? I mean—" Ian leaned across the table closer to her. For the first time since she'd known him, Ian seemed angry, even menacing. "What about the drawings you sold through Relay?"

"What?" Elm said.

"We reconnected at the auction and we've had dinner a few times. She's actually grown into a really nice person. She said you'd given her drawings to sell, which seemed strange to me. First, because you never said anything, at least not to me, which, by the way, I'm hurt about."

"Sorry," Elm said. "With everything on my mind I've just—"

"Why in the world would you give her drawings to sell instead of putting them up for auction at Tinsley's? Relay said she didn't know. And she hadn't thought to ask. Intelligence, not necessarily one of her most attractive traits."

Actually, Elm thought, claiming ignorance was a sign of acumen that Elm neglected to demonstrate.

"So I say to myself, 'Self,' I say, 'why is Elm pimping out drawings and not telling me?' Either she doesn't think they're worthy of the auction house, and in that case it's shitty to be foisting them on Relay, even though she doesn't know any better. Or she needs the money. Either way, it seems like something Greer would not be thrilled about, or it's potentially illegal. What are you involved in, Elm, and why didn't you tell me?"

Elm began to cry but she didn't avert her glance. "I need the money. Colin's going to lose his job; he has to testify in court. And yes, Relay's drawings were probably fakes. But they were convincing, and enjoyable, and, for all I know, possibly real. And it was helping out these Jews whose art was lost in the . . ." She trailed off. This was Klinman's line, his bullshit story. Suddenly, she understood Indira's attitude. Elm didn't care. She didn't care who got hurt as long as she could have Ronan. There were so many steps between Relay and Elm and Klinman, and the forger. . . . It was a gulf that stretched too wide to imagine, a snarling, rough sea. And it had swallowed her up and carried her out.

Her tears dried as she finally put the pieces together. But here was Ian, waiting for her to speak, to explain herself, to save their friendship, her job, and his.

"I didn't know," she said. "I didn't think it would get so huge. Indira's art looked authentic. We ran it through the paces."

"Yes, but to prove it was original, not to prove it was fake. It's different."

"What the fuck do I do now, Ian?" Elm looked up at him. His gaze was stern, like a father's. The disappointment radiated out from his forehead, wrinkled in dismay.

"Look, Relay won't say anything. And I'm not going to say anything. We never even had this conversation. Maybe the media attention will die down."

"An Englishman using the world's most famous ceramicist as a shill to sell fake art through one of the world's most venerated auction houses? Yeah, no one will want to hear about that," Elm said. She tried to catch the waitress's eye. She was famished. She wanted a grilled cheese sandwich so badly her knuckles ached. "Shit, shit, shit. Why didn't I just stay out of it?"

"More like, why did you drag me in?" Ian saved her by saying, "Excuse me," to the passing waitress.

"Grilled cheese, no tomato, please." Elm looked at Ian, who shook his head.

"How can you eat?"

"I'm not eating. The parasite is. What do you think I should do?"

"Lie low," Ian said. "Get lots of doctors' appointments. Can you get put on bed rest?"

"I don't know," said Elm. "I think I'm done with deception," she said, even as she realized that her deception ran so deep she would never be done.

———

Elm and Colin both took the day off before the long weekend. Moira ran around the living room singing at the top of her lungs, so excited was she to have vacation, and both parents home. Elm knew how little time she and Colin had spent together recently. She was also aware that though she had been living in the apartment, participating in family dinners and arranging pickups and drop-offs, playdates and meals, she had been with her family only in body. In spirit she had been . . . in a clinic, in France, getting impregnated with her dead child. Or on a beach in Thailand, watching as the wave came in to lay waste to her life.

Elm was making a dinner shopping list, which so far consisted of chicken and ice cream. She rubbed her lower back with her left hand, then felt Colin's hands on her shoulders, kneading the flesh there.

"We have to talk, Elmtree," he said.

Something in his voice, his touch, suggested sex. She was not in the mood, but she let herself be led to the bedroom after putting on a television show for Moira.

In the room, he sat her on the bed, and she could see he was no more interested in sex than she was. He began to pace, chewing on his hangnails as he did when he was nervous, so that she had trouble understanding what he said.

She asked him to repeat himself.

"It's over, Elm," he said.

There was a moment when she couldn't breathe. How had he found out about Ronan? Or had he done something else? Had he fallen in love while she wasn't looking? He wouldn't leave her six months pregnant, would he? He was so loyal; only the colossal lie of her pregnancy could make him leave her.

"I'm out," he said. "Don't look so scared; you're fairly pale. Do you need to lie down?"

Elm shook her head.

"I'll get another job, Elm. It's not like it's impossible. And I can stay home with the baby if nothing else pans up."

Elm deflated. He was leaving his job. Not her.

"Pans out," she corrected. "What happened?"

"HR scheduled a meeting on Tuesday. I brought home all the interesting files yesterday."

"And . . ." Elm still felt out of breath. Her heart was racing; she couldn't completely fill her lungs.

"They're not pursuing legal action. They are just going to shove it all under the rug and sweep away any crumbs. I'm a crumb. It's for the best, really. It's time to move on."

Elm nodded.

"It'll be okay, sweetheart. You're working. We have savings. It'll be all right."

"I, uh—" Elm held up her finger while she swallowed. Colin brought her the glass of water from the nightstand. Elm took a long swallow.

"Things aren't looking so great at Tinsley's right now. I have to . . . I wasn't—" Elm began to sob, then dry-heave. Colin, concerned, sat next to her on the bed, holding her while she made noises that hadn't come out of her since the days after Ronan's death, guttural grunts and wails. Moira knocked at the door.

"Not now, gobeen," Colin called. "Everything's grand. Go back to the television."

"I'm okay, go to her," Elm said.

"No," Colin said. "I'm here. Tell me. It can't be as bad as all that."

"It can," Elm said, calming.

"Mommy, I'm hungry," Moira called from behind the closed door.

"Wait a minute, sweetie," Elm said.

She took a deep breath. She would tell him. She could tell him and then this would all be over. She would tell him, he'd be angry, then he'd forgive her. He'd see that she had done the best thing for all of them. She put her hand on her belly.

"There was all this pressure. From Greer, and then your job thing, so I—"

"Elm, you're not making sense." Colin shook his head.

"Mommy, will you fix me lunch?"

"In a minute," they both chimed.

"Get a yogurt drink from the fridge," Elm called. "Okay," she said to Colin. "The beginning was before the auction, and Greer kept threatening me if I didn't get some good commissions. And then, suddenly, these two things came up. First, there was Indira Schmidt. Remember the ceramicist I told you about? The one who survived the Holocaust? She was profiled in *The New Yorker* a few years back?"

"All right . . ." Colin clearly didn't remember.

"She had this amazing collection of drawings, and this one Connois pastel that she said Blatzenger gave her when he went to France. They were having an affair. For years, apparently."

"From Nixon's administration?"

"It was, it is, a beautiful piece, and the story behind it is incredible. The poor lady, she's nearly blind. So I sent everything off to be authenticated, or rather, Ian did, and it went up for auction, which was a great success, remember?"

"Aye," Colin said.

"Okay, hold that in your mind while I tell you the rest of the story."

"I'll try," Colin said, his clipped tones betraying his confusion.

"Colette told me to call this Klinman guy in France."

"The reason you went to Paris, I remember," Colin said.

Elm felt a poke of guilt behind her ribs. The baby flipped inside her. "That, and . . . But initially, I didn't call him, because of Colette, right?"

"Colette the cow."

Elm smiled weakly at his attempt to cheer her with Irish slang. "You're not going to like this."

"I can tell."

"But his drawings were good, or they looked good. Not good enough for the auction house. But, I mean, decorative, convincing. Do you remember we went to that party in TriBeCa, and I met that art adviser? So I took Klinman's drawings and gave them to her and she sold them and we split the money."

"Elm." Colin's disappointment was palpable from the bass of his voice.

"Their provenances were—they were all stolen from Jewish families during World War II, and just recently returned. The families didn't want to come forward."

"I don't understand, Elm." Colin always thought the best of Elm, refused to recognize her faults, even when they were so obvious they might have been tattooed across her forehead. "The drawings were fake?"

"Well, that's hard to prove. But they weren't . . . right."

"Couldn't you X-ray them?"

Elm said, "FTIR is expensive, plus it's better for paintings." Elm looked at Colin, really looked at him for the first time since she began speaking. So far, she could tell by the set of his jaw that he was angry, but not so much that he would not forgive her. She wished she could stop talking, stop time, or stop her involvement in this story right here, at the part where her actions were merely bad, not despicable. But it was too late. She had to let it all out.

"Sounds like straight shite."

"Can you please not speak again until I'm done?" Elm said, impatience crowding her words. Stung, Colin stood, facing her.

"The whole thing blew up. Klinman was selling fakes and Indira Schmidt was one of his fences. And I was too dumb to suspect her because she's this famous artist. I thought someone just copied the authentic pastel. Now I think maybe that was a test, by Klinman, to see how good, or how bad, my eye was, how blind I'd become since . . ." She held up both her hands to stop him from speaking. "An article came out a few days ago in the paper. Klinman was arrested in some sort of international sting operation. Indira is a person of interest. It's only a matter of time until they come to talk to me." Elm paused.

"Are you done?" Colin asked. He said it so nonchalantly, like he was asking her if she was done with the half-and-half so he could put some in his coffee.

"I wish," Elm said.

"There's something more? Something worse?"

Elm nodded. She began to breathe faster.

"Wait, what did you do with the money?" Colin spat.

"At that party, in TriBeCa, Relay told me that your friends, the whoosits, from Budokon class, were cloning their pet."

"They've too much money and not enough sense." Colin sighed. Then his face paled. His arms fell to his sides and his eyes opened wide.

"What? Elm? That's impossible."

Elm began to cry again. "It's not impossible. I did it. This—" She pointed to her stomach. "This is Ronan."

"Motherfucking hell!" Colin yelled. In response, Elm heard the television volume grow from the living room. Cartoon Dora was screaming now too, slightly louder than Colin. It wouldn't be long before their grouchy downstairs neighbor came up to complain.

"Elm, you fecking eejit, what the hell have you done?" She had never seen Colin this angry; he spit a bit as he swore at her. His hands were curled now into fists. Elm was worried he might hit her, then hoped he would. She deserved to be hit, but he never would; he was not a violent man.

"Do you know how fucking illegal and experimental that is? How can you even be sure that it's really his DNA? What if it comes out with five heads, or a tail or something?"

"It won't," Elm said. "You've been with me to the sonograms."

"No one knows what happens to these clones." Colin began to pace. "No one knows what happens when they grow up, *if* they grow up."

"But—"

"No," Colin roared. "Now you wait until I'm done. How could you think you could replace him? By getting another body that looked like him? How do you even know that it's Ronan, that you didn't get duped by some sawbones? Do you know what happens to all these animals people are cloning now? They die, Elm. How dare you set us up to lose him again? How dare you?"

Elm said, "Human clones aren't like animal clones. . . . Something about the brain's ability to re-myelinate?"

He closed his mouth and looked at her. "Who the fuck are you?" He stood up abruptly and left their room. Elm followed him down the hall in time to see him grab his jacket off the rack in the entryway, and slam the front door.

"Where'd Daddy go?" Moira asked, unfazed, as always, by her mother's tears.

"Business trip."

Gabriel

On his way to Colette's house, Gabriel walked through the Passy Cemetery, a setting befitting his mood. The weather, however, was not cooperating. There was pale, cool sunshine and a light breeze, clouds passing quickly overhead, grouping and regrouping, forming interesting shapes. Maybe he could convince Colette to go to the park instead of somewhere fancy for dinner with her friends who spoke so quickly Gabriel had trouble following the conversation.

He had sensed that she was annoyed at him being in her apartment. She had begun to nag him to straighten up after himself, to do the dishes every once in a while. They had gotten into an argument, and Gabriel stormed off back to his apartment, where his roommates reintroduced themselves as a joke. Colette didn't return his calls for two days, even though he apologized profusely. Then a third day went by, and Gabriel began to worry, spinning fantasies of a crashed cab, a fatal illness, or, worse, that she'd met someone whose future might be brighter than his.

Finally he'd reached her on the fourth day and she sounded glad to hear from him. She accepted his apology and said yes to meeting up with him that afternoon. He felt oddly insecure about their relationship. He didn't want to examine what made him feel worried that she would dump him. Or, rather, that he would feel horrible *when* she dumped him. He was already feeling twinges of the humiliation, sadness, and self-loathing he would experience when it ended. Because it had to end. She was way out of his league. Beautiful, successful, popular, and, most important, French. She had the unattainable command of the French language and customs that he would never, ever master. She floated in and out of rooms, stores, parties, gliding through barely cracked door-ways with wit and popularity, while he stomped into barriers, fumbling and clumsy.

What if he broke it off before she could? Might that work? He was starting to scare himself. He rang her buzzer and waited. There was no response. He rang again. Nothing. Maybe she was late. He checked his phone. He texted her. After fifteen minutes he went to the corner and ordered a coffee, which he drank standing at the bar and looking at her front door.

She arrived an hour and a half after they'd planned to meet. Colette didn't even look around as she let herself in. Gabriel waited exactly five minutes. He ran through various fantasies in which he confronted her about her tardiness, her complete disregard for him or his time. In that scenario she apologized and confessed that she did it because she wanted him to break up with her; she loved him too much. Or, rather, she admitted to being purposely late so that he'd get fed up and dump her, saving her the trouble. In yet another reverie, he imagined her opening the door full of remorse, apologizing for the *métro* construction. Gabriel decided to say nothing to her and see if she would bring it up.

"Hey you." She gave him a passionless kiss; she had been eating cheese. Then she hugged him, grabbing her elbows around his back. "So, skinny. Don't you eat? Oh, sorry I'm late."

Colette didn't offer any further explanation. Gabriel swallowed a lump.

"Let's pretend we never fought. Want to go see a film tonight? There's a Billy Wilder retrospective at Action Christine."

"Again?" Gabriel never understood why the French liked seeing old movies in the theater when you could watch them on DVD just as easily in your house, for ten euros less.

"You'll get to spend time with me in the dark," she said suggestively.

"Fine," he agreed. He excused himself to the bathroom.

Once inside the tiny water closet, looking at the white tile above the toilet, dick in hand, Gabriel had a moment of self-pity, which he excused as clarity. Everything in his life started out full of promise, and it all petered out before it could be properly enjoyed. And why? Because Gabriel was always the wrong person. The right things happened, but they should not have happened to him. All these opportunities: the École, his mediocre solo show, his relationship with Colette, were doomed to expire because he was the object of them. This thought was comforting; it wasn't his fault. It wouldn't be his fault.

He pulled the chain and watched the liquid travel around in circles before it disappeared.

"What's wrong?" she asked as he came out.

There were no words. He blew a breath out of his lips.

Colette laughed. "What is it?"

"I feel like . . . We're fighting. My show, it only got attention because of Connois."

"Oh, don't start that again." Colette lit a cigarette. She changed out of her business suit, an act that was completely devoid of eroticism. "You exploit him too. Hell, you've made tons of money forging his work." Colette caught herself, and shut her mouth with an O. Seeing the awareness flood his face, she said, "You really thought I didn't know? Is it possible you're really that gullible?"

"That what?" Gabriel didn't know the word.

"That you believe the good in everybody?"

"No. I don't know."

"How do you think Augustus got rid of his drawings? Your drawings?" Colette put down her cigarette to pull a dress over her head.

"He sold them."

"Right." Colette nodded. She hung her suit in the small closet. "To whom? Without a provenance. How did he sell them?"

"Oh. Through you. To Tinsley's." Realization unfogged Gabriel's head. He looked inside himself, ready to be angry, but found only hurt.

"*Et bah voilà.*" Colette waved her hand like it held a magic wand.

"That's . . . that's . . ."

"That's . . . ?" Colette encouraged him.

Gabriel shut his mouth. What was he going to say? Illegal? Immoral? He was hardly blameless, but it surprised him that Colette was this capable of deceit. It made him see her in a new light, respect her a bit more, and fear her too.

"Well, that explains why you're with me," Gabriel said.

"You have the self-esteem of a newt," Colette said to the window, blowing out a ring of smoke. "Why would that explain that? What would that make me? Thank you for the compliment," she said sarcastically. "No, I'm with you because you fuck like you're scared shitless of me, and I like that in a man."

"Oh." Gabriel could think of nothing else to say. He wasn't sure if he was supposed to feel flattered or insulted.

Colette stubbed her cigarette out. "So forget about my uncle, and forget about art world political bullshit, and come here."

"I'm too scared," Gabriel joked. And Colette grabbed his shoulders, pulling him onto his back. When she kissed him he could taste the acidic, dusty remnants of the cigarette.

―――

Every year Gabriel's studiomates held a joint Christmas party, but with typical artistic languor, by the time they got around to organizing, it was February. Usually, there was a lot of one sort of food. One year everyone brought sausages and no one brought baguettes. Another there were eighteen bottles of wine and no food. This year, it appeared to be almost all side dishes: tabbouleh, *céleri rémoulade*, and shredded carrot salad.

Hans's wife had the baby in a sort of sling across her abdomen, and Hans inched as far away from her as possible. He looked tired, his skin hanging off his face. Didier started the grill, set up in the middle of the warehouse. He was wearing an apron that said "Kiss the cook" in English.

Gabriel brought Didier another beer.

"Hey," Didier said. "Where's Colette?"

Gabriel lifted the corner of his mouth and shrugged. He had been trying to get ahold of her for two days, but she wasn't even returning his texts.

"Are you no longer dating?"

"Why, do you want my secondhand kisses?"

"Ha," Didier said. He snorted and turned the lonely brochette 180 degrees. "I just wondered."

"I don't know," Gabriel answered the earlier question. "Yeah, I mean, I guess." He wanted Didier to ask him further, to probe a little bit so that Gabriel could admit he had asked her to the barbecue but she had blown him off. *I don't think it's my crowd,* she'd said.

Didier took the sole brochette off the grill and put it on a waiting plate. "Really? No one else brought meat?"

"I have some veggie burgers," Marie-Laure said.

"I'd rather eat Hans's shorts," Didier said.

"I like them," Marie-Laure said.

"Hans's shorts?"

"Don't be such a fucking adolescent."

Sitting down on the crates and broken folding chairs that made up the "courtyard" of the studio, Gabriel took his minuscule bite of beef and pushed the salads around on his plate. Everyone shivered in the cold.

Marie-Laure sat on her new boyfriend's lap, feeding him playfully. She was wearing a short skirt that revealed her underwear when she sat, white with red stripes. Didier was staring right at it. Hans took his turn with the baby, holding her in one arm and drinking giant gulps of beer with the other.

Gabriel felt clouds of gloom descend over him. He sometimes got this way, especially on Sundays. Everything in Paris was closed, the harsh metal grates like prison bars. Now, surrounded by friends, he was supposed to be enjoying himself, but instead he saw Hans trying to escape from his family; Didier acting like a fourteen-year-old, his fancy show having done nothing for his career; Marie-Laure giving too much to yet another loser; and Gabriel himself, his dreams of a solo show turning out to be not the success he'd hoped for after all. The lump in his throat got bigger, and he worried he might cry. He put down his plate to go inside, but his studio, dark, musty, full of his failures writ large on canvas, depressed him further. He went back outside to join Hans in drinking himself into oblivion.

He was finishing his third beer when his phone buzzed in his pocket. He took it out, assuming it was Colette, finally.

Instead, it was a text from Lise. "Must meet. Biche Blanche. 1 hr."

Gabriel stared at his phone. What could be so urgent? He felt pre-emptively guilty, like he'd done something terribly wrong and would have to beg forgiveness. But he couldn't think of what he'd done to Lise. Maybe she'd left her husband and wanted to declare her love for Gabriel. Maybe she'd gotten fired from Ambrosine's. Maybe Ambrosine offered her a show. Maybe Ambrosine wanted to offer Gabriel a show.

When he got to the café she was smoking and drinking a Cognac. He gave her two kisses and discovered that she smelled like cigarettes instead of her usual lemongrass perfume.

"You've read this, I assume." She plopped *Le Monde* down in front of him. Her tone was accusatory.

"I don't really read news. In French."

Lise was wearing a low-cut top. He could see the scaffolding of her ribs above the shirt. Too thin, he thought.

"Read." She nudged the paper at him again.

Gabriel held the paper out farther so he could read the small type. It took him awhile to read the article. When he was done, he read it again. Lise stubbed out her cigarette and lit another. His coffee came.

His mind spun. Klinman had been arrested? Think, he forced himself. He drank a sip of coffee, trying to hide behind the cup. Klinman arrested. Where was Colette? What would happen to Gabriel? Klinman could tell the authorities it was Gabriel who forged the drawings. But it hadn't happened yet, so it was possible Klinman wasn't going to implicate Gabriel. Except that Gabriel would be such an easy patsy, and he was totally expendable. The feeling of guilt, of needing absolution, returned to his stomach, and his legs began to bounce under the table. Lise was looking at him expectantly.

"The hotel drawings we did? Were those for this guy?"

"How did you know?" Gabriel said, not answering the question.

"What happened to them?" Lise asked.

"What do you mean? I don't know." This was not a lie. He truly didn't know. He hadn't thought about the hotel drawings in a while. Possibly they really were for a hotel. He resolved to ask Klinman about it. In fact, he had a lot to talk to the man about.

"Is there a chance they were used as fakes?" Lise blew smoke down toward her feet. "It's just, why would he be commissioning drawings for a hotel? Especially drawings in the specific style of certain artists."

Gabriel said nothing.

"That's my daughter," Lise said quietly.

"Sorry?"

"The drawing they talk about in the article. In the style of Ganedis. I sketched Hélène with our shih tzu."

Gabriel looked at Lise blankly. He had no idea what she was talking about.

"Here—" She ran her finger down the column. The nail had broken close to the quick. "There, they mention a gouache of a girl with a dog."

"That could be anyone," Gabriel said.

"My mother gave Hélène that yellow dress." She held Gabriel's gaze.

"I don't know what to say," Gabriel said.

Lise continued to look at him. She bit the inside of her cheek, and took another drag off her cigarette.

The urge to tell Lise everything was almost overpowering. He'd been forging drawings to make money, because he was pussy-whipped and weak. His girlfriend might have been dating him to keep his mouth shut. Even his show was probably a setup. He wished he could crawl into the ashtray with Lise's discarded cigarette butts. He wished he could vanish, go back to Spain, throw himself off the Eiffel Tower.

"You have something to say," Lise said. "Say it."

When he spoke, it came out harsh, like a stage whisper. "I can't tell you," he said.

"Why not?" Lise demanded.

Gabriel paused for a while, gathering his words, his composure. "Because I'm ashamed."

Lise grimaced and stubbed out her latest cigarette. She leaned closely in to Gabriel. For a second he thought she might try to kiss him, but when she spoke it was clearly not out of affection. "I don't know what you got yourself into. But you dragged me into it. If the police come after me, so help me God, I will kill you."

Gabriel nodded mutely.

"And I never want to see you again. Never. Understand?"

Lise spoke with such vitriol that little bubbles of spittle landed on Gabriel's chin. He didn't wipe them away. He'd never seen her so angry, never seen anyone so angry. It served him right. He *had* dragged her into it, even if it had been unknowingly. Never seeing her again was a suitable, terrible punishment. He watched her grab her purse and storm out of the café, praying, if he hadn't used up his celestial currency, that this whole mess would spare her.

He threw money on the table and took the paper with him to Tinsley's. He ran all the way from the *métro* stop, and was out of breath when he got to the building. He had to ring the bell twice before they buzzed him inside the building. After looking at the old, rickety lift in the center of the winding staircase, he charged up the stairs instead, and breathlessly asked the receptionist for Colette.

"She's not in at the moment. Do you have an appointment?"

"I don't need an appointment. I'm her boyfriend. Where is she?"

The receptionist recoiled a bit, now suspicious of him. "I'm sorry, I don't know. She stepped out. I don't know where she is or when she'll be back."

"Dammit," Gabriel swore. Other employees stopped their work to stare at him. He was struck by how shabby the office was, its paper peeling from the walls, the desks yellow with age. "If she comes back tell her to phone Gabriel. It's an emergency."

He ran into Colette as he left the building. "You owe me some explaining."

"I'm sorry?" Colette was carrying three oversized bags. She extended her hand to give him one, but he took a step back in refusal.

"What does this mean?" He pulled *Le Monde* from his back pocket.

Colette looked at it. "Fuck. Well, it took them long enough. Augustus was arrested last week."

"What is this bullshit?" Gabriel rarely swore in French. It didn't feel authentic.

"Kindly keep your voice down." Colette looked around, smiling too widely. "We can talk about this later."

"We can talk about it now," Gabriel said. "Or I can talk about it with the police."

Colette put her bags down wearily. "My little bear," she said, with a lilt of condescension. "All right, we'll talk about it now. Let's take a taxi."

Colette put the bags in the trunk of the cab. During the ride she narrated what they were passing as though he were a tourist.

"I do love Paris." Gabriel thought her voice sounded false, like she was doing an imitation of Audrey Hepburn or Jean Seberg. "Baudelaire has this great quote about Paris changing so much, but there's a lot that never changes."

He had calmed down by the time they reached her flat. Once inside, she began to make coffee. "Now, what would you like to discuss?"

"Please," he said. "I'm not an idiot."

"He'll be proven innocent. This will all blow over," she said. "It's unfortunate that Augustus takes the fall when that asshole Schnell goes free. But really, it's not your problem."

"It *is* my problem. What, I'm just supposed to believe you the way I was supposed to believe your uncle?"

"Believe whatever you want." Colette came over and sat next to him on the bed. She pulled his head into her lap and began to stroke his hair.

"I want to know. How much are you involved?"

"You don't want to know, little bear, actually." She stopped stroking suddenly.

Gabriel grunted. "And what if they found out I drew the art you sold?"

"First of all, as you well know, I don't 'sell art.' I facilitate its auction. And, not to mince words, it is not your work at all. Your work has netted you a piddling little show way out in the provinces."

Gabriel sat up, offended at her condescension but unable to defend himself. "It is my work. I drew it."

Colette nodded. "You have a very cunning hand, it's true." She held up his fingers, gripping hard when he tried to snatch them away. "What is it that you want, exactly? I wonder," she said.

Gabriel opened his mouth to answer, but she was still speaking. "I don't mean right now. I mean, what do you want out of life? Maybe you want fame. That's a good goal. You want people to admire you for your work and remember your name. Maybe you want money. That's a worthier goal still—and a hell of a lot more bankable than fame. Do you want to make great art? That's separate from fame and fortune, you know that. Art is a commodity. Maybe it used to be something else, but now, all it is is tradable currency that looks nice on a wall."

"I don't believe that," Gabriel said, standing.

"I thought you said you weren't an idiot."

"And me?" Gabriel said. His ire was returning. "Am I a commodity? Fuck me so I'll keep making your little drawings?"

"Don't be insulting," Colette said. Her voice was rising. She was offended. Good, Gabriel thought. I've finally hit the mark.

Colette continued, "I like you. I liked you. You're not untalented either. Like I said, a cunning hand. But we probably shouldn't be seen together for a while." She was crying a little, the way she did at sad movies, in a way that made her look no less attractive.

"I'm moving to New York."

Gabriel said nothing. She had never told him she was thinking about moving, and the idea that she had not even discussed it with him felt like a betrayal on par with discovering an infidelity.

"Someone's having a baby and they'll probably want me to replace her."

Gabriel said, "When were you going to tell me?" He wanted to sound angry but his voice came out a raspy whisper.

Colette shrugged. She found her cigarettes and lit one. Gabriel noticed that her hand was shaking.

"Take me with you," he begged. He hadn't planned on saying that, hadn't realized he felt so desperate until that moment, when the idea of a Paris without Colette was like sugarless coffee, all bite and no taste. He had changed since being with her. She had changed him, changed his life. Now he was going to have to go back to his previous self, a self he no longer recognized.

Colette shook her head slowly, breathing out smoke. "No," she said softly.

She walked over to her front door and opened it into the hallway. "You should go," she said. "*Adiós,*" she added in Spanish.

Gabriel stood and walked toward her. She stopped him by grabbing his arm and kissing him, her tongue searching out his closed lips. When she pulled back, Gabriel wanted to slap her. She seemed to read his urge, raising her eyebrows as if to say, *I'd like to see you try it.* Instead he took the stairs two at a time, almost falling out her front door.

Gabriel spent two weeks moping around his apartment. Then he took to the streets of Paris, spending whole days wandering around Clignancourt or out to the Périphérique and back. After a month, he sold the Piranesi sketch that Édouard had given him and lived off that. Two months later he took a job as an art instructor for seniors at the local community center. It paid poorly, but the seniors didn't seem to mind his accent, or the way he often lost his train of thought, staring out the window. They even politely ignored it (or maybe their eyesight was too bad to see) when he teared up.

When Klinman was released on bail, Gabriel attempted to confront him. But when he went to his apartment no one answered the bell. He called, but it went straight to voice mail. He even lurked outside for hours to see if Klinman would come in or out, but he never did, and Gabriel realized, as he shifted from foot to foot in boredom, that there would be nothing to say to him if he saw the man.

As he waited, his anger drained from him. Before, his rage was a circulating fountain, falling then returning in an endless loop. But now he felt empty. After so much animosity, he was exhausted, and he slept like he hadn't slept in years.

As far as Gabriel could tell, his connection to Klinman was never discovered. At any rate, no one ever knocked on Gabriel's door to discuss the forgeries with him. As the weeks went on, Gabriel's relief grew. The case against Klinman was dropped—there was some sort of procedural error. He thought he saw Colette once, across the street near the Bastille, but he couldn't be sure and she was gone before he could look again.

He didn't visit the studio for months, knowing that his materials would be either pilfered or ruined when he returned. If he returned. Late at night, he made wild plans, to move back to Spain, to travel through China, to go back to school to learn a new profession, to become a garbage collector or a toll booth operator, which required no thought and had no possible promotion. Work thirty-five hours a week and retire.

He had imaginary conversations with Lise in which he begged her to forgive him and she did, embracing him, not erotically, but the way she embraced her children, unconditionally. He told her he was quitting art, and she begged him to reconsider.

But in the morning the hope of those fantasies would ebb, and Gabriel would awake as stuck in his life as ever. Colette's voice ran like a sound track in his mind, reminding him that art was just a game, and that he needed to learn to play it. In one dream she laughed at him in a restaurant and ordered a twelve-centimeter man whom she immediately ate as Gabriel pleaded with her not to.

The Scandinavian students in his apartment were replaced with other Scandinavian students, who assumed their new roommate had always been that morose and misanthropic. Hans called him three times, but then stopped.

He went for long walks in the Bois de Boulogne, throwing pebbles in the pond. He admired their arcs, their long trajectories to the water, where they landed with a satisfying splash that rippled back to the edge where he stood. Once, a little boy near him picked up some pebbles and copied him, laughing. Gabriel had always been so angry. But now he felt pity. For whom? he wondered.

No one had forced him to be an artist. No one had forced him to fake the drawings. Being angry at the art world was like shaking your fist at the Obélisque in the Place de la Concorde. It was a structure too big to topple. He should stop railing at it. This realization brought him a sense of peace he hadn't felt in a while. He smiled at the little boy, who seemed not to be afraid of him, and they took turns throwing rocks in the water until his mother told him it was time to leave.

————

Just after class at the senior citizens' center, where Gabriel had given up trying to teach perspective and let the old codgers scribble over their paper like they wanted to, his phone rang. It had rung so seldom recently that he was surprised. The number was foreign.

"Hello?" an English voice said when he answered. "Is this Gabriel Connois?"

He responded automatically in French. *"Oui."*

She switched to French as well. "My name is Madelyn Hunter." Her accent was so thick that Gabriel could barely understand her, but she spoke fluently. "I represent the Academy of Arts in London. Have you heard of us?"

Gabriel's heart began to race. "Maybe."

"Then you know we sponsor an annual fellowship for a Mediterranean artist. It pays a stipend of fifty thousand pounds to live in the Academy in London and paint for two years." The woman might have been speaking from a script.

Gabriel had never heard of it, but was the fellowship about to be offered to him?

"Well, you are one of five finalists. You were nominated by someone on our board."

Gabriel felt the familiar relief of disappointment wash over him. A finalist. He knew he wouldn't win. So the phone call was a waste. Except that he *might* win.

"Do you understand?" the woman asked.

"Hmm," Gabriel said, too stunned for speech.

"We tell you this not to torture you but because we have to know if you're able to come to London for two years. Sometimes jobs and families don't allow—"

"I'm allowed," Gabriel said. That wasn't what he meant, but the word presented itself as available.

"Good," the woman said. "Can I verify your address so that we can send you the letter in two weeks? Regardless, now that you're a finalist, you're considered a member of the Academy."

"What does that mean?" Gabriel asked.

"It means you're part of the AOA," the woman repeated, as if Gabriel simply hadn't understood her French.

When the phone call ended, Gabriel stood in the street watching his students hobble glacially onto a bus. Was this a prank? he wondered. It couldn't have been. No one would bother to prank him. Especially not in French.

He returned to the studio and spent a few hours looking at his work. The stored canvases were rejects from the show. The drawings in his sketchbook were studies for pieces he did for Klinman. He ripped the canvases and tore the paper from the sketchbook, making several trips to the Dumpster. Then he examined his brushes. Gummy, gooey, frayed. He took the whole can outside and tossed it. His pencils were stubby, his turpentine cloudy. He threw them all away. He spent the day cleaning out his work space, getting rid of every vestige of his previous work, all the sketches in others' hands, all the half-begun paintings in his own style, the jar of ink. Then he decided to throw everything away, all his paints and pencils and brushes and palettes and solvents. As he tossed it all into the Dumpster out back, he felt wonderfully light, like a pebble winging its way to the pond.

Marie-Laure came outside. "If you were going to throw things away, I wish you would have asked if anyone else wanted them. Or at least recycled them."

"Fuck you," Gabriel said, the words sweet like a whistle in his mouth.

Marie-Laure spun and ran back to the studio.

He took the remainder of his Klinman money and went to Rougier & Plé, spending every last euro, buying more gum erasers than he would ever need just to get rid of all the cash. He had to hire a taxi to take him back to the studio, an expense he hadn't counted on, but with his purchases spread out before him he felt like he could begin again.

————

The following two weeks Gabriel walked around filled with anxiety. Now that leaving Paris was a possibility, he gazed at lintels, examined railings, went for long walks to breathe in the air. Sometimes he found himself smiling at odd moments. Maybe he would win. He was already a finalist. He considered, then rejected, buying an English dictionary.

"Good to have you back, man," Hans said. "I thought you were angry with me about the show still or something." Gabriel had accepted his invitation to have a beer. He told Hans about the possible fellowship.

"What are your chances, do you think?" Hans asked him.

"One in five."

"Ha."

"I don't know. I probably won't get it."

"Probably not." Hans paused. Gabriel hit him playfully. "But you might. I mean, no one made *me* a finalist."

"You're not a Mediterranean painter."

"True. It's harder competition for real countries. With actual economies, I mean."

Gabriel ignored the jibe. "I don't think I'll get it." But what if he did? It would jump-start his career, end his money problems. Two years in London at the Academy would mean he was really an artist. It was so difficult to hold these two contrary hopes in his head. On the one hand, not getting it would be a comfort. It would confirm what he'd always suspected. But getting it would place him firmly in the artistic elite—he wanted desperately what he had dismissed all his life as false and hollow. He would be the person he'd always hated, the one patronized by Big Art.

He waited around his apartment for the mail, ran several calculations of how long it would take for a letter to get there. They probably met on a Friday, he reasoned. So they'd mail the letters on Monday and it would get there on a Thursday. Unless they met over the weekend. Or if someone on the committee were out of town and they were waiting to meet until the following week. His speculations were pointless, which didn't dissuade him at all.

Finally, nearly three weeks after the phone call, Gabriel returned home from a lengthy walk during which he'd succeeded in forgetting about the prize for almost thirty minutes as he contemplated what pigeon genitalia might look like to find a letter in his mailbox with an English postmark. It was thin, and someone had taken care to line the stamp up perfectly with the edges of the envelope. The handwriting was formal, and it gave each part of his address its own line: the number, the street, the apartment, the city, the postal code, the unnecessary *région*, and the country.

He ripped it open so quickly that he tore the letter but still was able to read the first line: "*Félicitations/Felicidades*/Congratulations." It was embossed at the bottom. Gabriel let out a yelp that would make his neighbors check to see who was being assaulted in the lobby. And he would not notice until three days had passed, and he was trying to tape the letter back together, that it listed the board members of the Academy, among whose names was that of Augustus Klinman.

Elm

She thought surely he would be back by that evening, but at midnight she gave up waiting and went to bed. He'd be back by the next day. Moira seemed to understand the seriousness of the situation. She went right to bed when asked, and didn't even angle for a story.

He was right. How did she know that Michel hadn't simply implanted a random embryo? She certainly couldn't sue him if the baby wasn't Ronan. She had just trusted him blindly, the way she trusted Indira. She had confided in the wrong people, and pushed away the right ones, the ones who would have stopped her from this folly.

Elm spent the day examining the CVS results, comparing her blood type to Colin's to the fetus's, as if that alone would determine if it was a clone or a scam. She considered calling Michel, but then realized he would simply reassure her, and if he had been lying to her he would continue to lie in his smooth French accent. On Sunday, Colin still wasn't home. Elm left a message on his phone apologizing, asking if he would please come home just to talk, just for a minute. She wanted to call Ian, but she'd have to explain why Colin had left her. No, this was the bed of her making, and she would have to lie in it alone.

Moira said almost nothing the entire weekend. On Sunday she asked for a playdate, and Elm called up Patty and asked if Moira could go over to her house.

"You look pale," Patty said when they arrived. "Are you sure you're okay?"

"Yeah, I'm just worn out," Elm said. "And I'm a little anemic."

"Oh, dear. Do you want me to keep her overnight?"

Elm considered, standing in the doorway. The idea of being in her apartment alone was unappealing, but the freedom to weep and sulk and think won out. Elm thanked her, told Moira she was having a sleepover, and kissed her good-bye.

On the way home, a wave of melancholy overtook her, and for the first time since the days just after Ronan died, she considered that she could just disappear. She could take pills, or slit her wrists. No one would find her until it was too late. And then her mistake would die with her. It would upset Moira, of course, but she was young. The young were resilient. And Colin would be angry, but at least she wouldn't have to live knowing that she'd failed him, that he hated her. If there was a heaven, maybe she could be with Ronan there.

Even as she let these thoughts run their course, she knew she wouldn't do it. This was suicidal ideation, as her doctor called it. It was about figuring out your place in other people's lives, and re-upping self-esteem when you realized you were important. That you did matter. Plus, Elm felt strongly that suicide was for the weak. If there were people who cared about you, who depended on you, then you had the obligation to stick it out until the end. She had done this to herself.

Now she wondered if giving birth would even make her happy. She'd been so caught up in the logistics of it, the sheer science fiction of it, she never stopped to consider what her feelings might be once he was here. How could she have been so naïve to have expected that Colin would embrace this charade? That this would solve any of their problems?

On Monday, he sent her a text message: "I'm ok. Wld like to take Moira to dinner. Not ready to talk. 5 ok?"

Moira was excited once she was collected from her friend's house, baggy eyes revealing how little she'd slept. Elm told her that Daddy was coming home from his business trip early just to see her for a while, and she accepted this, the way children find it perfectly natural that someone would rearrange his schedule and fly across the country just for them.

When the doorbell rang, Elm had a grouchy Moira dressed in the cutest clothes she could find, as though she were presenting an orphan for possible adoption. She had tear streaks on her cheeks; she didn't want to wear the striped tights, didn't want to wear tights at all, but Elm had insisted. Moira flung her fists at her at the same time the baby gave her a jab. She felt she deserved both of these assaults.

Colin was wearing clothes she'd never seen before. Well, of course, he'd had to go shopping. He looked at her as if she'd changed something about her appearance that he couldn't put his finger on: Had she dyed her hair? Waxed her eyebrows? He wore a look of suspicion that Elm couldn't meet.

"She's a little tired," Elm said by way of hello.

"I am not!" Moira protested.

"She had a sleepover last night."

"Big girl," Colin said. He told Moira she looked pretty. "Back by eight," he said to Elm.

She nodded. When she closed the door on them, she burst into tears.

At work on Wednesday she sat in her office playing solitaire. Her phone didn't ring, and her e-mail box contained nothing of urgency. She called Colin. He didn't answer, and she didn't leave a message. Instead she texted him: "Pls talk."

An agonizing hour passed while she stared at her phone, stubborn in its silence. Then: "Thurs ok?"

She texted back, "Shd I get sitter?"

"No. After M goes to bed," he said. "I'll tuck her."

By midafternoon, when no one sent her an e-mail, called her, or stopped by, Elm knew the article in the paper must have circulated. The hall outside her office was deserted. If it weren't for the beeping of the receptionist's phone and the elevator chime, she might have thought she was the only one in the building.

She had to explain to Wania what was happening. The nanny wouldn't be content with the business trip story, so Elm said they'd had a large fight. She saw Wania's eyes widen in disbelief. "Mr. Colin gone then, ya? Him a dogheart."

Elm couldn't decide if she should pack him a suitcase, to show respect for his need for space, or whether that would show indifference to his leaving, even encouragement. She stood in the center of her bedroom, looking at a sock he had thrown toward the hamper, missing but not bothering to retrieve it. What if it never moved, what if it stayed there forever?

Whatever kind of heart Colin's was, she had broken it. He came over on Thursday with Thai food, making Moira yelp with glee. Again

Elm marveled at her willingness to be cheered. She wished that every hurt could be wiped away by takeout. If that were so, she'd already banked a thousand dinners of forgiveness.

Elm and Colin barely looked at each other, staring instead at their plates or at their daughter, who was animatedly telling the story of something unfair that happened on the playground. While Colin bathed her and got her ready for bed, Elm cleaned up. She put the leftovers in the fridge. Maybe Colin would want to take them to wherever he was living.

The noises ceased in Moira's room. She wondered fleetingly if Colin had kidnapped her, sneaking out through the window. Pregnant delusions; they lived on the twelfth floor. A half hour later, Colin came into the living room, rubbing his eyes. He'd fallen asleep.

He headed toward her stomach before he remembered, and instead sat down on the opposite side of the sofa.

"It's okay," Elm said. "It's the same baby as it was before. It's still ours."

Colin sighed and rubbed his eyes again, trying to stop the tears, which brimmed anyway.

"I just . . . I can't believe you."

Elm said nothing.

"I keep waiting for you to tell me this is all a joke, that you're kidding and ha, isn't it funny?"

"Right now I wish it were."

"I just keep coming back to, how could you?"

"I wanted him back." Elm burst into tears. "I want him back so badly . . ."

Colin waited for her to calm down. "We both want him back, Elm, but he's gone."

"He won't be gone anymore."

"Goddammit, Elm." Colin stood up. Even angry, he spoke in a stage whisper so as not to wake Moira. "This"—he pointed at her stomach—"is not Ronan."

"It's his exact DNA," Elm protested, cradling herself.

"But it's not him, it won't be, and to pretend is just . . . cruel."

"He'll look like him, exactly," Elm said. "And we have another chance. This time, we won't let him fall off the changing table and split his lip. We'll know to buy two of those bunnies he likes so when he loses one we'll have a backup."

"That won't make him Ronan."

"He won't have to go to my mom's funeral. We won't go to Thailand. You won't let him out of your sight so that a wave can sweep him away."

"So that's what this is." Colin's whisper grew loud. "You can't forgive me for losing him."

"I do. I mean, I try." Elm's tears were less urgent now, more painful. "I have."

"No, you haven't. I haven't forgiven myself completely either."

Elm shook her head. "It's my fault too."

"You can't forgive me," Colin said. "You can't trust me. We're done."

"No," Elm said calmly. "That's not true."

"And now you've done a thing I can't forgive you for."

"So we're even," Elm pleaded.

"That's not how this works. Two wrongs don't make a right. Two wrongs just prove it's wrong."

"Stop saying that."

"Elm, you've done something unforgivable. With volition. It's disgusting. It's immoral."

"It's *immoral*?"

"We don't get to decide what children we have, or what children get taken from us. I wanted a baby, not a science experiment."

"So now you're all religious."

"It's not religion, it's just morality, which I thought you had. My old wife had a moral compass. My old wife wouldn't embezzle funds to implant something illegal and lie to her husband about it."

"I was desperate."

"I can see that."

There was a silence that may have lasted a half hour. Elm could hear every beat of her heart, every beat of the baby's heart. She could feel the blood rushing through her, the volume of it increased because the baby needed it too. She felt her hands tremble. She was frightened. Terrified.

"I want to go back to Ireland," Colin said finally. "And I want to take Moira."

Elm pursed her lips. "That's not a good idea," she said. "I can't travel anymore."

"Not you." Colin stressed the last word so that Elm felt the sting of it. "Me and Moira."

"You can't just take her from me."

"I refuse"—he paused—"to subject her to another brother who is going to die. I refuse to do that to her."

"I won't let you. That's kidnapping."

"I don't think a judge would disagree with me when I tell him what you've done."

"Oh, so now you're blackmailing me?"

"You don't leave me a choice."

"You sound like a movie," Elm said. "It's not that hard. Please come back home, please. I'm sorry; I'm so sorry. I need you, I need help with our baby. I love you."

Colin appeared to be considering this, shaking his head lightly. "I've put out feelers for a job back home. There are a couple that look promising. "

"And where will I be in this scenario?"

"As far as I'm concerned, you can be in hell," Colin snapped. "I'm renting an apartment and Moira is coming to live with me in the meantime."

Elm was tired. She couldn't argue with him. He would just get angrier. "Fine," she said. "I want to see her, though."

"You can take her for dinner."

"I can't believe it's coming to this," Elm said, surveying the room.

"This is something you did," Colin said. "Remember that. This is not a tsunami, or a fact of nature. This is something you did to us, to me."

"*For* us," Elm whispered. Colin must have heard but he didn't take the bait.

"I'll have a lawyer be in touch. We should get all this in writing."

The air left Elm's lungs. She sank into the couch, without the breath for a response.

Colin went to the refrigerator and removed the boxes of Thai food. Then he draped his jacket over his arm and walked out, closing the door forcefully behind him. A few seconds later, Elm heard the elevator ding its arrival and then the doors whooshed closed and she knew he was gone.

———

Regret was not a strong enough word to describe Elm's feelings the next morning. She was sure Moira had heard them fighting. The little girl ran all the way to school, just to be away from her. Elm called in a personal day at work, understanding that she was giving everyone free rein to gossip about her.

She went into Moira's room to pack her a suitcase. How was it possible that she'd given away her daughter? She replayed the events of the previous evening. She had been expecting Colin to come home, that the sight of her pregnant with their child (with Ronan!) would tug at him in some irresistible way. She wasn't sure when it was that she had started being so horribly, horribly wrong about everything. She used to have good judgment, or at least, judgment that was not any worse than anyone else's. And now she was so mistaken all the time.

But really, what choice did she have? If Colin was ever going to forgive her, she would have to be as conciliatory as possible. Maybe she didn't deserve to see Moira.

Wania had left Moira's stuffed animals in a row; a dozen googly eyes stared at her like a jury. She opened Moira's closet. They had kept a few of Ronan's things, his favorite Yankees jacket, a suit he wore only once that Elm had never been able to give away, even when she finally got rid of his Simpsons T-shirt and his Lego collection. Maybe it reminded her of what he would have been if he'd lived, grown up to wear a suit to important occasions. Or maybe she was hoping against hope that his body would be found, that they could bury him. In any event, it hung there, limp, in Moira's closet.

What had been her plan, she wondered, for re-creating Ronan? She knew she couldn't literally replace her son, but she had been hoping that just seeing him would ease the cramp of missing him.

It was best not to fight Colin now; she didn't have the strength. But when she thought about packing up her daughter's life, it seemed so unfair. Poor kid, she'd have to move and lose a parent at the same time? Colin should stay in the apartment; Elm should move out. Maybe she wanted to punish herself, she admitted. But she also thought that a few generous gestures might soften Colin slightly.

She went back into her room to pack her own suitcase. The baby gave her a nudge. She felt worse now than she did in the first few weeks after she returned from Thailand. Then she had felt confused by grief. Days would slide by and then minutes dragged on for eternity. Now she had a clear view of the ways in which she was affecting the world. As much as she wanted to turn back time and redo the moments just before the wave hit, now she wanted to go back before the implantation, before that stupid party that gave her the idea, to go back to simply missing Ronan instead of plotting to resurrect him. He was just a kid. How had he become her messiah?

———

What struck her most was the unreasonable quiet. She had grown up in Manhattan; the sirens and the thuds of people living on all sides of her, their muffled sneezes through the bathroom vent, the slam of their doors when they came home, all were part of what Elm considered normal. Yet now she was living in a brand-new high-rise corporate residence, double-paned windows that didn't open and soundproofed walls and ceilings. She was so high up even the sunlight filtered through in an alien way, the strange glass reflecting its light into small particles that reassembled themselves to look like light, but were somehow different.

She could see her building from the window. Her own apartment was on the back side, so she couldn't see into it, but she had the strange sensation of watching herself from above, living in an establishing shot for a movie. When she called Moira in the evenings, she pretended to her that she could see into her room.

Moira had taken the news that Mommy was going to live down the block with her usual nonchalance. It was unclear whether she understood that her father thought this was likely to be a permanent arrangement, but they had agreed, for everyone's sake, to make it seem related to the birth of the baby. Moira made paper clothes for the child, and often brought home cards she'd drawn in school, her unadulterated excitement in sharp contrast to Elm's trepidation.

The oil painting arrived at her new apartment. It was large, two feet by four feet, and Elm took a deep breath before she opened it. It was lacking in any artistry, but the painter, whoever it was, had captured something about Ronan's eyes, the sparkle, from the school picture. Elm found it comforting, and instead of draping it back in the butcher paper, she leaned it against the wall, face out, where she stared at it for hours.

After work each day she went directly to her corporate apartment, resting until dinner. Twice a week she walked the couple of blocks to her home (she still considered it hers; it was still the place she lived, in her mind). Colin, now free during the day, made dinner, appallingly bad renditions of recipes from Rachel Ray's *30-Minute Meals*. Elm had little desire to eat anyway. She forked the food around her plate, attempting small talk.

And then she went back to her aerie and watched Lifetime television until she fell asleep. Often the television was still on in the morning, playing older and older dramas, so that she got out of bed to the hysteria of Pia Zadora in bad eighties hair escaping abusive men who looked like they were auditioning for heavy metal bands. Had Elm worn her hair like that? Probably. She could consult her pictures, except that they were at the other apartment. She had brought only two frames with her. One picture was from last Christmas, the three of them smiling on the couch. The other was the last photo of Ronan. She wished Colin had centered the picture better. Instead, Ronan's head was a little to the right, and the prow of a longboat seemed to poke him in the back. This was often the last image she beheld before curling up on her side and closing her eyes. Oddly, she slept dreamlessly, peacefully.

———

It was not surprising that Greer wanted to speak with her. What was surprising was that he suggested they meet in her apartment. Apparently, he wanted to keep Elm's situation quiet.

She had never seen him anything but placid and composed, but as she opened her door, his face was flushed. He took out a handkerchief and mopped his brow. He leaned forward to kiss her cheek, then thought better of it.

She invited him in, and when she stepped back from the door, he looked at her stomach, wearing an expression of disgust. His wife had had two kids, Elm thought; surely he understood that this is how they came into the world.

"It's very . . ." He looked around the apartment.

"Beige," Elm said. "It's very beige. Apparently corporate wonks like beige apartments."

Greer managed a forced smile. "Wow, is that—" He pointed to the oil painting of Ronan.

"Yes," Elm said. She knew she was supposed to explain why there was an extremely ugly convention center art show portrait of her dead son, but she took a perverse pleasure in letting Greer puzzle out what he was missing.

"Sit down?" Elm asked. "I'm afraid there's nothing in the house. Do you want some water?"

Greer shook his head. "Elm, do you know why I'm here to speak with you?"

"Greer, this isn't ninth grade. Spit it out."

"I've had a call from the FBI."

The scrunched and minuscule pouch that was Elm's stomach lurched. She'd been waiting for this.

Greer continued, "They're concerned about several pieces that we, well, that your department put up for auction last fall."

Elm nodded, pretending that what he was saying was news to her.

"And their connection to a certain Indira Schmitz."

"Schmidt," Elm corrected him. What had they said? she wanted to ask him. Get to the point, man. Was Elm going to jail?

"Since you've been . . . I asked Ian to look into it."

Elm breathed a sigh of relief. Ian must have covered for her. Wouldn't he?

"You are aware," Greer said. He was reciting from a script. Maybe he was wearing a wire. At the very least, he had been to see his lawyer. This did not bode well for Elm. "You are aware that she has been implicated in an art forgery ring."

Elm nodded. "Good," Greer said. "It's good that you're not denying it."

"I read the news," Elm said.

"Ian brought me the documentation of the authenticity investigations. It appears you did your due diligence."

"Of course, Greer."

Greer continued as though she hadn't spoken. "But, Elm, I looked at the report. If this pastel turns out to be a misattribution, then the implications for Tinsley's would be enormous."

"Look, Greer, I don't think it's misattributed," Elm said, sitting on the sofa opposite him. "And if it proves to be, I mean, I made a mistake. It happens."

"No, it doesn't," Greer said. "Not in my house."

Elm sucked her lips inside her teeth so she wouldn't say anything.

"Elm," Greer said. "It's come to my attention that there have been some other . . . dealings on your part. I recommend, I mean, my lawyer recommends, you say nothing."

Elm briefly thought about standing up and protesting this unfair treatment. He was acting on rumors and half-truths, and how dare he, etc. But she simply didn't have it in her to defend a principle she'd violated. She sat there, mute.

"We'll leave it there if you agree to resign, effective immediately."

Elm nodded as the tears started flowing down her cheeks. These were silent tears, tears of regret, not anger. She could say nothing to defend herself. Greer was right, horribly right. She had put the entire auction house in jeopardy. Her great-grandfather was really rolling around in his grave. But how had Greer found out about the drawings she sold through Relay, if these were the dealings to which he was referring? Ian must have told him. He was the only one who knew about her relationship with Relay. But why would he do that to her?

"I'll try to protect you from the law," Greer said, "but I want you to have nothing more to do with the auction house."

"Yes," she said. What hurt most right now, besides her fear, was that Greer, after acting superior to her in every way for years, did occupy that space now. As vile as he was, as mean and as hypocritical and as condescending, he had the moral hegemony that Elm could only dream about, a rightness she would never, ever recover.

"But, Elm," Greer said as he stood to go, his face even redder now than it was when he walked in. "I don't understand. Why?"

Elm thought. "None of your fucking business," she said.

———

In May, Moira and Colin left for Ireland so Colin could start his new job. Elm moved back into their apartment. It had once felt so small—a two-bedroom with four people living in it, all sharing one bathroom and one small living room; now it was an empty mansion. Colin had packed quickly; in their closet errant socks and summer clothing sat where they'd fallen.

Every morning Elm Skyped with Moira. "How's Ireland, honey?"

"I've been here before, 'member?"

"I know, silly goose, but how do you like it there now?"

"Good. When are you coming?"

"As soon as the baby's born and old enough to travel, pumpkin." Actually, nothing had been worked out. Colin's parents agreed to pick Moira up from school and take care of her while he worked. It was a perfect arrangement, and the fact that it didn't include Elm broke her heart.

Moira sighed, then got distracted by something away from the web-cam. She skipped out of view for a minute, then came back, fiddling with one of her dolls whose miniature plastic clothes were always getting lost.

"Have you made any friends at school?" Elm asked.

"Yeah, there's this girl, her name is Siobhan. She's nice. She has really really blond hair."

"Good. I can't wait to meet her." Elm hoped that Moira would attribute the crack in her voice to the imperfect wireless connection.

"She has a little brother too. And, Mom?"

"Yes," Elm said.

"It's raining here."

"It's raining here too, sweetie."

"But not the same rain?"

"No, sweetie. I think it's different rain."

Colin came up behind her. He looked different on the webcam, elongated, disproportionate. "Go on and wash your teeth," he said. Moira left without argument or good-bye.

"Hi," Colin said.

"Hi," Elm replied.

"Rain here too," Colin said.

"It *is* Ireland."

"Nothing?"

"Nope. I still have two weeks until I'm even full-term."

There was a long silence. Colin looked at his shoes. Elm wished she could reach her own feet to rub them.

"Elm?" Colin said.

"Yes?"

"I'm scared."

"Me too," Elm admitted. "I'm terrified." She wasn't sure they were speaking of the same fear, but Elm didn't want to pry; she wanted to let this small moment of agreement last for as long as it could.

———

Elm had thought Ian would come by with the contents of her office. Then she assumed he'd call to see how she was. She was upset at his silence, even as she didn't really blame him.

Finally, he came to see her bearing a large box of chocolates that sat uneaten on the coffee table between them. He was telling her some story that she wasn't really trying to follow, about someone from facilities who took it upon himself to talk up some buyers on the floor last week.

"Don't worry," he said, noticing her inattention. "The gossip will die down."

Elm smiled, a dissimulation so phony she didn't even convince Ian. In the past few weeks she'd received letters from both charitable organizations she worked with thanking her for her help up to now and wishing her good luck in her future endeavors. The museum on whose board she sat suddenly reorganized its trustees. Elm was not on the new list. The gossip would never die down, Elm knew. Even if there was no criminal prosecution.

"Did you tell Greer about Relay?"

Ian shook his head. "No. Elm, how can you think that?"

"I don't know, sorry," she said. "I'm just paranoid. Then who . . ." As soon as the words left her mouth she realized exactly who it was who ratted her out to Greer. How could she have been so clueless? Colette had brought her Klinman. She would have known all along. To think that Elm had been played by that—she didn't even like to say the word in her own mind—cunt. *Played* was the correct word. Toyed with. Colette would take her job. Elm thought about confronting her, storming into Greer's office to unveil the real Colette, maybe even telling the police about her. But that would do neither Elm nor Ian any good, and could have disastrous effects. Elm and Colette were mutually incriminated. As long as one didn't speak the other one wouldn't either.

"Oh, Elm," Ian said, sighing. He waited a long time before speaking, looking out her window. "Who's going with you to the hospital?"

"No one, I guess," she said. She'd been thinking about it, but there was no one to ask. It wasn't the kind of thing you asked casual friends, and really, that's all she had in the world besides Colin, friends by convenience and lack of effort, not true friends. Ian would have been that friend if she hadn't gambled him away.

"Will they even let you do that?"

"They'll have to." Elm shrugged. "I suppose it happens. . . ."

"I just don't understand how Colin could be that angry to leave you."

"It's complicated," she said. "I mean, yeah, he's angry, but he also got a really great job, and Moira's all settled. And it's not like the Celtic Tiger waits for people to have their babies."

Ian gave a tiger growl. "That always sounds like a drag name to me. 'Onstage next, the mistress of mischief, Miss Celtic Tiger.'"

Elm laughed.

"And then." It was a statement.

"Pardon?" she said.

"And then you're moving to Ireland."

"Yes."

Elm watched Ian's face screw up into anger and then release into a prim-mouth unhappiness.

"When will they announce your resignation?"

"After the baby, I assume. I'll stay home for more family time. I'm sorry, Ian. It's not that I don't, I mean, I want to, but I have to . . ."

"I get it," Ian said. "You know that without you I probably won't stay long at Tinsley's."

"I'm sure that's not true. I'll write a letter before I leave."

"No offense, Elm, but that might hurt the cause. You're not exactly persona grata there."

"You'll be fine," Elm said. Was she convincing herself or him?

"I know I'll be fine," he said. "I'm always fine."

"What do you want me to do?" Elm asked. "Stay here for your sake? Not go try to patch things up with my husband and raise our daughter and new baby? I should get rid of my family to make sure that you have a job?" Elm's voice was rising. She was angry, but as she spoke it simply sounded whiny.

"No," Ian said. "Don't be an idiot. I just wish that for once, just once in my life, I was someone's biggest consideration."

"I'm sorry," Elm said.

"And *not* the object of someone's pity."

"Besides your own, of course."

Ian smiled. "Besides my own. Elm, there's something about you that makes everyone risk themselves to help you, a risk that you would never, ever even consider making in return."

"That's a harsh thing to say," Elm said. Tears sprang to her eyes.

Ian shrugged, not taking it back. "Good luck. I hope . . ." He let the thought trail off.

———

She waited until she was sure they were actual contractions and not just indigestion, and then she took a bath, asking her back to relax. In the tub she rubbed her belly, amazed that at some point in the near future she and Ronan would be two separate people again.

She toweled off and sat on the toilet. When she stood, there was a plug of mucus and blood, shiny in the light. A calm settled over her. She felt clearly the air going in through her mouth, traveling through her lungs, and then back out. She would see him again, so soon, and it would be like letting go of a breath she'd held for years, the uncramping of a clenched muscle.

Soon, she told herself. Soon she'd be looking into Ronan's eyes; she'd have necromanced her son into rebirth. And in the face of that, compared with that eventuality, losing her job, her best friend, her husband, committing forgery, all that was inconsequential. It had to be. Please, she prayed, please let it have been worth it.

Part Five

Spring 2011

Elm and Gabriel

urry up," Moira whined.

"Moira," Elm said, "your brother has little legs. He can't walk that fast."

"Can so," Aiden said.

Elm looked at Aiden's gait, worried. He was still walking a little pigeon-toed.

"But what if we miss it?"

"You're not going to miss it," Elm said. "Mary is meeting us at the auction house and she'll take you. The carnival is going on all afternoon."

"But we're only in London for a week."

"Mama?" Aiden asked.

"No, I can't carry you," Elm said. "You're too much of a big boy."

"More like a big, slow turtle."

"That's enough, Moira. Come here and hold my hand while we cross."

It was a hot day, and Moira's annoyance was catching. Aiden continued to stare everywhere but in front of his feet, and Elm was dragging him. The back of Moira's neck was red and irritated. She was getting sunburned, but it hadn't occurred to Elm that one needed sun protection in rainy London.

"Da coming?" Aiden asked for the umpteenth time.

"Yes, baby, Daddy will meet us at the fair after his meeting." Probably. Maybe. Nothing was certain with Colin.

"After his meeting," Aiden parroted.

Aiden was meeting his developmental milestones; Elm waited for each one, sure that at some point his being a clone would manifest itself in a limitation, or a severe deficiency. She treated him carefully, and he was growing up timid and fearful, dependent. But so far they'd been lucky. Sometimes Elm forgot he was Ronan's clone; he seemed so himself, so Aiden.

Though Aiden looked just like his brother—his twin, really—with the long nose that Elm shared, Colin's blond hair and gray eyes, there were differences between Ronan and Aiden. Elm wasn't sure if this was some trick of memory or if Aiden really was taller than Ronan at this age (possible: foods were increasingly fortified; Elm was vigilant with his diet and had breast-fed him past one year). He was interested in music, which Ronan never was. And he was a ham, in the way of second children, forever competing for attention in a way that Ronan never had to.

Occasionally, during a late-night feeding, or for a moment in the bathtub, Aiden stared at her with Ronan's eyes and his genetics reminded her of her enormous loss, the grief that could only be salved, never cured. Though she would never admit it, those were the times when she regretted what she'd done. They were infrequent, but devastating, and flashes of hatred for this impostor were as strong and as fleeting as the impromptu feelings of recognition and adoration that same gaze could inspire. She would have to live with these contradictions. Always.

But then he'd look up at her in such a way that it felt like Ronan was there, inside him, and when he began to talk it was as though Elm were getting to regain what she had lost. At those moments she didn't care that she had sacrificed her career, her marriage, perhaps her happiness.

They stopped at the crosswalk near Phillips de Pury, and Elm strained to look for Colin's niece. She was supposed to meet them at the auction house and take the children for the afternoon, but Mary was notoriously unreliable. Yesterday she was an hour late returning home, bringing the children back full of sugar, having missed Aiden's nap. Elm couldn't explain to her how worried even a tardiness of fifteen minutes made her without seeming overprotective, crazy.

"Mary!" Moira squealed. She broke from Elm's hand and ran to hug her cousin. "Are we going to the carnival?"

"What carnival?" Mary feigned ignorance. "I thought we'd tour Buckingham Palace."

"No!" Moira giggled.

"Mary!" Aiden said. He knew better than to wriggle from Elm's grasp, but she could feel his urge to run to Mary. Elm was jealous; her arrival never provoked such fanfare.

"Hi, Mary," Elm said. "Thanks for taking them."

"No trouble," Mary said. She was wearing a long skirt woven with shiny threads that sparkled, her many bracelets providing an accompanying tinkling.

"Why do I say yes to this thing?" asked a nearby man, echoing Elm's thoughts. He was tall and thin, dark with a couple of days' stubble that looked purposeful rather than neglectful.

A young woman shushed him. "They'll hear you."

"I don't care." His accent was foreign. Was this the man she was supposed to be interviewing—Marcel Connois's great-great-grandson, himself some sort of artist? This was one of the auction house's gimmicks in the great global market collapse, an added value, an enticement to come to an underattended auction: meet the artist's descendant! What a change from three years ago, when people threw money at art as though they had it to burn.

Elm could not have cared less about meeting someone's relative (she of all people knew that blood ties were expendable), but the art rag she wrote for was interested in an interview. She considered approaching him now, but he opened his mouth and swore loudly, "Motherfuckers."

"Shhh," his girlfriend said again.

Moira gasped. "Mummy, who is that man?"

"I don't know."

"He said 'motherfucker.' "

"Don't, Moira, your brother will repeat it."

"Muddah-fakkah, muddah-fakkah," Aiden said.

"Stop it," said Moira. "It's a bad word."

"What is?" Aiden asked.

A representative from the auction house approached the foreign man and his girlfriend. "Mr. Connois? Welcome. We're very happy to see you. Come this way."

"Go ahead with Mary," Elm said. She reached down to kiss and hug her children, a drawn-out ritual that they all respected, one that would seem from the outside to be excessive. By the time she'd hugged

them and given Mary some money, Connois and his girlfriend had gone
inside.

————

"Ow, wait, there's a rock in my shoe." Karen pulled on Gabriel's
arm, and he stopped to support her as she fished something from her
platforms. "All right then, that's better."

As they continued toward the auction house, Gabriel could feel Karen's steps begin to slow. Or was it his reluctance that was slowing them
down? "We should have take a taxi," he said.

"Taken. No, it's all right."

In contrast to the crowd he feared, the pavement outside the auction house was nearly empty. There was only a woman and her kids, the
oldest a teenage hippie, the youngest not more than a toddler. How old
were they? He should know these things, start paying attention. The
woman was hugging and kissing each one in turn as if she were going
on a long trip.

He sighed. "Why do I say yes to this thing?"

"Shhh," Karen said. "They'll hear you."

"I don't care."

"Of course you do," Karen put her hand on her stomach, a signal
to Gabriel that he should practice his "worldly selflessness," one of the
personal tenets he'd adopted during the course at the Spirit Lotus London Meditation Center.

Appearing at this auction was part of the elaborately complicated
deal he'd worked out with his gallery. Someone owed someone a favor,
and thus Gabriel would show up, do some interviews, perhaps create a
little buzz around an otherwise lackluster auction in a sluggish economy.
In return, the gallery owner would place a painting of Gabriel's in the
collection of a well-known connoisseur. That would drive up the price
of his work, especially when the gallerist created an artificial scarcity of
work, storing Gabriel's canvases in a warehouse in Slough and allowing
only a select few to purchase them.

Favors. This was how the art world worked. How the world worked,
in fact. Since he met Karen, he felt like he'd grown taller, able to view
the world from a higher perch. He could see the way mutual interde-
pendence created intimacy, not vulnerability. He could accept a favor
knowing that the bestower was acting out of self-interest. That was only

natural. He could return the favor with his own motives securely considered. The Ngagpa had shown him this. His motives, for the first time, were clear: in three months Karen would have his baby, and he felt like the owner of a special secret.

What had not changed was the fact that he did not enjoy being paraded about like an accordion monkey.

They looked at the program posted in the window. "They bollixed your age again," Karen said. "You're fifty-five here."

"Motherfuckers."

"Shh. Don't worry. At least they'll say you look ten years younger."

Gabriel laughed and they went inside.

———

Elm took her place with the rest of the press corps, who were few at this low-level auction. She didn't recognize the other woman there, but nodded to the slouchy, overweight visual arts lackey of the *Guardian*. It must be a slow news day for him to appear here. The lights flickered once, twice, silencing the polite English crowd.

This auction was a sad simulacrum of what had been only a few years ago. Not only were fewer pieces making their reserves, but fewer pieces were even going on the market, when investors knew they wouldn't get top dollar selling them. There had been some fire sales (Lehman Brothers divested itself of an amazing collection, and some bankrupt investment bankers liquidated trophy pieces), but other than that, writing about the art market took all of Elm's imagination, and not a little bit of invention.

The auction began with the crack of a gavel. Elm watched dispassionately as the sparse crowd bid on a Sir John Tenniel cartoon satirizing the overtaxation of the middle class. A real snoozer, Elm thought, though it was better than the punning woodcuts that often came from *Punch* magazine's coffers. She scanned the crowd and found Marcel Connois's descendant. He seemed uncomfortable, shifting in his chair. There wasn't enough room between rows for him to cross his legs. His girlfriend, blandly pretty, a little round, was stroking his forearm. Elm thought of a few questions she could ask him. He was a recipient of the AOA prize, so he must be a decent artist in his own right. She looked at his bio, included with the auction materials. It said he was fifty-five. He certainly looked much younger; men were so fortunate that way. He had

had a solo show in France, and one in London. His paintings had been acquired by regional museums. Not bad. Elm decided she could talk to him about escaping the shadow of a famous ancestor. Elm knew a bit about that herself.

How had she sunk so low? she wondered, making cryptic notes on the sale price as the next lot came up. This was a rhetorical question. She had prostrated herself with a series of events that she alone had set in motion. Even after selling the apartment in New York, she would be paying off the debts she incurred to have Aiden for years.

She was lucky, she reminded herself, to have a job in art at all. She was lucky not to be in jail. Indira had died just as the investigation turned its eyes on her. She did have some other valuable art pieces lurking in her Havisham-like lair, but they were left to the United Jewish Appeal, which decided to sell the artwork through Christie's. Elm had resigned from Tinsley's by then, Colette ensconced in her place. Questions still bothered Elm—the extent of Colette's involvement, what and how much Indira knew—but she shoved her curiosity away, not wanting to stir trouble.

She hadn't spoken to Ian since Aiden was born. But she was living in the UK, and he was still in New York. He opened up an art gallery with Relay; Elm was on their Christmas card list, receiving annual postcards with a list of their upcoming shows. Sometimes she looked at his Facebook updates, invariably upbeat and funny. She felt a horrible sense of loss whenever she thought of him. He was yet another casualty of her machinations.

Elm forgot to pay attention to the next lot and had to look over the shoulder of the journalist next to her for the outcome. The woman retreated, shielding her steno pad. Elm couldn't imagine what she'd written that was too much of a scoop for a rival's eyes.

The next lot came up. Elm gasped. This pastel was Indira's—the scene of the market with the woman's uneven eyes. *Mercat*. On the block again? Elm quickly flipped through her catalog. There it was, listed, with no mention of Indira Schmidt. The title was given as *In the Square*. "Marcel Connois, 1825–1889. Signed by the artist. Pastel on paper. Provenance: Galerie Christopher Fuhr, Dusseldorf, 1938. Tinsley's, 2007. Literature: *Connois's Flights of Fancy*, 1901, illustrated. Exhibited: 'The Spanish Manner,' Frick Gallery, New York, 2010."

Elm stifled a noise. Incredible. In the three years since she'd seen the piece, it had acquired a gallery from before the war. It made it into Connois's catalogue raisonné with an illustration, and apparently the piece had conjured a museum exhibition. Someone within the art world (Tinsley's? The woman in blue who'd bought the piece? Someone else?) had decided it was authentic, despite all the evidence to the contrary, despite its tainted status. But Elm could say nothing. She had given up all her ability to criticize when she cloned her son. Having Aiden meant that she was no longer an art expert.

There was a rustle in the audience. She looked over. Connois was gritting his teeth, clenching and unclenching his fists. He must have sensed her looking at him, and he turned toward her. His eyes were slits, burning. They met hers, and both looked away in modesty and surprise. Still, in that split second, she felt that he knew.

––––––

Gabriel matched his breathing to Karen's, imagined that the fetus was breathing in time too. He tapped his foot and Karen put a calming hand on his knee. She didn't know why he was anxious. And he would never be able to tell her.

The bidding started. Gabriel's heart beat in his throat, roaring faster than Karen's now. He had no reason to be nervous; the pastel had been through two other owners since it left his hands, and along the way picked up a history that made it even more commercially attractive. There was no way anyone would tie it to him.

They had lit it poorly; the glass reflected the light back into the audience, and Gabriel joined in the polite applause that greeted its appearance. He saw his mother's face, her lopsided eyes staring at him. He had captured her, enshrined her forever. And that fucking dog whose proportions were off. No one had ever noticed. The signature was perfect. Gabriel squeezed Karen's hand and she obediently squeezed back. A brief cramp of shame gripped him, and he tried to employ the positive visual imagery he'd learned at the center. His Ngagpa's voice entered his head: *Every experience leads you to now. Accept the past and the future as your inevitable path, extending behind you and in front of you.* He let the shame flow out of him with his next breath, and took a fresh look at his work. He had created a thing of beauty; he had contributed to the world.

He felt himself being watched and looked over at the press pit. There was the woman who had said the overwrought good-byes to her children in front of the auction house. She was looking at him openly, and as his eyes met hers he could feel anxiety radiate from her pursed mouth, her flared nostrils. For a moment, Gabriel was unable to breathe, and he grew dizzy. Then he broke the gaze, forced his breathing to slow.

———

Elm felt a frisson; Connois looked away. She stared at the catalog for the rest of the auction, and left without seeking Connois out. She was unnerved. She wanted to see her children, have the comfort of them within her gaze. She hailed a taxi to go meet them, wondering what Connois's look meant. She put it out of her mind. It was impossible that he understood her constant awareness—when she laughed with her children, when she dealt with Colin, when she wrote about or looked at art, when she stared into the sleeping face of her youngest child, the features that were both Ronan's and yet not—that she was both the artist and the forger of her own life.

Author's Note

The world's most notorious art forger was Han van Meegeren, an alcoholic Dutchman who painted in the style of Johannes Vermeer. Though his original work was damned with faint praise by the art establishment, his fake *Christ and the Disciples at Emmaus* was authenticated by expert Dr. Abraham Bredius, sold for millions, and became the top attraction at Museum Boijmans in Rotterdam. In 1943, he exchanged his *Christ and the Adulteress* with Nazi second-in-command Field-Marshal Hermann Goering in return for 137 Dutch paintings that the Nazis had plundered during the occupation of Holland.

The painting was discovered by American servicemen in 1945 as part of a cache destined for the planned *Führermuseum*. Van Meegeren was arrested for collaboration, an offense punishable by death. During the trial in 1947, van Meegeren admitted he had forged the paintings, but claimed to be a hero, having saved the Netherlands' masterpieces from Nazi clutches and fooled Hitler's henchman. The court ordered him to paint another fake in a guarded and sealed room as part of his defense. The fake was convincingly authentic-looking; the collaboration charges were dropped, and van Meegeren was sentenced to one year in prison for forgery and fraud. At his trial he supposedly said, "My triumph as a counterfeiter was my defeat as [a] creative artist." He died of a heart attack before he could serve his term, a national hero.

Some art historians still claim, despite a multitude of scientific evidence, that van Meegeren's works are authentic Vermeers. His forgeries have become collector's items as well, and some forgeries of his forgeries have surfaced, van Meegeren's spiritual descendants trying to cash in on a hostile and capricious art market.

Acknowledgments

The author wishes to thank the following organizations and individuals:

Fundación Valparaiso, the Corporation of Yaddo, Paragraph Workspace for Writers, the Sami Rohr Prize for Jewish Literature, and the Jewish Book Council.

Sheila and Jim Amend; Nicole Hynson, Anthony Amend, and Corbin Kanoa; cousins David, Joan, Sam, Vivian, and William Adelman; Terra Chalberg; Ronit Feldman; Nan A. Talese; Carolyn Hessel; Margot Grover; Mark Baillie; Amie Siegel; Thisbe Nissen; Irina Reyn; Gina Frangello; Amy Brill; Leigh Newman; Lauren Creamer; Lynn McPhee; Jeremy Sisto; Addie Lane; Duncan Smith; Katherine Lee; Anna Helgeson; and the Delta Schmelta sorority: Sheri Joseph, Dika Lam, Margo Rabb, Lara JK Wilson, and Andrew Beierle.

Valuable information was obtained from Eric Hebborn's books *The Art Forger's Handbook* and *Drawn to Trouble* and from Musée d'art et d'histoire du Judaïsme in Paris.

In memory of Michael, whom the water took.